STANDING DEAD

ALSO AVAILABLE BY MARGARET MIZUSHIMA

The Timber Creek K-9 Mysteries

STANDING DEAD

A Timber Creek K-9 Mystery

Margaret Mizushima

CROOKED
LANE

NEW YORK

Copyright © 2023 by Margaret Mizushima

Published in the United States by Crooked Lane Books, an imprint of The Quick Brown Fox & Company LLC.

Crooked Lane Books and its logo are trademarks of The Quick Brown Fox & Company LLC.

Library of Congress Catalog-in-Publication data available upon request.

ISBN (hardcover): 978-1-63910-244-0
ISBN (ebook): 978-1-63910-245-7

Cover design by Melanie Sun

Printed in the United States.

www.crookedlanebooks.com

Crooked Lane Books
34 West 27th St., 10th Floor
New York, NY 10001

First Edition: March 2023

10 9 8 7 6 5 4 3 2 1

For my mother-in-law,
Sumiko Mizushima,
whom I love, respect, and admire

ONE

November, Pueblo del Sol, a small village in Mexico

As a deputy sheriff and K–9 handler from Timber Creek, Colorado, Mattie Cobb—who had recently changed her name to Mattie Wray—was out of her element.

Family meant everything to Mattie, and she continued to be drawn back to hers as certainly as her dog Robo was to his tennis ball. Her mother might not have been as dedicated to protecting her children as Mattie believed she herself would be, but still, she and her sister Julia were determined to see their mother again, to be held by her, to sit beside her and tell her that one of the bad guys she feared was now dead and another in prison.

The village was much as it had been when Mattie came to visit last July—small and quiet, with very few people on the boardwalks that lined the hard-packed dirt street. They'd driven an old pickup truck owned by Julia's husband past Tijuana and into the hills southeast of that huge city. Nerves made Mattie's palms sweaty on the steering wheel, and she continuously glanced at the rearview mirror to make sure no one was on her tail.

Julia sat in the passenger's seat gazing out the windshield with an anxious frown, hands clenched in her lap, fingers white from tension.

"Take a breath," Mattie said, trying to exude a confidence she did not feel. "This is going to be okay."

Julia turned her troubled gaze toward Mattie. "What if she's upset that we came?"

Though Mattie felt the same concern, she didn't want to voice it. She steered down the main street, searching for an inconspicuous spot to pull over. "I can't turn back now. Do you want me to drop you off at the café we just passed?"

"No." Julia plucked at the fabric of her capris. "I can't turn back either. I want to go with you."

Mattie spotted the *panadería* she'd parked near last time she'd visited—the time her mother had warned her never to return. She'd issued the warning out of fear of being found by the men who'd killed her husband decades ago, a violent act that she'd been forced to watch. Mattie understood the terror such an incident could induce, but she wasn't as convinced as her mother that danger still existed.

Even so, she'd watched to make sure she and Julia had not been followed.

Though familiar with danger and methods of self-protection, she felt responsible for her sister's safety. Mattie also missed her partner Robo, a one-hundred-pound German shepherd with dual-purpose training in patrol and narcotics detection. Robo would always protect her and anyone she was with. But she couldn't bring him with her, so she'd left him in the excellent care of Dr. Cole Walker, her fiancé and Robo's veterinarian.

Mattie had been investigating the shooting death of her father, Border Patrol officer Douglas Wray, a crime that had been committed decades earlier. Though law enforcement thought her father had been part of a smuggling ring and his case had never been a priority, a new detective, Lieutenant Sonia Alvarez, had joined the cold-case unit in San Diego, and she was willing to take a new look. This spurred Mattie to return to the village to encourage her mother, the only eyewitness they knew of, to come forward and be interviewed.

When Mattie decided to travel back to her mother's village, Julia wasn't about to be left behind. It had been thirty years since she'd seen Ramona, and she'd insisted that she would come too.

Mattie parked beside the plank boardwalk that extended down the street in front of the shops. "Let's buy cookies in there," she said, tilting her head toward the bakery.

Julia released her seat belt and reached for her small purse, slinging its shoulder strap over her head and across her chest. "Okay. Are we leaving the truck parked here?"

"Yes, the house is close. We can walk."

After exiting the truck, Mattie slammed the door, making her sister startle. Julia threw her an apologetic glance, and Mattie held her gaze for a moment, giving her a look that she hoped would steady her. Then Mattie turned and led the way down the boardwalk.

They were both dressed in denim capris, light-colored T-shirts, and tennis shoes. Mattie considered Julia much prettier than she was, but she knew they looked enough alike that most people would guess they were sisters, or at least related. Half Caucasian and half Latina, they were both brunette, though Julia wore her hair long and in a ponytail while Mattie's was styled in a shoulder-length bob. They both had brown eyes, tan skin, and fine features, with one difference: Mattie's nose bore a small bump on the bridge where it had been broken in a childhood fistfight, while Julia's nose was straight and narrow.

A bell above the door of the *panadería* jingled as they entered and stepped inside. A glass display case half filled with cakes, cookies, and pastries stood at the back of the room, where an arching open window afforded a view into the kitchen. A man dressed in a white shirt and pants covered with a white apron came through a swinging door behind the case to greet them with a friendly grin. Flour dusted one of his cheeks, and his glistening black hair was slicked back and held into place with shiny pomade.

"*Dios mío*," he said, his brown eyes twinkling with humor. He continued speaking in Spanish. "Have I died and the heavens sent two angels to bring me home?"

Mattie's heart sank. Last time she'd visited this *panadería*, a woman had been behind the counter. The woman had seemed bored and uninterested, and Mattie had sensed that she'd been considered one of the local customers, no one special. This man seemed interested enough in them to remember them later.

Still, she smiled as she replied in Spanish, "*No, señor.* We're on our way through town and decided to stretch our legs and browse your local shops before we drive on."

"It is my good fortune to have you stop in. What would you like to eat today? Fresh rolls? *Pasteles?*"

They selected a few of the pastries he offered and half a dozen cookies, which he placed in a waxy bag. He kept up a cheerful banter as he rang them up, flirting openly. His attention made Mattie uncomfortable, and she noticed that while Julia remained pleasant, her sister demonstrated a practiced art of diversion and made short work of their transaction. Soon they were headed down the boardwalk again, the bag of goodies in Mattie's hand.

"He was nice," Julia murmured as she strolled beside Mattie.

Mattie tossed a look over her shoulder to see if he'd come out of his shop to watch where they went. "Maybe a little too friendly."

She felt a twinge of alarm when the baker stepped out onto the boardwalk, his phone to his ear. He glanced their way and then turned as if looking up the street in the opposite direction.

Julia seemed oblivious of the baker. "Where to next?"

They'd come to the alley that Mattie had gone down the first time she'd been here. She turned into it, checking to see if the man noticed where they went, but he remained facing away from them. "This way. Over to the next street."

Despite it being November, the autumn sun warmed her tense shoulders as they made their way down the alley crowded with garbage bins, broken wooden crates, cardboard boxes, and old discarded furniture. The backs of small shops and restaurants lined both sides, and the scent of spicy Mexican food mingled in the air with the odor of decayed rubbish.

Mattie remained vigilant, but they encountered no one. At the end of the alleyway, they stepped out on a dirt street lined with adobe and clapboard houses, some with tiled roofs and others with shingles. As they passed by, hens scratched in the yards, uttering a contented, throaty murmur.

Ramona's home sat a few houses down the block, and as they approached, the first thing Mattie noticed was that the flock of hens her mother had been feeding the day she'd visited appeared to be absent. *And the yard isn't quite as tidy*, she thought, spotting weeds growing in the beds of flowers and succulents.

"Here we are," Mattie said quietly as she stopped in front of the house. Her stomach fluttered as Julia gripped her forearm. "Let's go to the side door. That's where she took me last time."

They skirted the side of the house, and Mattie tapped on the screen door. When there was no answer, she glanced at Julia, whose jaw appeared clenched. Mattie opened the screen door and knocked louder on the solid wooden one behind it.

The door swung open to reveal a bent and wizened woman with frizzy gray hair scraped back in a messy bun, the brown skin of her face lined and wrinkled. "*Sí?*" she asked in an aged voice. Gaps appeared between her yellowed teeth as she spoke.

Surprised, Mattie needed a half second to process and regroup. She could feel Julia pressing against her back. "*Hola, señora.* I'm looking for Ramona. I believe she lives here."

"No one named Ramona lives here." The lady took a step back as if to close the door.

Mattie placed her hand on the door to keep it open. "The lady who lived here last summer. Is she here?"

The woman shook her head. "That one moved."

"Moved? Do you know where?"

"No." She tried to close the door, but Mattie leaned on it with her shoulder, and the old woman gave her a stern look.

"Excuse me, *señora*, but I've come a long way and must see her. Can you help me?"

"I know nothing about where she went. She told me I could live here." The lady clutched the door, keeping pressure against it while Mattie pressed back.

"I believe you and respect that," Mattie said, although she had no idea if this woman was telling the truth or not. Right now, she was Mattie's only source of information, and if Ramona had indeed lent this woman her house, she must know something about her mother's whereabouts. "I'm not interested in this home. I only want to find the lady I visited here last summer. How can I contact her?"

"I don't know."

"Did she say when she'll be back?"

"No."

"How do you know her?"

The woman gave Mattie a suspicious look. "My daughter is her friend. Now, I must close the door. Please go away."

Mattie realized force might not be the best way to gain information. "*Señora*, please, I don't want to frighten you. I'm part of Ramona's family and have been here before to visit her. Please . . . I'd be very grateful if you would help me find out where she is." She offered the bag of pastries. "Here, we brought these *pasteles* for her, but you may have them."

The lady shook her head and made a shooing gesture, pressing against the door while Julia in turn pressed against Mattie's back. "I can't help you. Go."

"Who is your daughter, *señora*?" Also speaking Spanish, Julia threw out the question from behind Mattie. "She can probably help us."

A female voice came from behind them. "What do you want? Stop bothering my mother."

Mattie glanced beyond Julia and saw a stout woman, probably in her fifties, bustling over from the yard next door. She wore denim pants, a light-blue shirt, and an expression on her face that meant business. Glad that the daughter had arrived to end the standoff with the older woman, Mattie turned and stepped away from the door she'd been holding so that she could meet the newcomer head on. "*Hola, señora.* We don't mean to bother your mother, but we came here to visit Ramona and have just now learned that she has moved."

Now that reinforcement had arrived, the older lady stayed where she was, leaving her door open and watching with interest.

Mattie hurried on, hoping to avoid being asked to leave again. "I'm Mattie Wray, and this is my sister Julia. We're related to Ramona and planned to surprise her with a visit today."

"No one named Ramona lived here." The woman examined them both before gazing back at Mattie.

"I visited her here last summer. Ramona Martinez."

The woman squinted and studied them both. "I know her as Maria Martinez."

Mattie shouldn't have been surprised that her mother had decided to use her middle name and kicked herself for not realizing it. "Yes, Ramona Maria Martinez. Maria is her middle name."

"You look like her."

Mattie nodded and smiled. Though she hesitated to share too much information, she decided there was no reason to withhold how they were related to Ramona. Maybe it would help break the ice with these two ladies. "We're her daughters."

The younger of the two women nodded but didn't return Mattie's smile, and a guarded look remained on her face. "If you're her daughters, why didn't Maria tell you she was moving?"

That was a question Mattie wasn't prepared to answer. "We've been out of touch and have recently reconnected."

Julia spoke up, her voice anxious. "I hope you can tell us where our mother is."

The woman studied them for a few seconds. "Maria didn't tell me where she was going. She said that my mother could live in her house until she returned, but she didn't know when that would be."

Mattie remembered Ramona's husband. "Did my mother's husband, *señor* Juan Martinez, move with her?" She hoped mentioning his name to show she knew who he was would add credibility.

"Yes, Juan moved too." The woman's gaze remained suspicious.

Mattie sensed this lady would tell them nothing. She either didn't know anything or she didn't trust them enough to share. When Mattie first came to visit her mother in July, Ramona had said that her husband and his brother owned an auto repair shop here in the village. This brother would probably be their best source of information. "Thank you for your time," she said. "If our mother comes back or contacts you, would you tell her that her daughters want to talk to her? She knows how to contact me."

Tight-lipped, the woman nodded.

"Are you sure you won't tell us anything more?" Julia looked close to tears.

"I know nothing to tell," the woman said.

Mattie reached for Julia's hand to give it an encouraging squeeze. She hesitated, wondering if she should give this woman her business card, which identified her as a law enforcement officer. She decided it wouldn't hurt. She reached into her pocket for one of her cards and asked Julia for a pen to write her cell phone number on it. "Please call me if you hear anything that might help us find our mother. Or if she calls, please remind her of my number."

The woman took the card and scanned it. "You're police?"

"Yes. My mother knows this."

The woman pocketed the card, but the additional information didn't seem to make a difference in her willingness to talk. She stood in stony silence as if protecting her own mother.

As Mattie and her sister walked away, her mind raced through the possibilities. Had her last visit scared Ramona, causing her to bolt? Ramona had told Mattie that it was dangerous for her to come here and she wanted to remain hidden from the powerful men who'd killed her husband.

Or, despite Mattie's caution, had someone followed her and discovered Ramona's hiding place? But that didn't seem likely. Ramona had taken the time to invite her neighbor's mother to share her home, so she hadn't left town under extreme duress.

Had something else happened that scared her? Maybe Juan's brother would have some insight into why they'd packed up and moved.

"Mattie, what do you think is going on?" Julia's voice trembled with tension.

"I don't know, but we're going to find Mama's brother-in-law. He and her husband Juan own an auto repair shop here in town. Let's go find it."

"Oh," Julia muttered, sounding relieved. "I thought we were giving up."

"No, I just didn't want the neighbor to call him before we could find him. Force of habit—try to get to your information source before someone shuts him down."

Mattie led the way as they hurried back up the alley and made it to their truck. The baker was nowhere to be seen. She cruised slowly down the main street, looking for an auto repair shop of any kind. After a few blocks of tiny shops and a variety of cafés, she spotted a gas station at the end of the road leading out of town. A hand-lettered sign out front boasted *Martinez Auto – #1 Repair and Service.* From all appearances, the auto shop was not only number one but the only place of its kind in this small village.

Mattie parked out front and asked Julia, "Do you want to go in or wait here?"

"I'll go with you."

Mattie nodded, stepped out of the truck, and headed toward the main door of the station while Julia followed. When she opened it, a buzzer sounded beyond another open door that led into the service area. A short, slender man dressed in a grease-stained coverall came out from under a car hoisted up on the rack, wiping his hands on a rag he pulled from his pocket as he walked to the front to join them.

A smile softened his sharp facial features and crinkled the corners of his brown eyes. He was handsome, with a chiseled nose and cheekbones, a black moustache, and dark hair threaded with silver. "*Hola.* How can I help you, young ladies?"

"*Hola. Señor* Martinez?"

His smile turned into a friendly grin. "*Sí.* I am Tomás Martinez."

Mattie decided she might as well just get into it, offering a handshake as she made the introductions. "I'm Mattie Wray, and this is my sister, Julia."

He gave his palm a final wipe with the rag and inspected it briefly before showing his mostly clean fingers to Mattie. When she smiled and kept her hand extended, he gave a slight shrug and clasped her hand in a soft, polite grip before letting go. He gave her a quizzical look.

"I'm pleased to meet you," Mattie said. "You see, your brother Juan is married to our mother."

He raised a brow as if surprised, but his smile stayed firmly in place. If the presence of Ramona's daughters caused him any concern, he didn't show it. "You look like Maria. I'm very pleased to meet both of you, though I didn't know she had children," he said, including Julia in his gaze before focusing back on Mattie. "Have you talked to your mother or Juan lately?"

"Not lately. Have you?"

He shook his head, disappointment crossing his face. "I have not heard from them since they left town."

"Actually, we just learned that they'd moved. We've been out of touch with our mother and hoped you could help us contact her."

Tomás searched Mattie's face for a moment, and then he gestured for them to follow him to the counter in the back of the room. He stepped behind it, opened a drawer, and took out a black flip phone. "This belongs to Juan," he said, holding it up. "He told me he would call when they found a place to live, but I found this here on the counter after they left town. I don't know if he left it on purpose or by accident. All I know is that without this, I don't have any way of calling him myself. I've been waiting to hear from him, but so far . . . nothing."

Mattie thought he looked worried. "Are you concerned about them?"

He nodded. "They left so suddenly. Just packed their clothes and that's it. Left their house and furniture for their neighbor's *mamá* to look after. Not at all what I would expect from Juan."

"When did they leave?"

"On October fifth. Juan didn't give me any warning. He just came in and told me they were moving while Maria waited in the car out front."

That would have been almost three months after Mattie's visit with Ramona in July. Since she and Juan had packed up and left without warning, something else besides her visit must have frightened them. "So you're concerned about them," she confirmed.

He looked down at the counter for a few seconds before raising his gaze to meet hers. "At first I was angry, but yes, now I'm worried. It's not like Juan to leave his responsibilities and then just disappear without a word. He has not even called our own mother to tell her where he is."

Mattie had a bad feeling about it all, and she couldn't help but wonder if Juan and Ramona's sudden departure had something to do with her father's murder years ago. Discovery by his killers had been her mother's biggest fear when she'd last seen her. "Did Juan tell you anything about why they were leaving?"

"He said he and Maria needed to go somewhere out of town where they could be alone together for a while. I thought they had argued about our family, that maybe all of us living in this town together was too much for her or for them in some way, but he refused to answer any of my questions." His face was lined with concern. "One thing he said didn't make sense: 'It's safer this way.' I tried to get him to explain, but he wouldn't. We fought about him leaving me shorthanded with the business, and he looked ashamed but said it couldn't be helped. Then he left."

Julia remained silent, and Mattie could feel the tension radiate from her in waves while she tried to get more information that could help, but to no avail. She ended up leaving her business card after adding her personal phone number for the second time that day and asked Tomás to call if he heard anything at all from the missing couple.

He scanned the card briefly before looking up in surprise. "You're a police officer?"

She nodded, not knowing if this helped or hindered his trust in her. It certainly hadn't inspired faith with the ladies at her mother's house. "From Colorado. If your brother and our mother need my help in any way, I'll do what I can for them."

She glanced at the business cards on the counter, noticing that there were cards for both brothers. The cards were personalized with their photos, and she took one of each. The two men resembled each other, although Juan's hair was longer and wavier. "We'll call you if we hear anything at all from them."

Mattie and Julia said their good-byes and made their way out to their truck, where Julia dissolved into tears. "Oh, Mattie, I'm so afraid for her."

Julia knew everything about their parents' history: how Douglas had been executed in front of Ramona at the border guard station where he worked about thirty years ago; how the Cobb brothers had kidnapped Ramona, Mattie, and their brother Willie when Mattie was two and held them captive until she was six; how both Cobb brothers were now dead, killed in the same prison decades apart but their hits possibly arranged by the same gang of gunrunners and drug smugglers that had been active at the time of their father's death.

Feeling helpless, she reached out to embrace her sister, and the two hugged while Mattie's mind darted from one question to another. Had someone from this same gang shown up in town and threatened their mother, forcing her and her husband to run for their lives? If so, then who? Why now? And where had they gone?

As she started the truck and shifted into reverse, an older-model black Mercedes that was parked across the street and down the block caught her eye. It glided away as she pulled into the street, turning at the next block and speeding off as she began to approach. She noticed it had California plates, but it was too far away for her to determine the number. It gave her a funny feeling, but there was no reason to chase it. And it didn't follow as she turned onto the road leading out of town.

TWO

The next day in San Diego

Mattie didn't like it on this side of the table. She settled back, the plastic shell of her chair cupping her backside in an unwelcome hug. Julia took the chair next to her.

This interrogation room at the San Diego Police station wasn't much different from those at the Timber Creek Sheriff's Department where she worked—same austere atmosphere, no furnishings except a steel table and these plastic chairs. Camera lenses winked from recesses in the wall at the two corners of the room facing her. She'd noticed a third behind her before she sat.

Julia's knee bounced up and down against hers, telegraphing her nervousness.

Mattie stopped the bouncing with a touch of her hand. "We shouldn't have to wait long."

Julia nodded, leaning back in her chair as if to imitate Mattie but ruining the semblance of calm by twisting her hands together tightly in her lap. At least it was better than the jumpy knee.

A woman entered the room carrying a cardboard tray with three paper cups filled with dark brew. Mattie sized her up with a quick glance—iron-gray hair cut tight on the sides and longer on top, probably late fifties, about her own height of five foot four, stocky build, black horn-rimmed glasses around piercing brown eyes.

"I intercepted Marci as she was fixing your coffee." The woman set the tray on the table and extended her hand to Mattie. "I'm Detective Sonia Alvarez."

Firm grip. "I'm Deputy Mattie Wray from Timber Creek County Sheriff's Department in Colorado."

"Nice to meet you." Alvarez offered Julia a handshake. "And I remember you from when you were in high school. You've grown up, but you haven't changed much."

"It's good to see you again, Detective." Julia enclosed the detective's hand in both of hers. "I was glad to find out that you had moved to the cold-case unit. You were kinder to me than any of the others I've spoken with throughout the years."

"Yes . . . well, we had several openings lately, and I got the call." She smiled slightly as she took a cup of coffee from the tray and pushed it closer to Mattie and Julia. She looked at Mattie. "You and your sister were both missing persons from the Douglas Wray case back in the early nineties. It's unusual to find out about people the way we did with you, although it's always a pleasure when folks who are missing turn up alive."

Good to know that Sonia knew at least some of her background. "So is there a paper trail on me and our brother William?"

"Enough for me to know about you and where you work . . . and I'm sorry about the loss of your brother. There's a short summary in his missing person report about how he was abducted and killed a few months ago." Sonia included both Mattie and Julia in a sweep of her gaze before focusing back on Mattie. "You helped with the arrest of his killer, John Cobb, and I know that Cobb was killed last month in a Colorado prison."

John Cobb's death had started a landslide of terrible events that Mattie was still recovering from, but she didn't want to go into it all right now. "Sounds like you've got the gist of it. I can provide more detail and answer any questions you might have, but today, we're here to ask for your help with our father's cold case—Border Patrol agent Douglas Wray."

Sonia nodded as she took a sip of her coffee. "As you know, I'm familiar with the case, although I don't know many details. I did take a look at the file after we made this appointment. There are a few problems with the information we have on hand."

Mattie leaned forward, cupping her hands around the thick paper cup to warm them. "How so?"

Sonia leaned forward as well, placing her elbows on the table. "Back in the nineties, Border Patrol did a lot of their own investigations through critical incident investigative team units. Sometimes they called in the feds, sometimes we were called in, but in your father's case, no one was called. And there is very little information available."

Mattie decided to cut to the chase. "Do you think there was a cover-up?"

"I don't know. Why do you ask?"

She might as well just say it; based on what she'd heard from Julia as well as her first impression, this detective was open to listening and hadn't formed any hard-and-fast opinions yet. "From what I've been told about the case, the official belief is that our father was taking bribes and allowing smuggled goods and drugs through his checkpoint. I've wondered if that's why his case wasn't solved and why it hasn't received much attention throughout the years."

Sonia's gaze shifted to Julia and then back to Mattie. "Evidence of his culpability in smuggling is documented through Border Patrol records and is believed to be the motive for his killing—someone from the ring turned on him. As far as the case not receiving much attention throughout the years, that's anyone's guess."

"We believe Douglas Wray was coerced," Mattie said, gesturing toward her sister as Julia nodded agreement. She rushed on before Sonia could ask how she'd arrived at that conclusion, her mother's testimony being something she felt she couldn't admit to today. "He had a clean record prior to that activity. Our grandmother remembers that our mother was called to his checkpoint the night he was shot and we were abducted. Julia happened to be staying with her that night or she would've been taken too. We believe that it was a setup and that we were pawns used to threaten our father. He was killed trying to protect us."

Frown lines deepened between Sonia's brows as she focused on Mattie. "Were you a witness to any of this?"

Mattie put on her cop face to hide her emotions. "I was there, but I was two. I remember only bits and pieces."

She didn't want to go into detail about how she had repressed memories from that time in her life, between ages two and six. Things had been very bad for them while they'd been captives of Harold Cobb. Back then, she'd thought the man was her father, and he'd abused them all. "John Cobb told me shortly before his arrest that he and Harold Cobb were responsible for kidnapping us. I believe he was present when Douglas Wray was killed, but there were obviously others involved too. Others that might be active today."

Sonia nodded so slightly that it was hard to tell. "So your mother is the only living adult witness that we know of at this point, and she's still missing, correct?"

In light of recent circumstances, it was safe to agree. "Correct. She's missing and we don't know where she is at this time. But I wondered if there might be some evidence in the records that might lead somewhere. Or if other gunrunning or drug smuggling cases might be tied in that could give us other witnesses."

Sonia leaned back in her chair as she appeared to think. "The war on drug smuggling and border protection has come a long way since the nineties, but it's an ongoing battle. Comparing cases isn't easy, but I can do some research. As far as taking on the Douglas Wray case to try to find his killer, I'll have to run that by my supervisor."

The detective looked at Julia. "I've been interested in this case since I met you. You seemed to be a pretty self-reliant teenager at that time, especially considering your circumstances." She gave Julia a wry smile. "And of course, it's always a surprise when a missing person shows up at the station asking for help. That's hard to forget. Is your grandmother still alive?"

"She is," Julia said.

"It sounds like I would need to interview her. I know that others have spoken with her, but I haven't."

"She'd be willing to talk to you."

Sonia looked back at Mattie. "I'll take this case to my supervisor, and I'll see what I can come up with. I can't make any promises, because we have very little to go on here. How can I reach you?"

Feeling like this was the best outcome she could have hoped for, Mattie handed over her card. She wished she could've offered Ramona's eyewitness testimony to the detective, like she'd hoped. Before her mother went missing again.

THREE

Cole trotted down the steps in his home, closing the snaps on his western shirt as he ran. He'd had time for a quick shower, but he needed to help Mrs. Gibbs, his resident housekeeper, while she prepared for Mattie to arrive for dinner. When Mattie texted a couple of hours ago, she'd been halfway between Denver and Timber Creek, driving home from the airport and eager to see him, the kids, and of course, Robo.

Well, actually, she'd probably put Robo and the kids ahead of him in that lineup, but the thought made him smile. He didn't mind that she loved her dog and his kids as much as she loved him. In fact, that was one of the many things about her that *he* loved.

And now that she'd agreed to marry him and they were planning their wedding, he didn't care one whit who came first in her affections. They would soon all be one big family, something he looked forward to with joy, and joy had been hard to come by for him and his kids in the past year and a half.

He hurried into the kitchen, where Mrs. Gibbs was stirring a pot of beef chili on the stove. The spicy scent of chili powder and chopped Anaheim peppers filled the air, making his mouth water. "Mmm . . . smells good," he said, stepping over to the counter to retrieve a clean spoon from the drawer. "Quality control at your service."

Mrs. Gibbs gave him an indulgent smile and moved back to give him room. The hearty flavors of pinto beans, ground beef, peppers, and spices blended together on his tongue in a delightful bite. "Perfect!" he proclaimed. "Mrs. Gibbs, you are the chili queen of Colorado."

She snorted, shaking her head at him, her tight gray curls framing her face. "A chili queen from Dublin, aye?" she answered, her speech colored with her soft Irish accent. "What a charmer ye are. This is Teresa Lovato's recipe." Teresa was Mattie's foster mother, who still lived in Timber Creek and also still fostered homeless children.

He grinned at his housekeeper, grateful as always that this lady had come to help him take care of his home and children after his wife had left him. She would always be special in his eyes. "How can I help?"

"We need to set the table and get drinks for everyone. When do you expect Miss Mattie?"

"I'd say within the next fifteen minutes. The highway is clear, and the next storm isn't forecasted for days."

Robo came from the den as if summoned when he heard Mattie's name. The big German shepherd—mostly black with tan markings—ambled forward, looking up at Cole as if repeating Mrs. Gibbs's question.

"Yep, she'll be here soon, big guy," Cole told him as he took down plates and bowls from the cabinet. "You've been watching for her this whole week, and the waiting is almost over."

His youngest, Sophie, looked up from where she was sitting at the table doing her homework. She slapped her arithmetic book closed and started gathering up her papers. "He's going to freak when Mattie gets here," she said with a grin that bunched her freckled cheeks. Her brunette curls were tied back with a red scarf that she treasured, a gift from her aunt Jessie, Cole's sister.

"That he will, Sophie-bug. You know him well. Go ahead and give the dogs their food, okay? Robo might as well eat now, because he'll be too excited to eat later." Cole set the dishes on the table and went back to retrieve silverware while Sophie finished packing her books in her backpack. "Good job at doing your homework. Did you get it done?"

"Almost. I'll finish tomorrow." She put her backpack on the desktop that was part of the kitchen cabinetry and called to the other dogs while she gathered up their bowls. "Belle, Bruno, you'd better come eat dinner before Robo hogs it all."

Sculpted ears pointed forward, their Doberman pinscher, Bruno, rushed in from the other room, where he'd no doubt been lying on his dog bed. Belle, their Bernese mountain dog, followed at a more sedate pace, her limp from an old gunshot wound barely noticeable. All three dogs watched Sophie with eager eyes while she filled their bowls with kibble and then waited at her command as she set their bowls on the floor, a courtesy that Cole insisted upon so the dogs wouldn't rush their feeder and spill their bowls of food. With three big dogs in the family, manners were important.

Cole called upstairs for Angela, his sixteen-year-old, but when she didn't answer, he asked Sophie to run up and get her. She was probably listening to her music with earbuds in place.

The dogs chowed down, Robo and Bruno scarfing their food quickly and then settling down to watch Belle finish hers. They knew better than to try to take it away from the queen of the pack.

Sophie returned to the kitchen cradling Hilde, their six-month-old Siamese kitten, in her arms while Angela trailed behind. Sophie carried the kitten into the utility room to feed her, and Angie paused just beyond the doorway.

Cole noticed right away that Angie had changed out of the jeans she'd worn to school that day into leg-hugging black pants and a long open gray cardigan over a periwinkle shirt. She'd taken down her ponytail, her white-blond hair hanging long and straight past her shoulders, and she'd obviously spent time applying makeup that accentuated her vivid blue eyes.

"You look nice, Miss Angela," Mrs. Gibbs said.

"Thanks." Angie's pale skin flushed slightly.

Cole was wonderstruck for a moment as he took in how grown-up she looked and what a pretty young woman she was turning into. He smiled at her when she looked at him.

"Hey, Dad," she said as she headed for the refrigerator. "Is it okay if I go to the movies with Ben after we have dinner with Mattie?"

He had already realized she hadn't dressed up this way for the family and wasn't surprised that she wanted to go out later. She'd been dating Ben for about a month now, a kid he heartily approved of, although as a dad, he still worried about his little girl starting to date her first boyfriend. He'd been a teenage boy once himself.

"What time do you want to leave?" he asked.

"Not till a quarter to seven. We'll catch the seven o'clock show."

That allowed an hour and a half with family, which seemed reasonable. And he knew Mattie wouldn't care. The two of them needed some time alone together tonight anyway to talk about everything that had happened in Mexico and what she'd found out since. "I guess that would be all right, Angel. But you need to get home by ten o'clock."

She stopped midstride and turned to him, a look of disbelief stamped on her face. "That's so early. We want to meet up with Riley and Hannah and a couple of Ben's friends after the movie and get a Coke or something at the Pizza Palace. They're open until midnight."

The local pizza place catered to the after-the-movies teenage crowd on weekends. He'd become aware of their closing time the past month, even though it had never been important to him during the years before. There was little to do in the small town of Timber Creek, and he was glad that at least one place provided space in which the kids could hang out. He might as well face it and support the local business.

"How about we split the difference and say eleven o'clock?"

Angie gave him a charming smile. "How about eleven thirty?"

He glanced at Mrs. Gibbs, who was making no bones about openly watching. Her eyes twinkled and she cocked one brow at him. Sophie had entered the room, and she was focused on them too, as if taking notes for the future. Even the dogs seemed to be observing.

Cole weighed his options quickly—take a stand or give in? What about his plans for the night? Would he and Mattie stay here, or would they go to her house? Complications snowballed, but he decided to make a play for the end game. "Eleven o'clock is best for now. We'll consider changing that when you're older."

"Da-ad." Her voice was filled with disappointment.

One last plea, but he needed to stay strong. "Final decision, Angie. Take it like an adult. And I appreciate you including our family in the early part of your evening. Now, let's help get dinner on the table. What do you need us to do, Mrs. Gibbs?"

The lady gave him a nod, as if in approval, and began handing out duties like a sergeant rallying her troops. While they worked, she once again told Angie how nice she looked, how her new shirt was a great color, how her makeup was just right, keeping up a chatter to smooth out the edges and move on from the curfew confrontation.

She's gifted with kids and thank goodness for that, Cole told himself while he filled glasses with ice and water and thought about how his housekeeper had raised two daughters who each had daughters of their own. In his opinion, Mrs. Gibbs was a girl-whisperer.

Robo paced back and forth from the kitchen to the den, making Cole wonder about that sixth sense that dogs seem to have. As Robo reentered the kitchen, he paused at the doorway, his ears perked, obviously listening. He whined, whirled, and ran to the front door barking. The other two dogs followed.

"There's Mattie," Sophie said, trotting after them. "I'll let Robo outside."

Every bit as excited to see Mattie as her dog was, Cole rushed to the door that Sophie had left open, stepping out onto the front porch and into the frosty November air just in time to see Mattie drive up slowly to avoid the milling dogs. She'd evidently stopped at the station already to pick up her patrol car, a Ford Explorer tricked out as a K-9 unit that had everything equipped to meet Robo's needs.

After exiting the car, she stiffened against the closed door and spread her arms, as if bracing herself against Robo's rush. The big dog ran into her embrace, rising up on his hind feet and placing his front paws on her shoulders. As Cole moved down the sidewalk toward them, he could hear Mattie murmuring something unintelligible in Robo's ear, but no doubt it was a sweet message of love and greeting. It warmed Cole's heart to see the two of them reunite after their separation, and he stood back and watched, letting Robo have his turn first.

Robo wasn't nearly as generous with turn-taking. Even as Mattie tried to lower his front half to the ground, he hopped and danced around her, apparently unable to control his excitement in the midst of the other dogs and Cole's two daughters surging forward to greet her. Cole ended up wading into the melee to take control of Bruno and Belle, asking the kids to help him.

While he was busy sorting things out, both Sophie and Angie got a hug from Mattie, Bruno and Belle got pats and kisses, and Robo regained her attention as he gamboled about before jumping back into her embrace. Cole was beginning to feel like chopped liver when Robo suddenly twisted away and led Bruno on a merry chase around the yard, apparently his way of removing the Doberman from Mattie's space. Sophie and Belle sprinted after them, and Angie began to walk back up the sidewalk.

Mattie turned from watching the dogs run off and finally . . . *finally* . . . gave Cole her full attention, her beautiful brown eyes warm and soulful in the light from the front porch, a weary smile on her face. He opened his arms, and she walked into them. He felt her hands on his back as she encircled his torso with her arms, and he thought, *This is what I need—for Mattie to come home in the evening, every evening, to stay with me and the kids, to be a part of our family. This is what I want.*

"It's great to have you back home," he said, words that fell woefully short in expressing his true feelings. "How was your drive?"

"Long," she murmured, her face against his chest.

He could feel her muscles relax as she leaned against him, and he sighed with contentment. "I missed you."

"I missed you too . . . and the kids . . . and Robo and the dogs. It was a disappointing trip."

She'd shared some of the basics with him by phone, but not any of the details. Mattie was always guarded about what she said via cell phone. "Did Detective Alvarez have any leads on your dad's case?"

Mattie tensed in his arms, and Cole wished he could take the words back. His desire to provide a sheltered place for her to unwind was much greater than his need to know anything. That could've waited until later.

She leaned back slightly. "She's deciding if the case is worth looking into. She says there's little to go on."

He shook his head, trying not to overreact to her disappointment. "Maybe she'll decide to look harder."

Robo finished his circle of the yard and bolted back up to them. He bumped against their legs, jostling them apart. Using his nose as a wedge, he forced Mattie to take a step back. She leaned forward and gave him a hug, thumping his side vigorously.

Cole decided it best to let the dogs and kids do their magic. Taking her hand, he said, "Let's go inside. You look tired. Mrs. Gibbs has made dinner, and we can talk afterward."

The other dogs ran ahead with Sophie, but Robo stayed close at Mattie's heel. By the time they reached the kitchen, Mrs. Gibbs and Angie had everything ready for them to settle at the table.

The bright kitchen light revealed what Cole had suspected. Smudges darkened the skin beneath Mattie's eyes and stress lined her face. He imagined her insomnia had kicked in since she'd learned about her missing mother and stepfather.

Mattie greeted Mrs. Gibbs with a hug before taking her seat at the table. Sophie started a lively chatter, and Mattie and Angie briefly discussed Angie's plans for the evening while Mrs. Gibbs served steaming bowls of beef chili all around. Bruno had settled in beside Cole, Belle beside Sophie, and Robo had stationed himself next to Mattie's chair. She leaned to stroke the dark fur between his ears while she kept up with Sophie's banter, and soon Cole noticed the taut muscles in her face relax as kids and dogs—two of Mattie's favorite things in the world—seemed to ease her distress.

After eating, they lingered at the table while Angie told Mattie about the status of the litter of puppies Robo had sired, which had been born about four weeks earlier to Sassy, a beautiful German shepherd female that belonged to one of Angie's friends.

"They're so cute and furry," Angie was saying. "And so soft. Here, I have pictures of them." Out came her cell phone, and with a little squeal, Sophie jumped up from her seat and scurried around the table to stand next to Mattie so she could see too. Mattie's face lit up as she focused on the cell phone photos.

Cole realized that his kids had dominated the conversation throughout dinner and had now successfully captured Mattie's attention fully. And though she looked like she was enjoying herself immensely, he was beginning to feel a bit neglected. He told himself to be a man and buck up as he stood and began helping Mrs. Gibbs clear the table.

"Miss Angela, isn't it about time for you to get ready for your date?" Mrs. Gibbs said as she began rinsing bowls and putting them in the dishwasher.

Cole glanced at the clock as Angie rushed to put her cell phone in her back pocket and take her dishes to the sink.

"Thanks, Angie," Cole murmured as she passed.

She paused to look at him, one blond eyebrow raised.

"For staying for dinner and for being a good kid," Cole said, truly grateful for both.

She rolled her eyes before coming over and pressing a quick kiss on his cheek. "Good enough to stay out until midnight?"

Couldn't blame her for trying one more time. "I'm sure you are, but we agreed on eleven o'clock. I'll probably still be up, so I'll see you then."

Mattie tossed him a smile as she said good-night to Angie and carried her own dishes to the sink. Sophie skipped along beside her. "Mattie, will you read me a story tonight?"

"Of course. I've been looking forward to that."

"Me too! I've got a new book about these kids who solve a mystery."

"Sounds fascinating."

Cole gritted his teeth, thinking Sophie needed an early bedtime even if it was the weekend. He put away the leftover chili, and Mrs. Gibbs finished loading the dishwasher while Sophie ran to get her book. Belle and Bruno followed, but Robo seemed glued to Mattie's side.

"Why don't you two scoot while I finish wiping up?" Mrs. Gibbs said as she squeezed out the cloth. "Go grab a few minutes to yourselves, why don't you."

"Thanks for such a great dinner," Mattie said.

Mrs. Gibbs gave her a warm smile. "It was your Mama T's special recipe."

"I recognized that. Thank you. It was just what I needed."

Even though Cole had felt edged out by his kids earlier, he was cheered by the result. Mattie still looked tired but definitely happier than when she'd arrived. And that's what Cole lived for—making sure the people in his life had shelter, were well fed, and were content. Those were the things that mattered most in his world.

He led Mattie into the great room, Robo at her heel, and went to light the fire he'd laid earlier in the rock-lined fireplace. He loved the cozy feel in this room with its vaulted ceiling, the light glinting off the polished oak furniture and window casings, the shadows dancing in the corners after the lights were turned down.

Mattie sighed as she sank onto one of the leather sofas, pulling a chocolate-colored fleece throw over her lap. He smiled at her, loving the way she felt at home here in this room. "You're tired," he said.

She nodded as she returned his smile. "Tired but so glad to be home."

"I wish this was literally your home and you would be staying here with us tonight."

She nodded again, but instead of meeting his gaze, she stared off toward the fire, as if captivated by it. In the past, Mattie had pulled away from him when she was upset about something, and he grew uneasy that this might be one of those times. He knew she needed space to process and hoped it was just fatigue he was reading from her.

Sophie came bounding down the stairs and into the room to plop down on the sofa next to Mattie, who placed an arm around her so they could snuggle under the blanket together. Cole settled into an armchair across the coffee table from them so he could watch Mattie while she read to his daughter.

He was enjoying both the view and the story when his cell phone's ring shattered his mood. Mattie and Sophie paused to look at him as he glanced at the caller ID. He didn't recognize the number and excused himself to answer the phone.

He stepped into the foyer near the base of the staircase. "Timber Creek Veterinary Clinic."

"Hey there. Are you the vet?"

"I am. I'm Dr. Walker."

"My name's Tanner Rattler. I'm here near Timber Creek on a hunting trip, and I've run into trouble with my two horses."

"Good evening, Tanner. What's up?"

"They're real sick. I don't know what the heck's wrong with them, but it's bad."

"How are they acting?"

"They're wheezing, one's worse than the other one, and they both stumble, like they're losing their balance. I've been trying to keep them on their feet in case it's colic, but I don't know if I can keep them going."

This didn't sound like colic. "Can you bring them in?"

"They're sick enough that I'm afraid they'll go down in the trailer and get hurt or even die in there. I was hoping you could come out."

"Where are you at?"

"I'm at the campground between the Redstone Ridge and Balderhouse trailheads. Do you know the place?"

He sure did. It was the site where a young mother's body had been dumped last month. "It'll take at least thirty minutes for me to get to you, Tanner. This might not be colic. Have you temped them?"

"No. I don't have a thermometer."

"Okay. I'll leave now. If they want to lie down and they'll lie quietly, go ahead and let them. If they try to roll, like it's a colic, try to keep them up."

"Will do. Thanks, Doc."

After disconnecting the call, Cole stepped back into the great room, drawing Mattie's and Sophie's attention. "I have to go on a call," he said, his tone apologetic as he met Mattie's eyes.

She nodded, as if in complete acceptance. That was another one of the things he loved about her—her work hours were unpredictable and demanding, and she didn't fault him that his were too. "When do you think you'll be back?"

"The drive to and back will take an hour, so I'll probably be gone at least three." He thought he read a look of disappointment on her face. "Do you want to go with me?"

She hesitated as if thinking about it, then glanced down at Sophie before looking back at him. "You know . . . I'm beat. I think I'll finish reading to Sophie and then go home and try to get a good night's sleep. Can we get together to talk tomorrow?"

He'd been afraid that would be her answer, but he understood. Mattie looked entirely worn out. And maybe the dinner, warm fire, and soothing presence of the dogs and kids would help her get a good night's sleep in her own bed. "I'll call you in the morning. Are you scheduled to work tomorrow?"

"No, I have one more day off, although I might go in to the office to do some catching up with Stella."

Stella was the Timber Creek Sheriff's sole detective and one of Mattie's good friends. He imagined Mattie wanted to share what happened in Mexico with her and debrief, something he'd hoped to be able to do tonight. But that was not to be. "Maybe we could have lunch together. Or even brunch?" he asked.

"Sure. We'll be in touch in the morning."

He guessed that would have to do for now. He walked back over to the sofa and gave them each a kiss, wishing he could linger more with Mattie's but making it brief with Sophie observing mere inches away. Robo too—the big dog rose from where he was lying at Mattie's feet and sat, keeping a wary eye on him as if not trusting him with his partner.

Cole chuckled as he moved away, and Mattie gave him an amused smile. He left to tell Mrs. Gibbs where he was going before grabbing a coat and going through the kitchen door into the garage to climb into his truck with the mobile vet unit in the bed.

Most of the time he loved his work, but there were a few times, like tonight, where work got in the way of his life, and he would be the first to admit it. The phone rang in his pocket again before he could even pull out of the garage. It was the same number as before, Tanner Rattler.

"Hey, Doc," Tanner said, after Cole answered the phone. "My mare just went down, and she can't get back up. You'd better hurry."

FOUR

Mattie sighed as she drove up to the front of her home. She'd been this weary before, but it had been a long time since she'd felt this helpless. She could tell Detective Alvarez only so much, and she'd never shared that she'd been in contact with her mother. She'd promised Ramona in July that she would tell no one, and she'd kept that promise, misguided as it might be. So now, with her mother missing and unaccounted for, there was little she could do to initiate a search for her. She'd just have to trust that Ramona knew what she was doing and that she was keeping herself and her husband safe.

Wrapped in her own thoughts, Mattie functioned on auto-pilot as she parked the car. It was only when she released Robo and he bounded toward the front porch, chuffing a bark under his breath, that she awakened to her surroundings enough to sense that something was off.

The motion sensor lights in the front yard aren't working. "Robo, come!"

She and Robo had been attacked in their own yard before, and now her senses were on full alert. Robo did a one-eighty turn and came running back to her as she circled her vehicle to put it between herself and the house. Dressed in civilian cloth-ing, she didn't even have her firearm on her.

Scanning her surroundings, she opened the passenger side door and released the lock on the compartment where she'd stored her Glock. With her gun in hand and Robo by her side, she felt more secure. Nothing else seemed out of the ordinary: patches of snow on the north side of trees gleamed white in the moonlight, warm light glowed from her neighbors' windows, a chilly breeze sighed through the boughs of the huge Ponderosa pine in her yard.

A quick check told her that Robo didn't appear to sense imminent danger, although he stared up at her from her side, fully alert and waiting for a command. She knew he could sense her every mood. *If I'm alarmed, he will be too.*

Maybe there was a power outage or something while I was gone and the system needs to be reset. Keeping an eye on the shadows that surrounded her house, Mattie told Robo to heel and glided up the sidewalk, her Glock held low in front of her. Her breath hung in the cold air like a spirit. As she approached the porch, a white square became apparent on the screen door.

She feared an ambush. Two steps up and she was on the porch, her back to the wall, scanning the yard and the street beyond. Nothing. She'd hoped she'd been right about why the motion lights were inactive, but the envelope pinned to the screen door told her something might be amiss. Department protocol would dictate that she call someone for backup before entering her house under suspicious circumstances, but Mattie feared she might be overreacting.

She decided to have Robo clear the house. Leaving the envelope where it was, she unlocked her door and let him inside, following as he trotted into the living room. "Go search for a bad guy," she told him as she switched on the overhead light.

Everything was as it should be—her couch, one chair, coffee table, and small television on a simple four-legged stand were all in place. Robo took off toward the kitchen with his ears pricked forward and nose in the air, a dog on a mission.

She flipped on lights as she followed him, carrying her Glock low and in front. No one in the kitchen to the right side of the hallway, her bedroom and closet to the left, or the bathroom in the middle. Robo surged out in front each step of the way.

She watched his body language—no bristles on his back, no bob of his head to indicate he'd detected an unusual scent. She was beginning to think she'd let her fatigue and the tension from the past few days get the best of her and that she'd grown suspicious and alarmed for no reason. "Okay, now let's get that envelope and see if it's just someone inviting us to Thanksgiving."

Even though she'd decided the envelope likely contained something innocent, she retrieved it carefully, tugging on a pair of latex gloves before touching it and holding it between two fingertips at the corner. There was no address or salutation written on the outside. She carried it into the kitchen, laid it on the counter, and slit it open with a paring knife.

Call it a sixth sense or cop's intuition, but as soon as she slipped the note out of its envelope, the feeling of dread she'd harbored since finding her mother missing blossomed. She opened the note to read what it said:

> *Dear Mattie,*
>
> *You'll find him among the standing dead west of the Shadow Ridge Campground corral.*
>   *Until we meet again,*
>
> *A friend of your father's*

Her scalp prickled as she reached for her cell phone to call Sheriff McCoy.

★   ★   ★

It took only minutes for Mattie to change into her uniform, a long-sleeved khaki jumpsuit with the Timber Creek Sheriff's K-9 unit insignia at the top of the left sleeve. With long woolen underwear beneath, the heavy jumpsuit kept her warm when she worked outside in the high country. And that's where she would be headed tonight.

A quick check of the weather on her cell phone told her that the temperature had fallen to twenty-five degrees and the night was forecasted to be clear. Robo watched her every move, his eyes snapping with eagerness. Her partner loved to work, and he never complained about late-night duty.

She sat on her bed and tugged on wool socks and insulated hiking boots. "Okay, let's go."

Robo whirled to run to the front door. She picked up her Glock, dropped the magazine to check the ammo, even though she knew all would be as she'd left it, and then snapped the magazine back into place. She did a quick press check, pulling the slide back slightly to see the round seated in the chamber.

She holstered her firearm and shrugged on her heaviest coat, a brown Carhartt with a faux-fur collar and the department insignia on the sleeve. Her insulated gloves were in the pockets, and she grabbed her cap with the earflaps, the bag she'd placed the note in, and her backpack from the table beside the door.

Robo danced on his front feet as he waited, his nails clicking on the hardwood floor.

"Okay, buddy. Let's get your water." She snatched up the gallon jug of water she'd prepared and Robo led the way out to their SUV.

Stars shone brightly in the cloudless sky, and the moon lit their way. Tomorrow, she'd have an electrician come out to see why the motion lights weren't working. Tonight, she and Robo would be tracking down the mysterious "him" mentioned in the note to see if anyone needed to be rescued. Of course, at this point there was no way of knowing if the note was a hoax or a stupid practical joke, but in this kind of weather, they couldn't take any chances. Someone needed to investigate, and the "someone" most likely to succeed in finding a person was Robo.

Mattie loaded her dog and his water supply into the back compartment of their unit and drove across town to the station. She pulled into the parking lot right behind Stella LoSasso, the detective in their small county sheriff's department. Sheriff McCoy's Jeep and Deputy Ken Brody's cruiser were already parked in the lot.

Stella exited her silver Honda and waited for Mattie to unload Robo. He trotted over to greet her, bending his body around her knees while she leaned forward to pet him. "Hello, ya big galoot. I missed you." She raised her eyes to Mattie. "What a pathetic welcome home, huh? A note on your door."

"Can you believe it?"

"Yes, I can. After the kind of year we've had, I can believe anything."

Together they trudged toward the station door while Robo bolted out ahead of them. Stella was dressed in heavy clothing and hiking boots, new footwear that Mattie had helped her order to replace the more fashionable boots she wore for office work. These working boots had a heavy tread that provided better traction on rough footing, ice, and snow. Stella must be planning to go with them to search.

Robo stopped at the door, which was well lit from above, and stared up as if willing it to open.

Stella chuckled. "He never gives up, does he? Someday we should install an automatic door opener—that would blow his mind."

Mattie smiled at the image before sobering, the thought of the ominous message on the note uppermost in her own mind. "Wait," she told Robo as she reached the door, making sure he waited for Stella and her to enter first. It was a small bow to her being the boss but one she insisted on with this high-drive, alpha-male shepherd. It was easier if she kept him in line so he wasn't tempted to take over, like she'd been warned he might be by his trainer.

Waiting for others to enter first had become such a routine for him that he needed little prompting, but once inside, he rushed ahead to the dispatcher's desk. Again, Mattie was tickled by her dog's response when he spotted Sam Corns, the night dispatcher, at the desk instead of his good friend Rainbow. Robo skidded to a stop and waited for Mattie to check in. He looked back over his shoulder at her, and she could almost read the question on his face: *What's up with this?*

Sam, the bright light from the overheads glinting off his bald pate, greeted them as she and Stella approached.

"Sheriff McCoy and Brody are in the briefing room," he told them. "I made a fresh pot of coffee in there."

They both thanked him and headed back to the briefing room, Robo leading the way. The jolt of adrenaline Mattie received when she found the note no longer sustained her, and her energy flagged; black coffee would have to keep her going tonight.

Since the briefing room door was open, Robo rushed in, greeting Sheriff McCoy and Brody and receiving pats as if he'd been away for weeks instead of a few days. Mattie felt a glow of pleasure from the warm reception she and her dog were receiving after her week away. This team felt like family to her.

They'd been through a lot together the past year and a half since she and Robo had formed the first K-9 unit for this department, and for a moment she felt overwhelmed with gratitude for their support. As she swallowed against the lump in her throat, she told herself she must be tired to succumb so easily to emotion.

Brody had placed two load-out bags on the table and was zipping up one of them. They held GPS units, flashlights, radio equipment, first-aid kits, flares, and other emergency equipment. For the most part the bags were always ready to go, but the flashlights and radio equipment were taken from battery-charging racks and added at the last minute. Several rifles lay on the table, waiting to be placed in gun racks inside their vehicles.

Mattie laid the plastic sleeve that contained the note on the table. She'd placed the note open inside so they could read it through the clear protective cover.

Brody looked up after reading it. "You know this could be some type of trap."

"Ambush was my first thought," Mattie said. "But why?"

No one seemed to have an answer for that.

Brody unzipped one of the bags. "If it is, these will level the playing field," he said, taking out a pair of night vision goggles. "We've got two pair."

Mattie nodded. The night vision goggles would keep them from having to use flashlights, a sure way to become a target for a sniper.

McCoy picked up the note. "I'll secure this in my office for now. Do we have everything?"

Stella had filled two travel mugs with coffee, and she lifted them as if in answer to the sheriff's question before handing one to Mattie.

Originally, Mattie had thought that she and Robo might go with Brody as backup. She wondered why the sheriff felt the mission required all four of them and assumed it had something to do with the dangers they'd faced in the high country in the past and his concern that one of his officers might be following a siren's call.

Mattie grabbed a load-out bag and rifle while Brody carried the rest, and they trooped through the station lobby. They paused while McCoy took the note into his office and then came out carrying the satellite phone with him. He briefed Sam before turning to leave.

Mattie loaded Robo into his compartment at the back of their unit while Stella climbed into the passenger seat. Brody loaded their equipment into the back of the sheriff's Jeep before joining McCoy up front.

Mattie slid into the driver's seat, placing her travel mug in the holder as she glanced at Stella. "You ready to roll?"

Stella snapped the buckle on her seat belt. "Yep."

Robo came forward to poke his nose through the steel mesh at the front of his cage, and Mattie rubbed the top of his muzzle. Despite her fatigue, it felt good to be back at work with her partner.

Their headlights pierced the darkness as Mattie followed McCoy's Jeep out of town and onto the highway. They headed west, the moonlight illuminating patches of snow in the ditch banks. Being alone with Stella in the car gave Mattie a chance to update her on everything that had happened in Mexico and San Diego.

"So you have no idea where your mom and your stepfather went?" Stella asked.

"Right."

"How about why they picked up and left town?"

Mattie shook her head, her discouragement weighing her down. "Same. I hope it wasn't my visit that spooked her."

"That was months ago, and apparently she just left recently. I doubt if you made her run."

"I hope that's the case."

"If this detective, Sonia Alvarez, decides to take on your dad's cold case, there might be reason to share with her what you know about your mom. At least share what you gleaned from Ramona when you saw her last July."

Mattie had thought of that, and though her tendency was to withhold her trust from anyone new, she leaned toward changing her ways. "Julia and our grandmother are still afraid to share their secrets. Detective Alvarez has questioned them before, so Abuela has already withheld what she knew at that time. It's hard for her to come clean now."

"I understand that, but your mom's eyewitness account does shed light on your father's motive for cooperating with this smuggling ring. I think it's important."

Mattie nodded, sinking into silence as she mulled things over. She agreed with Stella's take on the case, and she'd felt guilty about withholding what she knew ever since she'd ended her interview with Alvarez. Her mother's disappearance changed how Mattie felt about sharing her location, especially if the San Diego police could help locate her.

When they turned onto the gravel road that would lead them upward toward Shadow Ridge, coniferous trees sprang up around them, the forest thickening as they traveled. It had been a warm fall, and even though they'd had a couple storms, the snow cover had melted for the most part, leaving patchy ice and snowdrifts in the shadows.

The road wound through the forest in a westward direction, gaining altitude slowly. Though they'd left the pavement and were now on dirt road, this particular route was well traveled by campers, horse trailers, and RVs that parked in the campground near the Shadow Ridge corral, so it was well maintained.

Soon the healthy green color of the pine in their headlights turned to gray. The mountain beetle that had decimated parts of Colorado's forests had hit this area surrounding the campground especially hard. Gray-brown patches of dead lodgepole pine covered the mountainsides, leaving them vulnerable to fire. Having originated primarily in northern Colorado, the pests were now spreading into southern forests, leaving swaths of standing dead pine in their wake. It was estimated that over three million acres of pine had been killed.

Standing dead. Her skin crawled as she remembered the note left on her door.

Mattie turned into the circular drive near the campground, noticing three pickup trucks parked among the needleless trees, one with an attached horse trailer. No people were visible, and she guessed the owners of these vehicles were asleep inside campers or RVs parked at sites within the campground. It was still rifle season for elk and deer, so even though the weather was below freezing at night, there would probably be hunters camped in tent sites as well.

She parked behind the sheriff's Jeep.

"There's a lot about this setting I don't like," Stella murmured.

Mattie knew how she felt. The presence of hunters in a mountain campsite felt very familiar, something she and her colleagues encountered frequently, and the dangers inherent in the situation were significant during a homicide investigation— if indeed that was what they were dealing with here. She still hoped that the note referred to a person who was injured or missing.

"Yeah, it's creepy here all right." Mattie released the latch on her door, making Robo rocket back and forth in his cage. "You wait here, Robo, until we see what we need to do next."

She stepped out of her warm vehicle, and the freezing air pinched her nostrils. She scanned the terrain as she and Stella walked up to join the sheriff and Brody. The corral the note had mentioned was constructed of lodgepole pine rails scraped free of bark, and their creamy color gleamed in the moonlight.

Several horses were tied to one side of the circular pen, nickering softly as they shifted their bodies and turned their heads toward the newcomers, their curiosity overcoming any fright that might have been aroused by the arrival of unfamiliar humans. Bales of hay were stacked outside the fence, well out of reach of the livestock inside.

Dead forest lay beyond the far side of the corral, the trees up front standing out like needleless skeletons jabbing at the stars while acres of the same loomed gray and dead beyond, a formless shape that stretched for miles. This was where Mattie presumed she and Robo would search for the male referred to in the note.

McCoy waved an arm in the direction of the dead forest. "Do you have enough light to get started searching in there?"

Mattie squinted across the corral at the trees. "The moonlight helps."

"We've got the night vision goggles," Brody said.

McCoy looked at Mattie. "Detective LoSasso and I will manage things here. I expect we'll have hunters coming out of their campsites soon to check on their horses. Deputy Brody will go with you."

It was what she'd expected. "I'll get Robo."

She turned her back on the dead forest to walk toward her unit. She had a bad feeling about this mission. The debris that had sloughed off the trees, dry twigs and needles, would make it impossible for them to dampen the sound of their footsteps while they searched, and anyone equipped with night vision goggles could observe their approach. This would be a perfect place to set a trap.

FIVE

Mattie's SUV swayed as Robo threw his weight around the back, and she could imagine his excitement. He was always ready to go.

She opened the back hatch and he stopped at the edge, prancing on his front paws. "You're ready to work, aren't you?"

Mattie slipped on his Kevlar vest, which had a blue nylon handle at the back that she could grab on to and hold if needed. Her dog was so obedient that she rarely needed more than a touch to signal him to be quiet and steady. This wasn't always the case with patrol dogs, and she considered herself lucky to have been paired with her remarkable partner.

"Let's give you a drink." She splashed a cup of water into his bowl, just enough to moisten his mucous membranes, important for enhancing his sense of smell before he searched for humans or objects.

Robo knew the routine, and after a few laps he looked up at her with bright eyes, his eagerness apparent. She invited him down to the ground, and he went directly to their unit's rear tire to lift his leg, another part of their ritual. Nothing stopped a search faster than a potty break, so Mattie always asked him to take care of business before they started.

"That's right," she murmured, reinforcing his independent thinking. "Take a break."

She strapped on her duty belt that she'd customized to hold Robo's equipment. Taking a short leash from a loop, she snapped it onto his collar and said, "Come with me," which allowed Robo to choose his own position, following along or at heel. She wasn't surprised that he chose to stick close to her left heel.

When she rejoined the others, Brody was carrying his AR15 rifle in a sling that hung from his back. Had they not experienced the past year of homicides and violence, she imagined things would have been different. They would have been much more relaxed about this mysterious note and wouldn't have suspected a trap or anything serious like they did tonight. But since the past year had been so tumultuous, Brody's rifle stood as a symbol of just how much they all felt on edge.

Brody handed her a pair of night vision goggles, and she slipped them on so she could adjust the strap. The green glow and illumination seemed eerie as she scanned the dead forest beyond the corral. Now able to see beyond the front line of trees, she could tell that the woods weren't as dense as she'd first thought.

A deep, rumbling voice from behind startled her. "What's going on out here?"

Robo whirled at her side to face the stranger. Mattie turned to see McCoy engage the hunter, who'd evidently been drawn out by the whinnies coming from the horses in the corral. Her goggles allowed her to see his face clearly—a male in his fifties with a swarthy full beard and a dark unibrow.

"I'm Sheriff Abraham McCoy. We've had a report of a missing person out here. Have you heard anything about that?"

The man denied any knowledge of a missing person while Mattie took off her headgear and tightened the strap. She listened as she and Brody tucked GPS units inside their pockets and made sure their radios were working.

"Drake Kelsey." He extended a hand, which McCoy clasped in greeting. "I heard your trucks and came out to check the horses. Do you need some help?"

"Not at the moment, Mr. Kelsey. You may return to your campsite for now."

"I'm happy to help if I can."

"We'd like to keep this area free and clear. If you have others in your party, you might tell them to stay at your campsite. We'll let you know if we need anything."

Kelsey apparently got the message, as he gave McCoy his campsite number and left. Mattie wondered if others would show up soon and if any of the hunters in this campground had something to do with the note.

"You two go ahead and get started when you're ready," McCoy said. "We'll deal with folks here and keep them out of your way."

Mattie met Brody's gaze and then returned his nod. He gestured for her to lead the way. Her eyes had adjusted to the moonlight, so she carried the goggles with her instead of putting them on as she picked her way around the rough terrain outside the corral and headed for the forest on the far side. Robo came along beside her at heel.

Once she reached the edge of the trees, she slipped on the goggles and made sure she'd adjusted the strap tightly enough for them to stay in place should she need to run or jog. When she looked down at Robo, his black shape and tan markings were clearly delineated. Tufts of grass, rocks, and ruts underfoot were also clearly visible, and here and there she noticed a disturbance in the terrain, a slight flattening of the grass. This would be a good spot to start, a place to see if Robo picked up human scent.

She removed the short leash from Robo's collar and tucked it back into place on her belt. She exchanged the shorter leash for a longer one, which she clipped to the ring at the back of his search harness. Then she began the talk they both knew so well, meant to rev up his prey drive enough to sustain him through a long search.

"Are you ready to work, bud? Do you want to find someone?" She continued the chatter, patting him firmly on his side until he gazed up at her, rising on his hind feet beside her in a pirouette. "Okay, boy. Let's find someone. Search!"

Robo had been taught to search for people several different ways. If Mattie had an article of clothing or something bearing the scent of a specific person, she could give him a whiff of it, and he would search for that scent alone. If there was no scent article but she knew where a scent trail started—such as when a person had left a parked car—she could direct his nose to the ground and ask him to pick up the track that way. Or, as in this case, if she was unsure where a track started, she could direct him into an area and he would quarter the ground, sweeping back and forth until he picked up the freshest scent trail of a human that he could find and started following it.

Robo put his nose to the ground and started sniffing along the edge of the forest where she indicated. He dodged around bushes, giving them a cursory sniff as he went. Mattie stayed close, tethered to her dog by the leash but keeping it loose between the two of them. Brody remained close by, standing still and waiting for Robo to strike out in a definite direction.

In cases like these, the start of a track was always the unknown factor. Was Robo picking up the scent midway? Was the track coming or going—which way should she encourage him to go? And if he found a human scent track, did it even belong to the human they were looking for?

But if there was one thing she'd learned in the last year and a half, it was to stand back and let her dog work. Searching for a human was different from searching for evidence. When searching for an unknown person, it was best to let him sort through the scents on his own and pick up a track if one was available.

As they reached the north side of the corral closest to the road, Robo paused and worked the ground. He sneezed as he poked his nose into the winter-brown grass but continued to sniff it thoroughly.

She studied him, looking for signs that he was onto something. His ears pricked and he advanced slowly, lifting one front foot and pausing as he sniffed. She could imagine those millions of scent cells in his nose and mucous membranes charging and firing as he cataloged each layer of scent: the earthy smell of the dirt, the dusty winter vegetation, the trail of rabbits or other wildlife. It was his job to ignore all that and search for human scent alone.

He lowered his foot to the ground, inching forward a few steps. Finally, he moved westward to the edge of the trees, sweeping his head side to side as he walked, increasing his momentum as he locked onto the track. When he surged forward, Mattie's adrenaline started to rise. He'd found a scent.

Mattie could tell that Robo was now certain of the scent he wanted to follow, and she kept up with him so she wouldn't hold him back. Brody fell in behind them.

They moved into the standing dead trees, and she slipped on her night vision goggles. Everything turned green and ghostly, but she was able to see the forest floor well enough to size up her footing. Deadfall was thick in this area, fallen branches and needles threatening to trip or turn ankles.

She could also see evidence that someone had been through here: broken twigs, disturbances in the dead pine needles, scuffs where shoes or boots had trod. These signs allayed any doubt that Robo was on a scent track made by humans. Though she hadn't doubted him at all. She'd learned to trust her partner, and he'd proven himself over and over.

Confidence in the power of her dog's nose bubbled over, and she offered him enthusiastic support. "Good job, Robo. Let's find someone."

Brown stuff crackled underfoot in the dead forest, proving her correct in what she'd expected. This footing would telegraph their approach to anyone waiting. She stared at Robo, watching for a change in his body language that might indicate an ambush up ahead. Nothing so far.

Robo continued to wind through the trees in a generally westward direction for at least ten minutes, keeping his nose to the ground. The scent must be fresh, because he didn't hesitate as he moved forward along a track that could easily have been traversed by a human. There was no backtracking, no climbing over deadfall, no stopping and searching for missing scent. He continued his confident trek along a trajectory that led in a beeline from the campground corral.

A breeze quickened from the west, chilling her cheeks below her goggles. Robo's head popped up, and he sniffed the air moving against his face. At that moment, Mattie recognized he'd switched from tracking the scent pattern on the ground to trailing it through the air.

Her pulse quickened as the hackles on Robo's neck rose, making the hair on her own neck prickle.

She grabbed the handle on his Kevlar vest and murmured, "Robo, wait," in a voice barely above a whisper. Turning to Brody, she held her finger to her lips and then pointed at Robo's back. In the goggles' green glow, she could see Brody nod his understanding. He held his rifle ahead of him at the ready.

"Search, Robo," she murmured, and let him lead her slowly forward. Skeleton pine surrounded them as they edged along, one careful step at a time. Mattie flinched as if she sensed a projectile piercing her back, and she immediately put a damper on her imagination.

She focused on Robo, trying to read him as they crept forward. When he hesitated, she raised her gaze to scan the forest. Trees with bare branches danced in and out of her vision as she swept the area ahead.

Then she spotted it—something different about one of the trees. She pinned her eyes on the bulky shape while Robo eased forward. The silhouette assumed the form of a human.

"Person," Mattie murmured to Brody, pointing at the form. And then to Robo, "Good job, buddy."

Her senses as alert as they could possibly be, Mattie followed Robo until he stopped and sat about five feet away from the tree. Though the person had long hair and a bowed head, she could tell he was a man. By this time, she could also make out the rope that tied him into an upright position against the tree.

The man looked as dead as the tree he was bound to—the standing dead. Mattie shivered, and Robo leaned against her leg. She stroked him, telling him what a good boy he was while she scanned the area in a 360-degree circle. Since Robo had not been trained to search for human remains, he must have tracked a live person to this location. Maybe that person was still out here.

Brody came forward, his head on a swivel as he scanned the forest. He removed his insulated glove, slipped his hand into his pocket, and withdrew a latex glove.

"Here, let me do that while you keep watch," Mattie said, taking the glove from him. "Robo, stay."

She tugged on the glove and touched the man. He was stiff, and she had a difficult time trying to move his head up so she could check for a pulse on his neck. Nothing. "He's been dead for several hours, I'd guess."

She felt chilled to the core as she extracted a flashlight from her duty belt and raised the goggles to the top of her head. Leaning close to the corpse, she examined his face in the more natural glow of the flashlight's beam. Long black hair shot with gray, grayish-brown complexion that matched the color of the tree, closed eyes . . . but the prominent cheekbones and the narrow shape of his nose looked oddly familiar.

Then it hit her. She remembered where she'd seen this man before. In fact, his business card with his photo on it was in her wallet, locked inside the glove compartment of her unit. Despite the chill, she broke into a light sweat as a new wave of adrenaline washed through her.

She would bet her next paycheck that this standing dead man was her mother's husband—Juan Martinez.

SIX

Fortunately, the ancient loafing shed at the Redstone-Balderhouse Campground provided some shelter. Inside the snug wooden structure, Cole leaned over the black-and-white paint mare lying in one of the stalls. This horse seemed sicker than the other one—at least the gelding outside in the corral was still standing. He removed the rectal thermometer to read the results. Elevated temp.

He smoothed the mare's trembling haunch before straightening. "She's got a fever," he said to Tanner, who was standing by with worried creases between his eyebrows. "Labored breathing."

He withdrew a penlight from his chest pocket as he moved to the mare's head and knelt. Lifting her eyelid, he shifted the light back and forth over her dark eye. The pupil remained dilated and fixed. He checked the other eye with the same result. *This doesn't look like colic. Is it toxicity or infection?*

Rocking back on his heels, he looked up at the owner. "What do you feed your horses, Tanner?"

A large man who probably weighed in at around 230 pounds, most of it solid muscle, Tanner Rattler had a round face framed by a full black beard that he'd probably grown out for hunting season. His dark eyes were intense and piercing under heavy black eyebrows.

"They get hay with a mix of alfalfa and grass this time of year."

"Any weeds in it?"

"No, it's clean, good quality. I grow it myself."

"Do you give them any supplements?"

"A little sweet feed when they're working hard. I had these two up in the mountains today."

"No vitamins or minerals, then?"

"Nope. Don't give them anything like that."

The mare opened her mouth and coughed, her belly heaving with the effort. Cole caught a whiff of a strong odor of garlic. He bent closer to smell her breath. Definitely the odor of garlic. He inspected her mane. It looked fairly normal, but when he bent the coarse hair at her neck, he thought it might be slightly brittle.

He gave Tanner a piercing look. He'd run into problems before with an owner who supplemented her racehorses with a powerful drug that made them deathly ill. The gelding in the corral demonstrated ataxia, which might be brought on by toxicity from something he'd ingested. "So you're not giving any supplements at all?"

Tanner shook his shaggy head. "Nothing like that. They get good hay and grain and that's it."

There was another line of inquiry to check out. "So these two were up in the mountains today. Did they graze on anything? Grass or weeds?"

Tanner appeared to be thinking. "Not that I recall. I took along some hay that I gave them midday, so they wouldn't have to change feed."

Cole thought this sudden onset had to indicate toxicity rather than infection. "Both horses were fine when you left this morning?"

"Completely normal."

"They probably ingested something they shouldn't. Think back on the day and see if you can come up with anything. I need to get some fluid into this mare's stomach to dilute what's in there, and I'll give her some mineral oil too, to try to prevent colic. I have to go to my truck to get some things. I'll be right back."

Outside, the air was crisp and clean and frigid. Stars twinkled in a clear sky, and the moon illuminated the gray planks that made up the shed walls. Cole gathered tubing, a jug of mineral oil, a stainless-steel bucket, and other supplies while his mind churned out the different diagnoses he could be dealing with.

The garlic smell on the mare's breath could be from selenium toxicosis. He'd seen it in horses before, but usually in a chronic form caused by grazing on grass or hay grown in soil with a high level of selenium.

Symptoms of chronic selenium toxicity included brittle hair, broken mane and tail hair, and sore feet. In severe cases, he'd read, some horses even sloughed their hoof wall, although he'd never encountered a case that bad.

There was little to be done for treatment—removing the source of selenium exposure and providing support for the symptoms was about it. He'd never seen an acute case of selenium toxicosis, although he knew it existed, primarily from selenium supplement overdose. Selenium was an important nutrient and supplementation became necessary in cases of deficiency, which could cause muscle cramping and reproductive problems.

Finding a proper balance for supplements could be tricky and overdose wasn't unheard of, but he believed Tanner when he said he didn't supplement his horses. Most ranchers who used their horses for normal work didn't need to. Typically, the owners of sport horses or racing horses were the ones who got into trouble when supplementing with selenium.

Carrying his equipment, Cole hurried back into the shed, feeling grim over the possible diagnosis. The bucket clanked as he set it down outside the stall.

Tanner knelt beside the mare, stroking her neck and shoulder, and he glanced up as Cole opened the stall door. "I went up to Shadow Ridge Campground to hunt today. When we got back to the trailer, I watered them at the stock tank in the campground pen. They also had water from streams when we were up in the high country. That's the only thing I can think of."

Contaminated water might do it, but it would have to be a high level of contamination to bring on this type of reaction. "I think we could be dealing with acute selenium toxicosis here,

Tanner. I'll draw some blood from both horses and see what's happening with their white blood cell count to rule out infection. I need to check on their liver function too. Let's see if we can get this mare to stand up."

Cole picked up the lead rope on the mare's halter while Tanner circled behind her to lend his considerable strength toward helping the mare lift her haunches from the stall floor. It took a great deal of tongue clucking, pulling, and pushing, but finally the mare straightened her forelegs and heaved her bulk up to stand precariously. Weaving, she staggered a few steps until she seemed to catch her balance.

Her strident breath sounds didn't bode well for her survival. Cole made short work of inserting the tube in her nostril, blowing gently on the free end as he advanced it into her stomach. He sniffed the gas that came back through the end of the tube, and the heavy odor of garlic almost made him gag. He was becoming more and more certain that this horse had overdosed on selenium.

Tanner had moved up to the mare's head to hold her halter. "That stinks."

"Yes, it does. What's it smell like to you?"

"Rotten garlic."

Using a stainless-steel dosing syringe, Cole injected a combination of water laced with mineral oil into the end of the tube. After he finished and removed the tube, he blocked the vein in the mare's neck and drew a blood sample. After withdrawing the needle, he capped it and slipped the sample into his chest pocket. He clipped a hair sample from her mane and hair coat, bagged it, and then scanned the stall floor.

A pile of fresh feces lay in one corner of the stall. "Is that from this mare?" Cole asked, pointing at the manure.

"She pooped shortly after I put her in here."

Cole turned a baggie inside out, scooped up a sample, and then turned the baggie back to normal so he could seal it. "Which campground did you say you were at today when you watered the horses?"

"Shadow Ridge." Tanner wore a frown of concern as he stroked the mare's neck. "I rode Keno here and used Boss as a packhorse. I'd left my truck and trailer parked at the campground, but I didn't shoot anything today. Didn't even sight any elk. I watered both horses before I loaded them. I remember that the tank was almost empty when Keno drank, and I refilled it while Boss was drinking."

That might explain why the mare was so much worse off than the gelding. "I need a sample of the water from that tank."

"I could go get one."

"You'll need to stay here and keep an eye on these two." Cole began gathering his equipment. "Let's get samples from Boss too, and then I'll drive up and get a sample of the water. If that tank is contaminated, there could be other sick horses up there."

He was glad to see that Boss was still standing in the corral, although the sorrel gelding wore that stoic, staring-into-the-middle-distance look that Cole associated with an animal's suffering. Cole noticed that the gelding's reddish-brown hair coat looked dull and lifeless.

Cole moved to the horse's head and gently opened his drooping lips to smell his breath. It carried a rotten garlic stench. "Smells like Keno's. Let's give him the same treatment. At least he's breathing easier than she is."

"He didn't drink as much as she did. I'm pretty sure that water tank is what made them sick."

Cole nodded. "We'll get it tested."

After treating Boss, Cole felt he'd done all he could for the two horses. "We should get some lab results back tomorrow. If this is selenium poisoning like I suspect, there's not much more we can do except keep a close eye on them and support them. I'm going on up to the campground to get that sample, and I'll stop back by on my way home to check on these two. If they want to lie down, go ahead and let them rest. But call me if one of them starts to colic."

"I'm not sure you'll have cell phone service up there, but I'll leave a message." Tanner stooped to pick up the bucket to help Cole carry his equipment back to the truck.

After repacking his instruments, Cole drove slowly away from the corral, lifting his hand to return Tanner's wave. His headlights pierced the darkness as he turned to go toward Shadow Ridge. He yawned and blinked hard to clear his tired eyes while navigating the hairpin curves that wound up the mountain through the pine forest.

His truck chugged up the steep road, and he was relieved when he spotted the wooden forest service sign announcing the entry into Shadow Ridge Campground. He made the last turn, carefully driving into the parking lot, and was surprised to see two Timber Creek Sheriff's Department vehicles parked among the trucks and trailers.

Beyond them was a string of yellow crime scene tape blocking the way around the near side of the corral. His gut tightened when he recognized one of the vehicles as Mattie's K-9 unit. Whatever was going on in this campground in the middle of the night couldn't be good. And Mattie was here, right in the thick of it.

SEVEN

Questions invaded Mattie's mind. Had someone killed Juan Martinez and then tied him to this tree? Or had he died standing alone here in the forest? Either way, was her mother being held captive by his killer?

The note she'd received taunted her, and she assumed the answer to her last question was yes. Nausea rose in her throat as she thought of what this meant for her mother.

Mattie directed the beam of her flashlight toward the dead man's face. She had to clear the tightness in her throat by swallowing before she spoke. "I think I know who this man is."

Brody glanced at the corpse and then resumed scanning the area around them. "Who?"

Robo whined, and Mattie smoothed the fur on top of his head. Her dog hated finding dead people at the end of a track. Robo had been trained to find live folks when he searched, although sometimes the trail ended with a dead victim. He'd also been exposed to cadaver detection as a young dog, so it wasn't a complete surprise when this happened.

Since the victim had been tied to a tree, it seemed obvious that someone had placed him there. If Ramona was in the hands of this man's killer, what Mattie and the team did next to process the scene would be crucial. The weight of responsibility overpowered the panic that was starting to build inside her.

"I've only seen a photo of the man I think this is, but I have that picture in my unit, so we'll be able to determine if it's a match." Mattie drew a breath to loosen the tightness that had gathered in her chest and spoke in a near whisper. "I think he's Juan Martinez. He's from Mexico."

Brody shifted, and the night vision goggles he still wore on his face turned toward her. "What? How do you know?"

The only people in Timber Creek who knew about Mattie's mother living in Mexico were Cole and Stella. It would be tricky to navigate this identification under the circumstances. "I have a business card in my unit with his picture on it. We can use it to compare."

"How do you have this photo?"

Mattie gazed around the area, wondering if any of the dead trees had ears. Fear for her mother's safety made her realize she would have to share more than she'd planned. She swept out her hand in a gesture that encompassed the forest. "We'll talk about that later. Once we've cleared this area."

Brody paused and then raised a hand to the radio he wore at his shoulder. "I'll call this in to the sheriff."

The radio receiver crackled to life as Brody pressed the button to talk. When he spoke into the mic, he chose to use ten-code, probably out of concern that civilians were still with the sheriff. "Alpha One, this is Alpha Two. We've got a 10-35 here and request 10-79. We're about a half mile straight west into the woods."

Major crime alert and request for the coroner. Mattie pulled her goggles back against her eyes as she scanned the forest. Danger seemed to lurk behind every tree trunk, even though they'd heard nothing. She glanced at Robo to see what she could glean from him. He remained sitting at her heel, alert and watching her for his next instruction.

The sheriff's response was quick and to the point. "Are you safe?"

"So far. Checking the area."

"We'll send in backup."

The fewer people back in here, the better, Mattie thought. "Tell the sheriff to hold on that for a few minutes. Let Robo and me clear the area."

Again, she could tell that Brody was observing her, but he passed on her message to the sheriff.

"Keep us informed," McCoy replied.

"Copy."

Though Mattie hesitated to send Robo into a dangerous situation, she'd decided that his body language told her they were alone out here. Even though the situation gave her the creeps, she figured her dog would have been acting jumpy if he'd smelled someone hiding in the deadfall. Especially in the presence of a corpse.

"What do you plan to do?" Brody asked her.

Mattie remembered how Robo's trainer had once told her that if she didn't learn to trust her dog, they as a team would never be any better than a human cop could be. But if she learned to let Robo do his job, there was no limit to what her partner could accomplish.

"I'll ask Robo to clear the area." She led him away from the corpse a few steps before bending to unclip his leash. Then, in a brisk and excited tone, she said, "Okay, Robo. Let's find a bad guy. Let's go. Search!"

Robo sniffed the air, trotted in an arc away from the tree, and then circled back. Sniffing the ground near the tree where they'd started, Robo appeared to pick up scent and headed back toward the parking lot, returning along the track they'd traveled before with his nose to the ground.

"Robo, wait." Mattie grabbed the handle on Robo's vest and checked in with Brody. "I think this area is clear. Someone made this body dump and probably went back to the campground. I need to follow Robo on this track."

"Go ahead. I'll stand guard here and check in with the sheriff."

Mattie released Robo, giving him lots of chatter to encourage him to resume his search. It would be amazing if he led her to the campsite of a killer.

Staying alert in case he was leading them both into an ambush, Mattie felt exposed without Brody at her back. Typically, it was her job to watch her dog for signals that he was onto something while Brody watched the environment for their safety.

The pressure of making every minute count weighed heavily on her. They had to work this scene and do a good job if they were going to find out who had left this dead man tied to a tree . . . and also whether her mother was out here somewhere being held captive.

Robo worked his way back to the parking lot, never once raising his hackles or pausing to search. As they came out of the forest, headlights from several vehicles lit the corral and the ground around it. Mattie pushed her goggles back to the top of her head.

Yellow crime scene tape glowed in the headlights, and she ducked under it as Robo led her around the edge of the corral. A crowd of people had gathered behind the vehicles in the lot.

McCoy moved forward from the group and stepped into the light. He raised one hand in greeting but didn't speak. He merely waited and watched as she and Robo finished their job.

Nose to the ground, Robo followed the invisible track past the lights and onto a darkened spot in the gravel lot. He sniffed around, for the first time hesitating, as if he'd lost the scent. Mattie knew that this might mean the person they were tracking had entered a vehicle and driven away, but she stood back and allowed him to take his time.

He evidently picked up the scent trail again, because he trotted back along the side of the lot, once again entering beams of light from the trucks. Mattie followed like a shadow as he passed through, going into the darkness surrounding the corral. She slipped her goggles back in place as she approached.

Robo trotted toward the water tank.

"Don't let him drink." Cole's voice came from behind her, surprising her with his presence. "It might be poisoned."

Mattie raised a hand to acknowledge that she'd heard, but she doubted if Robo was after water. He was still on the scent and just showing her where it led. As if to confirm what she'd thought, Robo circled the tank and then led her back to the dark side of the lot. There, he sniffed thoroughly, acting more and more frustrated as he tried to find where the trail led. By this time Mattie felt certain that the person he was looking for had left the area in a vehicle, so she told him to come to her and ended the search.

Mattie figured the same person who had left Juan Martinez in the forest had circled the stock tank. She praised Robo, and her pats made thumping sounds on his rib cage as she knelt and hugged him. He stole a kiss and wiggled with excitement. Backing away with his feathery tail wagging, he looked up at her with eager eyes lit by the moon. She pushed her goggles up onto her head so she could give him eye contact.

"You're a good boy, you know that." Hugging Robo against her leg, she turned toward the sheriff.

McCoy walked up close. "The trail ends here?"

It gratified Mattie that members of the team were learning to recognize Robo's body language. In most jurisdictions the success of a K-9 unit was enhanced by the support of the whole department and the backup the other officers provided.

She spoke quietly so the civilians couldn't overhear. "Robo picked up a trail near the victim he found. It looks like the trail led around the stock tank before ending here. Evidently the person entered a vehicle before it pulled away. We need to canvass everyone who's camping here to see if they know who was parked here on the edge of the lot today."

"I've called in Deputy Garcia to report up here and Deputy Hitchen to cover patrol. We'll have more help soon."

Garcia was a veteran in the sheriff's department, Hitchen a new recruit. "We need to keep the crime scene back there as clean as possible," Mattie said, gesturing with a tilt of her head in that direction. "I want Robo to search for evidence at first light."

McCoy nodded.

"And Sheriff." Mattie hesitated for a moment, but now was as good a time as any to divulge what she knew, while she had him alone. She spoke in a quiet voice. "I might be able to identify the victim. I have a business card in my unit with a photo on it that I think matches our victim."

McCoy straightened, his eyes on her face. "Who?"

"Juan Martinez. A business owner and mechanic from Mexico."

"And you know him?"

"We've never met. But I met his brother this past week."

The crunch of footsteps on the gravel came from behind the sheriff, and they both turned to see Cole approach. "The water in the tank might be poisoned?" Mattie asked him.

"I've got two sick horses who drank here earlier today. None of these horses have symptoms yet, but the tank has been filled several times by now. If there's still contamination, it's been diluted."

"Robo followed scent from the crime scene to here and over to the tank. Whoever left that track had to be messing around at the water tank earlier. What poison was used?"

"We don't know yet, but I'll send a water sample to the lab. I suspect selenium."

Mattie didn't know much about it. "Can it be deadly?"

"In high enough doses, yes." Cole turned to McCoy. "Do you need me to do anything here, Abraham?"

Cole was a member of the sheriff's posse, which was often called out to secure crime scenes or search for people who'd gone missing in the mountains.

"Not at the moment, but we might by morning. Are you planning to stay up here?"

"I have to go back to Redstone-Balderhouse Campground to check on the sick horses. But I can come back here afterward if you need me."

"Let's wait until we have more time to sort things out. I'll be in touch."

A compelling need to tell Cole how she was afraid for her mother grew inside Mattie while she listened to their exchange. This level of emotional neediness felt unfamiliar, and she didn't like it at all. This was not a time to spill her secrets in front of the others, and both she and Cole had work to do. She remained silent.

"Okay then. If I'm not needed here, I'll go." Cole looked from McCoy to her. "Mattie, can I have a word with you?"

"Sure." She turned to follow him.

McCoy spoke up. "I need to meet with you ASAP, Mattie."

"I'll be right there."

After leading her and Robo several feet away from the others, Cole turned. "Are you okay, Mattie? Abraham said Robo found a body back in that stand of beetle kill."

"I'm okay." Despite her hesitation, she thought she might tell him about Juan, but the man named Drake Kelsey and a woman she hadn't seen before separated from the crowd and moved their way, heading toward the sheriff. She touched Cole's arm, and he took her hand. "I need to get to work, and you do too. Let's talk as soon as we can."

"I'll be back in a couple hours."

"You should go home. Robo and I will be tied up here for the rest of the night."

Cole shook his head. "I'll be back."

She squeezed his hand before parting. As Cole walked away toward the vehicles in the parking lot, he and Kelsey passed each other without speaking. With a hollow feeling in her gut, Mattie headed for the sheriff. If this victim truly was Juan Martinez, they needed to locate her mother before she suffered the same fate as her husband.

EIGHT

"This is my wife, Edith," Kelsey was saying to the sheriff as Mattie approached. "What's going on out there in the woods?"

Kelsey's wife stood behind him, her hands thrust into her coat pockets. Though she was covered in heavy coveralls, boots, and a stocking cap, she appeared to be of average height and weight. Strands of silvery gray hair peeked out below the cap, but it was too dark to see her eye color. Kelsey also had strands of gray in the black hair of his full beard.

"We have evidence that a serious crime has been committed, Mr. Kelsey. We need your cooperation to stay back and let us do our work. We'll want to talk with everyone here, and it would be best if you waited in your vehicles or your campsites and stayed warm until we can get to you."

Agitated, Kelsey stepped up close to McCoy. "Are we safe? And what about our horses?"

Robo stiffened at Mattie's side as if he sensed a threat, and she backed up a few feet to keep an eye on the situation. The guy evidently had no idea what Robo's reaction would be if he laid a hand on the sheriff. She grasped the handle on Robo's vest just in case.

McCoy stood his ground. "I understand your concern. We have no reason to believe that anyone is unsafe at the moment, but I do want you to hole up in your vehicles for now until we can investigate this crime further. And Dr. Walker says the horses all look fine, but you need to water them from a bucket filled directly from the spigot until he can make sure the tank is clean."

"Yeah, yeah, he told us all that." Kelsey waved his hand in the direction of the corral. "But what's going on? Has someone been poisoned?"

"We don't know. We'll share what we can when we have more details. For now, though, I need you to go to your vehicle or your campsite so we can get to work."

Edith placed a hand on her husband's arm. "Let's go, Drake. I don't want to stand out here in the open. There could be someone with a rifle drawing a bead on us right now."

Mattie had to admit she wondered the same thing. She still had a feeling they'd been drawn out here into the forest at night for a purpose other than finding the dead man.

But Kelsey apparently wasn't ready to go yet. "So is it safe to leave our horses here?"

"As long as they're tied, I think so," McCoy said. "If you're concerned, you can stay in your vehicle beside the corral."

Mattie wanted to find out if they knew anything helpful sooner rather than later. "Before you go, can either of you tell me if you saw a vehicle parked out here at the side of the lot earlier? Say this afternoon or this evening?"

Edith answered. "There have been RVs in and out of here all afternoon. Most of them pulled out by evening."

"But did you notice anyone in particular parked at the side of the lot?" Mattie asked.

"Not really. I think they were just hunters coming and going."

"Did you see anything suspicious, like someone carrying a person or helping a person walk into the woods?"

Edith frowned. "Nothing like that. What's going on?"

Mattie shook her head. "If you remember anything, be sure you tell one of us."

"Wait a minute," Kelsey said. "I'm going hunting in the morning. We're here from out of state, and we don't want to spend our time sitting in the truck."

The sheriff gave him a stern look. "No one will be hunting out of this campsite in the morning until we clear it. After we have a chance to talk to you, we'll probably let all of you go to different campsites, but for now, I want you to stay put. We'll talk to you within the hour. Deputy Wray, come with me."

McCoy turned on his heel and strode off.

Mattie nodded at the Kelseys before following. "Thanks for your cooperation. We'll be with you soon."

Moving quickly, she and Robo caught up with the sheriff. "Can we go to my unit so I can brief you in private?"

He led her to her Explorer and got into the passenger's seat while Mattie let Robo into the back and then entered the driver's side. She opened the locked glove box and removed Juan Martinez's business card. "I think this is our victim," she said, shining a light on it. "I'll take this with me back to the body and see if it matches, but I'm pretty sure it does."

McCoy took the card and appeared to read it carefully. "Where did you get this?"

"In Pueblo del Sol, Mexico." Mattie drew a deep breath. "This man is married to my mother. I've never met him. I went to try to see her last week and found out that the two of them had left suddenly about a month ago. I spoke to his brother, and he didn't know where they went and hadn't heard from them since they left. I'm afraid my mother could be in danger now."

"So you found out where your mother lives?" McCoy gave her a keen look.

"I did. I found her last summer, and she begged me to keep her location secret." Mattie bit her bottom lip as she met the sheriff's gaze. This man had been her only fatherly role model, and she hoped she hadn't disappointed him. But she'd made her decisions based on her mother's fear, and she'd begun to believe that those fears had been well founded.

"All right." McCoy gave the card back to her. "If your mother is in danger, we have no time to waste. Take Detective LoSasso back to the scene, and I'll stay here to do crowd control and get started with interviews until Deputy Garcia arrives. I'll see if anyone spotted an RV that was parked where Robo led us. If this victim is a citizen of Mexico, I'll need to call the feds in, but I'm going to start with Rick Lawson from CBI. Anything else I need to know?"

Relieved that Sheriff McCoy seemed to be taking her secret in stride and had resumed business as usual, Mattie told him she had no further information. It would be great to have the

Colorado Bureau of Investigation and the FBI here to help. The sooner they could locate her mother, the better.

Within minutes, McCoy had taken Stella's place in the crowd and Mattie and Robo were leading the detective back through the dead forest to where Brody was waiting. Both kept a sharp eye on their surroundings while Mattie briefed Stella on their victim's identity. Her voice broke as she explained how scared she was for her mother's safety.

Stella had known the background already, and she squeezed Mattie's arm briefly in sympathy. "One step at a time, Mattie. Let's confirm this man's identity first. You say there's a brother we can contact?"

"Yes. We can phone him right away."

"Maybe Detective Alvarez in San Diego will help."

"I think she might." They were approaching the scene, and she called out, "We're here, Brody."

"Yo," he called back. As the standing dead man came into sight, Mattie's gut tightened.

"This is something you don't see every day," Stella murmured as they drew near.

Mattie retrieved the business card from her pocket and her flashlight from her duty belt and stood close to the victim. Brody shined a flashlight on his face while Mattie lit up the card.

Though the dead man seemed thin and drawn compared to the photo, the resemblance was undeniable.

"It's him," Brody said. "Now what?"

"Sheriff McCoy's calling CBI for help, and with the identity confirmed, he'll also contact the feds. We'll have a crime scene investigation team here by daylight," Mattie said, looking at Stella. "And hopefully Rick will be here as soon as possible."

Detective Rick Lawson with the CBI had helped them with cases before, and Mattie thought he was good at his job. He and Stella had been dating for about a month.

Stella was inspecting the corpse, shining her flashlight over the body and getting close to study it. "Can you see anything related to cause of death, Brody?"

"No blood that I can see, and no obvious knife or gunshot wounds. Of course, we won't know for sure until his clothes can be removed."

None of them would move the corpse until the coroner and crime scene investigation unit arrived. It would be a relief to release the poor man from his bonds, and then they could search his clothing and pockets.

Stella continued to study him. "He's awfully thin. Thinner than he looks in his photo. His clothing looks too big for him, and his hair looks brittle and dry. Has he been sick? Has he been starved?"

Anxiety rippled its way down Mattie's spine. At this very moment, was her mother suffering from the same treatment that had killed Juan Martinez? Was she close to death as well? She wished dead men could talk so Juan could tell her the answers. She gazed at the man—a stepfather she would never get to know—thinking out loud. "Or was he poisoned?"

Stella illuminated the grayish tone of the dead man's face. "My thought exactly."

Mattie explained to Brody. "Robo followed the track back to the parking lot and around a stock tank in the corral. Cole happened to be there, taking a water sample, because two horses drank there earlier today and have ended up with what he thinks might be selenium poisoning."

Brody raised his eyebrows in a look of consternation.

"We'll have this corpse tested for selenium during the autopsy," Stella said.

Brody spoke in a quiet tone. "Are you going to tell me how you have a business card from this man in your possession?"

Mattie explained the situation in as few words as possible, the same way she'd told the sheriff. As she told Brody what she knew and all she'd kept secret the past few months, Stella continued to examine the body with her flashlight, probing every exterior surface visually without touching.

Brody asked no questions, and Stella broke the silence that followed Mattie's summary. "It looks like Mr. Martinez has something stuffed into his right front pants pocket."

Mattie and Brody focused their attention on the spotlight Stella provided with her flashlight's beam. Juan's clothing did sag on his body, and the fabric at his pocket gaped so that a corner of what looked like a paper envelope peeked out a fraction of an inch.

"I noticed that earlier," Brody said. "But I waited for you, and technically we should wait for CBI to clear the body."

"Under the circumstances, I'm going to breach protocol," Stella said, pulling on a pair of latex gloves. "If this killer is holding Ramona Wray Martinez hostage, we've got to launch this investigation as soon as possible, and we know one note has been left already. If this is a cat-and-mouse game with this man's killer and he's left a clue, we need to know what it is."

With her thumb and index finger, Stella gently removed the envelope. It slipped out of Juan's pocket easily. Brody shined his flashlight onto the envelope while Stella held it under the beam. It appeared identical to the one left on Mattie's front door.

In fancy script, the envelope was labeled *Mattie Wray*. Stella opened the flap on the unsealed envelope and extracted a sheet of notepaper. Mattie's heart thudded in her throat as she leaned forward to read the note, which was penned in the same flowing handwriting as her name on the envelope.

Dear Mattie,

Since this man is your stepfather, you probably already know him. If not, I'm so sorry you had to meet him this way. Señor Martinez is what we in the business fondly call collateral damage because he died sooner than I wanted him to. But I still have your mother, and she's in bad shape. I'll let you know how you can help soon. Stay tuned, Mattie. Don't panic.

I look forward to seeing you again,

A friend of your father's

NINE

In the dark hours before dawn, the temperature plummeted and a bitter wind blew from the west. Even Mattie's outdoor gear couldn't protect her from the chill in the air and in her soul. She shivered as she sat in the back seat of the sheriff's Jeep, one arm around Robo, hugging him as close as she could. But the comfort of his furry warmth didn't penetrate the foreboding that the note had left in her heart.

McCoy and Stella occupied the front seats, with the car's heater turned up full blast. Stella turned to her now. "What do you think is meant by *a friend of your father's*? Do you have any ideas about that?"

Mattie shook her head. "I've racked my brain over it, but the only people I can think of who might have a vendetta against my mother and father are the Cobb brothers. And they're both dead."

"It must be someone from that time in your life, Mattie. Can you recall anyone who came to the house, anyone at all who seemed to have something to do with your parents?"

So many of Mattie's memories from the time when Harold Cobb held her, her mother, and her brother captive were elusive images that largely remained repressed. Mattie had tried therapy to find the key to opening up her past, and even though she'd benefited hugely from techniques to alleviate symptoms of posttraumatic stress, her cache of memories from that time remained untapped for the most part.

Her therapist had told her that certain events would surface when she was ready to handle the emotions that would result, and she had remembered many disturbing things from her childhood and had faced them already. But even though the words in this note were chilling, she could dredge up nothing that would explain them.

"I can't even recall John Cobb coming to the house when I was little, though I know he must have. My mother told me last summer that there were many people involved and that they were very dangerous."

"What about *what we in the business call collateral damage?*" Stella asked. "Any ideas about that? I mean other than the obvious—drug cartels and drug trafficking."

Mattie had been thinking about that part too. "What about military?"

"Or even law enforcement," McCoy added.

The sound of footsteps scuffing gravel came from the side of the car, and Robo leapt to his feet. He pressed his nose to the window, but instead of barking, his tail began to wave.

Knuckles rapped on the window opposite where Mattie was sitting. "It's me—Cole."

The sound of his voice gave Mattie a small amount of peace. She grasped Robo's harness and pulled him back to the middle of the seat so Cole could open the door.

McCoy lowered his window. "Go ahead and get in, Cole."

The killer had made things personal and turned this kidnapping and murder into a family affair. Though Mattie hated to drag Cole into it, she knew she wouldn't be able to shield him or keep him separate from it. They had discussed the danger of her work many times, and Cole had professed that he was able to handle it, but this situation brought a whole new level of risk. He needed to know the details.

As Cole slid into the seat and closed his door, Mattie reached to grasp his hand, keeping their clasped hands hidden from her coworkers behind Robo. Cole appeared to study her face while a look of concern blossomed on his. "What's going on?"

Where to start? "Cole, we've discovered the identity of our victim," Mattie said. "He's Juan Martinez, my mother's husband."

"From Mexico?" Cole couldn't have looked more startled. "But wait, does that mean . . ."

Mattie nodded. "The killer has my mother. We received a note." She explained about the two notes she'd received that night.

Stella turned in her seat. "Cole, you need to know that the note was written specifically to Mattie and expresses the intent to meet with her personally. We're taking it seriously as a threat."

Mattie squeezed Cole's hand and willed him to look at her. When he did, she tried to project an air of confidence. "We'll take precautions. I've got my guard up."

Cole's face reflected the seriousness of the situation. "I don't want you working alone."

"We'll make sure she's partnered up," McCoy said. "Don't worry about that."

Cole continued to stare at her, and Mattie knew he wanted to say more but was holding his tongue. Over the past year, she and Robo had survived several attempts on their lives, and Cole was fully aware of it. She'd also made it clear to him that her duties sometimes put her in harm's way, and he needed to accept her and her profession on those terms. They'd already sparred about this, and he'd indicated he understood. This was no different.

She gave his hand another squeeze to try to reassure him, and he returned it. "We all need to make sure we're backing each other up."

"Where are you at with the investigation?" Cole asked. "Is the body still out there?"

"Yes," McCoy said, sounding grim. "Dr. McGinnis has come, and we expect CBI's investigative unit soon. Once they clear the victim for transport, we'll send him to Byers County for autopsy."

"Will you need my help now?" Though Cole directed the question at the sheriff, he glanced at Mattie to check in with her. She shook her head subtly.

"Not right now," McCoy said. "I've interviewed almost everyone here at the campground, and Brody and Garcia will secure the scene until CBI gets here. Mattie wants to use Robo for evidence detection, and Brody's here to back her up."

Cole kept his gaze on Mattie. "I need to get back to the office to send out these samples to the lab. The sooner we know if there was something in the water, the better. I'll get results to you as soon as I can."

Mattie nodded. Just the few minutes she'd been able to be with Cole had soothed that part of her that needed him, even if only a bit. "I'll call you as soon as we come back to town."

"Plan to move into my house until this is over. I don't want you staying at your house alone."

Mattie started to protest that she would be all right at her own home, but the sheriff spoke before she could.

"That's a good idea, Mattie. We might not have the staff to provide twenty-four hour security, but we'll send a unit by Cole's house when you're off duty. Knowing you won't be isolated at your house will help a lot."

She hated to bring danger to Cole and his family, but she decided to sit still for now. If things changed before she went off duty, she could make adjustments later. And she and Robo could always sleep at the station. They'd shared his bed there before.

Cole squeezed her hand again before releasing it. "I'll head off, then. Call me if you need me."

He'd only been in the car for ten minutes, but Mattie felt stronger and less vulnerable after he left. Though she'd resisted depending on anyone emotionally almost her whole life, she realized she'd failed with Cole. Just knowing he was there—and now fully informed—helped shore her up.

But Mattie had developed a new fear for the rest of her family. Were Julia and her grandmother safe out in California? She needed to contact her sister as soon as possible, both to give her the bad news about their mother and stepfather and to warn her to take precautions to keep her and her family safe.

"It's only about a half hour until sunrise," McCoy was saying. "Glenna Dalton is on her way up to direct these campers to other campgrounds in the area." Glenna Dalton was the district wildlife manager.

"I need to drive down into cell phone range to call my sister," Mattie said. "She needs to know what's happening."

"You can use the satellite phone," McCoy said, handing it over to her from the front seat before opening his door to leave.

"I'll stay with Mattie," Stella said.

As she retrieved Julia's cell phone number from her list of contacts, Mattie realized that having a bodyguard with her at all times had begun. She plugged the number into the sat phone and listened to the sounds as it made a connection. The fear in Mattie's chest circled and tightened as the call forwarded to Julia's voice mail, forcing her to leave a message asking her sister to return her call as soon as possible.

★ ★ ★

Though the sun remained hidden behind the jagged horizon, dim light and an orange glow from the east offered the promise of sunrise. Sheriff McCoy had gathered the campers, telling them he had an update for them, while Mattie and Robo stood at the edge of the lot, downwind from the group. Mist from her breath wafted on the breeze.

A little over a year ago, during their first investigation as partners, Mattie had realized that Robo had cataloged the scent of the bad guy at the crime scene, though she didn't come to this conclusion until much later. If she'd been more diligent and read his signals better, she would have had a feel for the killer much sooner than she had.

She wished she could have Robo sniff everyone in the campground, but that type of search would be illegal. She would have to settle for watching his body language to see if he reacted to anyone with intense interest. Observations of a dog's body language would never stand up in court, but it gave a K-9 officer information that could be valuable in putting together a case and finding evidence that *would* be admissible.

Glenna Dalton was standing with Sheriff McCoy in front of an audience of about twenty-five people, all dressed in outdoor gear, many with arms crossed over their chests, gloved hands tucked under their armpits. Glenna had brought her dog Moose with her, a Rhodesian ridgeback that partnered with her just like Robo with Mattie. The ridge of hair along Moose's spine grew forward instead of back, standing out against the deep red color of his coat.

Glenna was a tall woman with large hazel eyes that now scanned the crowd from beneath a fur-lined cap, its earflaps snugged down and held in place with a strap under her chin. Mattie knew her well and considered her one of the friends she'd made during the past year. Physically, Glenna was strong and a powerful runner, one of few who could outdistance Mattie going uphill.

"We're going to ask you all to relocate," McCoy was saying.

The crowd murmured words of protest, and McCoy raised his hands to stifle them. "Now hear me out. Our primary concern is for your safety. As most of you know, a body was found to the west of the corral, and we suspect foul play. This isn't turning into a high-traffic area for wildlife this year anyway, and I've asked our local wildlife manager, Glenna Dalton, to come here to advise you about where hunting might be more promising."

Edith and Drake Kelsey were standing at the front of the crowd, and Edith raised her hand as she began to talk, projecting her voice so everyone could hear. "It's not that easy to just pack up and leave. Why can't you wrap up your police business and let us remain here?"

"We need to control traffic in and out of this area, so it's best to relocate everyone," McCoy said.

Drake evidently wanted to add his two cents' worth. "Well, we don't like that at all. And what are you doing to investigate the poisoned stock tank? That vet said it made some horses really sick."

"That's right," Edith said, squaring her shoulders. "We're just lucky our horses were tied, or it could've happened to us. Can you guarantee the water will be safe in the other campgrounds?"

Mattie wondered why the Kelseys had left their horses tied in the first place. Did they know the water had been poisoned and intentionally kept their horses away from it?

Sheriff McCoy assured them that contamination of the water tank was part of their investigation and then encouraged everyone to water their horses by bucket, since not every tank in the area could be tested.

Glenna started her spiel about other campgrounds while Mattie edged closer. As usual, Robo sniffed the breeze. Mattie watched for a head bob, a stare, an ear prick, any sign that her dog had caught a scent that interested him more than another, but she detected nothing that would indicate Robo had matched the scent from last night's track with someone in the crowd.

After Glenna finished, Mattie approached the Kelseys, keeping an eye on Robo as they drew near. His body language remained neutral except for a slight tail wave, which could indicate that he merely recognized them from the night before. She decided to take a friendly tack to try to glean information. "I'm glad your horses were tied last night so they stayed safe. That was lucky."

Edith seemed to take the bait. "We always tie first until we know the fences and gates are sound. Looks like from now on we'll have to keep our horses away from stock tank water too."

"We'll waste a whole day having to load up everything and relocate our camp," Drake grumbled. "C'mon, Edith. Let's get the inside scoop from the game warden about where we should move to."

Mattie decided the two were disappointed and focused on their own problems rather than the larger tragedy of a person's death. She supposed that was human nature, although since the homicide affected her so personally, their self-centered behavior was hard to dismiss.

As she continued to scan the crowd, a man and a woman who'd driven an RV into the parking lot only a short time earlier caught Mattie's eye. They stood apart from the others, and the man smiled at her in a friendly way before focusing his attention on Robo. The man was a burly guy who looked to be fifty-something, dressed in insulated camouflage coveralls and a bright-orange stocking cap. His face was covered in dark-brown scruff, dotted with gray, that appeared to be only a few days old.

Both Mattie and Robo grew alert when the stranger started coming toward them. The woman apparently noticed her companion had left her side and turned to follow him.

The man grinned and reached inside his pocket as he approached, making Mattie stiffen and place her hand on the release strap of her service weapon. But when he withdrew his hand from his pocket, all it contained was a baggie full of beef jerky.

"Can I give your dog a treat?" he asked as he opened the bag.

Mattie raised a hand to keep the man from coming closer. "No, not while he's on duty. But thanks for asking."

"Your dog's beautiful," the woman said, putting her hand on the man's arm as if to stop him. She looked to be in her fifties like the man she was with, her eyes a pale shade of blue and her cheeks pink from the cold. A long, silvery blond braid snaked from beneath her stocking cap. "Milo, the officer said not to feed her dog."

"I won't, then," he said, still grinning as he tucked the bag back into his pocket.

Robo was watching the man with an intensity that Mattie had been looking for, though it was entirely possible that the jerky had sparked his interest. "I noticed you two just arrived. It's very early in the day to be coming into a new campground."

"We were nearby and wanted to get an early start searching for elk this morning. We had no idea that something bad had happened here last night. What can you tell us?" the woman asked.

Mattie pretty much repeated what the sheriff had already told the campers. "Which campground were you at last night?"

"The one down the hill. What's it called? Cedar Canyon?"

It was a campground nearby, only about a mile away. "How long have you been there?"

"Two nights. We were thinking we'd move up here if we found a nice campsite."

"Our local wildlife manager can help you find a good place to relocate," Mattie said, gesturing toward Glenna. "And where are you from?"

The man continued to smile as he withdrew the bag of jerky from his pocket again and selected a piece to eat.

"We're from out west," the woman said. "A little town in Nevada. But we've been to Timber Creek before. It's so beautiful here, we try to come out every fall to hunt, and we don't care if we get anything or not. It's just great to camp."

"It's a cold time of year for camping."

"Not when you're dressed for it. And I love to snowshoe and ski. It's a shame there's not much snow this year."

Mattie kept an eye on Robo while she talked to the couple. *Yep, he's definitely interested in the jerky*, she thought as her dog gave his full attention to the man chewing the dried meat. "So you've been in the Timber Creek area before?"

"Many times. We love it here. The mountains are so beautiful; the air's so clean."

"And your names?"

"I'm Didi Carr, and this is my husband Milo."

Milo nodded, smiling while he chewed vigorously.

"Did you come to this lot yesterday?"

"No, we stayed and hiked around the campsite downhill."

"Will you be going back home soon?"

"Oh no. We'll move to one of the sites that the game warden recommends. We still have a week left for our vacation."

Robo had lost interest in Milo and was sniffing the breeze that was coming from the west, back toward where Juan's body had been found. The sun had crested the horizon, and it was light enough now to move into the forest to search for evidence. Mattie felt pressured to move on.

But even as she wished the couple well, she had an odd feeling about them. Milo's grin had flickered off and on the entire time she'd conversed with his wife, and he'd hardly said a word. Were the two of them hiding something?

But she'd suspected the Kelseys too. Was she just on edge and wanting to discover something—anything—that would help find her mother?

TEN

Even the birds had abandoned this part of the forest. All that could be heard in the eerie quiet after sunrise was the crackle of their footsteps as Mattie and Brody made their way through the dead trees back toward the crime scene.

Crime scene tape glowed yellow in the sunlight as they approached. Deputy Cyrus Garcia, built like a fireplug and a veteran of the force, stood leaning against a tree trunk outside the perimeter, drinking from the plastic cup of a thermos he'd evidently brought with him. He straightened and sauntered toward them as they drew near.

"Everything quiet?" Brody asked.

"As a tomb."

Brody looked at his watch. "ETA for the crime scene unit is thirty minutes. We'll search this area before they get here. The sheriff wants you to pull a double shift and remain on duty. We need you to continue keeping the crime scene log, but do you need a break right now?"

Garcia lifted his cup, and Mattie could smell the aroma of his coffee. "I've got my cup o' joe right here. I can hang for a while."

The crime scene log would document everyone who entered and left the protected area and the times. Mattie took off her backpack and dug out an energy bar to hand to him.

"Thanks, Mattie." Garcia took the bar and smiled down at it as he read the label. Then he turned the smile on her. "You're as good as my wife about being prepared."

"Just trying to make sure the kids are taken care of." Mattie tried to smile back but was afraid it turned into a grimace. Her effort at humor made her think of motherhood and therefore her own mother. She returned to business, always her comfort zone. She gestured with a sweep of her hand to encompass the forest. "We'll do a pass through this area around the tree and then go through a radius of about fifty yards. When the crime scene techs arrive, Sheriff McCoy wants you to stand guard while they work."

Garcia nodded, lifting his cup to his lips for a sip. Steam rose toward his nose. "Will do."

Mattie had given Robo a break from wearing his Kevlar vest earlier, but she'd put it back on before coming out here. Even though things had been quiet during the night, there were no guarantees that they would remain so. This entire situation seemed bizarre enough that she feared an attack even during daylight. And the presence of Juan's corpse still tied to the tree didn't help.

She pulled the blue nylon collar that Robo wore for evidence searching from a pocket on her duty belt. "Here you go, boy. Let's put this on."

Robo lifted his head and looked at her with adoration in his intelligent brown eyes while she buckled on his collar. It warmed her to be the recipient of such love, and she met his gaze as she stroked his head before dropping her face to his, cheek to cheek. She whispered in his ear, "You're a good boy, you know that. I love you. You're my good partner."

As she straightened, she thumped his sides and began the chatter that signaled the beginning of a search. "Do you wanta find something, Robo? Let's find something, okay? Let's go."

Robo pivoted on his hind feet and rose up beside her. He wagged his tail as he dropped back down to all fours, front feet on the ground, dancing in place.

Mattie did a quick check for a breeze, but the air had grown calm and windless. She wouldn't need to worry about starting downwind. Ducking under the crime scene tape, she led Robo into the area close to the tree where Juan's corpse was tied. Laying a grid in her mind, she held Robo's leash in her left hand and used her right to direct him. "Seek," she told him.

They'd done this maneuver hundreds of times in practice as well as at crime scenes, and Robo had dropped his nose to the ground even before she gave him direction. He swept his head from left to right, vacuuming up scent as they walked the grid together, covering swaths of about three feet in a back-and-forth pattern. Within five minutes, they'd covered the circle within the crime scene tape, and Mattie felt certain Juan's killer and any accomplices needed to carry him to this place and pose him had not left any items behind.

Brody stood by with Garcia while she and Robo did the close-in work, but when she ducked back under the tape to leave the immediate crime scene, he came forward. Mattie bent to unclip Robo's leash and flung her arm outward to encompass the surroundings, at the same time reinforcing Robo's command. "Seek! Let's find something."

Robo darted away, going through the dead pine with his nose in the air. Mattie jogged after him with Brody following closely behind, his AR15 held ready in front of him. They weren't taking any chances today.

Robo ranged out about fifty yards before Mattie whistled, signaling that he'd gone far enough. Then he started a zigzag pattern through the woods, quartering back and forth while he searched, mostly with his head up, sniffing the air, but occasionally with his head down. The forest was dry, except in damp patches where drifts from the snow a month ago had melted.

About fifteen yards almost due west from the tree, Robo slowed his pace, dropped his head, and sniffed the ground as he slowly walked forward. Then he sat. Mattie had been trotting behind him, so her heart rate had already risen, but it quickened even more when her dog gave her his signal that he'd found something.

At first she didn't see it, but as she came in close, she recognized slight dampness under some recently disturbed pine needles. She drew her dog up close beside her leg and patted his side. "Good boy, Robo!"

Brody came up beside her. "What did he find?"

"I think it's urine."

"Human?"

"I don't think Robo would hit on it if it was animal. Go ask Garcia if it's his."

"It better not be." Brody blew out an exasperated sound between his teeth as he turned to leave. About halfway back to the tree, he shouted to the deputy in question. "Hey, Garcia, did you take a leak over here?"

"No way!" Garcia called back, obviously offended. "I know better than that, jefe."

"Good man," Brody responded as he turned to come back. "Mattie, did you hear that?"

"I did." She'd extracted a short spike with six inches of orange flagging tape tied to it from a pocket in her duty belt, and now she leaned forward to plunge it into the ground next to the damp spot. "Let's get a sample of these pine needles and the dirt while it's fresh. With any luck at all, we've got a DNA sample from the perpetrators of this crime."

"Could be from one of the campers back there."

"It's possible, but I don't think so. The ground's still damp, so I think it was left after sundown."

"Good find, Robo! Good boy!" Brody grinned as he pulled latex gloves and a couple of plastic baggies from his pocket.

"I'll finish searching the rest of the area. Maybe we'll find something else."

"Nope, you wait right here until I can go with you. This will only take a minute." Brody squatted and began filling the bag with pine needles.

Mattie stifled her impatience and waited, knowing he was right to observe their safety protocol, but she was keyed up and raring to continue the search. She knelt beside Robo and hugged him close, ruffling the fur at his neck and murmuring words of praise. She let him know the search wasn't over yet.

"I hope this is what we think it is," Brody said as he scooped dirt into the second bag and sealed it. He tucked the two bags away in his coat pockets as he stood. "Let's finish up."

Mattie repeated the process of getting Robo's prey drive revved up and resumed the search. They were clearing the last quarter of the circle when—*crack*—a rifle shot echoed through the trees.

Instantly on alert, Mattie crouched and called Robo back to her.

Brody hunkered down beside her. "It came from the east."

Mattie slipped behind the nearest tree trunk, taking Robo with her. "Did you see a projectile hit?"

Brody had taken cover nearby. "No. I'm not even sure we were the targets."

Garcia called from behind. "Are you two okay?"

"Affirmative," Brody replied. "You?"

"Same. I think it came from east of the campground."

Brody pressed the button on his radio to check in with the sheriff. "Alpha One, this is Alpha Two. All clear. Checking on the shot fired. Anyone hit?"

"Negative," McCoy said, his words understandable through the receiver. "Shot came from the east."

"Might be a hunter?"

"Could be. Glenna left about fifteen minutes ago and headed east. I'll check in with her. CBI crime scene unit should arrive any minute."

"Copy that." Brody signed off and then turned to Mattie. "Let's finish up here before the crime scene techs take over."

Their reaction to what might have been a hunter's misfire was telling—both she and Brody were on edge. Mattie started Robo back on the search and finished up just as Stella brought the crime scene techs through the skeletonized trees.

Robo bumped his nose on the pocket of Mattie's duty belt that contained his tennis ball, his reward for a job well done. But Mattie knelt beside him, hugging him close. With a gunshot fired, people arriving on scene to investigate, and the general air of tension surrounding them, she didn't feel like she could play with him now. It would have to wait, and she whispered a promise in his ear that they would play later.

Brody's radio crackled to life at his shoulder: "Alpha Two, this is Alpha One."

Brody pressed on his mic. "Go ahead."

Sheriff McCoy's voice came through the speaker. "What's your status?"

"Finished the evidence search. Crime scene unit here and taking over the scene."

"Glenna Dalton does not reply. You and Mattie return to the parking lot."

"Copy."

As soon as the sheriff mentioned that Glenna was not responding to radio contact, Mattie's gut squeezed. In this type of situation, every officer was on alert, including those associated with wildlife management and the forest service. Glenna's failure to respond might mean equipment failure or injury. Mattie and Brody set off at a rapid pace through the trees toward the campsites.

Within minutes, they checked in with McCoy, who wanted them to go downhill one mile to Cedar Canyon Campground, where Glenna was supposed to be. The sheriff would stay to maintain command of the crime scene. Mattie loaded Robo into her unit as Brody took the passenger seat. She ran to the driver's side and climbed in.

Robo had lapped water from his collapsible bowl before he circled his cushion and plopped down, heaving a sigh. He'd covered miles during his searches, and he had to feel as weary as she did. She hoped he could rest while she drove.

After putting her Explorer in low gear, Mattie steered down the steep and narrow road, slowly winding downward toward where the forest was healthy. She kept an eye out for Glenna's green pickup, wishing Parks and Wildlife had used a color for their vehicles that wouldn't blend into the forest so well. Something like orange or yellow.

She was forced to drive slowly and carefully, and it seemed like it took forever to reach the Cedar Canyon overlook, a wide spot in the road that afforded a view of rolling evergreen forest that stretched out for miles. Just below this spot, Mattie turned right into an even narrower track that wound through trees beside a stream that would lead to another campground, this one isolated by narrow canyon walls.

"There." Brody broke their silence, pointing ahead. "That's her truck."

Mattie had spotted it too, and she steered toward the campsite where Glenna's pickup sat parked with the driver's side door open. Mattie pulled up beside it, set her brake, and jumped out to join Brody as he approached the truck.

No one was in it. Not even Moose.

Brody tried to contact Glenna by radio. No reply.

A feeling that something was terribly wrong gripped Mattie. They were close enough down here in the canyon that Glenna should receive their signal. Even though the truck was parked with the ignition turned off, it seemed unlikely that Glenna would have left the door open for a routine search of the campsites. People didn't risk running down a battery up here in the high country.

A deep bark boomed from the forest off to the right, and Mattie turned to see Moose come loping out of the trees, sunlight glinting off his burnished red coat, his long ears flopping as he ran straight toward her. She bent to brace herself for his typical exuberant welcome, but he stopped short about six feet away. He backed up and barked, looking up at her as if for help.

Moose trotted away a few steps and looked back over his shoulder at her. Mattie darted to the back of her unit and opened Robo's hatch. She grabbed a leash and clipped it to his collar. Robo leapt to the ground as Moose whirled and took off into the woods.

Mattie and Robo dashed after him. Brody followed, carrying his rifle.

It didn't take long to find Glenna. She was close to the northernmost campsite, lying on the ground faceup. Moose ran to her, jostling her body as he nudged her with his black muzzle. Robo hung back, looking toward Mattie as if asking her what to do next.

Drawing up beside her friend, Mattie knelt, gently pushing Moose away. Blood had soaked through the front of Glenna's jacket near the shoulder, and her head lay on a boulder like it was a pillow. She was out cold.

Placing her fingers against Glenna's neck, Mattie detected a pulse. "She's alive."

Brody hovered near, scanning the forest, his rifle ready in both hands.

Officers in the Timber Creek Sheriff's Department seldom had the luxury of being able to call an ambulance when confronted with an emergency in the higher elevations. They'd all been trained in first aid. Heart in her throat, Mattie was grateful for that.

"There's a first-aid kit in the storage compartment in the back of my unit," she told Brody. "There's a neck brace in there too. Way in the back."

The look on his face told her that he was torn about leaving.

She unsnapped the safety strap on her service weapon's holster before unzipping Glenna's insulated coverall. "Go ahead. Whoever did this is long gone."

He turned and raced off.

Mattie pushed back Glenna's jacket to find a huge red stain on her khaki shirt. She began unbuttoning the shirt so she could get to the wound, her mind spinning with possibilities. It looked like Glenna had lost a lot of blood, but her breathing seemed stable. Mattie hoped the projectile had missed her lung.

In her mind's eye, Mattie could picture the bullet hitting Glenna in the shoulder, knocking her backwards, and her head cracking against the boulder as she fell. She tried to calculate how long it had been since they'd heard the gunshot and guessed it was about a half hour. She glanced up and spotted the campsite a short distance away. It looked like Glenna could have been walking toward it when someone shot her.

Stop the bleeding. Focusing on Glenna's wound, Mattie gently pushed her shirt open to reveal blood-soaked white thermal underwear, the bullet hole obvious where it had punctured through it. Moose tried to sniff, but she told him no and asked him to sit. She knew him to be typically hardheaded and was relieved to see him obey on the first command. Robo was already sitting.

As she murmured praise to the dogs, Mattie fumbled to open a pocket on her duty belt, her hand slippery with blood. She withdrew a plastic evidence bag and slipped it beneath Glenna's undershirt to seal the hole. This should keep the opening from sucking air into her chest, causing a lung to collapse. She applied pressure to the outside of Glenna's shirt as she glanced up, hoping to see Brody. What was taking him so long?

Trying to jostle Glenna as little as possible, Mattie carefully felt under her shoulder, where she imagined an exit wound might be. A hole in the thermal undershirt surrounded by soggy, warm fabric told Mattie she'd found one. She placed another plastic bag beneath Glenna's shirt to seal the back wound, and then using her hands against the front, she leaned downward to apply pressure to both at once.

Brody sprinted through the trees, carrying the kit and the neck brace. "McCoy is on his way," he said as he halted and went down on his knees beside her.

"Front and back wounds are covered with plastic. Applying pressure. Her breathing is steady. Check pulse."

Brody placed two fingers against Glenna's neck. "Steady."

"She must've banged her head on this rock when she fell. Stabilize her neck, and then we'll apply a pressure bandage on this shoulder wound. No need to remove her shirt. It'll help hold the plastic bags in place. Let's get her ready to move when the sheriff gets here."

They worked together in silence, applying a pressure bandage to the shoulder wound. Glenna's skin was clammy and white, a sprinkle of freckles standing out on the bridge of her nose. She'd lost a lot of blood, and Mattie feared they would lose her before they could move her to safety and get her the medical care she needed.

ELEVEN

Cole taped the edges of the package that held all the samples he'd collected before placing it in the rack by the front door inside his clinic. A courier would be by within the hour to run them to the lab. His thoughts went to Mattie, and he wondered where she and her team members were at in their investigation. He couldn't help but worry about her and wished they would come down from the mountains and back to town, where it felt safer.

The door to his clinic opened, startling him. He wasn't expecting anyone this early, and in fact he had debated canceling routine visits this morning so he could go back to the campground to help in whatever way he could.

It was Angie, even more of a surprise. "Angel, I wasn't expecting you to come in this early."

She wrinkled her nose as if peeved. "I couldn't sleep. And I wasn't out that late last night anyway." She gave him a look that made it clear he was to blame for that sad state of affairs.

"Well, I'm sorry you couldn't sleep in, but I'm glad you made it home for curfew last night." He yawned. "I had an emergency, and I haven't been to bed yet."

"Oh . . ." Hearing of his sleep deprivation seemed to take some of the steam out of her, making him feel there was hope for this kid yet. He liked that she seemed empathetic toward him. She glanced at the clock as she crossed over toward the reception desk and computer, where they kept their schedule. "When is our first appointment?"

"In about an hour, but to tell you the truth, I was thinking I might cancel out the morning and reschedule for next week. Everything we have coming in is routine."

Angie had opened the schedule and was studying the screen. "You should get some sleep. I can reschedule."

Cole felt a glow of pride in her volunteering to take the initiative. It showed the level of maturity she'd gained the past year, and he felt he should honor it by sharing what was going on in Mattie's life right now. After all, he'd insisted that Mattie come to their home to stay when she was off duty.

"That would be great. But I need to tell you what's going on with Mattie and the sheriff's department." He summed up what he knew of the discovery of the dead man near Shadow Ridge Campground, leaving out the victim's relationship to Mattie. Mattie had insisted that her mother's location be kept secret from all of the family, including her foster mother, Mama T, as she believed this knowledge would endanger those who knew.

Angie's expression had gone from surprise to a pale look of horror. "A dead person? And Mattie was called out last night after I left?"

"That's right. I got an emergency call too, and it looks like the horses I treated might have been poisoned at the campground stock tank. So it could be that this is all wrapped up together." Cole gestured toward the package of samples in the rack. "The courier will pick those up soon, and we should get results back from the lab sometime today."

"Oh my gosh." Angie's fear registered on her face.

Cole wondered if his fatigue had clouded his judgment. Maybe Angie wasn't grown up enough to take on this type of worry, but then of course, there was more. "When Mattie's off duty, I've invited her to get some sleep at our house. I don't want her and Robo to be alone at her house. They can have my room, and I'll use Sophie's extra twin bed."

"Is she in danger?"

He didn't want to share the information about the notes—first of all because it was confidential to the investigation, but also because it was too frightening. "You know how they were attacked at her house last summer. I don't want her to be alone while she's sleeping."

Angie seemed to be processing what she'd been told, and she nodded as she turned back to the computer screen. "I'll take care of these appointments."

Cole placed a hand on her shoulder. "I appreciate your help."

She looked up from the screen at him and gave him a quivery smile. "Well . . . I had something to ask you, but with all this going on, I'm not sure it's the right time."

"Go ahead. I want you to be able to talk to me whenever you need to. Don't worry about waiting for the right time. In our busy lives, it might never come." He smiled to reassure her that he was open to listening.

"Well . . . um, Hannah needs a job." Hannah was part of the family who owned Sassy, the mother of Robo's first litter, and she was also one of Angie's friends. Cole's daughter looked at him with beseeching eyes, going on in a rush. "Her mom says she has to sell all the puppies so they can pay the rent and put food on the table for the family. Hannah wants to keep little Velvet, so if she has a job, she can help out with the bills, and maybe her mom will let her."

Cole drew up a lobby chair and sat, wanting to take his time with this dilemma. "So . . . where does Hannah want to work?"

"Could she work here?"

He'd thought this was where the discussion would go. Even his tired brain could see it coming. "There's a limit to how many employees I can have, Angel. I've already hired Riley, and I don't need any more help right now, especially during the winter months when things are slower."

Angie gave him her pleading expression. He'd had the pleasure of living with this child for over sixteen years, and he knew it well. "Please, Dad. Would you at least think about it?"

He sighed. "I'm sorry, Angel, but I know our limits at this clinic. I don't have extra work, and I don't have extra room on the payroll right now. What other jobs could Hannah apply for around town?"

"You know how hard it is to get a job in Timber Creek."

It was true. Their hometown was small, with a limited number of businesses. "How about working at Clucken House or the Pizza Palace? Has she tried there yet?"

Angie shook her head, her eyes downcast. "We thought we'd ask you first. You know . . . with me and Riley already here, we thought it would be perfect."

"Have her try there, and maybe at the grocery store." Preparing to haul his tired body up onto his feet, Cole leaned forward just as his phone rang in his pocket. He answered it instead. "Timber Creek Veterinary Clinic."

"Dr. Walker," the voice said on the other end of the connection, "this is Ruth Vaughn. Sassy and the puppies are sick this morning, and I hope you can work them into your schedule."

These were the puppies they'd just been talking about—Robo's first litter. "Oh no. What's going on?"

"They all have loose bowels. The puppies too."

He didn't like the sound of that, even with Ruth's euphemism applied. "How loose? Do they have diarrhea?"

"Yes, and it looks like blood in some of the puppies' stool."

His first thought was parvovirus. If it was parvo, he didn't hold much hope for the pups' survival. But Sassy had been vaccinated for it, so if she was sick too, perhaps it was something else. Even a reaction to something she ate could set the pups off. "Has Sassy gotten into any trash?"

Ruth paused. "Not that I know of."

"Has she been out of the yard?"

"Hannah took her on a long walk yesterday to give her a break from the puppies. Here, let me ask her if Sassy ate something she shouldn't."

There were murmurs as the two discussed it offline, and then Ruth came back on the phone. "She didn't eat anything, but there were some stray dogs in the park that came around, and they all sniffed each other. Hannah said she didn't let them play, but they hung around for a while."

Sassy could have been exposed to something that she'd then taken home to the puppies. It was rare, but it did happen now and then. "Are the pups still nursing?"

"They don't seem to have much appetite."

"How about Sassy?"

"She wouldn't eat this morning."

On the off chance that this could be parvovirus, Cole didn't want the bug brought into his clinic. "Okay, I'll come by your house to check on them. I can be there in about ten minutes."

Ruth released an audible breath. "Oh, thank you so much. We'll see you soon."

"And if any of the pups have the squirts before I get there, don't clean it up, okay? I'll need to get a sample."

After his conversation with Angie, Cole knew how much these puppies meant to the family. Sassy too. Not only were they beloved pets, but the income from the puppies was part of the family's livelihood.

Angie had been hanging on to his every word, so he briefed her quickly before going into his treatment room to grab supplies.

"They can't lose these puppies," she called to him through the pass-through window between the reception area and treatment room.

"I know, sweetheart. You don't have to remind me." He felt enough pressure, and he tried to keep his irritation from showing.

"Sorry, Dad." Angie pulled back from the pass-through.

Cole felt like a jerk. "Me too. Not your fault; I'm just tired and running on empty. Do you want to go with me?"

"No, I'll stay here and take care of the schedule. I'll call Hannah later."

It didn't take Cole long to drive the mile into town and then the few blocks to where Hannah lived with her mother and several younger siblings. Two other women who were once Ruth's sister wives as well as a passel of children who were Hannah's half siblings lived with them. The home was a small clapboard rental, and Cole had no idea how they all fit into it. But the adult women had found jobs in town and seemed to be making ends meet, and he supposed that was all that mattered. The entire situation seemed bizarre, but he hoped they'd found happiness here in Timber Creek now that they'd lost their patriarch.

Ruth was waiting on the doorstep. She was a demure woman who currently wore a puffy insulated coat over a blue denim skirt that Cole supposed she'd made herself. She waved as he parked out by the curb.

"Thank you so much for coming to help us," she said as he exited his truck. "Sassy and the pups are around back."

Cole snatched up his stethoscope and the parvovirus rapid test kits he'd brought, closed the truck door, and followed her around the side of the house to a gate. The yard had been fenced with five-foot-tall pine boards, and the area within was large and clean except for a few tricycles and bikes parked against the back of the house.

Ruth's blond hair was pulled into a bun at the back of her head. Everything about the woman and her home evoked the word *tidy*. She opened the door that led into an enclosed back porch, and Cole followed her inside.

Hannah was sitting beside a five-foot-square whelping box that contained Sassy. Blond like her mother but dressed in denim jeans and a sweatshirt similar to what Cole's kids wore, Hannah looked up with sorrowful eyes. "Did I make Sassy sick when I took her out yesterday?"

Cole's heart went out to her. This kid had worked hard to keep the runt of the litter alive after all the puppies were delivered by emergency C-section last month. "No, kiddo. Nothing's your fault. What's going on here?"

Sassy lay on her side on the padded floor of the box, which was now covered with partially soiled newspaper. Her eight puppies had been placed in a tall cardboard box away from her, and they lay in a dogpile in one of the corners, furry little four-week-olds sleeping in a heap.

"I usually keep the newspaper clean, but I left some of the poo after Mom told me to," Hannah said, a note of apology in her voice.

"Good deal." Cole squatted down beside the whelping box, and Sassy raised her head to look at him before letting it fall back, disinterested and listless. "Your mom said Sassy didn't eat this morning. Did she drink any water?"

"She did. And then she went outside and had the runs. Mom said you would need a sample, so I put it in that." She pointed at a small sealed container on the floor by the wall.

"It's fresh?"

"Five minutes ago."

"Good job." He was impressed by Hannah's efficiency. "And I see you've left some fresh piles here in the box for me too."

Cole took one of the rapid test kits from his pocket while he examined the pups' fecal matter visually. It was orange in color and runny. He detected a slight streak of blood in some of it. The pups were too young to have been vaccinated for parvo, so he decided it was important to test one of them in addition to Sassy.

"Has she vomited?" he asked.

Hannah shook her head. "No, she just has the runs."

He pulled on a pair of latex gloves. After opening a kit, he removed the top portion containing the cotton swab from the sample extraction device. He dispensed the buffer solution into the device and then coated the swab with feces before putting it into the solution and tapping it gently for a few seconds to mix it. He noticed that Hannah was watching his every move, so he began to explain each step.

"I need to have a flat surface where this won't get bumped," he said, taking the test portion of the kit out of the pouch.

Hannah pointed to a gardening bench that sat against the wall on the far side of the porch. "You can use that table right there."

Cole took the kit to the bench, and Hannah followed him.

"We put the sample here in this little well," he said, snapping off the top part of the sample extraction device and inverting it over the test portion. He squeezed gently and put five drops of the fluid into the well. "Now we let that sit for ten minutes, and then we can read it. One line in this window means negative, two means positive."

Cole took out his cell phone and set an alarm for ten minutes. After fifteen minutes, the test would become invalid, so timing was important.

"What are you testing them for?" Hannah gazed at the kit intently.

"Canine parvovirus."

With a look of shock, she raised her eyes to his. "Do you think that's what they have?"

"I have to rule it out."

"That could kill them."

Ruth, who had been silent the whole time, made a murmur of distress.

"So you know about parvovirus?" Cole asked Hannah.

"I've read about all the diseases that Sassy's vaccinated for. I thought the vaccine would protect her."

"It does. I doubt if that's what we have here, but like I said, I have to rule it out. Parvo is very contagious. We need to make sure she didn't bring the virus to the puppies on her fur." He took another kit out of his pocket. "Now we need to test Sassy's sample. Do you want to help me?"

When she agreed, he handed her a pair of latex gloves and then opened the kit. Together they set up the second sample and prepared the test portion, laying it on the bench next to the one from the pups.

"While this sits, let's listen to her heart and examine the pups," Cole said, checking the time before going back over to the whelping box. He knelt beside Sassy, adjusted the earpieces of his stethoscope, and then pressed the diaphragm to her chest. The thump of her heartbeat was steady but accelerated, probably from dehydration. The good-hearted dog then let him check her gums and press them gently. Her gums were pink, and after he pressed them till they turned white and then released them, the capillaries refilled and the tissue became pink again quickly—a good sign.

He palpated Sassy's gut. She flinched and raised her head to look at him as if to say, *Back off.* He said to Hannah, "She's got a painful tummy, and she's slightly dehydrated. I'm going to treat her with some Imodium to slow down the diarrhea, and I'll give her some subcutaneous fluids to make her feel better."

Cole scooted on his knees over to the box where the pups were huddled. The dogpile had begun to wiggle as the cute, furry balls of fluff awakened and began to sort themselves out. Yips and whines filled the air as they came awake. One of the larger male pups, approaching six inches tall and primarily black with tan markings like Robo, separated himself from the group and came forward to bark at Cole, his little pink tongue contrasting with his black muzzle and lips. The pup's ears still flopped forward, although one had begun to straighten except for the tip, giving him a jaunty look.

"Come here, tiger." Cole couldn't help but smile as he picked up the pup and snuggled him against his chest. He dipped his head to catch a whiff of the unique scent of puppy breath as the soft pup nestled into his hands and licked his chin. Cole looked at Hannah. "Did the puppies eat this morning?"

"They didn't eat as much as they usually do, but they all nursed," Hannah said as she reached into the box to pick up Velvet, the sable female that had been the runt of the litter and that Cole knew had become her favorite.

Velvet's fur was a mixture of black, brown, and gray, each individual hair bearing all three colors to give her coat a wolf-like appearance. She had caught up with most of the pups in size but still bore a delicate look and had a fine-boned head. She would be a beautiful female when she grew up, though all of the puppies showed promise of becoming gorgeous examples of the German shepherd breed.

The pup Cole held showed moist mucous membranes and good capillary profusion when he tested it. He quickly examined each puppy as they struggled for his attention inside the cardboard box, rising up against the sides and sliding down, their sharp nails making scratching sounds as they did. He was relieved that none of them seemed significantly dehydrated.

The alarm on his phone dinged its merry tune. "Let's read the test kits," he said as he stood.

He was relieved to see only one line in the test window, and he showed it to Hannah. "This means it's negative for parvo. Great news. I think Sassy either has gastroenteritis or she picked up canine coronavirus. Both affect the digestive tract and can cause diarrhea."

Ruth spoke up. "Can either one of these illnesses make our children sick?"

"No, neither one is transferrable to humans," Cole told her before turning back to Hannah. "You haven't changed her food lately, right?"

"No, we haven't."

"And she didn't eat anything she shouldn't when she went to the park?"

"Nothing like that."

"And no one slips her table scraps or food that might upset her stomach?"

"I don't think so." Hannah looked at her mother.

"I don't think so either," Ruth said. "It's hard to keep track of all of the children, you know, but I've told them not to."

"Okay, I think we're probably dealing with corona. I'll go out to the truck and get supplies to treat Sassy. As long as we support her and she can keep nursing the pups, they should be all right. You might add a little more water to the pups' food so they get plenty of fluid."

"Okay. I'll take good care of them," Hannah promised.

"Hannah wants to be a vet when she grows up," Ruth said, putting a hand on Hannah's shoulder.

As Cole left to go to his truck, he remembered how Hannah had patiently worked with Velvet to get her to suckle milk from a doll bottle and then to transfer her to Sassy. The weak puppy had required special care for several days, and Hannah had stuck with it, following every instruction and heeding his advice. She showed the type of persistence needed to do well at anything she chose to do in life. If she thought she wanted to be a veterinarian, it would be important for someone to expose her to the profession so she could make an informed decision.

He opened one of the side doors on his mobile vet unit and started gathering what he needed from the neat array of syringes, needles, medicines, and other paraphernalia laid out inside the sliding drawers within. He supposed that giving Hannah an opportunity to gain that experience would ultimately become his responsibility.

He sighed as he trudged back around the side of the house toward the back porch.

TWELVE

Mattie had steeled herself, blocking off her emotions while rendering first aid to Glenna and then transporting her halfway down the mountain. But now, after turning Glenna over to the EMTs, Mattie felt her hands trembling as she tried to wash her friend's blood from them. She wasn't sure if fear regarding Glenna's condition was what made her hands so shaky, or if it was rage that someone had shot her in the first place.

"We need to nail this shooter," Brody said, his voice a low growl.

"We do. I want to use Robo to sweep that crime scene."

She splashed a handful of cold water from Robo's supply onto Brody's hands and another onto her own, then rubbed her hands together vigorously in the frigid air. Water dripped through her fingers, hitting the dirty snowdrift beside her SUV and making pink streaks in the half-melted snow. It was no use. She stared at the maroon stains embedded around and under her fingernails. Without soap, no amount of water was going to clean her hands, and besides, she needed to save this water for Robo.

"I have some wipes in here," she said as she nudged Robo aside and opened the storage compartment. "We'll have to make do with those."

Robo lay down on his cushion and watched them while she and Brody scrubbed their hands with cleansing wipes that were not meant for skin, the odor of bleach filling the air. They leaned against the open back of the unit, working the wipes around their nails the best they could, while Moose sat in the passenger's seat, gazing soulfully through the mesh grate that separated Robo's compartment from the front of the vehicle. He looked as sad as Mattie felt.

Mattie and Brody had wrapped Glenna in a metalized polyester space blanket before placing her in the back of the K-9 unit. Mattie had ridden with Glenna, trying to hold her as still as possible as Brody drove downhill on the bumpy dirt road with Robo and Moose in front. It felt like it took forever to meet up with the ambulance and turn Glenna's care over to the experts. Her friend had remained unconscious during the harrowing trip.

Mattie drew a deep breath, trying to still the fluttering in her gut as she recalled Glenna's pale features and bloody wounds. They'd done the best they could. Now they needed to investigate a new crime scene, and they had nothing but theories regarding what might have happened to Glenna.

CBI Special Agent Rick Lawson had arrived, and Sheriff McCoy had sent him to the Juan Martinez crime scene while she and Brody transported Glenna. There were many moving parts in this inquiry, and things had become even more complicated. Rick's help was a godsend.

An overriding feeling of dread hit Mattie, weighing her down. Her mother was out here somewhere in this vast wilderness in the hands of a killer. Her stepfather had been killed and her friend injured badly, probably by the same person or persons. Mattie couldn't help but feel that Glenna's gunshot wound was her fault, since she was the one who'd drawn this killer to Timber Creek. And now the killer was playing cat and mouse with Mattie. She wished she could get the confrontation over with so she knew whom or what she was dealing with and could somehow find her mother.

She straightened and placed the cleansing wipe, now stained pink with blood, in the trash. Her fingers were partially clean and white from the chill. She pulled on her gloves, relieved to hide the discoloration still beneath her nails.

Brody eyed her while he disposed of his dirty wipe. "Do you want to drive?"

Her body weary, she thought of what she might give to lie down, even for a few minutes. "Actually, if you could drive, I'll stretch out back here with Robo. Do you mind?"

"Nope." He stepped away from the open hatch. "You gonna be able to keep going, or do you need to sleep for a few hours?"

"I can keep going. It's just that I was sleep deprived before this all started." Mattie climbed into the compartment with Robo, and Brody closed the door on them. Robo looked excited for her to join him, and he thumped his tail while she lay down beside him on his cushion and curled herself around him. It felt like heaven to be able to assume a reclined position, and she took several deep breaths to steady herself, stretching out the exhalation to twice as long as the in-breath.

Despite the Explorer swaying and jostling its way uphill, Mattie dozed, drifting in and out of wakefulness as they drove back to the Cedar Canyon Campground. When the vehicle stopped, she blinked her eyes, amazed at how even that little bit of rest had restored enough energy for her to sit up and move again. She stretched her tired and sore muscles while Brody ratcheted on the parking brake and came around to open up the hatch.

Robo stood and yawned, shaking every inch of his fur, including his tail. When Mattie slid out of the cage, he came to the edge as if ready to work again. She guessed they both were.

McCoy had stayed at the scene, and he'd already cordoned off the campsite where Glenna had been found with crime scene tape. He walked over to their car when they arrived. "I'll hand this scene over so you and Robo can complete an evidence search," he said, looking at Mattie. "I hope you can find something to use against this coward who shot an officer in cold blood."

Whereas Mattie had been feeling guilty about Glenna's shooting, she could tell that the sheriff had developed a healthy dose of anger. "We'll do our best."

McCoy gave her a confirming nod. "I know we can count on that." He included Brody in his gaze. "I've called Glenna's supervisor, and she's going to notify Glenna's family about what has happened and which hospital she's at. For now, I'll head back to Shadow Ridge and bring the crime scene techs here when they're done up above."

After McCoy left, Brody gestured toward Moose with his chin. "What do we do with him?"

"I'll put him back here after I get Robo ready." She put Robo's Kevlar vest on her dog, gave him some water, and then invited him to unload. Moose rocked the vehicle as he jumped side to side in front, looking for a way out. Mattie spoke to him soothingly as she pulled a short leash from her duty belt and went to the passenger's side.

Moose hit the door when she unlatched it, and she had to block him as she inched the door open, grasping his collar and telling him to sit. She clipped on the leash and he jumped free, trying to drag her back toward the spot where Glenna had been shot.

Poor guy. The big dog was hard to control, but she wrestled with him, trying to calm him, until he was willing to walk beside her to the back of the vehicle. With Brody's help, they lifted him into the cage, where she made sure he had water before closing him inside.

As they walked away, he gave a mournful howl. She needed to find a better option for the poor dog soon.

She and Robo joined Brody at the campsite, where he was bending forward, studying the ground.

"I looked for tire tracks that we might cast but haven't found any," he said, pointing as he walked slowly across the gravel. "This area is pretty rocky."

"I'm going to search a grid with Robo right here, and then we'll spread out toward where we found Glenna," she said.

The air continued to be cold and still, so Mattie started her imaginary grid where she thought the door to a parked RV might have been. After she prepped Robo for a grid search, they weaved their way back and forth, Robo sniffing every clump of grass, pile of wood chips from cut firewood, and mound of dead leaves and branches they came across. It was one of these mounds, about thirty feet away from their start, that Robo poked his nose into before he sat.

"What did you find?" Mattie squatted beside him and took out her cell phone to snap a picture. With a gloved hand, she gently pushed away the top layer of dead leaves. Nothing.

Brody came up beside her, and she handed him her cell phone. She didn't doubt Robo's nose, so she continued to sort through the small pile of leaves carefully while Brody documented her progress with photos. Midway through the pile, a glint of gold caught her eye. She rocked back on her heels.

"There it is," she said, pointing with one hand while she reached for an evidence bag with the other.

A brass casing lay partially buried beneath dried leaves almost the same color and against a bunch of dormant grass. If a shooter had looked for it, it would have been hard to find. It had taken Robo's skilled nose to detect it.

"Good boy, Robo," she praised him as she ruffled his fur and hugged him against her chest. He squirmed with pleasure.

After Brody documented the casing's presence with a picture, Mattie plucked it from its resting place with gloved fingers, being careful to avoid touching any potential fingerprints that might have been left on its side. She read the head stamp before placing it in the bag: *.223 REM.*

This was a .223-caliber round manufactured by Remington. The casing was slightly shorter than two inches long.

She sealed the bag and handed it to Brody—he was their expert on guns and ammo. "Do you think a professional would've controlled his brass?" She was thinking about how snipers often used a brass catcher at the rifle's ejection port.

"Might have been an unplanned shot. Or he could've been in a hurry and he didn't have time to set up." Brody held up the plastic bag and studied the casing. "Same round we use in our AR15s."

Mattie nodded. "Common enough ammo. Used in a lot of different types of guns."

"Semiautomatic, bolt-action rifles, lever-action rifles, and even some types of long-barrel guns the ATF classifies as pistols." Brody paused and looked at her. "But the point is, even though this round is legal for self-defense or sport, it's illegal to use for hunting deer in Colorado."

She knew that. "So why would a hunter have this ammo in his rifle? Points even more to our killer. I think Glenna came here and surprised the person or people we're looking for."

"That's what it looks like." Brody pocketed the evidence bag.

Mattie knelt beside Robo and hugged him. Evidence detection was a skill she worked on frequently with her dog, and she kept detailed records in her training journal to document his high level of accuracy for finds in the field. The journal accompanied her whenever she had to testify in court.

From a distance, she heard muffled howls start up again from inside her unit. She knew how Moose felt, and she wanted to join him in howling out her sadness, guilt, and anger about Glenna, Juan Martinez, and her missing mother. There was evil brewing in these woods. She could feel it.

As she glanced back at her vehicle, she spotted a brown RV nosing its way into the campground. The heavy vehicle jostled its way along the main track down by the stream that flowed through the campground, stopping just short of the crime scene tape. "We've got company," she said to Brody as he turned to look.

"Careful." Brody still held his rifle aloft, never having put it down since they arrived. "Let's tell them they have to leave. I'll do the talking."

Mattie knew that meant she was to stand guard and provide backup in case of a surprise attack. Approaching a vehicle was one of the most dangerous duties in her profession. A cop never knew who or what was inside, and it was a handy way to set up an ambush.

Scanning the area for potential cover, she told Robo to heel and followed Brody at a distance of about twenty feet. She released the safety strap on the holster of her sidearm as they went.

The driver hopped out of the RV as Brody approached, coming forward as if to greet him. Mattie recognized her immediately as Didi Carr, the woman she'd conversed with earlier at the other crime scene. The woman's husband, Milo, emerged from the passenger's side and circled the end of the RV to join his wife.

Both wore friendly smiles and didn't appear to be armed, although this was no reason for Mattie to let her guard down. She stayed back and let Brody handle the communication.

"Hi, folks," Brody said, stopping a short distance from the couple. "We've had an incident here this morning, and I'm going to have to ask you to leave."

Disappointment registered on Didi's face. "Oh no. The game warden said we could camp here."

"I'm afraid there's been a change of plans," Brody said. "You'll have to go to one of the other campgrounds in the area."

"We already had to leave Shadow Ridge." Didi glanced from Brody to Mattie as if to gain support. "We spoke to you earlier."

Mattie nodded to let the woman know she recognized her. She remained in place but projected her voice. "I'm sorry about this, but we can't let you stay. You might try the campground at Redstone Ridge. It's a nice one."

Redstone Ridge was a beautiful area, forever marred by death because of Mattie's past experience there—but these visitors wouldn't know about that.

Milo rocked back on his heels, lifting his toes for a brief moment, before leaning forward again. He thrust his hands in his pockets and turned as if to retreat to his side of the vehicle.

But Didi seemed to want more information. "What's going on here? Why are you closing this campground too? Did someone else get killed?"

Stepping back a few feet, Mattie let Brody handle the questions while she tried to keep Milo in sight. Robo stuck close to her left heel without need of further direction.

"I'm not at liberty to share information, but suffice it to say that this campground is closed until further notice."

Didi raised an eyebrow. "I assume that means yes, or at least another crime of some kind has been committed."

"Where did you go after leaving Shadow Ridge?" Brody asked. "It's been a couple hours since everyone vacated that campground, much longer than it would take you to drive here."

"The other campgrounds that the game warden mentioned were full, so we decided to come back here. Now I suppose we'll have to drive clear back into Timber Creek."

Milo was opening the door of the RV. He reached inside, pulled out the steps, and climbed in, shutting the door behind him. Mattie didn't like that he'd disappeared, and she wondered what he was doing.

"Do you mind if we take a look inside your vehicle?" she asked.

Didi frowned. "The detective already did when we were at the other campground."

"I'd still like to take a look, if that's okay with you."

Didi shrugged and walked around the vehicle. As she moved up the steps and tugged open the door, she said, "I guess Milo didn't understand that we have to move on. He's not feeling well today." And then she called inside, "Milo? Honey, where are you?"

"Back here."

His voice came from the rear of the RV, and Mattie heard a toilet flush. She waited outside with Brody.

The sound of running water came from inside as Mattie remained focused on the open doorway.

"Can you come outside with me, dear?" Didi said, coming back to the door. Milo followed, wiping his hands on his pants. They both came down the steps, and Milo put his hands in his pockets. "These officers want to take a look inside the camper."

"They already did," Milo said, giving Mattie a smile.

"I know, but they want to look again. Just come over here with me," Didi said.

Brody stayed outside with the Carrs while Mattie climbed the steps into the RV, taking Robo with her. She did a quick visual sweep, noting a neat galley kitchen, a short table and booth that probably converted into a bed, and a tiny bedroom in back with a bathroom that contained a toilet and shower.

"Do you want to find something?" she murmured to Robo. "Go find it."

She really didn't know what she was looking for, but if there was anything here that might point to illegal activity, she wanted to know about it. Anyone could be holding her mother captive, even this seemingly harmless couple.

Robo roamed inside the vehicle, and he sniffed each area thoroughly without hitting on anything. Mattie peered into closets and cupboards, finding only clothing, food, and household goods. Robo finished his search, ending by sitting beside the one locked cupboard that she couldn't open. "What's in there?" she murmured to him, wishing he could tell her.

She went to the open door. "Could you unlock this cupboard for me?"

Didi came up the steps. "Sure. That's where we keep our guns."

Made sense. Robo had hit on the guns and ammo. Mattie stood back while Didi unlocked the cupboard, leaving the door open. It contained three rifles of various types and some boxes of ammo, but none of the ammo boxes were labeled Remington .223 caliber.

"Thank you," Mattie said, moving to the door. "Let Deputy Brody take a look before you lock up the cabinet again."

She went down the steps, gesturing with her head as she told Brody she wanted him to take a look at the guns. Milo stood with his hands in his pockets, no smile on his face for a change, although one crossed his lips fleetingly as Mattie approached. He had a strange affect, and she wondered about it, but you couldn't arrest a man for smiling all the time.

"How has the hunting been?" she asked him. "Have you seen any elk?"

"Didi hunts. I don't." He smiled. "I go with her, though, but I don't remember if we saw any elk. You should ask her."

His answer made Mattie think that Milo might have some type of memory problem, which could also explain his way of interacting with people. Didi and Brody exited the RV.

Milo rocked forward on his toes as he smiled at his wife. "She wants to know if we saw any elk."

Didi returned his smile, her face softening as their eyes met. "No, but we've enjoyed going out to look for them, haven't we?"

"Sure have."

Mattie decided there was nothing here for her to worry about. These two appeared to be on vacation, and she believed they weren't hiding anything. She gave them directions to the campground between the Redstone and Balderhouse trail-heads. "It's farther west from Timber Creek, and it's in a beautiful spot. I hope you can find an open campsite in there. I think you'll enjoy that country, and maybe you can spot some elk."

Didi shrugged. "To tell you the truth, we don't care so much about bagging an elk. A lot of times we just hike without our rifles. Don't we, hon?"

The two grinned at each other before turning away to put the steps back inside and close the door. They said good-bye and went to their respective sides of the RV's cab. Mattie and Brody watched as Didi maneuvered the rig around the circle of the campsite and rumbled off down the two-track lane.

Brody looked at her. "Two of the rifles are hers—a Weatherby Camilla and a Savage Lady Hunter. They're both smaller, lightweight guns, and neither would shoot a .223-caliber round. The larger rifle is his, but it doesn't shoot a .223-caliber round either. She says he isn't hunting this year. She told me he got kicked in the head by a horse last summer and is still recovering from that."

"Oh man . . ." Mattie felt bad for the couple. "I thought he might have a memory problem."

Brody nodded. "Let's close off the entrance to the campground to keep people out of here until the crime scene techs can do their thing."

Once again, Mattie found herself fearing that her sister and grandmother could be in danger, a feeling that was becoming too familiar. "After they get here, I should drive down where I can catch a good cell phone signal. I haven't been able to talk to my sister yet, and I need to let her know what's going on."

THIRTEEN

"And you're sure it's Juan Martinez?" Julia asked.

Mattie gazed through the windshield of her Explorer at the green forest beyond the overlook where Brody had parked. He'd driven them down below the area of beetle kill to a spot where she could use her phone, and it felt awkward having to sit beside him while she spoke to her sister. "I'm as sure as I can be. We'll send photos to Detective Alvarez, and I hope she'll drive down to see if his brother can identify him."

Julia's voice was tight with tension. "Oh, Mattie, this is terrible. So you think Mom is being held captive somewhere out there?"

It was as if Julia couldn't believe what she'd heard, and Mattie understood how she felt. Her own brain was foggy with fatigue, and she'd crossed into that state where she felt as if she were dreaming with her eyes open. "We have strong evidence to that effect. And I think you and Abuela could be in danger too. Can you find a safe place for you and your family to stay for a few days? Don't tell me where right now. I don't trust these cell phone connections."

Possibly feeling the awkwardness as well, Brody stepped out of the vehicle and moved off to wait beneath the pine trees at the edge of the road. As if on guard, he took his rifle with him. Mattie squinted at him, trying to focus her tired eyes while hoping he was safe within the shelter of the trees. After Glenna, she felt on edge about everything out here.

"I know where I can go," Julia was saying. "We'll be okay. But how about you?"

"I'm being cautious. Don't worry."

"Should I come to Colorado and help you search for our mother?"

Mountains and forest stretched out for countless miles around Mattie in all directions. Searching for her mother in this wilderness seemed impossible, and Julia's safety was of utmost importance. It was best for her to stay as far away from this scene as possible. "No, you need to stay in California, where you can be in touch with Detective Alvarez. But please be careful. It would be best if you and Abuela could keep your family together at all times, at least during the next few days."

"You mean take the boys out of school?"

"If you can."

"I don't know, Mattie. That seems extreme."

Maybe Mattie was overreacting, but the fear of something happening to Julia, her family, or Abuela loomed large. She'd searched for her mother for decades before finding her. And now this. She couldn't bear the thought of her loved ones being in danger too.

"Maybe it is extreme, but we don't know what we're up against out here." She told Julia about Glenna being shot. "I don't think we can take any chances."

"I suppose it wouldn't hurt for the boys to miss school for a few days, but Jeff still needs to go to work."

Mattie would have preferred that Julia's husband remain with the family to protect them. "Talk it over with him and see if he could take a few days off. At least until you can get your security established. I don't want anyone to be able to get to you. Stay together at all times. Don't go off by yourself."

"All right, we'll see what we can do. But you take care of yourself too. When will you call me again? I have to know that you're okay."

"I don't have cell phone service up where we're searching, but I'll check back with you when I can. You can always call the station and get updates from Rainbow, our dispatcher. I'll give her clearance to talk to you."

"I guess that will have to do. Mattie . . . I can't believe this is happening. We were so close to being able to become a family again, but now . . ."

Mattie could sense Julia's pain. This was what being part of a family was like—you had to experience the bad times with each other as well as the good. Though Mattie had yearned for the connection of family, those years of being a loner hadn't prepared her for this type of emotional turmoil. "Julia, hear this. We're still family no matter what. And we're doing what we can out here to find our mother. Be tough. This isn't over."

She could tell that Julia was holding back tears when she responded. "I'm not as tough as you are, little sister. I love you."

Mattie swallowed against the knot that formed in her throat. "I love you too. We have to be strong together."

The radio in her unit crackled to life, followed by Sheriff McCoy's voice. "K-9 One, this is Alpha One. Do you copy?"

"I have to go, Julia. I'll call back when I can."

"Wait."

Mattie didn't want to cut her sister off. "Hold on one minute."

Evidently having heard the radio transmission, Brody opened the car door and pressed on the mic. "This is Alpha Two on board with K-9 One. Go ahead."

Mattie put Julia on hold while she listened to what McCoy had to say.

"We need a meet here at Shadow Ridge. What's your status?"

Brody raised a brow at Mattie.

"We can go right now," she told him.

While Brody relayed the message and gave the sheriff their estimated time of arrival, Mattie took Julia off hold and told her that she needed to say good-bye. After the sisters repeated reassurances to each other that they would be careful, Mattie was able to end her conversation with Julia at the same time that Brody ended his with the sheriff.

Brody started the engine, and Mattie settled back in her seat, turning to check on Robo and Moose. Both dogs were curled up in back, sound asleep. She wished she could take everything in stride like that. She leaned back against the headrest, closed her eyes, and tried to clear her mind of its fears and worries. She practiced her yoga breathing and focused on relaxing her muscles while the Explorer jostled its way up the road for the twenty minutes it took to reach the campground.

When Brody pulled to a stop in the parking lot, Mattie startled awake. She'd been dreaming of the last time she'd seen her mother in Mexico. The two of them had sat close together on her mother's couch despite the summer heat making them sweat. The purr of her mother's oscillating fan and the sensation of its breeze brushing against her skin lingered as she blinked her eyes to clear the cobweb of memories from her brain.

Vehicles from the Colorado Bureau of Investigation had parked in the lot—vans used by the crime scene investigation team and a familiar Jeep driven by Agent Rick Lawson, a detective who had helped them investigate a crime a month ago when several bodies near Redstone Ridge had been found. Rick was still working on that case, coordinating efforts with the FBI and the California Attorney General's Office to locate missing children and return them to their parents. They'd been successful in a couple of cases, and there was hope that more success was still to come.

Brody exited the vehicle, and Robo stood and stretched. Moose raised his head and looked at Mattie with sad eyes. She reached through the steel mesh of the cage and patted Robo when he came to her, stroking the smooth black hair between his ears. "You two wait here," she murmured. "Go back to sleep if you can."

She followed Brody to the sheriff's Jeep, where the team had gathered. The sun beamed down, warming the air and making it bearable to meet outside.

Rick was a good-looking guy, built like a wrestler. He wore his dark hair in a buzz cut and scrutinized the world with intense brown eyes. He greeted Mattie as she approached.

She returned his firm handshake. "I'm glad to have you here to help us. Thanks for coming."

"Let's address the elephant-in-the-room first thing," he said, his eyes searching her face. "This case is about as close to you as it can get, with the missing person being your mother. But I've seen how you work, even under pressure, and you have a skill set that we need, so we . . ." He gestured to indicate himself, Stella, and McCoy. "We've decided to include you in the investigation. But if at any time it becomes too much, let us know, and we'll do the same if we have concerns. Fair enough?"

"That's fair," Mattie replied, turning to Stella. "What's the status on the samples we've taken and the autopsy?"

"Rick sent the DNA sample to the CBI lab. We might be able to have results in a few days. We should have results on the water sample today, and I'll leave soon to attend the autopsy in Byers County."

This was part of why having CBI involved was so important. Rick had access to resources that would expedite the processing of evidence, all at no charge to their small rural department.

"Cole Walker has the posse on alert, and several of them are bringing food from the diner," McCoy said. "We'll set up a temporary command post here until the crime scene unit has finished processing this campground. For now, we need to develop a plan for finding Ramona Martinez."

Rick pinned Mattie with his penetrating stare. "It's time for you to come clean and tell me everything you know and anything you suspect."

Mattie didn't have time to feel guilty about retaining what she knew in the past, and she no longer felt remorse for breaking any promises to her mother. She laid out the information about finding her mother last summer in as linear a fashion as she could. "Last July, I learned that Ramona had witnessed my father's murder, and she was terribly afraid that his killers would find her. She said his killers were part of a gunrunning and drug smuggling ring through John Cobb in California and his brother Harold Cobb out here in Colorado."

Rick knew about the Cobb brothers' recent history, so she didn't need to go into detail. He had been a part of the investigation when John Cobb killed her brother, and he was aware that John had died in prison last month. He also knew that Harold had been killed decades ago while in the same prison.

She continued with information about her two recent trips to Mexico. "Ramona believed that her life might still be in danger, and she made me promise not to reveal her location. She said the gang who once held us captive was large and made up of very bad men. She swore that even though she witnessed them shooting my father, Douglas Wray, she didn't have any information that would give us leads on investigating his death, and I believed her. She said that he was coerced into allowing guns and drugs through his Border Patrol checkpoint because the ringleader threatened to kill Ramona and us kids. She said that Douglas was a good man who had just been trying to take care of his family."

Mattie paused for a breath. She studied Rick's face to see if she could determine his reaction, but all she saw there was a neutral mask that she associated with his cop face. She knew something about this mask because she was struggling to maintain one of her own.

"And you suspect that John Cobb was involved in Douglas Wray's homicide, but you don't have leads on any of the others," Rick said.

"That's right. I suspect both John and Harold Cobb were involved. And Ramona couldn't name any others either. My sister and I returned to our mother's house last week to inform her of John Cobb's death and to convince her to speak with Detective Alvarez in San Diego, but when we got there, we discovered that she and her husband had left about a month ago. His brother had no idea where they went."

"What's your take on why they left their home?"

"Anything I have to say about that is pure speculation." Mattie paused for a moment to think. "At first I thought it might be because I'd found her this summer, but then I decided that too much time had gone by for that. I think something, or more likely somebody, spooked her recently and made her run."

Rick glanced at Stella and then looked back at Mattie. "We need to have someone go to her town and see if they can get any information about why Ramona and Juan Martinez left. Maybe identify any new people who came to town recently. Interview shopkeepers and neighbors, see if they can track down any leads at all."

"Detective Alvarez might help with that," Stella said. "I've been in touch with her."

"In the meantime, I'll get back to the internet at the station and see what I can track down in our databases—anyone associated with John or Harold Cobb, back then or now. I also want a handwriting expert to examine those notes." Rick looked at Stella again. "I'll go down to Timber Creek with you."

The two had kept their romantic relationship quiet, and their interactions were all business when working a case. Mattie believed the two detectives were a powerhouse when they worked together, and they would do everything possible to help her mother.

Stella looked at her. "You should come down to Timber Creek too and get a few hours' sleep. Maybe by then we'll have some information that could help in the search."

Mattie desperately needed sleep, but she shook her head. "I can't. I think whoever took Ramona is still holding her hostage somewhere close. We need boots on the ground up here to cover more territory. I'll grab some sleep in the back of my unit if I need to."

"I'll check your house and make sure surveillance cameras get installed," Stella said. "We didn't have the staff to post someone there overnight. I'll see if there's another note on the door waiting for you."

Mattie remembered Moose, still waiting in her SUV. "Can you take Glenna's dog Moose down and drop him off at the Humane Society? Explain the situation and ask them to take good care of him until one of us can come get him."

Stella nodded. "Will do. Glenna would want him to be comfortable, and I'll take care of it."

McCoy spoke up, taking in both Mattie and Brody with a glance. "There are some folks living in Eureka just a few miles from here. Expanding our search to include that area would be a good idea."

Eureka was an abandoned mining town made up of tumbledown cabins, some more habitable than others. Mattie looked at Brody. "That seems like a good place for us to go next."

"We're on it," Brody said to the sheriff.

McCoy appeared to be studying the two of them closely. He glanced at his watch. "It's almost noon. Go to your unit and sleep for an hour," he told Mattie. "Deputy Brody, bunk out in my Jeep. By then the food will be here, and you two can grab some before you go."

Mattie started to protest. It felt urgent that they respond right away.

"That's an order," McCoy said. "You both need your wits about you in this environment. Get some rest."

His words rang true, and the thought of Glenna being shot while on duty drove his advice home. Mattie felt dead on her feet, and even an hour of sleep would do wonders for her condition. "All right. I'll get Moose for Stella to take with her. Wake us up when the food gets here."

★ ★ ★

Mattie jerked awake when Robo barked. As she sat up, stars wheeled in her vision. Her dog stood by the window, wagging his tail, and it thumped her in the shoulder. She scrubbed her eyes to clear them, thinking she must be dreaming when she heard Cole call her name from outside her unit.

"Sorry, Mattie." The glass muffled his voice. "I hate to wake you, but Sheriff McCoy said it was time."

Moving in slow motion, she raised her hand to place it against the cold surface of the window. Cole pressed his against the other side to match hers while Robo smudged the glass with his nose. She'd slept the deep sleep of forgetfulness, and now it all came rushing back to her—Juan's mask of gray-faced death, the handwritten notes, Glenna being shot, her mother in the hands of a monster.

"Let me wake up," she said.

Having locked her vehicle before falling asleep, she popped the hatch open and scooted to the edge while Cole came around to the back. The Explorer was toasty inside, warmed with heat from the sun and Robo's furry body.

"How are you holding up?" Cole asked as he sat on the edge beside her. Robo wiggled his way in between them, and Cole put his arm around both of them.

"I'm doing all right. Has anyone told you about Glenna?" She searched Cole's face, knowing that bit of news would have hit him hard. They all cared a lot about the new game warden.

Cole nodded as his expression turned grim. "Stella called. She'd been in touch with the hospital, and Glenna's condition is stable. The chest wound didn't hit anything vital, although she's still unconscious. There's a subdural hematoma at the back of her skull from hitting her head. It's small, but they might have to evacuate it if she continues to bleed into it."

Mattie looked down at the gravel in the parking lot and wished that boulder hadn't been behind Glenna when she was shot. But then, if she'd moved afterward, she might have been shot twice, so it could have been a blessing in disguise. "Do you have the results from the blood tests you ran on the horses this morning?"

"Positive for selenium. We received results from the water sample in the tank as well, and it tested above normal for selenium, although not high enough to cause toxicity. I suspect that if I'd taken a water sample yesterday when Tanner Rattler watered his horses there, the result would have been much higher."

Mattie shivered, and Cole stood to move to her other side. "Stay there, Robo. There," he said, as he tried to keep Robo in place against her while he snuggled close to her other side. "Maybe we can sandwich you in to warm you up."

"It's just a chill from waking up," she said, although she was thinking about the possibility that Juan had died from selenium poisoning. The thought was disturbing and painful. She supposed it might be later today or even tomorrow before they received the results from his autopsy labs. Mattie hugged Robo tightly against her. "How are the horses doing?"

"I'm on my way there next to check on them. Tanner says they seem a little better, so maybe he can bring them in to the clinic soon, where I can keep an eye on them. They'll be better off under shelter, where it's warmer."

"Stella had to take Moose down to the Humane Society."

Cole frowned. "They'll take good care of him, but I'll try to find a client to foster him until Glenna gets out of the hospital. It might be easier on him to be in someone's home instead of a kennel."

Mattie tipped her head against his shoulder. "That would be wonderful if you could."

"I'll see what I can do."

Mattie changed the subject. "Brody and I are going up to Eureka to see if we can find anyone who has noticed strange activity."

"There's a woman up there that you should look up. Name's Josie Baker. She's brought her cats in to the clinic before. Josie is an expert on plants and herbs, and she's lived up in a cabin on the north side of Eureka for a couple years now. Well, she actually comes and goes and only lives here part of the time. Her place is easy to find. It's on the north side, and her decor is different types of cat statuary. You'll know the place when you see it. Tell her I sent you, and maybe she'll be willing to talk. She's a bit of a recluse."

"Where does she live when she's not here?"

Cole's brows knit. "I'm not sure. Maybe she'll tell you."

Mattie yawned, covering her mouth before slipping her arm behind Cole's back to hug him. "I'm here between my two fellas in my favorite place, but I've got to get up and go back to work."

"Not before you grab some food," Cole said, standing up to give her room to move out of her unit. "We brought sandwiches, fruit, chips, energy bars, cake, and cookies, and the guys have built a fire to make coffee. You'd better get over there before Brody drinks it all."

As soon as he said *coffee*, the aroma tickled her nose. Or perhaps it was her imagination. Either way, it was just what she needed to feed her mission to find her mother.

Before she could turn away to go, Cole caught her sleeve. He looked deep into her eyes. "You'll be cautious out there, right?"

She gave him a thin smile. "I always am. Don't worry, okay?"

He returned her half smile with one of his own. "I always do. I can't help it."

FOURTEEN

The road to Eureka was narrow and winding but in good condition. Mattie steered around the final curve, which afforded a view of the small ghost town from above. She turned off the main road onto a rutted track that suffered from a lack of maintenance after last month's storm. Her vehicle rocked and slid down into Eureka Canyon, and she was grateful for her Explorer's four-wheel drive, which would probably be needed to climb their way out.

She threaded her way between healthy pine and spruce, passing tumbledown cabins until she came to an open space that had once made up the bulk of the small town. As far as she could tell, smoke rose from three chimneys. "I wonder if there are only three residents up here."

"I wouldn't doubt it," Brody said. "There's just one lane, so it won't be hard to find out."

"Cole said we should look up a client of his, Josie Baker. Lives on the north edge of town."

"We could start there. Let's drive to the end of the road and then come back through."

Mattie navigated the muddy lane, sloshing through gray snowdrifts that had not yet melted. She crossed a narrow bridge that spanned a shallow stream, noticing the remains of wooden sluices that ran alongside the water, remnants of someone's mining operation from the past.

They passed one ancient cabin with smoke pouring out of its chimney on the right side of the road but drove on toward the last cabin, the chinks in its boxy walls newly filled with white caulk. Black smoke from a coal fire rose from its chimney, and the pungent smell filled the air as Mattie drove up. A small, tan-colored RV was parked beside a Jeep Wrangler for off-roading. A variety of cat statues made of iron, ceramic, or wood dotted the front yard.

Mattie jotted both license plate numbers down on a pad on her dashboard. She pressed the talk button on her radio. "Dispatch, this is K-9 One."

"Go ahead."

She was a little surprised when Rainbow answered but glad to know radio reception could reach them in this shallow canyon. "Clear and list two plates." She passed on the license plate numbers so that Rainbow had them in case things went south in a few minutes.

"You're going to wait here," Mattie told Robo, who'd been standing behind her, apparently fully rested from his nap.

Brody came around from the other side, and together they proceeded down a short boardwalk that led to the cabin's front door. There he stepped aside while Mattie knocked on the rough surface.

"Who is it?" A woman's voice came from the other side of the door, sounding cantankerous at best.

Mattie glanced at Brody before introducing them both as Timber Creek sheriff's deputies to the closed door and the woman who was apparently standing on the other side.

"What do you want with me?" she shouted.

"We're investigating an incident that occurred in a local campground."

"I don't know anything about anything. Go away."

Brody raised his eyebrows in a quirky way that struck Mattie as humorous. Here they were, standing outside in the cold on the doorstep of a grumpy woman, investigating two major crimes just a few miles from here, and she was telling them to go away. Like that would happen.

"We're looking for Ms. Josie Baker," Mattie called through the door. "Dr. Cole Walker said we might look her up and talk to her."

The door cracked open an inch, and a small woman with eyes the color of blue columbine peered out at Mattie, giving her the once-over. "Why didn't you say so in the first place? Why does the doc think you should talk to me?"

A gray tiger-striped cat with white paws slipped through the opening and scampered off around the corner of the cabin.

"Oh no, should I try to catch your cat?" Mattie asked.

Josie smiled with half her mouth, her eyes crinkling slightly at the corners. She was an attractive woman, maybe late fifties, whose blond hair was turning white. "Nah, she'll stay close. No traffic for me to worry about, and she'll be back in mewling for her dinner before I know it."

Mattie rubbed her hands together to warm them. "May we step inside for a moment?"

The door swung open wider, and Josie gestured inside. "Mind your boots. If they're muddy, leave them on the door-step or stay on the mat."

Mattie gave the bottoms of her boots a cursory glance before stepping inside on the rug Josie indicated. Brody followed, and she edged over to give him room. Cops didn't take off their boots when making house calls, especially during a murder investigation.

A larger, bulkier version of the tiger-striped cat that had escaped lay on a wooden countertop in a tiny kitchen at the front of the cabin. An old round-shouldered refrigerator that resembled the one in Mattie's rental home sat against the wall along with a small two-burner gas stove, probably fueled by propane. What looked like dried herbs hung from the ceiling in bunches.

"Your cats are beautiful," Mattie said, hoping to establish some kind of rapport.

"They're my babies," Josie said, stroking the cat's fur and making him lift his face, all squinty eyed, for her to rub his chin. "Now . . . why do you want to talk to me?"

"We hope you can help us determine if there's been any unusual activity in this area. Have you noticed anything odd? Any outsiders who might be new coming in, folks who don't appear to be hunters?"

Josie lifted her face and squinted, reminding Mattie of her cat. "Folks around here sort of come and go. Most of them move out during the winter. When me and my cats are here, we stick to ourselves."

"Do you know who's here right now?"

"The boys down the road, Rope and Kent Gaffey. They're brothers. They just came back from somewhere. I don't really know where their home is. There's an old guy just across the road a bit who stays here year-round. Most of these buildings are abandoned and falling apart."

"Has anyone pulled a rig in down here to park?"

"Some do, but they don't usually come all the way down. The road's too iffy, so they back out and go somewhere else."

Mattie glanced at the ceiling, scanning the variety of dried plants that hung from the rafters. Her mind skipped from the thought of Cole's patient with selenium poisoning to wondering how the stock tank might have been poisoned to curiosity about these bundles, which were obviously carefully picked, prepared, and hung to dry. "You have quite a collection of herbs here."

Josie raised an eyebrow, looking suspicious. "What does that have to do with the price of tea in China?"

Mattie smiled, trying to regain the woman's congeniality. "I guess it doesn't, but it's interesting, and I couldn't help but comment. You have a huge variety of plants. Do you use these herbs in cooking?"

"Some," Josie responded, gazing at the plants. "Some are medicinal, some are used as poultices. Some are used to supply companies that manufacture health products."

This last comment surprised Mattie. "You gather herbs and plants as part of your livelihood?"

Josie shrugged. "It gives me some pocket money. I either ship them or transport them to the companies I work with, depending on whether I want to take the kids on a trip." As she stroked her cat again, one corner of her mouth quirked.

"Where do you live when you're not here?"

"I drive out to LA when I deliver the herbs myself. I usually stay in the RV. I don't have another permanent home."

Brody spoke for the first time. "What about that plant that looks like dried onions?" he asked, pointing to a bundle of spindly stems with tubular leaves and a puff ball at the top similar to an onion that had gone to seed.

Josie narrowed her eyes at him and gave him a suspicious look similar to the one she'd given Mattie. "Why do you ask about that one in particular?"

Brody shrugged one shoulder. "It looks like a plant I'm familiar with, one you wouldn't want to eat."

"Death camas," she said, her tone low and ominous.

Even the plant's name gave Mattie a chill.

"We used to look for it on the ranch where I worked during the summers when I was a kid, so we could get rid of it," Brody said. "It's toxic to livestock and most certainly to people."

"Aren't you a walking encyclopedia, smart boy? If you know that much, you should also know that if you prepare the root bulbs right, you can eat them."

Brody gave her a half smile. "Learn something new every day. Why do you save these poisonous parts?"

"Pack rat poison." Josie gave him a sour look before turning back to Mattie. "Are we done here?"

Given the brief exchange, Mattie didn't know if they were done there or not. And why would Josie set out poison when the cats might get into it?

But Brody asked the question before Mattie could. "Aren't you afraid your cats might eat the poison?"

Josie gave him another dirty look. "I use it in my RV and set traps the cats can't get into."

Deciding her explanation was reasonable, Mattie diverted the interview. "Getting back to my original question, have you noticed any unusual activity up in this neck of the woods?"

"I have not. I stick to my own business and hope that everyone else sticks to theirs." She threw a pointed glance in Brody's direction.

He gave her a thin smile.

Mattie decided that with the RV outside, the death camas hanging from the rafter, and the mention of Los Angeles, she needed to look further into Josie's business. "What do you know about selenium?"

Josie raised a brow. "It's used as a supplement, and people consider it an antioxidant, but the jury's still out on that. It should be used only as directed, because folks can overdose on it pretty easily."

"Are any of these plants used as a source for selenium?" Brody asked.

"Since selenium is found in the soil and many of these plants were harvested around here, where the selenium levels can be fairly high, there might be a trace of selenium in any of them. But if you're wondering if I harvest anything for the selenium market, the answer is no to that, smart boy. That's not my thing."

Mattie decided that taking a direct approach would be best at this point. "Ms. Baker, we're investigating a couple of major crimes. First of all, the death of a man at Shadow Ridge Campground yesterday evening. There was report of several RVs coming and going during the afternoon and evening. We don't know if an RV was involved or not, but I'd like to eliminate yours. Did you happen to go to Shadow Ridge in it yesterday and park in the lot?"

Josie raised her brows and scoffed. "Are you kidding me? No. I have no reason to go there. I was here all day."

"Like I said, it would be great to make sure of that and eliminate the possibility. No one else took your RV?"

Josie gave her a scornful look. "Absolutely not."

"There was also a shooting at Cedar Canyon Campground this morning. Were you anywhere near there?"

"What in the world is going on around here? This is what happens when too many people crowd into one place. Next thing you know, the crime rate around here will be as bad as LA."

Mattie repeated the question. "Were you anywhere near Cedar Canyon today?"

"I was not. I've been here the whole time both yesterday and today."

"Could I have your permission to take a quick peek inside your RV?"

"Why? What's so important about my RV?"

"We're also looking for a missing person, and we're turning over every stone trying to find her."

Josie shook her head, her disgust obvious. "Well, you won't find her in my rig, but you can look if it will get you out of my hair."

Mattie scanned the cabin, noting that everything seemed to be within this one room. Kitchen in one corner, a rocking chair and a recliner in front of the coal stove, a single bed tucked along the far wall, a bookshelf filled with books, and a cat litter box next to the bookshelf. There was one door at the back that might lead to another room. "Is there another room beyond that door?"

"Nothing out there but a pathway to my outhouse."

"Could I take a look in there too?"

Josie scoffed and crinkled her nose. "Be my guest."

"Thank you. Is your RV locked?"

"I'll open it for you. I have to get my boots on."

Mattie and Brody shuffled outside the door and circled to the back of the cabin while they waited for her. An outdoor privy stood about fifty feet from the back of the cabin, and the remains of several ancient cabins dotted the landscape out front. There was something about this ghost town that didn't sit right with Mattie, and she decided that using Robo to sweep the area would be in order before they left.

Brody strode over to the outhouse and looked inside before moving back toward the RV.

Josie joined them, her feet encased in fleece-lined rubber boots that appeared to be well worn. Mattie could imagine her tramping the hillsides in them, looking for her plants in late summer and fall.

Josie unlocked the door to the RV, and Mattie climbed up inside the small space. It contained a kitchenette, a table with boothlike cushioned benches that would convert to a bed, and captain's chairs in front for driver and passenger. Mattie opened cabinets and peered into the tiny bathroom in the back corner to make certain that her mother had not been hidden anywhere inside this vehicle.

She stepped outside. "Thank you, Ms. Baker. We'll be on our way now, although I'm going to use my dog to search on our way out. I appreciate your help and your cooperation."

"Always willing to help the police," Josie said with a sardonic smirk. "Don't let your dog attack my cat."

Mattie nodded as she pulled a business card from her pocket. "If you notice anything unusual up here, please give my office a call."

Josie glanced at the card before pocketing it. She locked up her vehicle and turned away to go back inside her cabin, evidently having nothing more to say.

Brody led the way to the back of Mattie's unit, and Robo jumped side to side as they approached as if he couldn't wait to be let out. It would be good to give him a chance to work again to release some of that energy. She had no concern about Robo chasing the woman's cat, even though some patrol dogs might be tempted. Robo was all business when he was on a mission, and he'd been trained to ignore other animals while working. Besides, by now he was well used to Hilde, Angie's cat.

"She was unusually cranky," Brody muttered as they climbed inside, where they could talk without being overheard.

"Cole warned me she was a recluse. I'll have to see if he can shed more light on that. Good find on that death camas."

"It's hard to say if it's important. But I did notice that there were no root bulbs on those plants."

"Yeah, me too."

"We'll need to tell Stella and ask her to talk to the ME about it," Brody said. "Maybe we should be looking at death camas instead of selenium poisoning. I'll radio the sheriff and ask him to pass the message on to her."

While Brody did just that, Mattie eyed the cabin across the road in her rearview mirror. When he completed his radio transmission, she started the Explorer's engine and backed out so she could head up the canyon. "Let's see who's at home next door before I take Robo out to search."

The sun had already begun its westward dip in the sky, and they still had a lot of work to do before nightfall. They needed to get to it.

FIFTEEN

Mattie parked behind a white panel van that sat outside the rustic cabin across from Josie Baker's and followed protocol to report the plate to dispatch. She told Robo to wait as she exited the vehicle and followed Brody along a grassy path that led to the front door. A ramshackle shed leaned against the right side of the cabin, and a collection of deer and elk antlers were arranged in clusters at the base of the front walls. This ancient cabin had an air of dilapidation, lacking the clean and tidy appearance of Josie Baker's.

At Brody's knock, the door opened quickly, as if the resident had expected them. Mattie figured it wasn't often that those who lived in this town received visitors, especially visitors in marked police cars.

"Yeah?" a man with a gray-streaked beard said as he opened the door. He stood in the doorway, a look of suspicion in his red-rimmed eyes under bushy gray brows. His hair was tousled, his blue denim overalls soiled and greasy, and he wore a red-and-black plaid flannel shirt with the dirty cuffs of what had once been a white thermal undershirt peeking out at his hands.

An unpleasant odor wafted from inside the cabin, and Mattie wished that Robo could decipher the scents and tell her what he smelled. While her nose could only tell her that she smelled something stinky, dogs sorted through scents in layers, so Robo would have been able to identify what that stink was composed of.

Brody introduced them while Mattie stood back a few feet. "And your name, sir?" he asked.

"Hank Thompson. What do you want?"

Apparently this man wasn't too keen on visitors either, like his neighbor.

"Do you mind if we come in to talk to you a few minutes? There's been a couple incidents up here that we need to inquire about."

"Don't have nothin' to do with me." He raised a brow and looked at Mattie for a moment before stepping back and leaving the door ajar. "But you can come inside."

Brody entered first while Mattie waited a few seconds, searching Brody's back for any signs of trouble. When there were none and he stepped aside for her to enter behind him, she found herself in one of the messiest places she'd ever seen.

This was another one-room cabin like Josie's, except that almost every square inch was covered with something. Narrow pathways led from one area to another. The kitchen was a mass of dirty dishes, dried-on food, greasy stove, old food containers; it was too much to even sort through and catalog in her mind.

Hank paused about eight feet into the room and turned to face them. As Mattie scanned the room beyond him, she could make out tables made with old doors and sawhorses upon which were spread guns and parts of guns, soiled rags, open boxes of ammo, and cans and plastic bottles of products used for gun maintenance. A large magnifying glass suspended on an adjustable stand sat near the window.

The familiar but overpowering odor of metal and gun oil filled her sinuses. Brody shielded her right side, and she placed her hand on the grip of her Glock and thumbed off the retention strap on her holster.

"Whoa," Brody said, his hand lingering on his service weapon. "You've got every type of gun known to man in here."

Hank thrust his lower lip forward and glanced over at the tables that filled much of the room. "I'm a gunsmith. I've got some guns here for repair, some I'm rebuilding, some I collect. What do you want to talk to me about?"

Mattie watched his hands, remembering one of the rules of engagement with anyone during a traffic stop or an unsecured interview—*always watch their hands*. His were in plain sight, his arms hanging down by his sides.

"There was a homicide at Shadow Ridge Campground last night and a shooting at Cedar Canyon this morning. We're talking to everyone nearby to see if anyone saw anything suspicious or knows of any suspicious activity in this area," Brody said.

Hank folded his arms across his chest. "So you thought you'd talk to me just because I have a lot of guns in my house."

"Actually, no. We didn't know that you're a gunsmith. Like I said, we're canvassing the area. That's why we're here."

Hank looked down at the floor for a few moments before looking back at Brody. "So somebody got killed up at Shadow Ridge? You say last night?"

"That's right. But the person or persons responsible might have been in this area lately, maybe even the past two weeks. Maybe they were in some type of RV. Have you seen an RV pull in here to park?"

Hank shook his head before gesturing toward Josie Baker's with his chin. "The gal next door has an RV."

"Has she taken it off the property and stayed somewhere else with it lately?"

He shrugged. "Not that I've noticed. But I don't keep tabs on her."

Mattie thought that was an odd answer, seeing as how he lived less than a hundred feet from where she parked the vehicle. "Are you sure about that, sir?" she asked. "Her place is pretty close; I'd think you might notice if her RV was gone."

He narrowed his eyes at her and reached for the chest pocket in his coverall, making Mattie's muscles tense. But all he drew out was a pair of wire-rimmed spectacles. He put them on and peered through the lenses. "I keep to myself and don't go out much. My eyes aren't as good as they used to be, so there's a lot of things in this world I don't notice."

Mattie scanned the room again, wondering how he could find anything in here and also wondering how anyone could search for something he'd hidden. There were piles of stuff in every corner and several piles in between. Even the bed that was against the far wall was covered with magazines, newspapers, and clothing. Only an overstuffed reclining chair with stained upholstery sat free of clutter next to one of the windows.

Brody persisted. "So have you noticed anything suspicious around here?"

"Can't say as I have."

Evidently Brody wasn't put off by the mountains of junk. He held out a hand palm up to indicate the premises while he spoke. "Our victim's wife is missing, so we're also searching for her. Do you mind if we take a look around?"

Hank's head swiveled to each side as if he'd been unaware of the mess around him and was taking it in for the first time. "Well . . . sure. You're here, ain't ya? Why not?"

Mattie thought there was only one way she could leave here feeling like they'd cleared this place, and that was by using Robo's nose. "Do you mind if I bring my dog inside to search?"

Hank's eyebrows rose in surprise. "I guess not. I've got nothin' to hide."

"Are we okay for me to go to the unit?" Mattie murmured to Brody.

"Affirmative." And then he said to Hank, "Tell me about your business. Who are your customers? I think I see an interesting rifle over there. Is that a Mossberg?"

Brody knew his guns, and Mattie left him to it while she went outside to retrieve Robo. The big guy was waiting for her, and he danced on his front paws as she approached. After opening the hatch, Mattie told Robo to sit so she could put on the harness he wore when searching for people. If her mother was hidden on this man's property, the chances of finding her without Robo were slim.

She clipped on a short leash and ruffled his fur before leading Robo back to the cabin. He was rested and ready to work. She opened the door and entered with him at heel.

Brody and Hank were standing near the gun tables, and Hank looked across the room to stare at Robo when he entered.

Mattie gave her dog the "Search" command that she used to initiate a search for humans. If Hank had any drugs on the premises, she had no doubt Robo would find those too. And she knew he would alert on gunpowder as soon as she got to that part of the room.

Robo pinned his ears when Mattie directed him to sweep the room while she led him down the narrow pathways between piles. He sniffed thoroughly around the base of tarps, old rugs, small appliances, car parts, dirty rags, empty whiskey bottles, *National Geographic* magazines tied in bunches . . . the items in the piles seemed limitless. When the two of them completed the circle of the room, Mattie felt satisfied that no human had been hidden within the mess. And if there had been a trapdoor below the flooring to hide people or drugs, she knew Robo would have turned that up for her too.

At the gun table, Robo sat and stared at the tabletop. She had prepared for the alert, and she told him he was a good boy as she gave him a Kong toy in lieu of throwing his tennis ball for him to chase. She'd been switching out his reward during training, since throwing the ball was not always possible in mountainous terrain, and Robo seemed very satisfied with the change. He chomped the rubber toy while he sat at her left heel.

Hank was lecturing about the merits of certain rifles and handguns, and Mattie knew Brody had been taking inventory of every gun and box of ammo on the homemade bench. And she would bet her next paycheck that he could list it all from memory by the time they reached the car.

"We're done here inside," Mattie told Brody. "I'd like to clear the outside buildings."

"So your dog can smell what yer looking for, ma'am?" Hank said, staring at her through lenses that enlarged his reddened eyes, making Mattie wonder if it was alcohol or eyestrain that made them so bloodshot.

"He can find people and drugs. Apparently you don't have either here in your cabin."

Hank snorted. "That's a safe bet. You can look outside too. He won't find nothin'."

Mattie figured his complete cooperation signified that he was innocent of any illegal activity, but she wouldn't pass up the opportunity to sweep his buildings. She told Robo to drop his toy, and he reluctantly let her take the slobbery, wet cone from him.

Brody gave Hank his business card, asking him for his help and to call if he noticed anything suspicious, and then they all went outside. Hank stood on the doorstep with Brody while Mattie and Robo circled the cabin, finding a shooting range out back that had steel plate targets set up against a hillside. They swept the old shed and the outhouse as they came to them, and as predicted, they turned up nothing.

Hank shook Brody's hand like they were old friends while they said their good-byes, and Mattie figured the two of them had probably bonded over the guns. Out at the Explorer, she and Brody huddled.

"He's got .223 ammo and several rifles that are built for it. He says he's repairing those guns and uses the ammo for testing and sighting after repair," Brody said, keeping his voice low and quiet.

"There's a shooting range out back for target practice."

Brody nodded. "He says he's losing his eyesight, but he hasn't been seen by a doctor. Says his mother went blind at a young age and he figures there's nothing that can be done for him."

"What is he, in his sixties? A lot has changed since his mother went blind."

"Yeah, I told him that. Told him the county has resources that can help him if he needs help. He said he doesn't, but he'd keep it in mind."

Brody was getting soft in his old age, and Mattie appreciated knowing how he'd handled the guy. "So you don't think he had anything to do with Glenna?"

"Nah, I don't like him for it."

Mattie felt the same and turned her attention back to the rest of the town. "This might be a bust, but I think we should sweep this area just in case."

Just in case of what? She felt like her mouth had betrayed her, but Brody didn't ask what she meant. They both knew that she would be looking for a body dump. Robo wasn't trained for human remains detection, but if she asked him to search for a person and he came upon a body instead, he would let her know he'd found something, even if only by raising his hackles like he had last night when he found Juan's corpse.

She gestured toward the dilapidated buildings on each side of the lane. "I don't think we need a warrant to search here. These properties are apparently abandoned and none of the buildings are completely enclosed, so there's no expectation of privacy in them. I know it's a gray area."

"Exigent circumstances are on our side with a missing person. It won't hurt to clear these ruins before we see if someone is home at the first cabin. We'll need to get a warrant or permission before we search that property, since it's obviously inhabited."

"Agreed. I'll take Robo through here on foot. I think it's safe enough that you don't need to back me. Maybe you could drive the unit down toward the first cabin and just sort of follow along behind us."

"All right. I'll stay close."

It didn't take much chatter to prepare Robo to work; he was still ready to go. A slight breeze flowed through the valley, and they were downwind. Mattie unclipped his leash. Flinging her arm out to encompass the area, she told him to search.

He lifted his nose to the breeze and took off, turning left to set up the sweeping pattern he used to quarter an area. Moving back and forth, left to right and back again, Robo would systematically cover the ground until he caught a scent.

A human—or for that matter, anything that Robo had been trained to find, like a stash of drugs or gunpowder—generated scent that flowed from the point of origin in a cone shape that handlers called a scent cone. As Mattie jogged after her dog, she kept one eye on her footing and one eye on him, watching for changes in his body language that would indicate he'd found scent and was working the cone. In that case, he would work back and forth, moving in and out of the cone as it narrowed down to its origin. At that point, her dog would indicate that he'd found something.

But Robo continued to move back and forth in a wide sweeping pattern as they moved through the town. The grasses and weeds were damp with snowmelt, which fed the stream that ran down the middle of the abandoned town. Robo hopped smoothly through the water while Mattie stayed close but avoided wading each time he crossed. Her pants and boots grew wet from the slushy terrain, and the damp conditions were excellent for holding scent.

As agreed, Brody stayed close behind her as they approached the Gaffey cabin. About fifty yards away, Mattie noted the changes in Robo that she'd been watching for—he lifted his nose, pricked his ears forward, and began closing in on a scent. She suspected at least one of the Gaffey brothers would be home and occupying the cabin, but she stayed close to Robo in case he'd scented something in a nearby outbuilding.

Her dog led her right around the backside of the cabin, where two men in camo were dressing out the carcass of an elk. Brody had parked and left the vehicle beside a newer-model Jeep Wrangler out front, so he was right beside her as she followed Robo to the origin of the scent cone. Robo had found not just one human but two.

Both men looked up from their work and didn't seem surprised to see them; she supposed they'd been aware of visitors since she and Brody drove by earlier. The men lay down the knives they'd been using on the carcass and wiped their hands on nearby paper towels.

"Hello," one of them said, a tall, lean guy with dark eyes and a black beard. He looked to be in his forties.

Brody greeted him and introduced himself and Mattie. Robo had sat on his haunches, his method of indicating a find. He was looking up at Mattie proudly, so she took a moment to tell him what a good boy he was and give him his toy for finding these people while Brody handled the introductions.

"Pleased to meet you," the tall guy said, raising his blood-stained hands with a smile. "I'll skip the handshake for your sake. I'm Kent Gaffey, and this is my brother Rope."

Rope was dark and swarthy like his brother, although he was a few inches shorter and stockier. He dipped his head and echoed Kent. "Pleased to meet you."

"We're investigating two major crimes," Brody said, evidently deciding to cut to the chase. "A homicide at Shadow

Ridge Campground last night and a shooting at Cedar Canyon this morning."

Surprise took over the faces of both brothers. "That's terrible," Kent murmured.

"Have you noticed any unusual activity up here lately? Anyone coming into Eureka to park an RV?"

Rope glanced at his brother before speaking. "Josie's RV comes and goes."

"How about yesterday? Here or gone?" Brody asked.

"I'm not sure. We've been out hunting every day. We filled one tag, but we've got another one to fill."

"What time did you get in last night?"

"It was after dark. I think Josie's rig was parked there by her cabin when we got in," Kent said, glancing at his brother. "Did you notice?"

Rope wagged his head, looking down as if trying to think. "Yeah, I'm pretty sure it was here."

"Any other RVs come in here to park?"

"Not anyone who stays," Kent said. "But they're all over the campgrounds."

Mattie decided to move on to more pressing information. "The deceased man's wife is missing, so we're searching buildings and rigs so we can eliminate the possibility of her being inside. Do you mind if I take a look inside your cabin?"

The two men looked at each other before Kent, who appeared to be older, answered. "You can look, but the cabin's a mess. It's just the two of us, so . . ."

"Nothing wrong with a messy cabin. It's important we clear this entire area so we can move on." Intending to take Robo inside with her, Mattie reached for his toy and told him to drop it. She tucked it back into a pocket on her duty belt.

Rope moved to the back door of the cabin to open it for her, and Brody came along behind, stopping at the doorstep. "Stay outside here, please," he told Rope as Mattie prepared to enter.

Rope raised his hands slightly and stepped back into the yard with his brother. As Brody peered inside the cabin, Mattie stayed back where she could respond if either of the brothers made a move. Brody turned back toward her. "Okay," he said.

This meant that his visual sweep indicated an all-clear inside. Mattie told Robo to heel and took him inside while Brody remained on the stoop, guarding her back.

The cabin was as messy as promised. Clothing, blankets, firewood, utensils, trash—just about anything you could imagine cluttered almost every surface.

Mattie guided Robo quickly around the room in a sweep that revealed nothing but the obvious disorder. Certain that her mother was not on these premises, Mattie felt discouraged but satisfied that they'd searched everything they could. She moved back outside, intending to take a quick look inside the privy before they left, although she figured Robo would have hit on the building if a human had been inside.

The radio speaker at Brody's shoulder crackled to life, and McCoy's voice came through the static. "Alpha Two, this is Alpha One. Do you copy?"

Brody pressed on his mic. "Copy."

"Return to command, ASAP."

"Copy that. ETA fifteen minutes."

Mattie exchanged a glance with Brody as she snatched a business card from her pocket. She handed it to Kent. "Please contact us if you see anything suspicious or if you discover anything that might help us find the missing woman. She's in her late fifties, Latina, black hair with strands of gray, brown eyes, about five feet three inches tall with medium build," she said, before gesturing toward the outhouse. "Is it okay if I check that building on our way out?"

Kent waved a hand, palm up. "By all means."

Mattie nodded and swung by the privy on her way off the property. Opening the door revealed nothing, and she hurried to load Robo into her unit. There had been a sense of urgency in McCoy's transmission, and she was eager to see what had transpired.

But as Mattie settled in behind the wheel and started to drive back to Shadow Ridge, she had second thoughts, and a dreadful premonition squeezed her gut. The sheriff wouldn't have called them back unless something bad had happened.

SIXTEEN

When Mattie pulled into the campground parking lot, she spotted Sheriff McCoy standing next to his Jeep with their new hire, Deputy Lester Hitchen. Hitch and the sheriff were deep in conversation, which ended upon Mattie's arrival as they both looked at her. She knew the sheriff well enough to know that his face was filled with concern, and her stomach dropped.

She told Robo to wait as she glanced at Brody. His expression was serious, and it looked like he also expected bad news. He came around to her side of the Explorer as she steeled herself and stepped out to join him. The two of them walked toward McCoy together, and Brody's presence by her side felt like the support she needed.

Mattie could read sympathy in McCoy's eyes. She swallowed before taking a breath. "What happened?"

The sheriff didn't mince words. "We've just heard from Detective Alvarez in San Diego. Your sister Julia is missing."

The world swayed, and Mattie felt Brody's hand at her elbow. "Since when?"

"Her husband phoned in about an hour ago."

"The kids? My grandmother?"

"They're with him, and they're all safe. Julia went to the grocery store before going to their new location. She went alone."

A wave of anger pushed at the shock and dismay she was feeling. She straightened, and Brody's hand at her elbow fell away. "I told her not to go out by herself."

McCoy gazed at her steadily for a few seconds before speaking. "Detective Alvarez has issued a BOLO for Julia in the state of California, and the FBI has extended that into Nevada, Arizona, Utah, and Colorado. We suspect this is a kidnapping that will cross state lines."

Mattie knew what that meant, and a hollow feeling grew inside her. "You think whoever has taken her plans to bring her here."

"That's right." McCoy's gaze became intense. "It's even more important that we keep a guard on you at all times, Mattie. We can't risk your safety, and all of us believe they'll be coming for you next."

It made sense, and she didn't doubt it. "But how can we handle that in our small department? And don't forget that I do have a partner who's very protective."

"We'll do double duty." McCoy's face softened, showing Mattie how much he cared. It was almost her undoing. Then he became all business. "Deputy Hitchen, Deputy Brody, and Detective LoSasso will share duty, depending on where you're all needed and what assignments you're taking. We might enlist Cole as well."

Mattie shook her head. "He's a civilian."

"But he's a trained member of the posse. We'll keep him in mind but only use him as a last resort. I understand your concern."

Fear for Cole and his family came to the surface of Mattie's tangled emotions. She met McCoy's gaze. "I can't bring danger to Cole or his family. It's imperative that we keep them at a safe distance."

A muscle bulged at the sheriff's jaw. "Point taken. We'll have to convince Cole of that. But for now, you need to return to the station so you can talk to Detective Alvarez on a secure line. I'll have someone set up a cot in one of the interrogation rooms for you. I want you to stay there and get some sleep until Detective LoSasso returns, then we'll determine next steps."

He looked at Brody. "You stay here with me, and Deputy Hitchen will follow Mattie back to town. He'll stay at the station to take any calls that come in while we finish up here." Then he said to Mattie, "Agent Lawson is still at the station, so we'll have you well covered."

"I'm not sure that a twenty-four-hour bodyguard is necessary." But even as she spoke the words, Mattie remembered being hit in the back with a large animal tranquilizer dart in her own yard and being taken against her will, helpless to prevent it or to protect herself. But since then, safety measures had been put in place around her house.

The sheriff was giving her a stern look, so she continued quickly. "But I'll go now and remain there until we can determine our next move."

Brody followed her to her unit. "I'll keep canvassing the campgrounds up here."

Mattie thought of Glenna—these people were dangerous. "Stay safe, Brody. Wait until there's another officer who can go with you."

Brody shrugged. "I'll see what the sheriff has in mind."

As she drove away, he gave her a short salute before turning to rejoin McCoy. Deputy Hitchen followed her in his own cruiser.

Steering the Explorer back onto the road to head downhill, Mattie let her shoulders slump as an overwhelming feeling of helplessness washed through her. From all appearances, Juan's killer had some type of vendetta against her or her family. And thinking of Glenna, she knew that even her friends were not safe. Her only hope was that the sheriff and the others were right to believe that Julia was being kept alive to be transported to Colorado.

If she was given the chance to save her sister and mother, she would grab the opportunity. No matter the consequences.

★   ★   ★

As if Robo sensed her mood, he stayed close when Mattie let him out at the station instead of beating her to the door and waiting for her as he always did. She opened the door and entered first, remembering to tell him it was okay to come in, then went in search of her friend Rainbow, the department's dispatcher. Hitch had parked his vehicle beside hers, and he followed her and Robo inside, where he remained at the doorway as if standing guard. Apparently he was taking his assignment seriously.

Rainbow sat at her desk, her headset atop her blond head. When she spotted Mattie, she jumped up, pulled off her headset to lay it aside, and charged over to give her a hug. "I can't believe what's happening. I'm so sorry."

Fluid brimmed Rainbow's blue eyes and made Mattie's burn with her own unshed tears. She took in the warmth of her friend's hug briefly before stepping back. Rainbow was a free spirit, favoring tie-dyed tunics, leggings, and gauzy scarfs, which made her an unlikely candidate for friendship with someone as straightlaced and regimented as Mattie considered herself to be. The two had found a happy balance between them, and Rainbow's caring personality was just the balm Mattie needed when haunted by her past. But today, nothing could lighten her spirit. "Is Stella here?"

"She hasn't returned yet from the autopsy, but I expect her to call any minute to tell me she's on her way." Rainbow walked with her as she went toward the staff office. "Agent Lawson is in the briefing room. He said to let him know when you arrived. And I made a bed for you in the second interrogation room. I made sure the audio and video were disabled in the observation room, so you'll have privacy. I'll also make sure no one bothers you."

Mattie grasped Rainbow's hand and squeezed it. "Thank you. I'm going to call Detective Alvarez first. Would you tell Lawson that I'll check in with him as soon as I get through talking with her?"

"Sure. I made a fresh pot of coffee for you, but you might want to wait until you've had a few hours of sleep. Sheriff McCoy said—"

"I know. We're all worn out, and I'll grab some sleep if I can." Mattie assumed McCoy had enlisted Rainbow in his mission to make sure his staff got rest when they could.

"And Mattie . . . Cole said to call him as soon as you arrived."

"Does he know what's going on with Julia?"

"Evidently Sheriff McCoy told him."

Mattie squinted at her friend, feeling torn in ways she wasn't used to. She knew Cole would want to be her protector, but it wasn't his place. And she wasn't convinced yet that she needed protecting anyway. "Go ahead and let him know I arrived but that I'll be tied up for a while. Tell him I'll call when I can."

"I'll take care of it," Rainbow said, before turning away to go back to her desk.

Mattie followed her dog into the staff office, where he stepped up onto his cushion beside her desk and went down in a play pose, his signal that he wanted a treat. After reaching into the dish where she kept his chicken snaps, she gave him one with one hand while pulling up Sonia Alvarez's number with the other. "Lie down," she said as she dialed.

Robo hastily complied as he settled on his bed with his treat. *Usually he has to work for his treats*, she thought absently as she listened to the phone ringing on the other end of the line. She pinned her gaze on her dog as she tried to alert her fatigued brain and brace herself for the upcoming conversation.

The detective answered her phone. "Alvarez."

"This is Mattie Wray." The voice through the phone became her sole focus.

"Are we on a secure line?"

"Yes."

"Three hours ago Julia left her home to go grocery shopping. After your suggestion to go to a safe location, they were planning to go to the condo they stayed in last month."

Mattie couldn't help but respond, as if she had to defend herself. "I told her not to go anywhere alone."

"Well, that was good advice, but evidently she didn't heed it. When she didn't come home, her husband took their kids and your grandmother and went looking for her. He found her car parked at the store, but she was nowhere to be found. She wasn't answering her phone either, so he contacted me directly."

Mattie released a pent-up breath. "Thank goodness he had your number."

"Yeah, well, I was able to get on it right away. CCTV at the store showed a white panel van parked at the rear of her car but blocking the view of the action behind it from the camera. Two guys dressed in black with hoodies obstructing their faces jumped out after they pulled up behind her. I think they swept her up and put her in through the side door. We haven't been able to find a camera with a direct view, but that's a good guess. The driver ran back around, hopped in, and the van took off. The grab-and-go took thirty seconds. We got a clear view of the plates and put a BOLO out on it. Street cops found the abandoned van about a half mile away."

"Any cameras there?"

"Nada. This looks like a professional job, organized, quick, and effective. The van had been stolen from off the street and discovered missing about the same time we were searching for it. The plate had been stolen from a different van, just to mix things up a little, as if they knew the camera would get a picture of it. Julia's cell phone and purse were left in the van . . . along with a note."

Mattie's stomach churned. She could already guess for whom the note was intended.

"Addressed to you, and I quote: *Yes Mattie, we have your sister now. We'll see you soon. Stay tuned. Fondly, A friend of your father's.*"

"That takes out the guesswork of where they're headed."

"Yeah. We've got the highway patrol looking for Julia, but since we don't know what type of vehicle to look for, it makes her pretty hard to find."

Mattie remembered something. "There was an older-model black Mercedes that might have been used to surveil us when we went to Mexico last week. It had California plates, but I didn't get a number."

"I wish you'd told me you two knew where your mother was and that she had gone missing a second time recently. I felt out of the loop when Detective LoSasso called to tell me about the Juan Martinez homicide. It's hard enough to work a cold case without being given all the information."

Mattie felt chastised, but at this point, they just needed to move on. "I'm sorry about that, Detective, but I was keeping a promise I'd made to my mother to keep her location secret. And given these recent events, I'd say the fear she held for her safety and the safety of her husband had merit. And anyway, by the time we talked to you, she was already missing again."

"Okay . . . I get all that. Back to the car you and Julia spotted—these guys seem to be good at changing plates, so maybe a plate number isn't important. I'll update the BOLO with the car description and send this additional information out."

"Sheriff McCoy said the FBI has been notified."

"Yep. Everyone will be on the lookout, and it's all coming your way. We'll stay on it here on our end and see if we can track down any other leads. I was about to leave for Mexico to get an ID on Juan Martinez, but I sent a guy from our unit to do it. I'll be working with Missing Persons on this in the immediate future."

"I believe all this has something to do with my father's murder all those years ago."

"Tell me what you're thinking."

"Before he died, John Cobb seemed convinced that my mother had stolen money from their operation. She swears she didn't, and that she never had any money at all while she was captive. From what I remember as a child, I believe her. There was never enough food in the house, and we lived a poor life. She took the best care of us that she could, and I'm sure she wasn't hiding money."

Sonia paused as if thinking. "I don't think we can be so sure of that. Maybe she was able to stash something away for when she could try to escape."

"I thought of that, but . . ." Mattie wanted to believe Ramona would never have abandoned her children if she had a cache of money to depend on. "But the point is that John Cobb *thought* she'd taken some missing money, and so the people he worked with all those years probably believe she did too."

"Hmm . . . thirty-plus years seems like a long time to carry a vendetta over some stolen cash when this smuggling ring was more than likely bringing in hundreds of thousands per year."

Mattie thought it over, her mind sluggish with fatigue. "Maybe so. But I still think Ramona was afraid that men from her past would track her down, even as late as this last summer, so I think someone from her past showed up in her village and made her run. Like you said, these scumbags are professionals. Somehow they got to her."

"It's as reasonable a theory as we have to go on, although it doesn't necessarily explain all the difficulty they went through to kidnap Julia. She was never involved in the original kidnapping."

"True, but if they want a way to make my mother talk, why not go after her children?"

"Agreed. And I have turned up some information on problems between Border Patrol agents and critical incident investigative teams around the time of your father's homicide. It's preliminary and I haven't tied it in to the Douglas Wray shooting, but I'll keep working on it." She paused for a moment. "I'll also contact my guy who's headed down to see Tomás Martinez and have him try to dig up anything he can about why Ramona left town so suddenly. And maybe I can dig up something on John Cobb and his associates."

"We're doing that here on our end too. We'll get back to you if we find something promising."

"In the meantime, we're working that van over in our lab to see if we can pick up prints, DNA, fibers, or latent evidence of any kind that gives us a lead. I'll keep you in the loop."

"And you know how to reach Sheriff McCoy if you can't reach me."

"I do. We'll be in touch."

It meant a lot to have someone in California trying to help her family. "Detective . . . thank you."

"I hope we can make progress here. Watch your back, Mattie."

They said their good-byes, and Mattie hung up the phone. Robo had settled onto his cushion, and he blinked up at her, a sleepy look in his eyes. "Do you want to stay here, or do you want to go with me to talk to Agent Lawson?"

Robo stood and stretched, his front legs out and shoulders lowered in downward dog. When he beat her to the doorway, Mattie figured that was her answer.

At the briefing room door, she tapped twice before she opened it. She found Rick Lawson sitting at the table with his laptop and printed pages spread out around him.

"I heard you wanted to talk to me," she said, entering the room with Robo beside her.

His brows shot up when he saw her. "How long has it been since you had some real sleep?"

"I'm not sure."

"Well, pull up a chair. We'll make this brief," Lawson said, combing through some of the papers on the table. "I have an autopsy report from Stella."

Mattie sat across the table from him, eager to see what progress had been made.

"First of all, livor mortis indicates that Juan Martinez died while lying on his back. He wasn't moved into standing position until blood had pooled and colored the entire backside of his body." Rick paused for a moment before continuing. "He had internal congestion in the lungs and kidneys that might be consistent with heart failure, but the additional information about the potential for selenium poisoning made the ME look more carefully. There was also a subtle orange-brown discoloration of the organs and his fingernails that might have been overlooked. His hair was slightly brittle, and he had a patchy irritation on his scalp—again, something that could have been attributed to being held captive for a few weeks, but also something that could point to selenium poisoning. The ME believes it could be acute poisoning rather than chronic, since some of these symptoms would indicate the condition hadn't been long-term."

This was confirmation of their suspicion; she was grateful that Cole had given them this lead to follow. "When will the cause of death be confirmed?"

"Blood tests have been sent to the lab. We'll hear by this evening or tomorrow at the latest."

"How could he ingest enough selenium to be toxic? Food supplement overdose?"

"There have been cases of overdose from liquid food supplements, typically caused by the manufacturer using too high a concentration in the product. These cases were typically accidental and caused illness rather than death. But there are cases on file of murder and attempted murder by using gun bluing."

Mattie was surprised. Bluing was a solution used to treat gunmetal to help preserve it. The chemicals turned rust to black iron oxide, which gave the metal a blue tint. "Gun bluing? Readily available through a gun store."

"Actually, even available through major discount stores."

"But it has a steel-like odor, and it must not taste very good."

"It evidently can be disguised in food and drink under the right conditions. A couple tablespoons will do the trick."

The things humans came up with to do damage to one another always amazed Mattie. "They say poison is a woman's weapon of choice," she mused.

"True, although men are guilty of using that method to kill someone plenty of times."

"Brody and I just interviewed a gunsmith named Hank Thompson who lives up near Shadow Ridge. I'm sure he had gun bluing on his workbench. He had .223 ammo too."

Rick's brow shot up. "Does he look good for this?"

Mattie drew a breath and let it out in exasperation as she remembered their conclusion about the man. "He's elderly, has failing eyesight, doesn't look in very good health, and neither of us liked him for it. Robo searched his cabin and outbuildings and didn't turn up anything."

"We'll still keep him in mind. Could anyone else have access to his stuff?"

"The woman next door, Josie Baker, might. She's a more likely suspect."

"Okay then, I'll keep them both in mind. The only other thing I have to add is that I'm having a forensic handwriting expert examine the notes that have been left for you. The report should be coming in soon."

"Sounds like a good idea."

"So that's all for now. McCoy said to tell you to get some rest, and we'll touch base soon after Stella gets back."

Mattie didn't want to lie down, but she had to admit she was dead on her feet. When she left the briefing room, Rainbow hurried from her desk to join her. "Cole wanted to talk to you, but he said he'll be tied up with the horses he's been treating. He said to tell you to get some sleep and to call him when you wake up."

Mattie had to admit she was glad she didn't need to navigate a conversation with one more person, even one as beloved as Cole. "I'll go lie down on the cot you made for me."

Rainbow beamed. "You'll probably want to take Robo's bed in there with you. Here—let me help you."

She and Robo led the way, Mattie trailing behind. Back in the staff office, Mattie saw that Hitch was there, working at his desk. He glanced up and nodded at her but focused his attention back on his computer monitor without comment. She'd been around the new guy long enough to know he was an experienced officer who rarely spoke, which suited her fine. He seemed to be observant and learned by paying attention, though Brody had done most of his orientation, so her conclusion was based on random observations.

Rainbow picked up the bulky dog bed with no apparent strain, showing Mattie once again how strong her yoga-teaching friend was.

"Let me help," Mattie said, reaching for the bed.

"No, I can carry it. Just open the door, okay?"

Mattie hurried to stay ahead as Rainbow lugged the large cushion back into the hallway toward the closed doors of the interrogation rooms.

"It's room two," Rainbow said.

Mattie opened the door and flipped on the light switch before standing back to let Rainbow enter. A cot from the jail had been set up, complete with a thin air mattress covered in a sanitary plastic liner. But what set this bed apart were the pink floral sheets, soft-looking pillow, and mint-colored fleece blanket that Mattie figured Rainbow had brought in from her own home. A pink sheet had been pinned up with thumbtacks to cover the observation window. The plastic chairs were lined up on the opposite side of the room, while the table had been left close to the center to display a small bouquet of tiny pink carnations, red rosebuds, and white baby's breath in a pint mason jar.

Tears pricked Mattie's eyes as she took in the room. She recognized the time and attention her friend had given to transform this cold interrogation space into an inviting and restful place to soothe her weary mind and body. As Rainbow plopped the dog cushion down beside the cot, Mattie reached to give her a hug.

Rainbow returned the hug, patting her lightly on the back. "Now you get some sleep. I'll wake you if anything happens, okay?"

"Thank you for this," Mattie said, indicating the room with a gesture.

Rainbow closed the door on her way out, and Mattie sighed as she sat to take off her boots. Her dog edged in close, nudging her arm until she stopped to pet him. She sat with him for a minute, eye to eye and then cheek to cheek, and gathered what comfort she could before padding over to the light switch. "Are you ready for a good nap? Go ahead and lie down."

After circling a few times, Robo settled on his cushion. Mattie turned off the light and moved to her cot in the darkness. As she felt her way to the top of the bed so she could pull back the soft blanket and crisp sheet, her mind conjured an image of Julia, bound and gagged and trapped in the dark space within the trunk of a car.

Fully clothed, Mattie sank onto the cot and tucked into a fetal position under the blanket, trying to erase the picture of her sister from her mind's eye. Combining yoga breathing to quiet her inner trembling with utter exhaustion, she forced herself into the oblivion of deep sleep.

SEVENTEEN

The sun hovered over the jagged peaks to the west as the Rattler truck and trailer rumbled up the lane. Cole had waited at the clinic to admit Tanner's horses so he could treat them and then settle them into stalls under the shed. He went out to meet Tanner and waved him up onto the concrete pad alongside the covered box stalls where he could park. Tanner jumped from the driver's seat, and a woman Cole didn't recognize exited the passenger's side.

"Things are a little better this afternoon," Tanner said as he circled to the back of the trailer.

Cole could see that both horses were standing upright in the trailer and facing forward, a good sign. "Looks like they made the trip okay."

The woman joined them. She was attractive, with shoulder-length brunette hair and jade-green eyes framed with long lashes. She appeared to be the same age as Tanner, maybe mid-fifties. She wore navy denim jeans, a puffy down coat, and cowboy boots with a square toe.

"This is my sister Althea," Tanner said as she approached and offered a firm handshake.

"These are my horses," she said, looking Cole in the eye, "and I'm not pleased that they're this sick."

"I can imagine. But they do look better than they did last night. I'm glad you could bring them in where I can keep an eye on them. I'll put them inside box stalls, where they'll be warmer too."

"Sounds good." Althea unlocked the trailer gate and swung it open fully before stepping up inside to untie the first horse.

"Are they eating yet?" Cole asked.

"Not really. They don't seem interested," Tanner said as he stood back, waiting for his sister to back the sorrel out of the trailer.

The sorrel stepped off the edge, his shod hooves clopping onto the concrete, making a scraping noise as he scooted back on his hind feet until his front hooves hit the ground. Althea led the gelding out of the way while Tanner went into the trailer to untie the paint mare.

Cole studied the sorrel, noting the gauntness of his frame, the ribs showing on his sides. "Is he drinking yet?"

"A little," Althea said.

"How much?"

"Maybe half a bucket each."

"Let's take him into the treatment room and put him in the stocks." Cole gestured toward the open double doorway of his equine treatment area, watching the sorrel's gait as Althea led him away. He worried that these horses could develop laminitis, a hoof condition associated with heat and inflammation that often caused severe lameness. The horse definitely walked like he was sore.

Althea led the gelding into the metal stanchion designed to keep a horse still while it was being worked on as well as keep the humans around it safe. Cole swung the side bar closed, connecting the rear bar with a heavy steel clasp.

"Go ahead and tie him up front," he told Althea, wanting to keep the horse from lying down in case he took a notion to. "I'll put the paint in the portable stocks outside. I'll be right back."

Tanner stood outside, holding the paint's lead rope. Cole directed him to his extra stocks, which were anchored to a heavy plank bottom rather than concrete like the one in his treatment room. The mare minced along behind Tanner as he led her forward, her gait indicating soreness as well. She went into the stocks easily, though, and Tanner secured her head to the front.

Cole bent to feel the temperature of the mare's coronary bands, the place where a horse's hoof attached to the skin above it. As suspected, they felt warm, indicating the presence of laminitis. He noticed that Althea was standing at the open door of the treatment room, where she could keep an eye on the sorrel but still see what was going on with the paint.

He projected his voice to include the horses' owner. "Looks like we've got some laminitis here."

Althea uttered an expletive. "Not a surprise. I could tell they were both sore."

"I'll give the mare some more anti-inflammatory paste and IV fluids. From the looks of it, we'll need to do the same for the gelding."

"How the hell did this happen?" Althea's glare took in both her brother and Cole.

Cole thought he saw Tanner flinch under his sister's scrutiny. "The water sample I took at the stock tank at Shadow Ridge showed elevated selenium levels, although not enough to cause this kind of damage. But I figure the selenium had been diluted with a couple different fillings by the time I went there to take a sample."

"Are there other horses who got sick?" Althea asked, her anger still apparent.

"Not that I know of. I suppose other horses might have consumed water at the same level of toxicity but were trailered out of the area before needing a vet. It's hard to say." Cole spoke as he went back to the treatment room, where he bent to feel above the sorrel's hooves. "He's got the same heat in the coronary bands as the mare. I'll treat them both again and get fluids started."

It would probably be a couple of hours before Cole was able to see Mattie. He hadn't heard from her since learning that Julia was missing, which would have hit her hard. It was frustrating to be tied up with work instead of taking care of someone he loved.

A muscle clenched in Althea's jaw, and she narrowed her eyes. "So it looks like someone contaminated the water in that tank with selenium?"

Cole moved past her to get supplies from the cabinet. "That's what it looks like."

"Are the police aware of this? Is someone trying to catch the bastards?"

"The local sheriff has been informed." The contamination of a local stock tank was the least of the sheriff's worries at the moment, except for the fact that it might be related to a man's death and therefore a lead in a murder investigation. "They're working on it."

Althea's mouth formed a sarcastic smirk. "Like that's going to help. Small-town cops."

Her smug attitude got to Cole. While he'd first classified her anger as typical for an owner who was upset over intentional or accidental damage to her animals, this turn in her reaction made him wonder. Especially combined with Tanner's obvious discomfort at being her target. *This is a woman with a nasty temper*, he thought. "The sheriff's office does all right. They're a competent group of professionals."

"Hmm . . . well, I hope so. My next stop is to go file a report. If I get my hands on whoever did this to my horses, I'll throttle them."

Cole refrained from comment as he uncapped the tube of anti-inflammatory paste and stepped up to give the sorrel an oral dose. The focus on work was a convenient cover for diverting the conversation. The IV he'd inserted into the gelding's neck was still intact, taped into place and buffalo capped, so he hung a bag of fluids on a pole next to the stocks and connected the tubing, adjusting the flow once it was established.

"There," he said, gathering the supplies he needed for the other horse. "If you'll keep an eye on this one, I'll go treat the mare."

Althea stepped into the open doorway. "Tanner, get in here and watch this horse so I can help the doc with Keno."

Tanner looked startled, but he did as he was told without protest. As Althea followed Cole to the other horse, he realized he wasn't going to avoid getting an earful.

"The incompetence of some people," she was saying. "I can't believe my brother didn't realize something was in that water tank."

"The concentration of whatever was used could have been enough to be toxic without discoloration of the water. And it could've also diluted any odor. I don't think you can blame your brother for what happened."

She snorted. "Oh, you don't? You don't know Numbnuts very well, do you? He can pretty much mess up anything you put him in charge of."

Cole administered the treatment for the mare and redirected the conversation. "Tanner said you're from Nevada. Near Reno, right?"

"That's right. We own a ranch there together, handed down through our family. If I could buy him out, I would. He's about as dumb as a fence post when it comes to managing horses. I should've known better than to let him bring them here to hunt with."

Cole straightened after connecting the tubing to the IV on the mare's neck and reached to hang the bag of fluids to a pole attached to the front of the stocks. "I hope you can take these two home in a couple days. It's a positive sign that they're feeling better than they did last night. Now if we can reverse the laminitis and keep them from developing colic, we'll be in good shape."

"We'd better, or there'll be hell to pay."

"I've got everything under control here and can keep an eye on both horses while I run these fluids. You can go now if you have other business to take care of," Cole said, hoping Althea would move on and take her venom to the sheriff.

"Nah . . . I'll stay here and make sure everything's okay and these two are in their stalls. We brought hay, so we can keep them on the same feed. If you'll show me where you want it, I'll get Tanner to unload it."

Cole gritted his teeth and braced himself to endure this woman's company for the next hour or so. Maybe her temper would improve with her horses' condition . . . or at least he could hope so.

★ ★ ★

After the Rattlers drove away from the clinic, Cole needed to check on Sassy and the pups. He dialed Hannah's cell phone.

She answered on the first ring. "Hi, Dr. Walker."

"Good evening, Hannah. How is Sassy doing?"

"She's better. She's been sleeping a lot, but she hasn't had the runs once this afternoon."

"Good. The Imodium helped. Has she eaten yet?"

"No, but she got up twice to drink water. She drank a whole bowlful."

"This is all good news. How about the pups?"

"They're better too. I'm still keeping them separated from Sassy unless they're nursing."

Sounded like Hannah had followed his instructions. "When did they nurse last?"

"Just an hour ago. They also ate their puppy chow, and I put extra water in it like you said to."

"How about the runs? Are the pups still having problems?"

"It tapered off this afternoon. Their poo looks pretty normal now."

"That's good. Give them another half ration with extra water before you go to bed and let them nurse one more time. Let's keep them separated from Sassy during the night, though, so she can have more recovery time. Sounds like the break has done her some good, although I'd like to see her eating again soon."

"Do I let the pups nurse during the night?"

"At one o'clock, if you can, and then again at six in the morning."

"Sure, I can do that."

Her eagerness to do whatever was needed impressed him. "Keep the food and water available for Sassy. Maybe put a little warm broth on her kibble—nothing heavy or fatty, okay? That might tempt her to eat, but we don't want her to get sick."

"Right. Mom has some homemade chicken broth. Should I use that?"

"Sure, if you want, but store-bought is fine too."

"Mom makes most of our food."

Cole would've guessed that—just as Ruth sewed their clothing. "I think Sassy and the pups are going to be fine now,

Hannah, but don't hesitate to call me if you have any questions or concerns at all. Even if you need to call at one o'clock in the morning, that's perfectly fine. I sleep with the cell phone next to my bed."

"Okay. And . . . thank you for helping us with our puppies."

"You're very welcome, kiddo. You're doing a great job." Cole said good-bye and disconnected the call. It looked like he needed a helper like Hannah at his clinic after all. He'd work her in part-time until summer, when things got really busy and he could increase her hours.

As he was shutting off lights to leave for the sheriff's station, his cell phone rang in his pocket. He reached for it, hoping it was Mattie.

But it wasn't. Caller ID showed a number he didn't recognize. "Timber Creek Veterinary Clinic."

"Doc?" a female voice asked.

"Yes."

"This is Josie Baker. I need help with Buster." She sounded stressed and upset. "He ate something poisonous."

Buster was Josie's large male cat. "What did he eat?"

"Some flowers and seeds from death camas."

Cole wondered how Buster had gotten into something like that, but some cats would eat anything, and his size hinted that he might be one of them.

"How much did he eat and when?"

"I don't know. I think maybe he got a few of the seeds and flowers, but he stopped eating when I yelled at him. I think he ate it just now, right before I noticed what he was doing. Oh, what do I need to do to keep him from dying?" Her words choked off in an upward keen.

"Take a deep breath, Josie, and try to calm down. You've got to make him vomit, okay? Do you have ipecac on hand?"

"No, no!" His advice to calm down seemed to have had an opposite effect on her.

"Okay, how about mustard or vinegar?"

"Yes, both."

"Use whatever you've got to get him to swallow some. You might have to force feed him with a dropper or something."

"I have a dropper I can use." She sounded a bit more hopeful.

"Good. Use the vinegar; it'll probably go down easier. Try to get him to vomit before you leave home, but bring him in to the clinic."

"I'll get there as soon as I can."

"Don't skimp on getting him to vomit. That's an important step. If we can stop the digestive process, we have a good chance of saving him." Cole wished he could be there to help Josie, but she lived too far away for him to be able to make a difference. Emergency first aid would have to be her responsibility. "Be careful driving to town. Is there anyone up there who can help you?"

"I can handle this." She sounded determined, more like the Josie he knew. "I'll be there soon."

She disconnected the call before Cole could say good-bye. Since he wouldn't have time to go to the station now, he decided to call Mattie. But before he dialed, he called Rainbow instead to see if Mattie was awake.

Rainbow answered his call right away. "Timber Creek Sheriff's Department."

"Rainbow, it's Cole Walker. I'm calling to see if Mattie's available."

"She's still sleeping, Cole."

"But she's there at the station, right?"

"Yes. I set up a bed in one of the interrogation rooms, and we have three officers here now, so she's safe and sound. You don't need to worry."

It was a relief to know she was being sheltered by those she worked with; it was more security than he could provide for her at home. Especially tonight, when he wasn't sure he would even be able to get home. "Would you tell her to call me when she gets a chance? I'm afraid to text or call, because I don't want to wake her."

"Sure, I'll leave her a message."

As Cole disconnected the call, his stomach growled. He decided to go home, check on the kids, and grab a sandwich before Josie arrived with Buster. It was going to be a busy night.

EIGHTEEN

Josie bent over the cat carrier and pinched the latch to open the door. "He irked up the vinegar and some seeds at home, but I think he barfed again inside here on the way down."

"That's actually good news," Cole said, drawing on some latex gloves and grabbing a paper towel. "Here, let me wipe that up so I can examine it before he spreads it on his way out of the carrier."

Josie held the door closed until Cole was ready, and then he reached inside to wipe up the mess, noticing that part of it was a large hair ball. That was one way to clear the cat's digestive tract, albeit not the best. Buster hunkered at the back of the crate, hissing and spitting.

"I think he disapproves of his treatment," Cole said, examining the paper towel, where he saw several seeds and undigested stems. He laid the towel on the counter and turned back to look at the angry cat, whose gray-striped fur had puffed up to make him look as large as a tiger cub. Buster growled, a long, drawn-out message to stay away. "Let's let him settle down a bit before we bring him out."

Josie leaned forward, looking into the carrier and cooing. "He's a big sweetheart, he is. He won't hurt his mommy." And she reached in before Cole could stop her.

The cat continued to growl as Josie smoothed his fur and spoke more baby talk, but within a minute the growling stopped. Josie pulled Buster out of the crate, snuggling him close to her chest. The cat's green eyes, wild and dilated, darted around the room as if he were looking for a place to hide.

"There, there, my big fellow. Mommy's right here. You're going to be okay."

The cat remained pretty worked up, so Cole thought his heart rate would be accelerated. He approached Buster cautiously and was able to pet him while Josie held him in her arms. Slipping his stethoscope's diaphragm onto the cat's chest, he listened to the *ka-thump* of his heart, rapid but strong and steady.

"You've done very well, Josie, and getting him to throw up twice will go a long way toward reducing the toxicity of the plant. But I think we need to give him some activated charcoal to bind the toxins left in his stomach and help prevent them from moving into his bloodstream. All right?"

"Whatever you think is best."

"It means I'll have to tube him to get the charcoal into his stomach, and that means I'll have to sedate him, Josie. There's always a slight risk whenever I have to sedate an animal, but there's a greater risk the toxins can damage his organs if we delay."

Josie held her cat close and nodded. "We have to go ahead and do it," she said, sounding resigned.

Cole had already laid out an esophageal tube and dosing syringe on the counter, so now he hurried to measure and liquefy the charcoal powder, mixing it in a small vial and placing it on the counter within reach. He drew up a dosage for sedation into a syringe. "If you'll put Buster there on the table and stand back, I'll give him the shot by myself."

He held Buster by the scruff of his neck, staying away from the sharp teeth and claws to administer the injection. Within minutes, the cat lay prostrate on the table under sedation. Cole passed the esophageal tube quickly past the needle-sharp teeth so he could deliver the activated charcoal directly into Buster's stomach. He reached for the dosing syringe filled with the liquefied charcoal, attached it to the end of the tube, and began pushing it through.

"How did he get into death camas this time of year, Josie? You said you found him in your kitchen?"

She shrugged, looking guilty. "I use the root for food and keep the stems to make pack rat poison. I had no idea it could shed pieces of it and become a danger to my babies. I'll get rid of it."

Cole nodded, thinking it odd that she would use that type of plant for food. He'd never seen a death camas root bulb, but it couldn't have been that large, and he didn't think of it as very appetizing.

Josie stood by, stroking the fur of her motionless cat and looking worried. When Cole finished, he pulled the tube out and tried to reassure her. "I think he'll do fine, Josie. But I have to repeat this in about four hours. You'll need to leave him here overnight."

"Oh, I thought you'd say that," Josie said, looking up at him. "I brought Mittens down too. She's in her crate in the RV. I'll stay here overnight with the both of them."

Cole felt a frown take over his face. He wasn't set up for overnight guests in his clinic, and allowing clients to stay here unsupervised just wasn't something he did. As animals came out of sedation, there was usually a great deal of floundering about and moaning. They were best left in a confined space where they couldn't get hurt, and the noise and uncontrolled movement were upsetting for their owners. He explained as much to Josie. "I'm sorry, but I can't let you stay. It's best for you and Mittens to go back home. I can call you after his second treatment if you want me to and keep you updated."

Josie's jaw set. "No, he'll be better off if he knows I'm here. Mittens can go in the cage beside him so he'll feel at home. I have a reclining lawn chair that I'll set up right beside his cage, and I'll stay by his side. I won't bother your stuff, if that's what you're worried about."

Cole felt pressed. He knew that the Rattlers were coming back to check on their horses too. It was going to be one of those nights, he could tell, and he was going into it completely exhausted. His small clinic was beginning to feel like Grand Central Station. "I'm not worried about you getting into my stuff, Josie. Why don't you just stay outside in your RV and get a good night's sleep?"

"You look like you could use one yourself, Doc." She picked up her limp cat and held him close to her chest. "No,

Buster needs to know I'm beside him when he wakes up. Now if you'll show me where you want me to put him, I'll get him settled and then bring in Mittens and my chair to set up for the night."

Josie headed for the door into the kennel room, and Cole figured he couldn't stop her. Maybe after Buster's second treatment, she would be satisfied enough to leave. He led the way to set up cages side by side for her cats. Josie would be disappointed when she saw that the cages were designed so the animals wouldn't be able to see each other, but it was the best he could offer.

★ ★ ★

Mattie gasped and sat straight up in bed, waking suddenly with a sense of doom. The room was pitch-black, no moonlight streaming through her open window. Wait . . . no window at all. Her recurrent claustrophobia kicked in, and she clutched at the edge of her bed.

Not my bed. Robo came to her in the darkness and nuzzled her hand with his wet nose. She stroked the velvety fur between his ears as she remembered where she was—the interrogation room at the station. Her other hand went to the soft fleece blanket that Rainbow had left for her, its texture also a comfort. Between Robo and the blanket, she grounded herself and pushed away the panic brought on by the dark, closed room.

It came back to her at once—the death mask on Juan's face, her missing mother, Glenna's shooting, and now Julia. For a brief moment, she wished she could go back to sleep and escape. Where was Julia now? She felt certain her sister's kidnapper was bringing her to Colorado, and she'd better be awake and alert for his next move.

"Time to get up," she told Robo, even as she wondered how long she'd slept. She swung her legs out from under the blanket and could feel the coldness of the linoleum floor even through her heavy woolen socks. She padded to the wall by the door and flipped the light switch, flooding the room with harsh light from above. The flowers Rainbow had decorated the room with still looked sweet and fresh.

A glance at her phone told her it was shortly after six o'clock, so she'd slept only a few hours. But it was the most sleep she'd had at once in the past few days, and it would be enough.

She yawned, and a shiver ran across her shoulders as she sat on the bed and pulled on her boots. Robo sniffed at things around the room, stopping at the door to stare at it as if willing it to open.

"Do you need to go outside?" she asked him as she stood to push aside the makeshift curtain so she could see herself in the two-way mirror. She looked like a mess: bleary eyes, flattened hat hair. She ruffled her shoulder-length bob, trying to restore some lift but mostly making her look even more disheveled.

Giving up, she let Robo out of the room and followed him into the hallway that led to the staff office. "Let me get my coat, and I'll take you outside."

His energy fully restored, Robo gamboled alongside, looking up at her with adoring eyes. This dog did much to boost her mood, even when she was at her lowest, and she vowed not to let her fear and worry interfere with her ability to think.

No one was in the staff office, but as Mattie went to her desk to grab her coat, Hitch entered behind her. "You're awake," he said, stating the obvious, his voice low-pitched and rather gruff. As he eyed her putting on her coat, he asked, "Where are you going?"

It wasn't that unusual for one officer to ask another where they were headed, but Hitch's tone was enough to remind Mattie that she needed to heed the sheriff's warning to cooperate with the bodyguard system he'd ordered for the time being. "I need to take Robo outside, and then I thought I'd see if Stella was here. Do you know if she came back from the autopsy?"

"She got back a couple hours ago. I'm not sure if she's in her office or in the briefing room with Agent Lawson."

"Have you been out on patrol?"

"It's quiet in town, so I've been hanging out here. The sheriff and Brody are expected back any minute."

Mattie zipped her jacket.

"I'll go with you," Hitch said. He had probably been told to stay close until the sheriff returned to the station.

"That's not necessary. I'll just step outside to take Robo to the grass. We won't be long."

"Sheriff's orders." He shrugged on the coat he had draped over the back of his chair.

Robo led the way, scurrying back and forth to the door. In the lobby, Rainbow was talking on her headset, and she and Mattie exchanged finger waves as Mattie passed through. Outside, the sun had set behind the peaks to the west and dusk was turning to dark. The temperature had plummeted, and her breath hung in the air.

An unfamiliar Lexus SUV with Nevada plates sat in the parking lot, a trail of cigarette smoke coiling out the lowered passenger side window. A man turned his dark-bearded face toward them and stared.

Hitch approached to within ten feet of the vehicle. "Can I help you?"

Mattie noticed the way her fellow deputy's hand hovered above his service weapon. She called Robo to her side and stood by, waiting to intervene if needed.

"I'm waiting for my sister," the guy said. "She's inside talking to the sheriff."

"He's not here." Hitch's skepticism was apparent.

"Well, she's in there talking to somebody about how our horses got poisoned."

Mattie realized that this was the guy who had called for Cole's help—could it have been only yesterday evening? She moved up to stand beside Hitch. "Your horses were poisoned up at Shadow Ridge?"

"Yeah, you know about that?"

"We do. We're investigating it."

"That's good to know." He flicked ash out his window.

"What can you tell me about it?" Mattie asked. "What time were you there?"

"Oh . . . I don't know . . . maybe about six o'clock yesterday evening."

"Was anyone else there?"

"Actually, yeah, a guy named Drake."

Mattie thought of Edith and Drake Kelsey, the guy with the full black beard and heavy unibrow and his wife. "Were Drake's horses in the corral at the time?"

He paused as if to think. "They were tied at the fence."

That's interesting. So Drake never did water his horses at the tank. She still wondered if his staying away from the water source held any significance. "Anyone else around?"

"Not there by the corral. Others were probably in the campground."

"Is that where you were camped?"

"We stayed over in Redstone-Balderhouse."

Mattie decided to leave it at that and go give Robo a break. "Hope your horses will be okay. They're in good hands."

The guy nodded. "Hope so."

Mattie turned and led the way around the building to the grassy area that stretched out alongside it. While Robo patrolled the lawn, marking his territory as he sniffed his way from one bush to another, Mattie and Hitch stood in comfortable silence under the shelter that covered the staff picnic table.

She knew that Hitch had come to them directly from the sheriff's office in Mesa County, and he brought with him years of experience in rural law enforcement. He appeared to be in his midfifties, had gray-streaked blond hair and pale-blue eyes, and had grown up in Willow Springs. He'd been eager to move back closer to his old hometown.

Hitch stood with his hands in his pockets, his stance casual, but Mattie noticed that he kept his eyes on the street and that his head moved side to side as he scanned the area, frequently looking back to the edge of the building near the parking lot. She'd been doing the same. Apparently neither of them trusted having a stranger parked so near. "Did any news come in while I was asleep?" she asked him.

He shook his head. "Not anything that was shared with me."

"What do you hear from the sheriff . . . like . . . when does your shift end?"

"I'll be around for a while. I think he plans to send Brody and Garcia home to get some sleep."

Mattie nodded. Figuring that was enough small talk for both of them, she called Robo, who led them toward the front door. It opened while she was still about ten feet away, and Robo darted back to stay at her left heel.

A woman was exiting the station, and as usual, Mattie took in her identifying features: black hair; light-colored eyes, although it was hard to define their exact color with only the light above the door to illuminate her face; about Mattie's own height of five feet four inches; average build. Her outstanding feature was pale skin that all but glowed in the dim light from the parking lot as she stepped away from the door. Since her skin appeared so delicate, it was hard to pinpoint her age. Maybe somewhere in her fifties?

Hitch held the door open while Mattie stayed back a few feet with Robo at heel. She could almost feel the woman's gaze touch her as she gave Mattie the once-over, finally settling on Robo. The women's intense interest felt eerie.

"What a fine shepherd," the woman said. "So this is your partner?"

"It is."

"It must be a pleasure to work with a dog instead of another person."

This had always been Mattie's feeling, though she didn't want to share that thought in front of Hitch.

The woman extended her hand. "I'm Althea Rattler. Two of my horses were poisoned at Shadow Ridge, and I understand your department is investigating it."

Mattie returned Althea's firm handshake. The poisoned stock tank was a part of the larger picture that the entire case presented, so she had very little to say about it. "Yes, ma'am."

"Well, if there's someone around here who has such little regard for animals, you'd better watch your dog." Althea started to reach out to pet Robo but withdrew her hand as if she thought better of it. Robo stood at attention by Mattie's side, neither friendly nor threatening but definitely on guard. "Well, I won't keep you. I've already talked to the detective. Good night."

"Good night." As Mattie watched Althea walk around to the driver's side of the Lexus and get in, she noticed that the man in the passenger seat appeared to be observing her, though he looked away as soon as they made eye contact.

The encounter felt strange. Was Althea warning her as one animal lover to another? Or had she made a threat? Mattie turned away to enter the station with Hitch, wondering if she was being overly sensitive under the circumstances. She was starting to see threats everywhere, whether they existed or not.

NINETEEN

Stella was waiting in the lobby at Rainbow's desk when Mattie entered. She had gathered her auburn hair into a ponytail, and dark smudges of fatigue colored the fragile skin beneath her hazel eyes. "I see you met Althea Rattler."

Mattie nodded. "What did you think of her?"

Hitch stood back a short distance, as if unsure that he should join them.

"Angry, threatening to sue everyone, used to being in charge, but this terrible thing that happened to her horses is out of her control. Blames her brother, blames the person who poisoned the tank, blames us."

"So the guy in the car is her brother?"

"I don't know. She didn't say her brother was with her."

"They look nothing alike, but I guess that doesn't mean anything. They could still be siblings."

Stella gave her a thin smile. "Withhold judgment until you have the facts."

It was a new version of Stella's motto: *Don't jump to conclusions.*

"Go ahead and get some coffee if you want, and then join me and Agent Lawson in the briefing room," Stella went on to say. "We both have info to share."

Hitch followed Mattie and Robo into the staff office. Mattie filled her cup, the dark brew's aroma wafting up to tease her appetite. She realized she was hungry and tried to recall when she'd last eaten. Sometime this morning, she thought. She peeked inside a pastry box sitting by the coffeepot and found it empty. "Looks like you'll be pulling a double?" she asked Hitch.

"Part of the job. I heard the sheriff's having food delivered."

"Something to look forward to."

Robo trotted toward the briefing room as Mattie entered the lobby. Sam Corns, the night dispatcher, was now sitting at the desk, and Rainbow was putting on her pink puffy down coat. Mattie crossed over to give her a hug. "Thanks so much for fixing up the room. I slept like a log."

Rainbow's blue eyes lit up, and she broke into a wide grin. "I'm so glad. We'll leave it that way for a while. No telling who might need it."

Mattie nodded, suddenly fearful for anyone she felt close to. The past couple of days had proven that her loved ones weren't safe. "Why don't you sleep here tonight?"

"Oh, Mattie, that's not necessary. I'm totally fine. There's no need to worry."

She hoped her friend was right. "Be careful. Call the station if anything seems out of the ordinary when you get home. Text me when you're settled inside your house."

"I will. But I need to pick up some groceries, so don't expect to hear from me right away. I'll be back at six in the morning. Oh, and Cole wants you to call when you have a chance."

They said their good-byes, and Mattie went to the briefing room, where Robo waited outside the closed door. She tapped on the door before opening it.

Stella and Lawson sat on opposite sides of the table, staggered so that both of them could spread papers in front of their open laptops.

Stella glanced at Mattie and gestured toward the chair at her end of the table. "Go ahead and have a seat." As Mattie settled in her chair, Stella got right to it. "Rick said he already gave you preliminary information from the Juan Martinez autopsy. The ME said if he hadn't known we were suspicious of selenium poisoning, he might have been tempted to diagnose cause of death as congestive heart failure. Of course, he did add that the body being left tied to a tree would have alerted him to dig deeper. He said to thank the vet who made the connection." Stella gave a nod to Mattie, her face set in a look of approval. "As it is, COD is pending until return of results from the blood samples. He should get those in tomorrow."

Being able to arrive at the proper diagnosis was huge, and Mattie felt grateful to Cole too. But fear for her mother and Julia rose inside her. Were they being subjected to the same type of poisoning?

Stella stood and went to the whiteboard, which she'd already set up with an enlargement of the tiny photo from Juan Martinez's business card at the top. It was grainy and pixilated, but this was better than having to use a photo taken after death. Stella had recorded a summary under a column labeled *Autopsy*, so she moved on to a column labeled *People Near the Scene*.

Under that she had written a short list of people from the campsite, including Drake and Edith Kelsey and Milo and Didi Carr. She added Althea and Tanner Rattler. "Who did you talk to when you and Brody went to Eureka?" she asked Mattie.

Mattie took her notebook from her pocket to make sure she remembered the names right. "Josie Baker in one cabin, Hank Thompson in another, and brothers Kent and Rope Gaffey in a third."

Stella added them to the list. "What did you think of them?"

Mattie described finding the bundle of dried death camas hanging from the rafter in Josie's kitchen. "But if we find out that Juan was killed with selenium, I guess we can rule out death camas."

Stella narrowed her eyes. "Yes, but why would she have a poisonous plant on hand?"

"She said the roots were edible if you know how to prepare them, and she uses the poisonous part for killing pack rats."

Mattie went on to tell them about the gunsmith and his ammo. "So he probably not only has gun bluing on hand, which Rick already mentioned is a source of selenium, but he also had the same ammo used in Glenna's shooting. Brody questioned him about the shooting in Cedar Canyon, and he said he only shoots at targets in back of his house and has never even been to the campsite in question. He also said he's losing his eyesight, and there seemed to be evidence of that—thick lenses on his glasses, a large magnifying glass for him to work under."

"We have to keep all this in mind," Stella said, writing *Notes* on the board to start another column. "Anything suspicious about the two in the third cabin?"

Mattie shook her head. "They were processing an elk carcass and appear to be hunters who come to their cabin for that purpose. Robo cleared all the buildings."

"All right," Stella said, finishing up notes on the people from Eureka. "Rick has a preliminary report from the forensic handwriting analyst."

Lawson had been quiet, but now he cleared his throat and angled his computer screen so that both Mattie and Stella could see the picture on it of the note that had been left on Mattie's door. "As you see, this note is written in a cursive script, and when you turn over the note to view it from the back, there are indentations that show it was written with heavy pressure. You'll also notice a variety of angles and what the graphologist calls 'cover strokes,' places where the writer reverses direction abruptly and covers the previous stroke. These features combined with others that we'll talk about next suggest a personality type that is rigid and controlling."

Mattie tucked the information away, hoping information about the personality of the note's writer would help them find her mother and sister.

"This coiled shape," Rick said, pointing to a curlicue the writer had made inside the capital S, "and the amount of others like it suggests a person who is extremely self-centered. Both of these notes, the one found at your home and the one found on Juan's body, were written by the same person, while the other one definitely was not."

"And the person who wrote the first two notes probably remains here in Timber Creek, while the other one participated in the kidnapping in California," Mattie said.

Stella gave her a steady look. "So I had Althea Rattler fill out an incident report while she was here, but to my untrained eye, her handwriting wasn't a match. We'll have the expert look at it and also go back and get writing samples from others who were in the vicinity of the crime scene."

Rick pointed out other features in the handwriting sample. "You'll see there's an extreme right slant here. That combined with the heavy pressure can predict a buildup of frustration that might erupt suddenly. And these long *t* crosses—see how they cover the whole word in some cases? This might signify that this person is willing to go to whatever ends he can to achieve his goal. But what's important is that the graphologist looks at the entire sample to come to these conclusions, combining all of these features. Just one feature or another doesn't tell the whole picture."

"So we're dealing with a very determined person who'll do anything to get what he wants," Stella said, locking her gaze on Mattie's. "And he wants you."

"I think we knew that."

"Maybe so, but I can't stress it enough, Mattie. You've got to be careful, and I know you. I bet you already want to go off on your own to your house, to Cole's, wherever. But we need you to make sure you're with one of us all the time. There's safety in numbers."

Mattie was getting antsy to be on her own for a while, so Stella had gotten that right. But she didn't want to go to Cole's house. She was determined not to bring danger to him or his family, and if anyone was out there stalking her, she didn't want him to think Cole's property was a good place to find her. "I hear you, Stella. I'm not going anywhere, although I do need a shower and some clean clothes."

"We'll arrange getting clothes, and you can shower here. But before we go, Rick has more information to share."

The door to the briefing room opened, and Mattie turned to see the sheriff and Brody enter. They both looked beat. The gray streaks in McCoy's beard stubble stood out against his ebony skin, and his eyelids were puffy. He'd been showing his age lately, and Mattie feared the demands of his job were hard on him. Brody's scruffy beard and bloodshot eyes made him look like he'd been on a bender.

Rick stood and moved to pull up another table and some chairs for them, the table screeching against the linoleum floor.

The noise made Robo lift his head and prick his ears as he watched. Brody set his coffee mug down on the table and straddled one of the chairs.

"The crime scene technicians have finished with both sites, and we've opened up both campgrounds again," McCoy said, sighing as he settled into a chair and placed his mug on the table. He scanned the whiteboard as he rubbed his chin. "Interesting that you've got the Kelseys and the Carrs listed up there. Both parties came back to Shadow Ridge right as we were leaving."

"Did you talk to them?" Stella asked.

"They both said that other campgrounds were crowded," Brody said, his voice gravelly with fatigue. "Kelsey wanted to bring his horses back to the corral. He wanted to know if the stock tank was safe, and I told him it had been scrubbed and emptied, so we think it's safe. He said he'd use buckets to water the horses tonight. And Didi Carr said she liked Shadow Ridge better than Redstone, so as soon as she heard it would open for tonight, she headed back."

"How did she hear it would open?" Mattie asked.

"Shortwave radio. She listens in to open channels. Picked it up from forest ranger correspondence."

"Any additional evidence found or anything new to report?" Stella asked McCoy.

"They'll try to identify where the rope that tied Juan came from. They'll do a close check for fibers and DNA on his clothing. We'll know more tomorrow."

Stella updated McCoy and Brody on the autopsy report before moving on. "Rick has some more information he wants to share with the team."

McCoy nodded at Rick, giving him the floor as he lifted his coffee mug to his lips.

"Thirty years ago, there was a San Diego agency called the Critical Incident Investigative Team, or CIIT. This unit was called out to investigate incidents that involved Border Patrol."

Any vestige of fatigue that Mattie felt seemed to drop away as a wave of adrenaline hit her system. This information was about her father's case.

"Over time, there was a mingling of officers from both agencies, as CIIT often recruited Border Patrol agents. Later there were reports of covering up crimes that BP agents might have committed because their cronies who were investigating them swept evidence under the carpet. I decided to follow this trail to see if I could find anything about Douglas Wray."

Mattie scooted to the edge of her seat. Robo sat and put his chin on her knee, and she absently stroked his head as she listened. Her dog responded to her mood, and she was definitely in turmoil at the moment.

"During that time, the San Diego PD often deferred to CIIT for investigations, and a lot of the time SDPD didn't become involved. So I called in a favor from a cohort of mine who works for the California Attorney General's Office. He was able to ferret out an old report on the Douglas Wray shooting that had been buried in a storeroom holding old CIIT files."

Rick paused and looked at Mattie, but she couldn't speak. She waited, bracing herself for what he had to say.

"The file says that border agent Douglas Wray was involved with passing drugs and guns through his checkpoint, and the ring he was involved with turned on him, reason unknown."

Mattie managed to respond, her throat tight with tension. "My mother said he was coerced under threat that they would kill his wife and children, but he had decided to no longer participate."

"The interesting part is that none of the gang that shot him that night were identified, but a witness whose name was redacted from the report said there were three men and a woman who went into the station, shot two agents, and took a Mexican woman with two children outside with them when they left."

"That woman and her kids were me, my mom, and my brother." Mattie couldn't help but say it, the spoken words making it real.

Rick acknowledged her comment with a nod. "Evidently they all drove away in a van that the witness gave a description of, but there was no report saying it had been found. In fact, it appeared that very little investigation was done later. The agent who filed the original report is deceased, so we can't talk to him, but his name was listed later on a report of fraudulent agents. He died before the investigation even started, so charges weren't filed against him, and he was never prosecuted for that crime. The Douglas Wray case got filed away, and evidently it didn't get picked back up until years later, when it was reported to the San Diego PD. As far as we can tell, this original report was buried until now."

Silence fell over the room until McCoy broke it. "So there were three men and a woman who shot Douglas Wray. We know that John and Harold Cobb were there. Who are the other man and the woman?"

"That's the pivotal question," Stella said.

Mattie's gut churned. "It's a safe assumption that at least two people were involved in the Juan Martinez killing, and at least two involved in Julia's kidnapping. Since the Cobbs are deceased, could the others mentioned in the report still be in play?"

"Ramona never mentioned a woman involved in your father's shooting?" Stella asked.

"Never. She just said a lot of very bad people. Everything she's said about the night my father was killed and we were taken has been vague, although she was still traumatized and afraid the bad guys would come after her."

Mattie sat staring at the table, trying to digest this information to see if it connected to anything else she might know or remember. Most of her memories from her childhood were scattered, brief flashes that surfaced now and then, sometimes in dreams that she couldn't even say were real. She couldn't pull out a memory of a woman from her childhood . . . it had always been men who hurt her and the people around her.

While her thoughts churned, she grew more and more afraid for the safety of her loved ones. *Look what had happened to Glenna and Julia.* Her grandmother and Julia's family had relocated, and Detective Alvarez had assigned a guard to watch over them. But what about Mama T? And Cole and his family?

She looked at McCoy. "We need someone to watch over Teresa Lovato and her family of foster kids. And even Cole and his family."

A tap at the door preceded Sam Corns cracking it open to peek in. "Pizza Palace delivered the pizzas. Shall I bring them in?"

McCoy rubbed his eyes and then pulled his hand down over his face, looking at Mattie as if trying to determine what she was thinking. "I guess you might as well," he said to Sam.

Pizza had sounded good earlier, but Mattie had lost any appetite she'd had previously.

"Let's talk to Cole and set something up with him to assure his family's safety," McCoy said. "I'll have to pull someone in from the sheriff's posse to guard the Lovato residence, but that can be done as soon as possible. Do you want to let her know someone will be stationed outside her house, or do you want me to?"

Although Mattie wanted her Mama T to be cautious, she didn't want her to be overly frightened. "I'll call her."

McCoy nodded. "After dinner, I want us to get some sleep in shifts. We need to be prepared when we hear from the kidnappers next, and I suspect that will be sometime early tomorrow. If they drive through the night, they should arrive with Julia by then."

He looked at Mattie, and she met his gaze and nodded. It was what she'd been thinking too.

McCoy continued. "Mattie, Brody, and Stella, you sleep the first shift. Agent Lawson, can you stay up until about one o'clock AM?"

"Yes, I slept last night, so I'm good to keep going," Lawson replied.

"I'll stay here too until then. We'll sleep during the second shift." McCoy looked at Mattie and then Stella. "Mattie, do you want to sleep at Stella's for the first shift?"

Having just awakened, Mattie wasn't sure she could sleep again, despite the sheriff's careful planning. Right now she just wanted to get away from the others so she could find a quiet place to think about this mysterious woman that Rick had mentioned. "If I can get some clothes from home, I'll shower and sleep here tonight."

"I'll go with Mattie to get some clothes," Stella said.

"No, you go home and get some sleep," Rick said. "I'll go with you, Mattie. Just let me know when."

"I need to feed Robo while I make those phone calls, so I'll be in the staff office for about fifteen minutes. Then we'll go." Mattie stood to leave the room, and Robo leapt to his feet to go with her.

When she opened the door, she discovered Cole on the other side, his hand raised as if about to knock.

TWENTY

Mattie looked pale, tired, and stressed beyond belief, and Cole wanted to take her in his arms. But she gave him a look that told him not to touch, so he stepped aside to let her pass, falling in behind to follow as she headed toward the staff office. She stopped suddenly when she reached the doorway, and over the top of her head Cole spied the new deputy seated at his desk, eating a slice of pizza. The man looked up, and his eyes narrowed when they met Cole's.

Mattie opened the interview room door on the left, flipped on the light, and entered. The new deputy watched Cole until he turned and followed Mattie into the room. Robo pressed past Cole to stay close to Mattie. The space had been transformed into a comfortable bedroom. Mattie gestured to a chair that sat against the wall, and Cole pulled it up close to the table, where another chair had already been placed. The light scent of flowers on the table caught his attention as he took his seat and Mattie sat in the other.

He reached for her hand, and she held on tight. "Did they fix this up for you?"

She nodded. "Rainbow did."

"It's nice. I thought I'd stop in and see if you wanted to come to my house for the night. You look like you need a break." He looked at his watch. "I imagine it will take at least ten more hours before Julia could be brought here."

"I can't come to your house, Cole. I can't lead these people to your family. It's best if I stay right here or go home with Stella."

Cole had figured she'd say that, and he didn't want to argue at the moment. "What's the latest on the investigation?"

Mattie told him about a report that Rick had found from an investigative unit in San Diego. It seemed preposterous that the report had been buried all these years. "Were there any names involved that Rick could follow up on?"

Her lips thin and set, Mattie shook her head. "There might be a man and a woman from that gang who're responsible for all this—my mom's and Julia's kidnapping, Juan's murder, even Glenna being shot. But I can't remember anything about a man other than the Cobb brothers from my childhood, and I certainly don't recall there being a woman."

"It was a long time ago. Thirty years is a long time for a child to remember details, even without the trauma you were suffering at the time."

"You'd think I could do better."

"Don't be so hard on yourself. You're doing the best you can."

Mattie looked at him, her eyes strained with fatigue. "I need to meditate and see if I can pull up anything else from that time. Who is this woman? I know there have to be men involved in all this; there's been a lot of heavy lifting in these kidnappings and Juan's murder. But I can't help but wonder about this woman."

"Tell me why you think she's important." Cole hoped he could help her by talking through it.

Mattie focused on the flowers, but he could tell she wasn't seeing them. "I don't know. I keep wondering how my father became involved with this smuggling ring. They obviously had connections, probably to the cartel that had power at that time, and they were running guns between Mexico and Canada as well as smuggling drugs into the US. So why did Douglas Wray get involved with them in the beginning? What was his motive? Money?"

Mattie stared at him, and he could see the pain in her eyes. He thought he could read her mind. "And you're wondering if this woman got Douglas involved?"

She nodded. "Someone with a vendetta against my father, and now she's carrying it out against my mother."

"*Hell hath no fury like a woman scorned?*"

"Something like that. It's hard to say, but it's possible."

"So your parents were how old when your dad was killed?"

Mattie straightened, and her eyes widened. "He was my age. Thirty-one. My mother was twenty-eight."

"Okay, then she's about fifty-eight now. John Cobb was sixty-two. If this woman is still around, she'd probably be in the range of midfifties to midsixties."

"Seems reasonable." She sat for a moment, eyes on the flowers again as if thinking. "What can you tell me about Josie Baker?"

"She's at my office right now."

Mattie looked surprised. "You're kidding."

"Her male cat ate some death camas that she apparently had in her house. We're treating him for the poison."

"I saw the dried plant today, and the cat too, for that matter. She said she uses death camas for pack rat poison. But at the risk of her cats getting into it? Does that seem likely to you?"

Cole thought about it. "No, it doesn't."

"How well do you know her? How long has she been your client?"

"I don't know her all that well. She brought the cats in about three months ago for the first time. She seems to be very dedicated to them—a cat mom."

"Does she have a temper when around you?"

"Not really." Cole remembered how strong-willed Josie had been about staying at his clinic with her cat. She'd set up camp before he left and didn't show signs of budging. He'd locked all of his drug cabinets and left the clinic to her. "She does seem determined to have her own way, though."

"She was downright cantankerous when Brody and I met her. She didn't seem to hold back, which is not the usual persona associated with a criminal. They're usually more manipulative and wily than that." Mattie looked at him with a frown of concern. "But I don't like the idea that she's on your property. What if she's the one?"

Cole thought about the likelihood of Josie Baker being a kidnapper and a murderer, and it didn't sit right. "I don't think so, Mattie. She wouldn't have poisoned her cat on purpose just to get to you through me. She's dedicated to those cats, makes sure their inoculations and health needs are up to date. She lives alone and hasn't mentioned a partner. I can't imagine she's the one."

"Everyone is a suspect during an investigation. There's a man that lives right next door to her who is a gunsmith. That's where she could have obtained the gun bluing to use for selenium poisoning. And even a gun to shoot Glenna with the .223 ammo."

Cole sat with this for a while, thinking it through.

Mattie's fear was obvious by the look on her face. "I want you to take the kids and Mrs. Gibbs somewhere safe. I don't want any of you here in Timber Creek where they can get to you."

"I've got a clinic full of sick animals, Mattie. I can't leave them." He hadn't told her that Sassy and her pups were sick too, and he didn't want to alarm her even more with that information now.

Her grip on his hand tightened. "But we can't put the kids at risk, and you need to be with them."

Cole's mind was spinning through the information, trying to sort through what was fact and what was speculation. He didn't want to discount Mattie's fears, but exhaustion and the stress of having her family in the hands of a killer could be making her see demons where they didn't exist.

Still, she was right. There was no way he should be putting his family in harm's way, and against his better judgment, his clinic had been taken over by strangers tonight. And here he was, at the station, while his other loved ones were alone and unguarded in their home.

"You're right," he told her. "I can't leave those animals without care, but I need to go and get the kids to a safe place. Maybe move them to my parents' ranch?"

She shook her head. "If they've done any reconnaissance on me at all, and it looks like they have, they'll know you have parents who live here. Then none of them would be safe."

"Garrett," Cole said, thinking of his friend. Garrett was a member of the posse and a trained sharpshooter. He would lay down his life for Cole's kids, though Cole certainly hoped it would never come to that.

Mattie's face lightened a bit. "That's perfect. Just make sure you're not followed when you take them out there. It's dark. Drive around town before you head out to his ranch, and watch for headlights behind you. When you hit the highway, watch for headlights that turn off suddenly."

"Got it." Cole stood. "I'd better get started and call Garrett to make sure he and Leslie are willing to do this."

Mattie stood with him, still gripping his hand. "Text me when you have everyone secure."

Cole bent and held her for too brief a moment before sharing a kiss that was more tender than passionate. "Take care of yourself. I think you're more at risk than we are, although I don't discount your feelings. I'll make sure I settle the kids and Mrs. Gibbs somewhere safe. You're better off here at the station, if you can stand sleeping here tonight."

"Sheriff McCoy wants everyone to get some rest before tomorrow, but I think I'd rather be here than at Stella's. Rick might go bunk at her house for a few hours, and I don't want to get in the way."

"It might be safer sticking with the two of them."

"Hitch is going to pull a double shift. He'll be here at the station, and I'll be fine."

In the back of his mind, Cole felt a twinge of fear and hoped the new man was who he purported to be. Now he was doing it—seeing demons where there probably were none—but he couldn't dismiss his fear without warning Mattie. "What about Hitch? Are we sure he's who he says he is?"

Mattie appeared to think about it. "He passed a thorough background check."

"I can imagine McCoy was thorough in hiring him. I'm just worried about everything, I guess."

"I'll watch out for myself."

Cole hated to leave her, but he said good-bye and headed toward his truck in the parking lot. On his way, he called Mrs. Gibbs and was relieved to find out that everything was fine at home. Both kids were present and accounted for.

"I'm on my way home. Could you make sure all the doors are locked, and don't open them for anyone?"

"Oh my sweet heaven, what's going on now?"

"I have several folks coming and going at the clinic, and I'm taking some precautions." He'd kept Mrs. Gibbs informed about some of what was happening with Mattie and her family during the day, although she didn't know the extent of it. "Some things have shifted with Mattie. I'll tell you more when I get there."

He reached his truck and said good-bye, although he could tell his typically unflappable housekeeper was alarmed. As he powered his engine and maneuvered his truck out of the parking lot and into the street, he speed dialed his friend Garrett, who answered right away. Garrett was also aware of what was happening with Mattie's family and had been on call all day, waiting to see if the sheriff's posse was going to be activated.

"Hello, Cole. What's up?"

Cole gave him a brief summary of the latest, including their concerns for the safety of his family. "Would you and Leslie be willing to have Mrs. Gibbs and the kids out at your house tonight?"

"Of course. Kip is a great little watchdog. No one will be able to sneak around here without her making some noise," Garrett said, referring to the border collie he'd adopted last month from a family that didn't want her anymore. "Why don't you bring Belle and Bruno out too. With the three of them on guard, we'll be locked up tight and secure."

"That's a great idea. Thanks, Garrett. I definitely owe you one for this."

"You know you and Mattie can count on us anytime. I'll help Leslie get some rooms ready."

It was a known fact that Garrett and Leslie loved Mattie. She and Robo had solved their daughter's murder a little over a year ago, and the two of them showed their gratitude in many ways. Having both been raised on cattle ranches outside of Timber Creek, Garrett and Cole had been friends and there for each other since they were kids.

As Cole ended the call, a text came in from Althea Rattler, saying that she and her brother were going to have dinner and then would be out to check on the horses. Before pocketing his cell phone, he decided to call Josie. She answered right away.

"How is Buster doing?" He could hear the cat yowl in the background.

"He's coming out of it, poor baby. He's hunkered in the back of the cage, looking at me with bleary eyes and complaining about it. Kind of wobbling around."

"That's to be expected. Josie, I have another call to take care of and then I'll be back. Are you okay to hold down the fort?"

"Absolutely. I have my chair, a cooler with my dinner, and my cats. That's all I need."

"All right. See you a little later." As he disconnected, he wondered if he was talking to a murderer, but that still didn't feel right. Josie seemed like a concerned pet owner, and even though she was quirky, he didn't think she was dangerous.

He agreed with Mattie on one major thing, though. Juan's murder and Julia's kidnapping showed they were dealing with ruthless and organized people, and since he couldn't stay at home and watch over his family, he needed to get them somewhere safe and off his property. And he needed to do it now.

TWENTY-ONE

As Mattie watched Robo eat, she realized she needed fuel too. She used to think of food as something nurturing, a gesture of love like the creations from her foster mother's kitchen. But since she'd become Robo's partner, she'd realized that food was a source of energy, something to keep her body going so she could keep up with her dog.

She snatched a slice of pizza from the box in the staff office and laid it on a napkin to leave on her desk while she called Mama T.

Her foster mother answered right away. "*Hola, mijita.*"

"*Hola, Mama.* How did you know it was me?"

"You're the only one who calls me from that number. I recognized it."

Mattie imagined her foster mom on the other end of the line—plump and soft and always dressed in a worn housedress. Her long black hair threaded with gray would be drawn back into a bun at her nape, and she would be smiling into the phone. Her mama was a good woman who would never imagine she might be in danger. "What if it had been Sheriff McCoy instead of me?" Mattie teased her.

Mama T chuckled. "Then I would have a nice chat with the handsome sheriff."

In an attempt to sound normal, Mattie forced herself to laugh too. "There's something I need to tell you, and I don't want you to be too alarmed, okay?"

Mama's chuckle this time sounded slightly nervous. "Okay, but . . ."

When she didn't finish her sentence, Mattie did so for her. "But now I've made you frightened, right?"

"A little bit."

Since Mama T didn't know that Mattie had been in touch with her mother, she felt she couldn't share all the details about Ramona and Juan Martinez. Instead, she carefully explained that she had grown nervous about the safety of her loved ones because of some threatening notes that had come in to the sheriff's station.

But her mama showed she was more astute than Mattie had assumed. "Have you been threatened, *mijita*?"

"Well . . . yes, but we're taking precautions, and that includes putting a guard outside your home to keep watch over you and the kids. I want you to make sure your doors are all locked and you don't open them for anyone but people you know from the sheriff's office. Okay?"

"*Sí*. Don't worry about me . . . I'll get out the baseball bat and put it next to my bed."

Mattie reacted with a thin smile as she recalled her foster mother's go-to means of protection. "And I hope you never have to use it, Mama. I'm sorry I have to cancel breakfast with you in the morning, but I'll call you later. Don't be scared. We're just being very careful here to make sure everyone is safe and sound."

"You take care of yourself too," Mama T said. "I'll talk to you in the morning, then."

"Sometime tomorrow, yes. I'm not sure yet what my schedule will be."

"I have to go now. I have bathwater running for the younger ones. I love you, *mijita*."

A lump thickened in her throat. "I love you too, Mama."

Mattie regained control of herself after disconnecting the call. She settled in with her pizza and watched Robo while he crunched his kibble. He took a few pieces in his mouth and noshed them while gazing into her eyes. This made her think again about food being a gesture of nurture and love. And that made her think of Rainbow.

She checked the time. Even if her friend had stopped at the grocery store, she'd had plenty of time to get home . . . but still no text. As Robo finished the last crunchy in his bowl, Mattie dialed her friend.

She waited, a pit growing in her stomach, while it rang and rang. No answer.

There must be an explanation. Rainbow had probably arrived home and, forgetting that she'd promised to text, climbed into a hot bath. After all, it had been a long day for her as well.

Mattie left a message. "Rainbow, give me a call, okay? I want to make sure you're home."

Hitch looked up from where he was eating at his desk. "Didn't she leave about an hour ago?"

"Yes. She said she would text when she got home, but I haven't heard from her."

"Want me to run over to her house and check on her?"

"Do you know where she lives?"

"I guess not, but I'm sure I could find it if I had an address."

Rainbow lived outside of town in a cabin located near the waterway called Timber Creek, for which the town was named. Mattie doubted that an address would help Hitch find her place. "She lives in the country. I'll go with you. Let me tell the sheriff where we're going."

Taking her coat from the back of her chair, Mattie went looking for McCoy. He wasn't in his office, so she moved on to the briefing room, where she found him talking to Rick. He turned her way when she entered the room, looking somewhat revitalized. Evidently the food had helped fuel him too.

"I asked Rainbow to let me know when she arrived home," she told him, "but I haven't heard from her yet, and she doesn't answer her phone. Hitch and I are going out to check on her."

McCoy's brows knit in a frown. "Try her again."

While Mattie made the call, McCoy looked at Rick. "I think we should go instead. Rainbow lives out of town, and this could be a trap to get Mattie."

When the call went to voice mail, Mattie disconnected, feeling even more urgent about the need to check up on her friend. "Still no answer."

"Rick and I will go," McCoy said as he rose from the table. "You and Deputy Hitchen stay here."

"We might need Robo," Mattie said, unwilling to be left behind. "Even if this is a trap, you're going to need all of us."

The sheriff didn't protest as they moved into the lobby, where Hitch was waiting. McCoy checked out with Sam while Mattie shrugged on her jacket.

Outside, McCoy headed for his Jeep. "Deputy Hitchen, take your cruiser. Agent Lawson, you ride with Mattie."

Within seconds, Mattie had loaded Robo into the back and they were on their way. When they reached the highway that ran west of town, McCoy switched on his overheads, and Mattie followed suit, picking up speed as they drove with lights but no sirens toward the western mountains. Behind her, Hitch turned on his overheads as well, setting up a three-car convoy with flashing lights.

The sun had set behind the horizon earlier, but the moon had not yet risen high enough to light the sky. Their headlights penetrated the darkness as they drove the fifteen minutes it took to reach the turnoff to Rainbow's cabin. Mattie's heart was in her throat as she followed McCoy's Jeep into the short lane.

The first thing she spotted was Rainbow's small Chevrolet Spark parked in front of her house, the back hatch open, the lights inside still on. Something was wrong.

Mattie drew up beside McCoy's Jeep, threw her vehicle in park, and ratcheted on the brake, leaving the engine running. Rick was already out of the car, his service weapon drawn.

"Hitch, Mattie, stay here," McCoy said, running toward the front door of the cabin, his firearm also drawn and held ready. "Lawson, come with me."

Drawing her own service weapon, Mattie forced herself to stay on guard at the front of the cabin. Heart pounding, she scanned in all directions, seeing nothing but darkness. If this was a trap of some kind, she and Hitch would never see it coming. She used the popper button on her duty belt to open Robo's cage door. He bailed through it and out the doorway that Mattie had left open, rushing to her side when she told him to heel.

Their headlights lit the front of the cabin. Lights came on throughout Rainbow's home, one at a time. Mattie imagined

McCoy and Rick methodically clearing each room in turn. Within minutes, the floodlight out front flashed on, and both men appeared in the cabin doorway.

"She's not here," McCoy shouted from the front step. "I'll check out back."

Rick went with him as he circled around the side of the cabin. Mattie stepped up to Rainbow's car and searched the contents. Two bags of groceries were in the hatch, one of them tipped to the side and spilled. In the back seat were a cap with a visor and a sweater—scent articles, something she'd been wishing she had from her mother since finding Juan's body.

Mattie ran back to her SUV, switched off the ignition, and grabbed a set of night vision goggles. She put them on and scanned the area, seeing nothing but a small barn and various types of trees that surrounded the cabin: willows, aspen, cottonwoods, and pine. No people aside from Hitch, no sign of Rainbow. She pushed the goggles to the top of her head.

She snatched up her dog's tracking harness and put it on him. Already excited, Robo wagged his tail and reared up on his hind legs, bouncing around Mattie without touching her. McCoy and Rick came back around the front.

"No one," McCoy shouted.

With Robo at her side, Mattie joined up with McCoy and Rick while Hitch stayed back, standing guard at a short distance. "I'm going to track her, even if it just leads to the road and a dead end," Mattie said.

McCoy nodded. "Go ahead. Rick, you back up Mattie. I'll check the barn. Hitch, stay where you are, keep your eyes peeled." He turned away, heading toward the barn.

Mattie slipped on gloves from her pocket and took the hat from Rainbow's seat. Her dog was already familiar with Rainbow's scent. The two of them were best buddies—he'd snuggled with her, stolen kisses from her, and tracked her during training sessions.

"Scent this," she said, holding the cap where Robo could smell it. He wagged his tail while he buried his nose inside the cap, as if taking in his friend's aroma gave him pleasure. It dawned on her that while she was feeling nothing but fear,

Robo thought this was a game. No matter; he was revved up and ready to play, and that's all she needed from him.

Carrying the cap with her, Mattie led Robo to the back of Rainbow's car and gave him the scent article again. Her dog was already putting his nose to the ground when she unsnapped his leash and said, "Let's go find Rainbow!"

She tossed the cap inside the hatchback as Robo vacuumed up scent behind the car. She hoped he would pick up the hottest track, the freshest scent that Rainbow had left in front of her house. Dogs were hardwired for that, and it was what handlers counted on both in search-and-rescue and in tracking fugitives.

It took mere seconds as Mattie's fears and hope hung in the balance, but then Robo's body language told her he'd picked up a track. Ears pricked, tail waving, he scurried forward, heading not toward the road as Mattie expected but toward the trees about twenty yards off to the side of the cabin.

"He's on track," Mattie murmured to Rick as she sprinted after her dog. Rick fell in behind her.

Robo didn't miss a beat when he followed the track into the darkness of the trees. Mattie pulled down her night vision goggles, adjusting them on the run. She could use her head lamp, but if this was a trap, there was no reason to give her stalkers a target to shoot at.

As darkness closed around them, she heard Rick stumble and curse softly. Robo picked up speed and she did too, rushing to follow so she wouldn't lose sight of him in the trees. His tail was waving and his head up, as if he was closing in on his quarry. Mattie dared hope that her friend was near.

Sprinting behind Robo, Mattie looked beyond him and spotted someone standing upright against a tree. Then she heard muffled sounds, whimpering. She didn't care if this was a trap—she wouldn't let her dog go in alone. With a burst of speed, she ran after him.

Robo got there first, and he jumped up against the tree. Though there was no color in the view of her goggles, Mattie recognized Rainbow's puffy coat. Then she saw the hood over her head, a gag binding the fabric and forcing it into her mouth. Rope bound her friend upright to the tree.

But she was alive! Robo wouldn't be acting so happy if she were dead. And Mattie could clearly hear her muffled cries for help.

Mattie reached the tree and hugged her friend's bound form. "We're here, Rainbow. We've got you. You're safe."

Rick came up behind her, shielding her back. "Look for explosives," he warned, handing Mattie a pair of latex gloves.

Mattie had already taken out her Leatherman tool from her utility belt and had extended the blade. "I'll cut away this gag, Rainbow. Hold on."

She reached in back with the knife and cut the gag near the knot that she wanted to preserve as evidence. She lifted the hood to expose Rainbow's white face, sobs coming from her open mouth.

"Let me have it," Rick said, reaching to take the cloth gag and hood from Mattie.

Robo jumped in excitement, dodging around the tree.

"Robo, sit," Mattie told him, and he reluctantly obeyed. She took off the goggles and leaned forward to touch her cheek to Rainbow's. "We'll get you untied. Are you okay? Are you hurt?"

Rainbow was shivering so hard her teeth chattered. "I'm okay. My wrists hurt. My hands are numb."

Mattie's flashlight revealed that Rainbow's wrists were bound tightly with a zip tie. She replaced the blade and then extracted a tool to snip the zip tie free, plucking it away to hand to Rick. In the flashlight's beam, she could see where the harsh plastic had lacerated her friend's wrists.

Rainbow's sobs urged Mattie to move quickly as she examined the rope with her flashlight. Rainbow had been bound at her shoulders, her waist, and right below her hips with three separate lengths of rope. Mattie murmured encouragement as she checked for any sign of explosives. "It looks clear," she told Rick.

"Cut the ropes and hand them to me."

She made short work of it, cutting her friend free while Rick took care of collecting the evidence. After the last of the ties peeled away, Rainbow collapsed, sinking down to sit at the base of the tree.

Mattie knelt beside her to take her in her arms, and Robo rushed in to lick her face. Robo looked like he'd figured out that this was no longer a game and he wanted to help make his buddy feel better. Rainbow reached for him.

They stayed in a three-way embrace while Rainbow sobbed until McCoy arrived at the scene, huffing and puffing and murmuring words of concern and gratitude that Rainbow was safe. Knowing how he felt, Mattie lifted her face to the sky and uttered "Thank you" under her breath.

"There . . . there's a note in my pocket," Rainbow said between sobs, her teeth chattering. "He told me . . . before he left."

TWENTY-TWO

Her hands still gloved, Mattie took the sealed envelope from Rainbow's pocket and handed it to Rick. With an arm around her friend, she asked, "Can you stand up?"

"I th-think so." Rainbow trembled as she tried to stand.

McCoy and Mattie lifted her to her feet, and while Robo ran ahead, they each put one of her arms over their shoulders and helped guide her back toward the cabin.

"Let's get you inside where it's warm," McCoy said.

Rainbow started to tell them what happened, her speech pressed and breathless as if she couldn't get the words out fast enough. "They came from behind me. I don't know where they were hiding. There were two of them . . . strong. I only caught a glimpse of one guy before they put that thing over my face. He was tall, dressed in black, a black ski mask over his head. I screamed, but one of them held me while the other put the gag in my mouth."

When Rainbow paused to take a breath, Mattie tried to get specific information. "What did their voices sound like?"

Rainbow became steadier on her feet as they slowly made their way to her cabin through the trees. "No one talked until the very end. When I wouldn't walk where they wanted . . . I thought they were going to load me into a car, and I didn't want them to take me anywhere. Nothing good ever comes of that." Her breath caught, and she moaned as if the thought of it was too much to bear. Being employed by law enforcement, Rainbow would know. "When I wouldn't walk, one of them just picked me up and threw me over his shoulder. I was helpless, Mattie. I've never felt that way before. So scared."

Mattie tightened her grip around Rainbow's waist. She knew the feeling only too well. When she'd been kidnapped, she'd been tranquilized and completely helpless too. "You're safe now," she murmured. "Did you recognize the voice of the one who spoke, Rainbow?"

"No, not at all. But it sounded deep and gruff, like he was trying to disguise it."

The floodlight from the cabin's porch flickered through the trees as they approached. The shadowy form of a man walking toward them became backlit and loomed larger than life, and Rainbow gasped.

"It's okay," Mattie said, squeezing her tightly again. "It's just Hitch. He waited here to watch your house."

"Oh."

The word sounded tiny and vulnerable, and Mattie could barely stand hearing her happy-go-lucky, full-of-life friend sounding so defeated. "Let's go inside."

Mattie and McCoy helped her up the steps while Rick and Robo followed behind. Hitch stood in the doorway for a moment and then stepped back onto the porch, closing the door behind him, as if to give them privacy or to stand guard. Perhaps both.

The living room of Rainbow's cabin remained as always: colorful pastel rugs on the wooden plank floor, a comfortable sofa and an assortment of plush chairs arranged around a glass coffee table adorned with candles and seashells. A small television sat against the wall, and patchouli scented the air. It appeared the intruders hadn't come inside for a robbery. They'd come for one purpose—to send a message—and they'd accomplished it well.

Mattie settled Rainbow on the sofa and then sat beside her, taking her gloves off gently so she could examine her wrists. The zip ties had cut the skin enough to make it bleed, and Rainbow's dried blood stained the tops of her gloves as well as the ends of her pretty pink coat sleeves. Mattie wanted to weep, knowing how painful it must have been to stand tied to a tree in a remote area in below-freezing temperature for over an hour, not knowing if anyone would come to the rescue. Thank goodness Robo had found her before she succumbed to the elements.

Robo pressed up against his buddy's knees, and Rainbow leaned forward to wrap one arm around his neck and kiss his cheek. "You saved me," she murmured. She squeezed Mattie's hand and looked at her with teary eyes. "You too."

Mattie heard the soft shushing sound behind her as Rick slit open the envelope. She knew the note inside it would be for her, and she was anxious to know what it said, but her place right now was with Rainbow. "Let's go to the bathroom and clean up your wrists."

Bent forward and stiff, Rainbow moved with Mattie to the bathroom, decorated with hanging crystals and stained-glass flowers in the windows. A variety of bottles containing bubble bath, skin cleansers, and hair products lined the edge of the tub.

Robo tried to press into the small bathroom behind them, but Mattie told him to wait outside the door.

"It's okay, I want him here," Rainbow said, stepping aside to give him room to enter.

With a thin smile, Mattie allowed him in. "He'll be dogging your tracks for days."

"He's a hero."

The brief exchange seemed to establish a small bit of normalcy between them. She pushed the sleeves on Rainbow's sweater up to her elbows. "I'm sorry, but I need to photograph your injuries before we clean them."

Rainbow nodded. "I know you do."

After Mattie took pictures with her cell phone, she turned on the water in the sink, placing her fingers in it to tell when it was warm enough. She lightly rubbed her friend's cold fingers. Everything she said, every movement she made, was quiet and slow, intended to soothe Rainbow's traumatized nervous system. "Do you have the feeling back in your hands?"

"Pins and needles. My poor wrists." Rainbow's bottom lip trembled, and she bit it in an effort to control her shakiness.

"Here, the water's warm but not too hot. Put your hands in."

Rainbow sucked in a breath as the water trickled onto her wounds but began to rub her hands together under the warm stream. Mattie helped her bathe the dried blood from her wrists, cleaning them enough to see that the lacerations weren't too deep.

"It looks like you probably won't need stitches, but we still need to take you to see Dr. McGinnis. He might have salve or something to use on them to help them heal."

"I can just use the ointment and gauze I have in that drawer." Rainbow pointed to a drawer in the vanity. "I don't need to see a doctor."

Mattie agreed that a doctor probably wasn't needed for the physical wounds, but she wondered if it might not be a good idea to let Rainbow talk to Timber Creek's kind family doctor about the emotional toil the night had taken. "I'm pretty sure Sheriff McCoy won't give you the chance to choose. We'll take you to see Dr. McGinnis."

Still holding her hands beneath the warm water, Rainbow glanced up at her with a look of panic. "Mattie, I don't think I can stay out here tonight."

Mattie felt the slow burn of anger start within her chest. "No problem. Let's grab some bedding and some clothes, and you can bunk with me. I've got the best room in the house at the station all picked out. Do you have a camping mattress I could use on the floor?"

"I do. But I'll sleep on it."

"Nah . . . Robo will be all over you if you're down on the floor with him. You won't even have a chance of getting any sleep." Robo beat his tail against the floor, and she was rewarded with a trembling smile from her friend. "Do your hands feel any better?"

"They're okay. If you'll get that ointment out of the drawer, I'll put some on."

When she opened the drawer, Mattie was surprised to see regular antibiotic cream rather than some type of organic healing compound, which was what she'd expected. She squeezed the tube while Rainbow applied the cream cautiously to her wrists, and Mattie was happy to note that some of the color had returned to her pale cheeks.

"Now repeat after me, Rainbow: I am safe, and those scum-bags are not going to get me down."

Rainbow giggled, another sign of recovery that delighted Mattie. "What is this, affirmation therapy?"

"I guess so. Use the yoga breath you taught me if you start to feel afraid. And don't let it replay in your head too much."

Rainbow met her gaze, her eyes wide and serious. "Is that what you had to do when you were kidnapped?"

"Absolutely, that among other things. It helped to have Robo living with me." It dawned on her how perfect it would be for Rainbow to have a protection dog if she was going to live out here by herself. "You know, that's something to think about—getting you a dog. A big dog."

"I don't know. I'm such a pushover. I'm not strong and firm like you. A big dog would probably just walk all over me."

Mattie snorted at the image, and Rainbow smiled. "You *are* a softie, and you spoil Robo terribly. But I could help you with training if you wanted me to."

It felt like Rainbow's well-being had been somewhat restored, fragile though it would be for a while. "Let me wrap your wrists, and then we'll gather some things to take with us."

When they emerged from the bathroom, both McCoy and Rick were looking grim. Mattie decided to ignore what was coming for a bit longer. She took her friend by the elbow and steered her toward her bedroom. "We're getting some things, and Rainbow is coming with us back to the station."

McCoy nodded as Mattie turned away. As if out of energy, Rainbow sank down on the bed and stared at the dresser. Mattie found a large, paisley bag on a shelf in the closet and began prodding her friend for help.

"You'll need to sleep in sweats or yoga pants and a T-shirt, something like that, for tonight. Can you get those? And a set of clean undies and clothes for tomorrow. I'll grab some shampoo and stuff from the bathroom. I think you and I are going to shower in the staff locker room tonight. We'll put a *ladies only* sign up on the door. Now, let's get a clean coat and gloves too."

She was chatting away to distract Rainbow and gathering her friend's things when the sheriff came to the doorway. "Mattie, we need to go," he said.

Surprised, she looked at him and saw the concern on his face. "What's going on?"

"I've been trying to reach Cole, and he doesn't answer." He gave her a plastic evidence bag that held the note, which was faceup so that she could read it.

Mattie,

You must know by now that I can get to anyone you care about, including the good doctor and his two daughters. If you don't cooperate, I'll take everyone you love, one by one, until you have no one left. Remember this when I give you instructions tomorrow.
 Until then,

A friend of your father's

Her heart dropped as she looked up from the note and met the sheriff's gaze.

McCoy took it from her. "Rick will go with you to check on Cole, and Deputy Hitchen will back you up. I'll take Rainbow to the doctor."

Rainbow was murmuring a protest about not needing a doctor as McCoy stuffed her things in the bag. "Dr. McGinnis is expecting us," he said, holding her coat as Rainbow turned compliant and slipped her arms into the sleeves. "I'll call this in to dispatch, Mattie. Call me directly when you get there and check things out."

Mattie knew the sheriff would take excellent care of her friend; he was a sensitive and kind man, and Rainbow knew him well. Her thoughts now were filled with Cole and his kids . . . and the fear that they were in danger. She rushed into the living room and found Rick waiting in the doorway, talking to Hitch.

Without speaking, she hurried to her unit with Robo at her side. While Rick climbed in front, she loaded her dog, fired the engine, and headed down the lane to the highway, Hitch in his cruiser close behind. "How many times did the sheriff try to reach Cole?" she asked Rick.

"Twice, but only a few minutes apart. He decided we shouldn't wait longer."

Mattie nodded. She flipped on her overheads and accelerated to full speed, running lights with no sirens into the darkness. The moon and stars were now out and the air clear and frigid. "ETA ten minutes," she said to Rick as she focused on the highway, the white stripes in the middle flashing by.

They met very little traffic, and the few cars they approached pulled over to give them plenty of space to pass. Mattie slowed as she reached the town limits of Timber Creek and sped up again on the other side of town, rushing that final mile to Cole's house. "ETA one minute," she told Rick. "Notify dispatch. Tell him to stand by."

"Got it," he said, then used her radio to update Sam.

Her headlights swept the lane and surrounding grass as she made the last turn. She killed the overheads and headlights and steered her unit to park under the cottonwood tree outside the yard. The front of the house was dark. "I'll take the lead."

Releasing the safety strap on her holster, Mattie popped open the door to Robo's cage, and the two of them bailed out the driver's side door. Robo usually came here to play with Bruno and Belle, so she told him to heel in a firm tone that indicated he was here to work.

Hitch parked his cruiser twenty feet down the lane. Bent low, he ran to join them.

"Stand by here," she told him. "I'll signal if I want you to move in."

She and Robo glided up the sidewalk with Rick following close behind. When she reached the porch, she could see through the picture window that a light shone from the kitchen on the other side of the den.

She tried the knob. Locked. She checked on Rick and saw that he was aware they could be seen through the window and he had taken cover away from it. She pounded on the door and rang the bell. Cole had installed an alarm system, so she didn't want to force the door open unless she had to.

Stepping over to where she could peer inside, she saw Cole jog down the stairway and come into the light from the kitchen. He was dressed in sweatpants and a tee and was toweling his hair. Relief hit her as she realized he'd been in the shower.

"Cole, it's me," she called, thinking how strange it felt to not have Belle and Bruno barking on the other side of the door. Where were they? She said to Rick, "He's alone. Looks like he was in the shower."

Rick had holstered his service weapon by the time Cole flipped on the porch light and opened the door, smiling a greeting. "Mattie! What a nice surprise."

★ ★ ★

Mattie told the new deputy to check in with dispatch and go back to the station. When she and Rick stepped inside the entryway, Cole could see the strain on her face as she told him about Rainbow and the threat to him and the kids in the latest note. Rick Lawson stood by, not saying much, but his mere presence made Mattie put on her cop persona and come across as all business.

"The kids and Mrs. Gibbs are out with the Hartmans, and all of the dogs are there on guard," Cole explained.

"Good." She seemed to relax slightly. "Could you let Garrett know about the note, just so he stays especially alert?"

"I will."

"And will you come with us to the station for the night?"

"I can't, Mattie. I've got horses and a cat at the clinic that I need to treat during the night. I thought I'd get a few hours' sleep here first. I'm dead on my feet."

"Is Josie Baker still at the clinic?"

"She is. I have her locked up inside, and I told her not to open the door for anyone."

Mattie raised a brow. "I'm not worried about her safety. I'm concerned about *you* being safe from *her*."

Cole shrugged. "I think she's all right. I really do. But I'll watch my back."

"What about the Rattlers? Are they there too?"

"They called after dinner and checked in by phone. They're not coming back until sometime in the morning."

Mattie looked at Rick, as if asking his opinion.

"Josie Baker is a person of interest, not a suspect," the agent said. "You have an alarm system here at the house, Dr. Walker?"

Cole nodded and gestured toward the alarm controls on the wall.

"Make sure it's armed before you go to sleep. Check in with our dispatcher when you get up to go to your clinic during the night. Keep us posted of your whereabouts until you're locked back in your home and secure."

"That won't help if he's taken by surprise," Mattie said, looking back at Cole. "What time do you want to go to the clinic? We'll send Hitch or Garcia to go with you to make sure everything's okay."

"You're stretched thin enough at the station, Mattie. It's not necessary."

"What time?"

He could tell she wasn't going to back down. "One o'clock. But I tell you what. Let me call Frank Sullivan and see if he can come stand by," he said, referring to one of the posse members who was highly trained in protocol and procedures.

Mattie paused, apparently thinking it over before she reached for his hand. "All right."

Rick gave a salute as he stepped through the door onto the porch, apparently intending to give them some privacy. "Don't hesitate to call if you sense anything suspicious at all, Dr. Walker. Stay alert."

When the door closed behind him, Mattie tightened her grip on Cole's hand, and he pulled her into his arms. She settled against him, turning her head to lay her cheek against his chest.

"You're the one I'm worried about," he said.

She shook her head slightly and put her arms around him to hold him close. "We've got the station buttoned up, and Rainbow and I will be sharing the interrogation suite together."

"Is she okay?"

"Banged up and pretty shaken. I hope she'll be able to put it behind her in a few days. By then, maybe we'll have arrested the guys and have them safely under lock and key."

"I hope so."

She tipped her head back and looked him in the eye, dead serious. "You take care of yourself, you hear? I don't think I could handle it if anything happened to you."

He wished she would stay here with him, but he knew she would be safest back at the station. He placed his hand under her hair at the back of her neck and tilted his face down toward hers. "The same goes for you. Don't leave the safety of the station unless you have someone with you."

This time, the kiss he gave her was more passionate than tender, making it all the harder to let her go. After saying good-bye, he watched her stride purposefully down the sidewalk toward her Explorer, her dog on one side and Agent Lawson on the other. He offered up a prayer for her protection to the powers that be as he closed his front door and set the alarm.

TWENTY-THREE

The early hours of Sunday morning

Mattie awakened in the dead of night with words ringing in her ears: *No one cheats destiny.*

At first disoriented, she lay still, focusing on the glowing numbers on a digital clock above her and figuring out where she was. Four thirty-four—the interrogation room at the station.

Rainbow had brought the clock in to set the alarm. She was determined to relieve Sam on dispatch when her shift started at six. It was probably better that way—work always helped Mattie when she needed distraction from life, and she hoped it would help Rainbow as well.

She listened to the sound of her friend snoring softly from a few feet away. Rainbow had tossed and turned in the early part of the night but then decided to take the sleeping tablet Dr. McGinnis had given her. Soon after, she went out like a light.

Mattie reached across the floor to stroke the soft fur between Robo's ears. She rolled faceup on the air mattress and bent her knees to stretch her back. *No one cheats destiny*—she could have sworn someone had shouted it into the room. Of course no one had, but the words still echoed in her mind.

It didn't take much to figure out why the phrase had popped into her head. Though this night seemed like the longest one in history, morning approached. And with the coming of the new day, some kind of instruction would be sent from the person who was holding her mother and sister hostage.

If you don't cooperate, I'll take everyone you love, one by one, until you have no one left. Remember this when I give you instructions tomorrow. That's what the note said. That was her destiny. The day had arrived, and within hours it would be dawn.

The thought of Julia being taken and transported to Colorado filled Mattie's heart with pain. She felt terrified for her sister and determined to do whatever it took to save her from harm.

Julia wasn't used to being mistreated. Mattie couldn't help but believe she herself was much better prepared for what Julia must be going through right now. She wished they could trade places. She needed to stay focused, and when she received her instructions, she needed to take out these scumbags.

Mattie reached for her phone and saw she had a text from Cole that had come in at around two while she'd been asleep. It read, *Animals treated and I'm back home in bed, locked up safe and sound. Wish you were here.*

Turning off the light that backlit her screen, she gazed toward the ceiling in the darkness. She wished she were there too, watching over him.

It felt urgent to try to remember the woman the CIIT report had mentioned, the one who'd been present the night her father died. Mattie had been present too, although the horrible incident was a memory her two-year-old mind had repressed. If only she could remember what this woman looked like.

Her therapist had told her that her memories might surface when she could best handle them. Deciding to meditate and clear her mind, she set the intention of remembering that terrible night. She began to relax by controlling her breath and quieting her thoughts. Inhale . . . exhale. Gradually she lengthened her exhalation until it was about twice as long as her inhalation.

No one cheats destiny. The words kept resurfacing. She shifted position on her air mattress to try to get more comfortable and refocused on her breath. An image of the gray skin on Juan's lifeless face popped into her mind, followed by one of Rainbow standing tied to a tree with a hood over her head and a gag in her mouth.

After about five minutes of no success at getting her monkey mind to stop its shenanigans, Mattie sat and reached for her hoodie to pull over her T-shirt and yoga pants. Robo stirred on his cushion, and in the dim light from the clock, she could see that he'd raised his head and pricked his ears.

She smoothed his fur and whispered, "Stay here with Rainbow. Stay," as she rose to her feet and slipped out of the room. She paused a moment in the hallway to make sure he remained on his cushion and then soundlessly eased the door shut.

The light was still on in the staff office, and Deputy Garcia now sat at the desk he shared with Hitch. *This must signify the changing of the guard*, she thought as she padded into the room on socked feet.

Garcia looked up and smiled. "Good morning, sunshine."

Self-conscious, she ran her fingers through her tousled hair. "Do I look as bad as I feel?"

"You always look beautiful, *mi amiga*. I made a fresh pot of coffee just about an hour ago." He gestured toward the coffee station. "My wife sent some grapes and homemade doughnuts."

She realized she was hungry. "That was good of her. Did Virginia have a short night too?" Garcia's wife was a social worker who also worked for the county.

"Not too bad; she can sleep through anything. But she knew we'd all have only a short break, so she made these before she went to bed."

"She's a good person."

"Too good for my sorry tuchus."

"I'd say you two were pretty well suited for each other." Mattie poured a cup of coffee and reached inside the minifridge for milk. "Is Stella around yet?"

"She came in for coffee about a half hour ago."

"And Rick?"

"I think he left when she checked in." Garcia rose from his chair and began pulling on his coat. "Now that you're awake, I'm going to make a quick patrol through town to make sure everything is quiet. I'll swing by Teresa Lovato's house too."

"Thank you. Keep us posted if you need help with anything."

He nodded and left the room. Mattie selected a couple of doughnuts, put them on a napkin, and took some grapes for good measure, leaving plenty for Rainbow, who would probably want only fruit for breakfast. Picking up her coffee mug, she headed off to find Stella.

Sam was at the dispatcher's desk, and he raised his mug as if toasting her as she went through the lobby.

"Is everything quiet, Sam?"

"Haven't heard a peep out of anyone the past few hours."

"I hope it stays that way." It felt bizarre being here like this, dressed in civvies and gliding through the station on stocking feet without Robo at her side. Stella's office was dark, so Mattie headed for the briefing room, where she found her sitting at the table with her laptop and coffee.

Stella looked up with a smile.

"Help yourself," Mattie said as she set the doughnuts and fruit on the table.

Stella pushed some spare napkins toward Mattie. "I've already had mine. Delicious but sticky. How is Rainbow?"

"Sleeping. Rick briefed you?"

"He and the sheriff. I wish he'd called me."

"He decided to let Rick handle it. You needed the rest." Mattie selected one of the glazed pastries, pinching it between two fingers to examine it. "How in the world would one go about making these things?"

Stella snorted. "I don't want to know. They're irresistible."

"I think Rainbow is going to be okay. Dr. McGinnis treated and dressed her wrists and gave her a few sleeping pills. She took one, so she's snoring away right now with Robo on guard."

"I wondered where your sidekick was."

"She's got such a positive outlook on life . . . I think she'll consider this a bump in the road eventually and never look back. Or at least I hope so." Mattie took a bite and chewed. "We can't let her continue to live out there by herself."

"I know what you mean, but that's her decision."

"We at least need to get her a dog."

"Rainbow seems like more of a cat person."

"A little dog, then. Even a little dog would have alerted her that someone was on the property."

"Mattie . . ." Stella leaned forward. "Those guys were there for a purpose, and a little dog would've probably been hurt. You have to remember that this was a one-time thing."

"Because of me." Mattie placed her doughnut on the napkin, the guilt and dread over what was happening to her friends and loved ones stealing her appetite.

"Not your fault." Stella gave her a stern look. "You should know that. You've been in law enforcement long enough to know that sometimes innocent people get in the way of scum."

Mattie didn't know what to say, so she nodded and took a sip of coffee.

Stella looked at her laptop screen. "Rick's contact dug up another report. This one has more detail."

"Wow. What does it say?"

Stella raised an eyebrow at her. "Have you been able to remember anything?"

"I wish I could tell you yes, but I haven't."

"This one has more detail about the people who went into the checkpoint before the shooting."

"Same witness?"

"Yes. We still don't have a name." Stella focused on her computer screen to read aloud. "There were four people who entered the checkpoint—two Caucasian males, one male believed to be Hispanic, and one Caucasian female. The female had long blond hair, was of average size, no distinguishing features other than the hair, which was described as light blond and worn in a ponytail that came to her shoulder blades. She wore a cap and dark clothing and carried a rifle."

Stella glanced up with a frown. "You'll see here as I read this why this report didn't offer much more to the case than the first one we found. Other than the description of the woman, that is." She continued reading. "One of the Caucasian males was described as about five foot ten, average build, no distinguishing features, wore dark clothing and a cap, and carried a rifle. The other Caucasian male appeared to be an inch or two taller but otherwise dressed the same. He also carried a rifle."

Stella raised her eyes from her screen again to look at Mattie. "I figure those two individuals were the Cobb brothers."

Mattie nodded, her attention riveted. "How about the Hispanic male?"

"Well, that's vague." Stella focused back on her screen. "The third male was described as *probably* Hispanic, although the witness was unsure because of the dim light. He was average height but heavier built than the two Caucasian males. The witness said, 'Not heavy as in fat but heavy as in muscular. Like a football player with thick shoulders.' He also wore dark clothing and carried a rifle. The witness knew little to nothing about weapons and wasn't able to identify the type of rifles they carried."

Stella paused, giving Mattie a sympathetic look. "This leads now to an earwitness report and might stir some memories. Okay if I continue?"

"Absolutely. That's what I'm hoping for."

"Bear in mind that this witness was apparently inside a car a few vehicles in line south of the checkpoint, preparing to enter the US, and the incident occurred at approximately eleven fifteen PM. After noticing the four individuals enter the building—this witness initially thought they were Border Patrol agents—the witness heard shouts coming from inside, both male and female voices. No words could be deciphered except for screams for help that were believed to be from a woman. These screams were cut off suddenly by gunfire that, and I quote here, 'came in rapid bursts like a machine gun.' The gunfire ended after several rounds, and the four individuals described above left the building with, and again I quote, 'a Mexican woman and two little kids,' end quote."

Mattie was on the edge of her seat, trying to relive the event as the words on the screen played out. But she received nothing. She realized the muscles in her shoulders were as tight as Robo's when he prepared to spring. She drew a breath and shrugged, exhaling slowly as she dropped her shoulders.

Stella was studying her. "Pretty hard to hear?"

"Yeah." Mattie stretched the muscles in her jaw by opening her mouth, inhaling and letting out a puff of air. "But I've got nothin'."

Stella pursed her lips as she stared at the table. "You know . . . that's okay. Maybe this is enough for now. We know the two white males were the Cobb brothers. Currently, we have no Hispanic male on our radar, although we don't know who carried out Julia's kidnapping in San Diego. Two questions that come to mind are: Is the woman who was involved in your father's shooting still in play and involved in our cases here? And if so, is she still working with this Hispanic male that's in this witness report?"

"Gut-level reaction—I feel strongly that we are dealing with a woman here. Not just because of the poison, because like Rick said, plenty of men use poison to kill too. But more on a level of the feel of the whole thing—cat-and-mouse play with the notes, stringing us along, the organized approach to the kidnappings. I know, all of these things could be done by a man too, so I guess all I have here is a hunch."

Stella seemed to be observing her carefully. "Yes, maybe all you have is a hunch, but is it a hunch based on a repressed memory? Somewhere in your psyche, you might know that this woman is important."

That resonated with Mattie. "Exactly. I've felt that way ever since I learned a woman was involved that night. And I think a woman is involved now."

Stella got up and went to the whiteboard. "So we have plenty of women listed here. Josie Baker, does she have blond hair?"

Mattie pictured Josie in her mind. "Blond turning silver. I'd say late fifties, early sixties—right age range. No partner that we know of, but she has a neighbor who is a gunsmith. We already talked about that. She's at Cole's clinic right now, which makes me crazy, but he believes she's nothing but a client who is attached to her pet. But would she poison her cat to get close to Cole, the kids, and me? That doesn't make any sense."

Stella nodded, her eyes on the whiteboard. "Moving on to Althea Rattler. She actually came in to the station, which could be reconnaissance to gain intel on your whereabouts and what we're doing to protect you. Dark hair, but I would guess that came from a bottle. Average build, appears to be in her late fifties with no gray hair—thus my assumption about the hair color."

"Again . . . would someone poison their own horses just to get intel on me?"

"A ruthless person would," Stella said. "Remember how the graphologist said we were dealing with a person who would go to any lengths to have their way? If this individual has carried a vendetta for your mother for thirty years, whether male or female, we *are* dealing with a ruthless person."

"Agreed." The doughnut Mattie had eaten had formed a greasy ball in her stomach. "We've also got Edith Kelsey at the campground with her alleged husband Drake. She has blond hair, fair skin with freckles, sort of looks like the all-American girl. She's average height but stocky build—so is Drake. Even though he's Caucasian and not Hispanic, he has darker skin tones and a black beard. The thing about them is they had their horses tied, remember? Their horses didn't get poisoned."

"True. And that has seemed suspicious from the get-go."

"And the Carrs, Didi and Milo. They were there at the campground but not really hunting. Didi has very long blond hair that's turning gray, worn in a braid down her back, average build, no horses. They popped back up at Cedar Canyon after Glenna was shot. They have guns but not one that shoots .223 ammo. Her husband Milo apparently has a brain injury, which she reports was from a horse kicking him in the head. Unfortunate, but it happens."

"It does indeed." Stella stared at the whiteboard as if it could give her answers. "Anything else that stands out about Didi Carr?"

Mattie paused to think and remembered something from her first interview with them. "Robo acted interested in Milo when I first met them, and I thought it might mean that Robo recognized his scent from the track the night before. But when I found out Milo had jerky in his pocket, I thought that might explain the interest."

"Okay, so Robo isn't above showing some interest in beef jerky when he's on duty." Stella looked at Mattie, and they shared a smile.

"At least he didn't hit on it." Serious again, Mattie went on. "But I can't say it means Milo Carr did or didn't leave the scent trail. Robo is an amazing dog, but I didn't train him to specifically perform a scent ID from a track. Although it's a skill I should consider adding to his repertoire."

"And while you're at it, teach him to talk." The phone in the room buzzed with an internal call from dispatch, and Stella rose to answer it. "All right. Good. Patch her through." She covered the phone's speaker and murmured to Mattie, "It's Glenna's sister from the hospital. Glenna's awake."

Mattie felt a wave of relief wash through her, and she watched Stella's face while she listened.

"All right. If she remembers anything, let us know immediately. Thank you so much for keeping me posted. It feels good to know that you're there with her."

Stella disconnected the call and came back to stand by the table. "Glenna's awake but doesn't remember much about the shooting. She remembers an RV at the campground, and that's about it. She thinks that when she was shot, she was going to inform them about the homicide at the other campground and that they could remain where they were, but she's not sure. She says she can't recall being alarmed about anything or having a confrontation with the campers. The shot seemed to come out of nowhere."

"And that's all she remembers?"

"Yes, darn it."

"All right. We just have to deal with things as they come. We should get instructions from Juan's killer soon."

"Tell me what you're thinking, Mattie." Stella was giving her that penetrating look.

"I need to be ready when these instructions come in."

Stella narrowed her eyes. "But you know that it might not be possible for you to follow through with the next directive."

"Maybe that's so, but maybe not. We'll have to take it a step at a time."

"I don't like that determined look on your face, girl. We're a team here, and you need to remember that. The team will make decisions on how to respond."

Mattie scooted to the edge of her chair, wanting to make sure she expressed herself clearly. "If I get the opportunity to be in the same space as my mother and sister, I'll take it. They aren't used to dealing with criminals like I am. If we can negotiate with these people, we will. But negotiation might not be possible."

"Your safety is of utmost importance as we proceed."

"And I think my mother's and sister's safety and the safety of everyone around me is of utmost importance. I'm tired of playing games with notes."

"We all are, but we can't get impatient and go off half-cocked. You know that."

Mattie looked down at the table to escape Stella's gaze. "What I know is that it tears me up to think of Julia being transported here to Colorado, probably bound and in the trunk of some vehicle. And my mother . . . who knows what she has endured? Has she been poisoned with selenium, like Juan? I need to get answers."

Stella's jaw muscle clenched. "We'll have to see, Mattie. Remember that we're dealing with a killer here. A ruthless person."

Mattie nodded. "I know. Someone who will go to extremes to get what they want. But I'm determined too, Stella. I'll go to extremes to get what I want too."

TWENTY-FOUR

It was lonely eating breakfast without the kids and Mrs. Gibbs. Cole had cooked scrambled eggs and toast and was eating at the table, wishing his family and Mattie were there with him. He picked up his phone to check again for a text from Mattie, but to no avail. He wanted to call . . . but what if she was sleeping?

Instead he dialed Garrett, who answered on the first ring.

"Good morning, Cole. Everything's good here on our end. How about yours?"

"All quiet here. I'm about to get started on my morning rounds."

"The girls are still asleep, but Molly's here having coffee with Leslie. Want to talk to her?"

"Sure."

Since Cole and the kids always used the more formal title *Mrs. Gibbs* when speaking to their housekeeper, it seemed odd for Garrett to call her by her given name. The lady sounded chipper when she greeted him on the line. "Top of the morning to ye, Doctor."

"Good morning. How are you getting along?"

"I'm having a splendid holiday with Leslie and Garrett. We'll make some breakfast here shortly. Do ye want us to come home soon?"

"I'd rather you stay there until after I finish my rounds. Then I'll call you and we can decide. Is it okay if we decide later?"

"Whatever you say. We'll stay here as long as the Hartmans will let us. I don't want to put these two girls in jeopardy."

"Same here. I'll check in with Mattie after a bit and get her opinion. I'm glad you're content where you are."

"Oh, it's been lovely. We played pinochle until midnight. Miss Angela might be a wee bit antsy about going home soon, but Sophie seems happy."

"Thanks. Tell Angie that she can call me if she wants to when she wakes up. Take the pressure off you."

Mrs. Gibbs chuckled. "Good idea."

After disconnecting the call, Cole finished his breakfast in a few bites and cleared the table. He filled a travel mug with coffee and snagged his jacket before heading to the garage. The double door rattled up on its rollers, allowing the cold air to rush in.

Cole drove the couple hundred yards farther up the lane to his clinic, thinking it had actually worked out quite well having Josie Baker keep watch over Buster during the night. He'd told her he would keep his cell phone close and to call if she had any concerns at all, but he'd not heard from her. Her RV was still parked out front where it had been when he'd left last night.

Inside, he found Josie where he'd left her, ensconced on the lawn chair she'd set up next to her cats' cages. She looked up at him rather bleary-eyed when he peeked into the kennel room. "Good morning," he said.

She ran a hand over her face. "If you say so."

Cole entered the room and handed her the mug of coffee while he scanned the two cages. Both cats seemed settled, lying down toward the back of their cages. "How did Buster do after his last treatment?"

"Same yowling and wobbling around his cage like before, but he came around soon enough. I didn't have to call you. Figured we both could get some sleep."

"I'm glad it worked out. Let me take a look at him."

As if Buster knew he was being discussed, he rose and then crouched in the back of his cage, eyeing Cole suspiciously.

"If he's doing well, you can probably take him home," Cole said.

He began to reach for the cage door, but Josie motioned for him to wait, groaning as she stood. "I'll get him." She stretched, one hand against her back. "Oy, it seems I'm getting too old to sleep over in a lawn chair."

He led the way into the exam room with Josie trailing behind, carrying Buster. As soon as the door swung closed behind them, Mittens started yowling in her cage. "She must not like being left behind," Cole said as he waved toward the exam table, an invitation to place Buster on it.

"I told you they don't like being away from each other. If I'd have left her at home, that's what he would've been doing all night."

Cole completed a thorough exam and deemed Buster well enough to go home. "He might be a little slow to get back on his feed, but he looks like he's typically a good eater, so I think he'll do fine. Let me know if you have a problem."

"All right." Josie picked Buster up and cuddled him against her. "Oh, by the way. There was a note under my windshield wiper that I found early this morning. I put it on that stack of papers on your lobby desk. It was addressed to Mattie. Is she that cop you sent up to my place to talk to me yesterday?"

Cole felt a jolt of alarm. "A note? Did you touch it?"

"Of course. I said I put it on your desk."

He hurried to the lobby and stared at the sealed envelope like it was a swarm of bees. There it was, lying on a pile of papers, so he hadn't noticed it when he came through earlier. The handprinted lettering on the front of it spelled out only one word: *MATTIE*. "Josie, do you know who left it there? Did you hear anyone drive up?"

"No and no. I heard you leave last night, but no one else came that I know of. I fell asleep after Buster settled down."

"Did you leave the front door locked?"

"Sure. You told me to. I didn't go outside until this morning. Pretty odd for it to be left on my vehicle like that, don't you think?"

He wished he'd had surveillance equipment installed at the front door, but he hadn't thought it necessary. He reached for his cell phone to call the sheriff.

★ ★ ★

Mattie left Cole's office feeling completely frustrated. After she and Stella had driven out to retrieve the note, Stella had questioned Josie Baker about who might have left it and how she'd found it, trying to glean at least some information. But Josie denied hearing or knowing anything, and she stuck to her story.

When asked if they could take her fingerprints to eliminate hers from the envelope, she refused to cooperate. Said it was her right to decline, and if they wanted her prints, they could get a warrant. Cole had tried to persuade her, but she became huffy even with him. In the end, Josie took her cats home and Mattie and Stella took the envelope, sealed in a plastic baggie, back to the station.

Cole stayed at the clinic to check on the Rattler horses, but as Mattie left, he told her to expect him at the station as soon as he finished. He'd said, "I need to know what that note says."

They all needed to know. The team gathered in the briefing room, including Rick, who'd arrived after getting little sleep. Mattie felt her nerves flare as Stella gloved up and carefully slit the top of the envelope. After removing the note, she opened it and laid it on top of the plastic baggie.

With Robo beside her, Mattie stood across the table from Stella. From her position, it looked like the same cursive handwriting as that on the other notes.

McCoy stood at the head of the table, where he probably couldn't see clearly. "Go ahead and read it," he told Stella.

She cleared her throat and began to read:

Dear Mattie,

The time has come for you to join your mother and sister for a little tea party. They are both alive and, though not so well, they are still able to participate in a family reunion. If you don't come, you'll find each of them, one at a time, among the standing dead at various spots in the forest.

Meet me at the twenty-six-mile marker on the road past the turnoff to Eureka at eight o'clock tonight. Come alone, and don't bring that dog of yours. Leave your car on the road and walk a hundred yards straight north into the standing dead. If there is any sign of anyone else in the vicinity, I'll disappear and the next note you receive will contain the death notice of one of your loved ones. Your mother looks like she'll be the first to go.

It's your choice. Cooperate or prepare for a funeral.

Always,

A friend of your father's

When Stella stopped reading, all in the room remained quiet. Mattie turned to walk a few paces away from the group, digesting the information with her back to the others.

Brody's growling voice came from behind her. "You're not gonna do this. We'll find another way."

"Agreed," Stella said.

"We'll station someone up in that area ASAP and prepare to intercept whoever goes there," McCoy said. "Deputy Brody, you could find a position nearby without anyone seeing you. We'll get an unmarked vehicle to drop you off up above, and you could hike in."

"Absolutely. With camouflage, I could find a surveillance point and get in there hours before eight o'clock. We have plenty of time to set up an ambush."

Mattie turned and eyed the others. Probably sensing her turmoil, Robo hovered at her left heel. Brody's face was dark with rage, while the sheriff and Stella frowned in concern. Only Rick's expression remained neutral. "I'll do it," she said. "Anything else puts my mother and sister in jeopardy."

McCoy shook his head. "But that puts you in harm's way with no backup. I can't allow that with one of my officers."

Mattie looked at Rick. "What kind of tracking device could you put on me? Do you have anything small enough to avoid detection?"

Lines deepened between Rick's eyebrows. "I could set you up with a mini tracking device, about a half inch in diameter, that we could sew into the hem of your shirt or your pants. It could go undetected unless they use a certain type of wand."

"The people we're dealing with here will most likely have that type of wand," Stella said, her voice tense. "It's too risky."

"Maybe they would, but odds are against it. Our devices are military grade and impossible to detect with ordinary equipment," Rick said.

Stella stared at him, and he lifted one shoulder in a slight shrug.

McCoy narrowed his eyes as if thinking. "We could do a combination of the two ideas. Set up surveillance and make sure you wear a tracking device."

"I have a feeling that these people are already watching that part of the forest," Mattie said. "One deviation on our part, and my mother will be killed."

"We don't know that for certain," Stella said. "They want you. If our activity is detected, they'll probably call strike one and start with a new plan to get at you."

"I disagree," Mattie said, feeling pressure start to build inside her, a mixture of adrenaline and dread. "I think we're dealing with someone who wouldn't hesitate to kill. This person signs the letters *a friend of your father's*. I'm not sure what that means exactly, but it probably goes back to the time they worked together to smuggle through his checkpoint. They used my mother and us kids as pawns to hold over my father's head back then, and I believe they have no regard for her or us now."

"There's some type of revenge this person is enacting," Rick said. "That's one theory that would hold up to thirty years of incubation. Hatred and revenge last a good long time."

"Not necessarily the money that John Cobb referred to," McCoy said. "Seems like Ramona stealing money was a long shot anyway. She didn't have money during or after the time she spent with Harold Cobb. Revenge sounds likely."

"Well, Mattie didn't do anything as a little kid that would merit revenge," Stella said. "This is a plot against Ramona."

"I called the police on Harold, which resulted in him being incarcerated," Mattie said, locking eyes with McCoy. He'd been the young deputy that responded to the call that night, and he, more than anyone, knew what conditions had been like in that household. "This might be revenge against Ramona, but it could also be directed at me."

Stella uttered a sound of frustration. "So how do you propose to defend yourself when you give yourself up to these killers? They're not going to let you carry any weapons."

Mattie looked at Rick. "Any ideas?"

"I have a slew of options: a tiny stun gun, small enough to conceal in the hem of your shirt along with the tracker; brass knuckles that look like an engagement ring; another type of ring with a hidden blade; a tactical self-defense pen with a stun gun and a handcuff key. There are others, but these are the ones that come to mind."

"The rings are pretty obvious, and there are no guarantees you could keep any weapons you might have hidden," Stella said, with some heat. "It's not acceptable for you to even consider playing their game, Mattie."

"A stun gun small enough to hide in the hem of my shirt?" Mattie asked, eyeing Rick.

"Yes, I can bring in a set of items I have in my car, and we can look at them."

"Sounds good," Mattie said.

After Rick left, Stella renewed her protest. "Sheriff, I'm not in favor of this."

"This might be our only chance to get into their circle and rescue Julia and Ramona before they're killed," Mattie said, appealing to McCoy. "Stella, I know it's risky, and I'm willing to accept that risk. This is a chance to save two innocent civilians from a group of ruthless criminals."

"That's just it," Stella said. "We don't even know how many people we're dealing with. There have to be at least two men here who attacked Rainbow, and enough out in California to pull off Julia's kidnapping. And there must be at least one other person here who stood guard over your mother and sister last night when those two men were busy at Rainbow's house."

Mattie shrugged. "It's hard to say. Those two could have Ramona confined somewhere they can leave her. She's probably sick and immobilized at this point, and Julia wouldn't have been in Colorado yet last night."

Stella threw up her hands as if exasperated. "That's splitting hairs. Point is, you won't be up against only one person, and you know it."

"Stella, I don't want to argue. And the real point is, I do know it, and I'm willing to take the risk. Now help me figure out how we can mitigate as much of that risk as possible so we can try to save the lives of my mother and sister."

Stella stared at her for a long moment, lips pursed in the way Mattie had come to recognize as her thinking mode.

McCoy spoke up. "I haven't made a decision yet, Mattie, but I think we need to explore ideas on how to make this work. Then we'll decide as a team, but I have the last say."

Brody cleared his throat. "It's possible that once they have Mattie, they'll kill all three of them. I still say I can get in there to set up an ambush, but I have to leave here soon to do it."

"No," Mattie said. "The sheriff's right. We need to talk this over as a team, and I don't want to put Ramona and Julia in jeopardy before the mission even starts."

Rick reentered the room, carrying a box full of his tricks of the trade. They began to sort through them, tossing out ideas as they dug in and analyzing theories to come up with a plan that might work.

TWENTY-FIVE

Cole arrived at the station about an hour later than he'd hoped. Althea and Tanner Rattler had turned up at his clinic shortly after Josie Baker left, and they kept him there longer than he'd planned, asking all sorts of questions. It felt like he would never be able to wrap up and leave.

While driving into town, a quick call to Hannah told him that Sassy was eating and drinking this morning and the frequent diarrhea had ceased. He told Hannah it looked like the worst was over and to keep an eye on Sassy's intake for the rest of the day.

After parking beside Mattie's unit, he hurried into the station and was surprised to see Rainbow at the dispatcher's desk. She looked up and waved when he entered.

He extended his hand, and she reached out to clasp it. "Rainbow, it's good to see you here. How are you doing?" He squeezed her hand and released it.

Her eyes brimmed with tears, but she swiped them away. He noticed the bandages on her wrists. "I'm okay. I really am. Just had a bad scare. There's no reason to take off from work. And I don't want to be home, you know."

Cole felt for her. "I understand. Do you need a place to stay?"

She shook her head. "No . . . no, it'll be all right. I-I'll figure something out today."

"If you need help, let me know, and we'll put our heads together and work on it. I'm not sure my place feels any safer right now."

"Stella offered her place, but I might just stay here. I'll see how the day goes. But thanks, thanks anyway."

"Of course." Cole scanned the empty lobby. "Is Mattie in?"

"She's in the briefing room with the others." Rainbow stood and turned to head that way. "Let me tell her you're here."

"I can do it," he said, starting after her.

She half turned and held up a hand for him to wait. "No, wait here, okay? Sorry. I'll see what the sheriff wants and if she can come out."

The change of routine disturbed him. Since he'd joined the sheriff's posse, he'd been included in many a briefing, and he wondered why he was denied access now. But he didn't have to wait long, because Mattie came back with Rainbow straightaway, Robo trailing along behind and then trotting ahead when he recognized Cole.

"I'm glad you're here," Mattie said, holding out her hand. Robo wagged his tail in greeting, sidling up to press against his knees.

While using one hand to pet Robo, Cole took Mattie's hand with the other as he examined the signs of stress and exhaustion on her face—dark smudges below her eyes with tightness at the corners and around her mouth. "What did the note say?"

"Come with me." Continuing to hold his hand, she led him to the same interview room where they'd met last night. Only now it was crowded by the addition of an air mattress on the floor. She bent and heaved it up onto the bed so they could sit in the chairs. Robo squeezed into the room with them and settled into a spot on his cushion.

Sitting knee to knee, Mattie took both his hands in hers and gripped them tightly. He had a feeling he wasn't going to like what she had to say. "The note is an invitation for me to join my mother and sister, and it includes a threat to kill them if I don't cooperate."

Cole's gut tensed. Even though he'd known this latest note would contain some kind of demand similar to this, he really hadn't fully prepared for the inevitable. In fact, he'd been so busy that he hadn't prepared for the news at all.

She appeared to be reading his face. "I know it's a lot to take in. We're discussing what to do about it as a team, but I wanted to tell you what's going on in private."

After a pause, during which she seemed to be giving him some time to catch up emotionally, Cole blurted out exactly what he was thinking. "What's to discuss? You're not going to give in to their demands, right?"

Her lips tightened, and so did her grip on his hands. "I have no doubt my mother and sister will be killed if I don't cooperate. We're—"

Cole interrupted her. "We don't know that for sure. It could be just a threat."

"I don't think it's an idle threat." He started to interject, but she shook her head at him. "I was going to say that we're discussing ways we can respond while mitigating the risk. We're examining our options."

"I hope giving in to these killers is not an option. That's not something you would even consider, is it?"

Her expression turned sad. "Actually, I am considering it, Cole. After they got to Rainbow and then threatened you and the kids, I hoped for an opportunity to end this game they're playing."

"Not by risking your life." Cole realized he was beginning to sound angry, his go-to emotion when he was afraid. He tried to soften his voice. "I'm worried about you, Mattie."

Mattie looked down at their intertwined hands for a moment before meeting his gaze. "Cole . . . listen . . . I tried to find my mother almost my whole life, and I waited here in Timber Creek, hoping she would come back someday and find me. But finding Julia first, that was a huge gift. Think about it . . . I didn't even know I had a sister, and then she turns up. You remember, you're the one who suggested I submit my DNA to the database. You remember what a thrill that was when I found out I had a sister, right?"

He nodded, unable to deny that Mattie had changed then. She'd seemed happier, lighter and less serious about everything. And she'd seemed less fearful about opening her heart to let in his love.

"Then my sister and grandmother led me to finding my mother. Finally, I dared to dream that one day we could have a true family reunion; that they could join us here in Timber Creek and we could all be together for Christmas or Thanksgiving or something like that. To do things together like a normal family . . . you know, like the family you had when you were growing up."

The fear circling inside Cole's chest began to grow. "I know what you mean. I want that with you. I want that for *our* future."

"See, I can't give up that dream. I can't turn my back on my mother and sister and let some psychopath kill them. I have to do everything in my power to help get them back."

"But you said it, Mattie. This is a psychopath we're dealing with. You can't play this game on their terms."

Her eyes became fierce. "Do you suggest I wait until either Julia or my mother is killed and tied to a tree in a dead forest?"

Her words were like a slap in his face. He released the pressure on her hands, and they both let their hands part and fall into their laps. "You know that's not what I want."

Mattie shook her head, the anger gone as quickly as it had arisen. Now she just looked resigned. "I know it isn't. I know you're afraid, and I am too. But we've got to think this thing through with our heads, not our hearts."

"But Mattie, that's what you're doing, don't you see? You're thinking of your mother and sister with your heart."

She stared at him for a moment before nodding. "You're right about that. I get a pain in my chest every time I imagine my mother being ill from selenium poisoning, so ill she might die, just like Juan. When I imagine Julia bound and gagged and riding in the trunk of a car all the way from California, it tears me apart. I would do anything in my power to end their suffering."

Cole was speechless. He could see her point. Wouldn't he feel the same way about Angela or Sophie? Wouldn't he feel the same about Mattie? He would trade his own safety and even his life for any of them.

When he didn't respond, she went on. "The team talked strategy this morning, and we've gone over all kinds of ideas. We weighed the pros and cons of different approaches. We all believe that these offenders consider Ramona and Julia expendable, and they're in grave danger."

He didn't need to say it again; he could tell she knew she would be in danger as well if she joined them. The fear in his chest ballooned into a monstrous thing and threatened to boil over into anger again. Not at this woman he loved. This stand she had taken was so Mattie; he could have predicted this would be the choice she would make. His rage was aimed straight at the vermin who were holding her loved ones hostage. He wanted to go with her and thrash them all.

"But I can't see how turning yourself over to these people would do any good. You can't take any weapons. You would be helpless, and that's not going to free Julia or Ramona."

Mattie leaned back in her chair and studied him. "I'm a law enforcement officer. I think differently than they do. I also know the food and water are poisoned, so I wouldn't eat or drink like Juan did, and like my mother probably has."

"You can't keep that up over time."

"We're talking about a way to track me, so I won't have to keep it up for long."

Cole imagined how easy it would be to detect a tracker. "I can't see how you'd get away with that."

"We've found a way to hide a tracker so it won't be detected. We've pored over maps of the area so we can cover all the roads and trails if they try to escape. We're going to add to our force to have enough power to overtake them. We're also talking about how to camouflage agents in the area. I won't truly be alone."

His chest felt tight, and he raised his eyebrows. "You will be alone, Mattie. You'll be alone and in the hands of a killer."

Mattie leaned back and released a pent-up breath, disappointment on her face. "I thought you'd see that I have to do this. I thought you'd understand and help with our plan."

Cole sat back for a moment, hating that she was disappointed in him. He bent forward, elbows to knees with his hands holding his head as he stared at the floor. "Give me a minute to think."

It felt crazy to even be considering it. But he could tell she was determined, and when Mattie decided to take something on, she stuck with it to the end. And this was her family—he could understand that. Once they married, her sister and mother would be part of his family too.

He knew her well enough to know he wasn't going to be able to talk her out of this. If he refused to help, she would be hurt, maybe even weakened in her resolve to come out of this mission alive. And what if there truly was something he could do to support her and he declined . . . what then? He would be responsible for diminishing the strength of the plan to keep her safe.

There was a lot at stake here. Did he love her enough to support her no matter what? He'd told her countless times that he supported her career in law enforcement, her decision to serve and protect; but when it came down to her putting her life on the line, was he really and truly behind her? And in reality, she put her life on the line every day she went to work. Could he handle that year after year, throughout their lifetime together after they were married?

It all boiled down to this: could he match his words with his actions?

She shifted in her chair, and he imagined her growing impatient with this forced inactivity. That was also what this was about. She was a woman of action, and she'd grown tired of being cooped up in the station and staying under forced guard. She was ready to form a plan and get to work. He could understand that completely.

He lifted his face, propping his chin with his hands, and made eye contact. She'd put on her cop face while she waited. His heart wasn't in it completely, but his head had told him what he needed to do. "How can I help?"

Her neutral expression crumpled into a look of relief. She took his hand and stood, tugging him to stand with her. It felt good to hold her in his arms and feel her encircle him with hers. He knew how hard it was for her to trust others, and he felt he'd passed a test. He just wished it wasn't a test involving life and death.

She lifted her face to his and returned his kiss, long and sweet. At the end, she leaned her head back and looked him in the eye. "Come into the briefing room with me, and we'll tell you the plan we've come up with."

TWENTY-SIX

By late afternoon they had completed their plan and everyone had dispersed to put the pieces in place. Cole had left earlier to go to his dad's ranch to get four horses ready in case they were needed. Mattie expected him to come back to the station before it was time for her to leave.

Disguised in camouflage coveralls, two additional agents from CBI and two officers from the Colorado State Patrol had arrived at Shadow Ridge Campground in two different four-wheel-drive vehicles. This afternoon, they had hiked the area below and above Eureka, acting like hunters scouting for elk but doing a quick reconnaissance of the terrain to familiarize themselves with the surrounding area. They were careful to stay away from the exact location that Mattie had been instructed to go to that night.

Mattie and Rainbow were in the interrogation room that they now jokingly called their home away from home. Stella had run to Main Street Diner and brought back Mattie's favorite meal: a cheeseburger, fries, and a vanilla shake. She sat at the table, eating what she could to prepare for her mission, but her stomach turned queasy every time she thought of what lay ahead. She took a bite of the burger and focused on chewing.

Rainbow sat cross-legged on the bed with needle and thread, sewing a mini tracker into the hem of the black T-shirt that Mattie planned to wear under a flannel outer shirt that night. She didn't know how much time would be spent outdoors, and she wanted to at least stay warm and ready to move.

The night forecast called for it to be clear and cold, and the moon would be three-quarters full, which would give Mattie some light in the ghostly terrain of the dead forest. She swallowed the lump of food she'd been chewing and sucked on the straw inserted in the sweet milkshake, trying to focus on the flavor instead of her thoughts. She welcomed Rainbow's conversation.

"I'll sew the tracker on the side with a secure stitch, but I can use a basting stitch to hold in the switchblade. Then you can rip it out easily to get to it."

Mattie glanced up from her food. Her friend was sitting in a serene yoga pose and talking about hidden switchblades, something she never would have guessed might occur. "That sounds good. Could you put the knife in the back?" She was thinking that if they tied her hands behind her with rope, the blade might be easier to reach.

"Sure." Rainbow unspooled a length of thread, snipped it before licking the end, and squinted at the eye of the needle as she tried to thread it. "Now where is Robo going to be tonight?"

Robo pricked his ears and looked back and forth between the two of them as if he listened for the answer too. "He'll be with Cole and Brody. They're going to be in an unmarked Jeep a few miles from my drop site."

"Okay . . ."

Mattie could tell that something bothered her friend, and she could guess what it was. But she didn't want to initiate the conversation. Rainbow would if it mattered enough to her. It didn't take long to discover that it did.

"I can't imagine going into this like you are, Mattie. It's so scary." Rainbow stopped sewing and placed her hands on the shirt that lay in her lap, looking at Mattie with wide eyes.

"I know. It's scary, but I'm ready for it. I've seen it coming for a while now, and I'm ready to get started."

"How can you eat right now?" Rainbow put one hand against her stomach. "My belly is heaving."

Mattie shrugged. "I have to stay fueled and hydrated. It's part of the plan."

Tears brimmed Rainbow's eyes, and she swiped at them with the back of her hand, the sewing needle gripped between her fingers away from her face. "I think you're the bravest person I know."

Mattie couldn't help but release a nervous chuckle at the solemn look on her friend's face. "Either brave or foolish, right? I guess we'll find out. C'mon . . . let's finish so you can braid my hair."

Rainbow picked up her sewing while Mattie took another bite of what she knew to be a savory hamburger. But her gut quivered, and her mouth had lost its ability to taste anything.

★ ★ ★

Using his dad's truck, Cole trailered four saddled horses to Frank Sullivan's ranch, just a few miles from his dad's place. He turned off the highway, rattled across the cattle guard, and headed up the lane to the white stucco house with a green roof. The sun was sinking fast in the western sky, and it was only an hour or so until he would have to say good-bye to Mattie.

Frank came out of the house to greet him, dangling a set of car keys from his fingers. As soon as Cole exited his truck, Frank handed them to him. "The tank's full of gas and ready to go," he said, nodding toward his Jeep Wrangler that sat parked nearby.

"So is the truck," Cole said. "The goal is to get up to Shadow Ridge Campground before dark and mingle with the people there. Try to blend in, ask for good places to find elk, things like that." He walked Frank to the back of his dad's pickup. "I threw in my tent and a cooler with some food and drink for tonight if you want it. Make it look like you're just up there searching for a campsite."

"Sounds good. Dave Harris is coming with me," Frank said, referring to another one of their buddies on the posse. "We can pull this off."

"There's a radio in the front. Make sure you're inside the truck and ready to pull out by eight o'clock. Sheriff McCoy will be up there too, also in an unmarked vehicle. He'll let you know if we need the horses and where to meet."

"I'm ready to go now. I'll pick up Dave and head up to Shadow Ridge."

Cole felt antsy to get back to the station. "I'll leave you to it, then."

Frank walked him to his Jeep, gripping Cole's hand in a quick shake as they said good-bye. "Tell Mattie we'll be there for her. And I'm sending my prayers for her safety."

As Cole pulled back onto the highway, he thought about the many times the posse had banded together this past year to support the sheriff's department and especially Mattie whenever they worked up in the wilderness area. The whole group rallied behind her and Robo, celebrating their successes. Her success was the town's success, and she and her dog had gained quite a reputation.

He reached into his pocket to update Garrett, who was chomping at the bit to go with the posse up into the forest tonight but would remain steadfast at his post, guarding Cole's family. Friends like Garrett didn't come around often, and Cole treasured him even more than he had before.

★ ★ ★

Mattie was in the briefing room, completing a final equipment check with Rick. The tracking system worked well and was tapped into the radio network for increased range. The team should be able to follow her even if she was taken into the rugged terrain of the wilderness. And if she was taken down to the highway to be transported elsewhere, it would be all that much easier to track her.

Cole entered the room and hesitated just inside the door. Mattie caught a glimpse of the anxiety on his face before he rearranged his features into one of the smiles that he seemed to give only to her. Her chest ached as she realized what she was putting him through, but there was nothing she could do about it. She needed his support tonight more than she'd ever needed anyone's.

"Are we done here, Rick?" she asked.

"Everything checks out fine. We'll be able to keep up with you while you make contact. Once you reach a stable spot and are no longer on the move, we'll form a perimeter and close in."

Mattie glanced at the clock; it was almost time for Cole to leave with Brody to go to their surveillance point. She pushed her chair back and stood, making Robo jump up to stand beside her. He was sticking to her like a hummingbird to a feeder, as if he possessed a sixth sense that told him something out of the ordinary was going down. "Then I'll take a break now and say good-bye to Cole."

Mattie took Cole back to the interrogation room, the only space where they could meet in private. Robo squeezed in behind them and plopped down on his cushion, watching Mattie with his intelligent brown eyes. She stepped into Cole's embrace and hugged him with a fierce grip that had nothing to do with passion and everything to do with love and a deep need for reassurance. She wished she could hold him tightly forever and never let go. Thinking about what she would do in a few hours made her weak with terror.

He returned her grip, and they stood holding each other for a long moment. Finally, she pulled away.

"I need to show you how to put on Robo's vest," she said, picking up the Kevlar vest that she'd carried in from her unit earlier. "Go ahead and put it on him shortly before eight o'clock, in case you need to respond quickly. He can wear it for several hours, but when you take it off, he likes to have his fur ruffled up where it's been matted down."

She put on the vest, fastening the buckles and then taking it off so she could tousle Robo's fur. "And make sure he has plenty of water available. If you take him out to track, be sure and give him water before you start."

"I will," Cole said softly, making her look at him. He wore a thin smile.

"I know you know all this," she said with a grimace. "I can't help myself. I just need to go over it again."

"We've practiced. I can handle him if I need to, Mattie. Don't worry. He knows me."

It was true that she and her dog had spent many an evening at Cole's house with him and the kids, and Robo was as comfortable and bonded with Cole as he could be, considering Cole wasn't his handler.

Mattie tried to shake off her nerves. All she could do was voice what she hoped for. "Everything's going to be all right. This will all be over soon."

"That's right." Cole met her gaze, his face raw with fear, his eyes strained and reddened. "Now kiss us both so we can leave, and we'll see you again soon."

After their kiss, he turned away, as if trying to hide tears that threatened to surface. Mattie sank down on the bed. Robo came up to her and placed his head on her knee. She scooted to the edge of the mattress and slid to the floor, putting her arms around his neck and kissing his cheek. He licked her face while she clipped on his leash. "Go with Cole," she said, holding back tears of her own as she handed Cole the leash.

"I'll take good care of him," Cole said, taking the end of the leash. He opened the door and stepped into the hallway. "Robo, come."

Robo threw her a confused glance as he followed Cole out the door. She pulled herself back up to perch on the edge of the bed. "I know you will," she whispered, feeling alone and vulnerable without the presence of her partner and Cole.

★   ★   ★

When it was time to leave the station, it was clear and dark outside, and the moon had topped the eastern horizon. Stella and the sheriff had already left to take their positions below her drop-off point. Dressed in her warm Carhartt coat, Mattie left the interrogation room for the final time. Hitch came from the staff office and stopped her in the hallway.

He offered a handshake, a frown of concern between his eyebrows. "I wanted to wish you luck tonight before you leave, although you won't need it. You're well prepared, and you're a solid officer. I wish I was going to be up there to back you."

Mattie returned his firm grip. Hitch would be the only officer left at the station tonight. Everyone else would be located somewhere on the mountainsides surrounding Eureka. "I appreciate that you're here keeping watch over Rainbow and

Sam. Take care of them, okay? That gave me a scare last night when those dirtbags attacked her."

"Me too. I'll be here, although I think all the action will be in the high country tonight. Stay alert. Be strong."

She gave him a short nod and turned to go into the lobby, feeling very strange without Robo trotting ahead of her. Rainbow stood and came from behind the desk to throw her arms around Mattie. "Oh, I don't want you to go," she whispered.

Mattie tried to hide her own fear as she hugged Rainbow and spoke quietly. "It's going to be okay. You'll see."

Her friend gave her a fierce squeeze and then backed away, blinking back tears. "I'll see you soon, then. Be careful."

"Always." Mattie gave Sam a casual salute, which he returned, and left the safety of the station to go to Stella's car in the parking lot. A new silver RAV4, it would serve as a civilian vehicle, which she would leave parked on the road as instructed. They'd all decided it best to leave her unit at the station to avoid it being commandeered by the riffraff they were dealing with.

The snug SUV started right up, and Mattie tried to avoid thinking as she pulled out of the parking lot. Rainbow stood at the glass door inside the station, and they gave each other one last wave.

The streets of Timber Creek were fairly empty even this early in the evening, and there was no traffic on the highway. Moonlight cast shadowy images across the landscape as she drove west. The winter-dormant grasses in the meadows stretched out on both sides of the road, giving way to foothills with rock formations and evergreen trees beyond the ranches she drove past.

This was the familiar territory where she'd grown up; the people who lived in the ranch houses she passed were her people. She turned her thoughts away from wondering if this would be her last time to travel this road.

Everything she believed about keeping her community safe and exacting justice on those who would threaten others, she'd learned while serving in the sheriff's department of this county. And tonight . . . well, she needed to believe that tonight was just one more step in her career.

She pumped herself up with positive thoughts about going undercover with a team of disciplined and trained officers to support her. She drove steadily into the night, seeing ahead only as far as the headlights would allow. She decided it was symbolic of the mission that lay ahead—she could only see ahead one step at a time. The rest of it would play out and reveal itself very soon.

The compact SUV made its way up the gravel road that led to Eureka with no difficulty, the steering and brakes responding well as it hugged the hairpin turns that looped back and forth up the mountain. She passed Eureka about ten minutes before eight.

As she approached the mile marker above the town that would be her insertion point, she realized her breath was coming in shallow puffs. She focused on yoga breathing, deepening her inhalation and slowing the rate of her exhale. There was a narrow pull-off at the marker. She steered the car into it and parked. Her headlights illuminated an envelope fastened just below the mileage sign.

"What the . . ." Mattie set the brake and exited her car. She slipped on her insulated gloves and plucked the envelope off the post. Back inside the vehicle, she opened it and read the note she found inside.

My dear Mattie,

You're doing great! You've come this far, but you need to go just a bit farther—two more miles. Turn right onto the jeep trail and drive one hundred yards. Leave your vehicle there. Walk one hundred yards into the woods toward the east. Remember to cooperate. Keep your hands up where we can see them.

As always,

A friend of your father's

So that's how they wanted to play—it was still a game. She wasn't concerned about the change in plan. She and the team had discussed how this could happen. In fact, the new insertion point was positioned two miles closer to where Brody and Cole were located. Rick would track her movement as she drew near and let them know.

Fueled by aggravation at the game playing, Mattie no longer felt fear. She was eager and determined to get this ball rolling. Rick had placed a tracker on her car as well, so he would know she was on the move and still inside her vehicle. She pulled back into the narrow dirt road, making note of the mileage on her car while also looking for the mile markers.

Two miles farther uphill, she began searching for the entrance into the jeep trail and spotted it just ahead in the glow from the headlights. She slowed and eased down into the barrow ditch, the RAV4 rocking side to side as she slowly maneuvered onto the two-track jeep trail. The car bumped down the rutted track until she reached a distance of about one hundred yards. She found a grassy spot where she could pull over, park, and kill the engine.

Relieved that there was no apparent note fixed to a tree or boulder, she drew a deep breath and prepared to exit the car. She tucked the key under the passenger seat and took a final swig from her water bottle. After stepping outside the car, she closed the door and raised her hands to the level of her head.

The moon showed her which direction was east. Keeping her hands raised, she slowly walked to the edge of the tree line and looked into the shadows cast by the beetle-killed pine in this part of the forest. They were thick in here, so there wasn't as much light as she'd thought there would be. She stepped carefully past the first skeletal pines onto the dense mat of dropped needles, twigs, and branches. There was no need to try to muffle her footsteps—she wanted to be heard and seen as she approached.

Each step led her deeper into the darkness until she was unable to see her footing. Feeling her way along, she continued for what she thought was about thirty yards. How would she be able to traverse another seventy yards in the dark?

Just as the thought crossed her mind, they came out of nowhere from behind. One snatched her wrists and twisted her arms behind her back, making her flinch with pain. The other crammed a cloth hood over her head.

"I'll cooperate," she said, hoping to get the guy behind her to ease up on her arms. "No need to get rough."

In silence, they bound her wrists with what felt like a zip tie as it cut into her flesh. One of them turned her, giving her a slight push from behind to get her to move. She took a tentative step forward, unable to see a thing.

"I'll walk, but I can't see. We'll have to go slow."

Still not uttering a word, one of them picked her up and slung her over his shoulder. He was a big guy. The contact knocked the breath out of her, and she tried to refill her lungs as he carried her off.

TWENTY-SEVEN

Cole and Brody sat in Frank Sullivan's Jeep on a logging trail about four miles north of the mile marker originally thought to be Mattie's drop-off point. It was 8:40, and Rick had notified them all that Mattie had driven her car farther up the road two miles. Cole guessed he was now only two miles away from her position.

He wished he were there beside her.

Robo ranged around the back seat, going from side to side to look out the windows. Though he'd been somewhat content to go with Cole and Brody, as soon as Cole dressed him in his Kevlar vest, he'd become restless. Cole figured Robo was as eager as *he* was to get out of the confines of this vehicle.

The radio crackled to life, followed by Rick's voice. "Alpha Team, this is Bravo One. She's out of the car. Heading east into the trees. She's not on the main road." He rattled off her GPS coordinates.

Brody pressed on the mic. "Bravo One, this is Alpha Two. There's a jeep trail two miles north of the original mile marker."

"Copy. Hold your position."

They waited in silence, and Cole had to remind himself to take a breath. Robo moved forward, looming over the console to stare through the windshield, ears pricked. There was nothing to be seen out there except trees decimated by beetles, left standing stark and gray in the moonlight.

It seemed like forever before Rick's next transmission came, although the time on Cole's cell phone showed only ten minutes had passed.

"Alpha Team, this is Bravo One. She's headed back toward the car. She must've got another note and they're leading her on a goose chase. Stand by."

"Copy," Brody replied.

Cole squirmed in his seat. Ten minutes and another eternity later, Rick came back on the air. "She's on the move without her car. Looks like she's moving fast in another vehicle and they've got her. She's back on the main road headed south toward Eureka. Hold your positions."

"Copy," Brody replied.

This time McCoy chimed in as well. "Copy that."

Stella and McCoy were posted below Shadow Ridge Campground, so Mattie would now be sandwiched between them and where Cole and Brody waited. Rick was located south of Mattie as well, between Shadow Ridge and Eureka.

Cole put an arm around Robo and stroked the fur at the front of his neck. If there'd ever before been a time when Cole had felt this jumpy, he couldn't remember it. They held their position and waited.

★   ★   ★

Although it was hard to tell with the hood over her head, it felt like Mattie was moving in the direction from which she'd come. The guy carried her slung over his shoulder for quite a ways while she fought to regain her breath. It didn't help having her hands tied behind her back, but it was way too early in the game to try to break free. She could hear the other guy tromping behind her through the deadfall beneath the trees. With the hood over her head, she couldn't see a thing, but her other senses remained sharp.

Hanging upside down made her think of Rainbow and how frightened she must have been when she received the same treatment. Maybe it was because Rainbow had survived it, but Mattie didn't feel afraid. She just felt disgusted with these two goons who would manhandle her this way.

When she felt she'd been carried farther than the distance she'd traveled from her car, she actually started to feel slight admiration for the big guy's stamina. Though she wasn't tall, she didn't consider herself a lightweight either. Not like Rainbow. Mattie had worked to build muscle on her frame, and she was strong for her size. She'd have to remember that this guy was even stronger when she had a chance to take him on.

She heard a car door open, and the man deposited her inside. He bounced her against the seat unceremoniously, and she fought to right herself to keep from falling sideways. The tie bit into her wrists as she leaned back against her arms.

She felt someone climb onto the bench seat beside her and decided she must be in the rear of the vehicle. Two doors shut, one to her left, one ahead and to her left. She determined she was in the back seat on the passenger side.

The engine fired and they started to move, jostling her side to side. "Seat belt," she said.

Evidently amused by her request, the guy sitting beside her snorted.

"It'll be easier on both of us if you just belt me in."

"Shut up," he said, his voice deep and gruff.

Mattie thought he might be trying to disguise it, but she was glad she'd made him say something. Crazy as it might seem, she felt a small sense of accomplishment for making the big lummox speak. Nevertheless, she decided not to prod the bear any further. Even though her wrists had taken a beating, at least the rest of her body had escaped that kind of treatment so far. And she was grateful they hadn't put a gag in her mouth like they'd done to Rainbow.

They made a sharp left-hand turn, and the road smoothed out a bit. She wondered if they'd driven back to the main road; a left turn meant they were headed back toward Eureka. After a few minutes the car stopped.

Both doors to the left opened and closed. A hatch in back opened. What were they up to now?

Her door opened and the guy grabbed her by the arm, wrenching it sideways as he dragged her out of the car. She stumbled to her feet.

"Hey," she said, letting her anger show. "You don't have to get rough. I want to go with you, remember? Just tell me what to do, and I'll do it." She wanted to add *you dumb shit*, but again she decided not to prod the guy, even though the term was probably accurate.

She stood still for a few seconds until she heard a familiar beep. A wand. She held her breath, but she knew instantly that they'd found the tracker in her shirt.

One of them cut the tie that bound her wrists. Her hands tingled as blood flowed back into them. She rubbed her sore wrists.

"Take off your coat." The same gruff voice.

Mattie complied, letting her coat drop to the ground. He raised her arms and made her stand with them outstretched. Another beep.

She felt a cold circle of steel press against her neck, and she knew it was a gun.

"Take off your clothes."

"Why?"

"You know why." He jabbed the gun harder against her throat. "I gotta nine-millimeter here to remind you to cooperate."

"It's freezing out here, man. I can't take off my clothes. You can take the undershirt. That's where the tracker is."

"I've got somethin' you can wear."

So they'd planned for this possibility. Organized. Calculating. She and the team had guessed as much from the previous kidnappings, and this confirmed it.

"Strip." He jammed the gun up against the corner of her jaw, making pain shoot into it.

"Okay, okay. You don't need to get testy." Mattie took off both her warm flannel shirt and the T-shirt beneath and dropped them on the ground. The frigid air made her shiver, and she crossed her arms over her chest. She heard the wand beep as they evidently passed it over her pile of clothing.

"Pants and shoes too."

"You've got a wand. You know there's nothing in my pants and shoes."

"Take 'em off."

Wanting to get it over with, Mattie did as she was told. Standing in only her underwear, her feet against the frozen ground, made her feel vulnerable and angry. She'd just lost her switchblade, but she felt confident that Rick's plan would work.

The guy shoved a piece of clothing into her hands. "It's a coverall. Put it on."

By touch alone, Mattie figured out quickly how to put on the clothing. It was roomy and long sleeved, not as warm as the clothes she'd given up but not as bad as it could have been.

"Get back in the car."

"My boots."

"No can do, girl." He placed a pair of tennis shoes in her hands. "Use these."

Mattie felt her way to the seat of the car and climbed in, taking the shoes with her. Once inside, she put them on, noticing they were close enough to her size that the fit wasn't too bad. She tied them quickly, found the ends of her seat belt by touch alone, and buckled herself in. She placed her hands in her lap and sat there quietly, leaving her hood in place.

She hoped they would leave her hands unbound, but no such luck. One guy zipped her wrists together again, this time in front and not so tightly.

The twosome returned to their seats, and the car started back up. The driver executed what felt like a three-point turn, and she thought they headed back uphill toward Cole and Brody.

Without her warm coat, the cold air sapped her body heat, making her shiver. She fought the feeling of claustrophobia the hood was giving her.

★　★　★

Waiting for Rick's next transmission, Cole continuously tapped his knee with his fingers. "Where do you think they're headed? Do you think they'll head downhill to the highway?"

"Hard to tell. Just wait it out," Brody replied.

In the dim moonlight, Cole could see Brody's jaw muscle bulge, a sign that he wasn't as calm and patient as he was trying to let on.

Even though he'd been waiting for it with bated breath, static erupting from the radio made Cole jump. Rick's voice came across the airwaves. "Alpha Team, this is Bravo One. She's stopped. They're about a mile south of where they started. Still on the main road. Hold your positions."

There was silence for ten minutes while Cole and Brody waited. Then: "Alpha Team. The tracker is still in the same spot. Hold on for another ten minutes."

The next ten minutes seemed never ending. Finally: "Alpha Team. Still in the same place. Alpha Two, you're the closest. Move down and check it out. Drive by if you spot a vehicle." He gave them the GPS coordinates.

"Copy," Brody said into the mic.

Thank God, Cole thought. *At least now we can move.*

Cole tapped the coordinates into his GPS while Brody fired the engine and followed the two-track logging trail back to the main road. After a left-hand turn they were off, the only vehicle on the gravel road. "Three miles ahead," Cole said.

They met no oncoming traffic on their way downhill. Hunters and campers were apparently buttoned up for the night.

Brody gestured off to the left as they passed a rarely used jeep trail. "That's the trail I think she went up before. We'll probably find Stella's car up that way."

Cole nodded, glancing up the jeep trail but unable to see anything but forest. He focused back on the road and their general surroundings, keeping watch for anything out of the ordinary.

Brody slowed as he approached the last turn. "We're close to the mile marker in the note. Watch the trees on your side."

What if this whole thing was a farce and these thugs had already killed Mattie and left her on the side of the road? Cole pushed the thought from his mind and kept his eyes glued to the ditch and trees. As they approached the mile marker, he saw something at the edge of the headlights' glow. "There!" He pointed ahead. "There's something in the ditch."

Brody pulled up, his headlights giving detail to the lump beside the road. Cole released a pent-up breath when he saw it wasn't a body.

"Stay in the vehicle. It could be a trap. I'll check it out," Brody said.

"You stay; you're behind the wheel," Cole said, opening his door.

Brody shut off the headlights. Ducking low, they both approached. Brody directed his flashlight and illuminated a pile of Mattie's clothes. Her coat and boots were lying beside them.

TWENTY-EIGHT

Mattie was grateful for her seat belt because it kept her from sliding into the goon sitting beside her. Still hooded and with her hands tied, there was no way she could prepare for the bumps and dips in the road. Right now, they were tipped at a forty-five-degree angle, her side of the vehicle up. Rocks and potholes made the ride even worse; sometimes it felt like the very ground beneath their tires had dropped out from under them. A Tilt-A-Whirl ride from hell.

Although her lack of ability to see left her somewhat disoriented, she figured they had taken her back to the jeep trail where she'd left Stella's car. Once they left the main road, the two-track had become harder and harder to navigate, slowing their speed to a crawl.

The growl from the engine and the cold seeping into the vehicle told her she must be in some type of off-road vehicle. Probably a heavy-duty Jeep with a canvas top—something like that.

They must be counting on the secrecy of this particular trail into the wilderness, but *she* counted on Brody and Cole knowing all about it. Those two men had grown up in Timber Creek, and they had hunted, fished, and otherwise combed this area of the forest their entire lives. She would bet they were figuring out where she was headed.

"Geez," she said as their vehicle bounced down to a short stretch of level road, only to heave back up at a severe angle on the other side. "This is the worst road I've ever been on. Where does it lead?"

"Shut up," the guy next to her said.

He's a man of few words. Wherever they were headed, as long as her mother and sister were at the end of the trail, that was all that mattered to her. That was her goal, and she wouldn't make waves with these two until she connected with her family. She ignored the coldness inside the vehicle and the pain in her wrists and hung on for the wild ride.

★ ★ ★

Parked at the side of the road, Brody sent a transmission to Rick and the others that they'd found Mattie's clothes and the main tracker they'd been following. Though Brody sounded all business, Cole was feeling anything but. The temperature was below freezing. Had Mattie's captors provided her with other warm clothing? Was she out in the elements without protection? Had they molested her? Was she all right? Questions without answers bombarded his brain.

And the zip ties left in the pile of clothes had traces of blood on them. He wished he could get his hands on the guys who had taken her. He hoped he would have his turn with them soon.

Rick responded to Brody's transmission. "This is Bravo One. The backup tracker is still online. She's on the jeep trail you passed a mile north. What's down that road?"

Straightening his spine against a wave of relief that almost left him limp, Cole rummaged in the console for a head lamp and a topographical map he'd placed in there earlier. Putting the lamp's strap around his head, he focused the light on the map, looking to see if the trail was even marked. He'd been on it before, although he hadn't ever followed it to its end. "Hardy Pass," he said to Brody.

The response Brody spoke into his mic let Cole know he was familiar with the trail too. "Bravo One, that's a jeep trail over Hardy Pass. It's rugged, even for a four-wheel drive."

"Where does it lead?" Rick asked.

Brody replied, "Uphill, but once they hit tree line, it will be packed with snow."

The pass was an ancient trail, first used by Ute natives who lived in this country before the white man took over, then used by miners on horseback. In modern day, it had been widened enough to allow all-terrain vehicles to cross over, but the higher in elevation it climbed, the more treacherous it became, so it was rarely used and couldn't be traversed with an average four-wheel-drive vehicle.

And Brody was right—during this time of year, these high mountain trails were never maintained, and they became choked with snow early in the winter season. No one would be able to get through until spring. They had discussed the possibility of these criminals using snowmobiles to escape capture by law enforcement, and that seemed to still be a viable option.

McCoy's voice came through the speaker. "This is Alpha One. We can't get the horse trailer very far down that road. We'll have to unload close to the trailhead and send riders up."

There was a pause; Rick was evidently thinking things over. The danger in that plan was that the offenders might take Mattie in a whole new direction or even come back toward them, ruining law enforcement's ability to take them by surprise once Mattie was reunited with her mother and sister.

Cole pointed to a spot on the map to show Brody. "Right about here is an abandoned shack and another one close by. I think they're committed to this trail, and one of those shacks could be where they're headed. I haven't been up there this season, but I bet the road is still accessible that far up."

"I know the two old huts you're talking about. There's another trail even deeper into the woods to the north that they might use to try to escape."

Brody summed up their conversation and guesswork in another radio transmission to Rick and McCoy.

Rick came back over the speaker. "How long will it take horseback riders to reach one of these shacks?"

Cole responded. "Not a lot longer than a Jeep. That trail is steep and rough—slow going."

Brody repeated Cole's reply into the mic and then added a thought of his own. "The Jeep we're in is the only one that's going to make it up that trail. We're going to have to all go in one vehicle."

"I'll guide the horseback riders," Cole murmured to Brody.

Rick's reply came through the speaker. "Alpha One, notify the cavalry. We'll all meet at the base of that jeep trail."

"Copy," McCoy replied.

"Copy that," Brody said, firing his engine and making a three-point turn to head back uphill.

Robo nuzzled the bag that Brody had placed Mattie's discarded clothing in, and Cole reached into the back to stop him with a quiet command. He stroked the satiny hair between the dog's ears when he obeyed and went back to looking out the front windshield. Cole had the sense that somehow this dog knew they were going to go search for his partner.

Cole studied the map, figuring they had about four miles to go deep into the wilderness. They were placing their entire bankroll on this one bet—and they'd better be right. All he needed was to get within Mattie's vicinity, and he and Robo would do the rest.

★ ★ ★

The vehicle Mattie rode in bucked and rocked, creeping up a steep trail that obviously wasn't made for motor vehicle travel. She shivered, hunched in the back seat, trying to keep her spine from rattling apart. Her hands had gone past aching to feeling like numb lumps of ice. The clothing they'd given her didn't offer warmth or protection at all. She'd even begun to feel grateful for the hood. At least it acted like a hat and contributed a bit toward keeping her body heat from escaping via the top of her head.

She had a feeling that these two guys were merely errand boys and the real brains of the operation awaited her at the end of the trail. She decided she had to speak up. "Hey," she said, projecting her voice in hopes of reaching the driver, since the guy beside her had proven unhelpful. She allowed her teeth to chatter. "I'm about to freeze back here, and hypothermia is setting in. If you plan to deliver me to your boss alive, I need a blanket or a coat or something. What do you have?"

"Put the blanket over her," the driver growled. "What are you trying to do?"

The guy beside her uttered an expletive, but after a short pause she heard the crackle of a foil space blanket being unfurled. He placed it over her, roughly tucking in the sides at her shoulders.

"Thank you," she told him while thinking some pretty dark thoughts about what she wished she could do to the guy. Evidently he'd been supposed to take better care of her.

Mattie lost all track of time as the painful ride went on. There was no way she could keep track of the direction they were headed. All she could tell was that it was uphill and across some wild country.

Finally, after what felt like hours, the vehicle stopped. The driver shut off the engine, and she heard him ratchet on the parking brake. The door in front opened as the driver said, "Carry her."

"If you'll take this hood off, I can walk," she said, hoping to regain some level of independence.

Without replying, the guy beside her opened his door. She felt him get off the seat they shared and then heard him slam the door shut. When her door opened, he tugged off her blanket, and the frigid air took her breath away. He grabbed her by the arm, wrenching her shoulder when the seat belt held her still. The tie cut into her wrists.

"My seat belt," she shouted at the guy.

He unbuckled her and tried again, this time dragging her from her seat. Having her wrists bound in front didn't keep him from putting her over his shoulder facedown. She suppressed a groan as pain shot through her arms and blood drained to her head.

He carried her a short distance over uneven terrain before stepping up onto what sounded like a wooden platform. A door opened, he carried her across an indoor space, and she heard another door open. He deposited her on the floor and she stumbled, trying to get her feet under her.

She heard the crackle of the space blanket as it fell beside her. The door closed. Silence. She stood still for a moment working to get her bearings. Her hands were still tied, and she still wore the hood. Though she felt stable flooring beneath her tennis shoes telling her she was inside a shelter of some kind, frigid air bombarded her from all sides.

Not wanting to make a move that could be misinterpreted as being uncooperative, Mattie remained still and quiet, awaiting instruction. But when none came, she decided to venture a question. "Is anyone here?"

"Mattie?"

The voice was weak and hoarse, but it was unmistakably Julia's! Mattie reached up and fumbled with the hood that covered her face. Her numb fingers could barely manage to grasp the fabric as she eased the hood off her head without dislodging the military tracker that Rainbow had braided into her hair. She didn't trust that the two men were finished transporting them yet.

Mattie blinked. The room was pitch-black. No windows, no light coming in from under the doorway. She spoke softly. "Julia?"

"I'm here." Though still spoken near a whisper, more energy behind the words told Mattie that her sister knew who she was. "Against the wall. Be careful. We're on the floor."

Without the hood, a stench that could only be from human body fluids assaulted her nose. "Is Mom here?"

"Yes. But she hasn't responded to me for a while."

As Julia spoke, Mattie edged her way across the floor toward the sound of her sister's voice. "Is she alive?"

"I think so. Yes, she's still breathing, but she's so cold."

"So you're together? You can touch her?"

"Yes. Here . . . here we are."

Mattie's toe struck the edge of a pliable barrier. She bent to feel what it was, but her fingers were too numb for her to tell. Her sister's arm knocked against hers as she leaned forward, and a zing of pain ran up to Mattie's shoulders as Julia grabbed her hands. Mattie gasped before she could stop herself.

"Oh," Julia said under her breath, "your hands are tied."

Mattie sank to her knees onto what she'd determined was a thin mattress. Julia sobbed and ran her hand gently up Mattie's arm to touch her cheek. "I . . . I'm so sorry. So sorry," she said. "I keep going over and over it in my head. I . . . I should've listened to you."

"Don't worry about that now." Mattie edged forward on her knees until she could grasp Julia's hand between her own. She had to find a way out of this zip tie. "What is this, a mattress?"

"Right. Mom's right here beside me. She's been so sick. Me too, really, but she's much worse."

"Did you drink or eat anything?"

"I drank an energy drink they gave me. I resisted as long as I could, but I was so thirsty. I thought it might be okay, since it was in a bottle, but it made me throw up."

Energy drinks or sweetened drinks were often used to disguise the taste of poison. Mattie remained kneeling, holding Julia's hand in both of hers. "Throwing it up was probably a good thing. I'm sure it was poisoned. Can you help me get this tie off my hands?"

Mattie released Julia's hand and squeezed hers together until she felt her sister's fingers at her wrists. "Go ahead and try to pull it off while I try to wiggle my hand through. It's not as tight as the first one they put on me."

The two of them pulled and tugged while Mattie tried to narrow her hand as much as possible to slide it through. The tie bit deep into her skin, but she wasn't willing to give up. Her wrist grew warm and slick.

"Mattie, you're bleeding." Julia stopped pulling at the tie.

"Don't stop now. I think I can wiggle my hand through if it's slippery." Mattie gritted her teeth against the pain as they continued to work together. She felt the tie cross the meaty part of her palm, and her hand slipped free. A wave of euphoria washed through her. "There! We did it."

She dropped the tie onto the floor and hugged her sister as sensation flowed back into her hands, creating excruciating stabs of pain. "Where's Mom?"

"Right here." Julia guided Mattie past her toward her other side. They exchanged kneeling positions on the mattress, and Mattie tried to assess her mother's condition by touch alone, but pins and needles prickled her upper extremities.

After her sense of touch had been restored a bit, she was able to tell that her mother was covered with a thin blanket. Ramona was wearing a coat, but her face above the collar was cold and dry, and her hair felt brittle and broken. Spasmodic shivers ran through her body at Mattie's touch. "She's probably been poisoned with selenium, and she's now dehydrated."

"I told her we couldn't drink the water they gave us."

"You were able to talk to her when you first arrived?"

"Yes, she was awake and recognized me. I told her about the poison. She asked about Juan, but I just couldn't tell her, Mattie." Julia began to sob.

"That's okay. It's better that way. Did she know who took her?"

"She said it was a woman that was there the night Dad was killed. She didn't know her name. She just kept saying she knew this woman would come get her someday."

This confirmed Mattie's theory. She wished her mother had told her this much before, although what could she have done about it then? Probably nothing. "Did you see who took you?"

"Two big gorilla guys, but they wore ski masks on their faces. They had a van they put me in, and then they transferred me to the trunk of a car. I was in there for a long time. It felt like a fast, smooth ride, so I assumed we were on a highway. Then they transferred me again into what felt like a Jeep—and at that point they passed me off to two other guys. There was a hood over my head, so I couldn't see anyone, but I could tell the guys changed. It was very cold by then, so I think we had reached Colorado. The last part of the ride was horrible— rough, and they bounced me all over the place. Mom was already here when they dumped me off."

"Yeah, the road up here felt like it was barely even a jeep trail. Did they ever say anything to you to explain?"

"No one spoke to me at all. They just manhandled me to get me to where they wanted me."

It felt good to hear the spunk in Julia's voice. Mattie could tell she was also mad about the way she'd been treated. "The men who brought me here didn't talk much either. I wonder if it was the same two guys. The one who carried me was tall and big. I couldn't tell anything about the driver."

"Same here, but I agree the one was tall and big. Both of the guys in San Diego were huge. These seemed a bit smaller, but still large."

Mattie stroked her mother's hair back from her face and murmured her name, hoping to get a response of some kind. Her mother moaned and moved her legs. Even though that was the only acknowledgment Mattie could elicit, she was glad to see that her mother's level of unconsciousness wasn't that deep. She wished she had some uncontaminated water she could give her to help wash the poison out of her system.

"How did they get you, Mattie?"

"Actually, they invited me to join you and Mom. I couldn't resist."

Julia uttered a low moan. "Oh no . . . Mattie, you shouldn't have done that. You should've stayed safe."

"I want to see if I can negotiate your release." She needed to be careful about what she said in case this place was bugged. She couldn't tell her sister that even as they spoke, law enforcement officers were surrounding this place. "Wait. I think the guy dropped a space blanket into the room beside me when we came in. Let me see if I can find it."

"Be careful. There's a bucket that we had to use nearby. It's nasty."

"Which direction?"

Julia grasped her sister's hand and indicated off to the left of where Mattie knelt. Mattie backed off the mattress, stood, and then carefully turned to go in the direction she thought she'd come from. Bending to search the floor by feel as she edged forward, she inched along until she found the space blanket. After picking it up, she continued forward until she came to a wall. Feeling her way in the darkness, she discovered the cracks of a doorway with a solid door built of rough-cut lumber. No doorknob. No hinges on this side.

Mattie pushed at the door with her shoulder to see if she could open it, but it wouldn't budge. Using the tips of her fingers, she tested whether it would open toward her, although the lack of hinges on this side made her believe it would not. She didn't spend much effort on the door when she could tell it was solid. Besides, she couldn't leave her mother, and Julia seemed in no condition to make a run for it either, so she would just have to bide her time and wait.

Mattie quickly moved back and forth against the perimeter to get an idea of the room's size. Probably about ten feet. If she estimated right, the room was about ten feet deep as well. Getting her bearings at the door, she carried the space blanket back toward the mattress.

"Found it," she told Julia when she returned to the mattress. "While we wait for these guys to come back, let's warm up. Do you think there's room for three of us here?"

"We can make it work."

Mattie found a spot on the far side of her mother where she could fit. She spread the space blanket over all three of them and huddled under it. For a brief second she feared the tracker might not have worked, but she banished the thought and hoped her teammates would be able to zero in on her position. If not . . . it would all be up to her.

TWENTY-NINE

Moonlight filtered through the trees, giving Cole a degree of visibility on the rocky trail. It was worse than rugged, at times clinging to the mountainside with a sheer drop of a hundred feet or more on the open side.

He led the way on Mountaineer, his roan quarter horse built stout and low to the ground. He trusted Mountaineer to stick to a trail and take him anywhere, even in semidarkness. Brody, Rick, and Sheriff McCoy were on horseback in a string behind Cole, and other reinforcements were following behind in Frank Sullivan's Jeep.

"We'd better stop soon." Rick spoke quietly in the stillness of the night. "We're getting close enough that we need to leave the Jeep. We'll have to go on by foot."

Cole turned to reply over his shoulder. "We'll stop as soon as we come to a wider spot in the road."

He scanned the way ahead, using the light of the moon to search for a suitable place to pull over.

★　★　★

Huddling under the space blanket did a lot to restore everyone's body heat. Mattie felt better, and even Ramona had stopped shivering. After at least an hour of waiting, Mattie heard footsteps approach the other side of the door. She eased out from under the blanket, tucking it in tightly against her mother.

"Stay here with Mom," she whispered to Julia, steeling herself for the upcoming confrontation.

As Mattie positioned herself at the front of the mattress, the door opened, and light spilled across the threshold. Someone aimed a spotlight directly at her face, and its light blinded her. She raised her hand to shield her eyes. The bright beam lowered to sweep over her mother and sister, and she could make out the shapes of four figures behind the flashlight.

"Isn't this cozy?" The voice was definitely female and sounded familiar, but Mattie couldn't quite place it, though she thought she could eliminate Josie Baker. She blinked, trying to help her eyes adjust to the light. Who were these people in the shadows?

"Come with me," the woman said, turning to go back through the door and taking her flashlight with her.

One of the others followed the woman while two stayed, both turning on flashlights to focus on Mattie. "Don't try anything," one of them warned. She recognized the voice of the driver, while at the same time she saw light glint off the barrel of a gun.

"I won't," Mattie said, lifting her hands to keep them in sight and away from her body. If they noticed she'd removed the zip tie from her wrists, they apparently didn't care. She passed the two guards and followed the woman into the other room. "I want to talk things over as much as she does."

The room was larger than the one she'd been in but not by much. There was a rough plank floor, log walls, and boards where windows once had been. She was relieved to see a small rock fireplace in one corner, its hearth filled with ash and partially burned logs but no fire. This space was just as cold as the one she'd left. Several foldable canvas camp chairs sat in the middle of the room, but there was no other furniture present. A battery-powered lantern sat on the floor, casting enough light that she could see the two who'd entered ahead of her clearly.

Didi and Milo Carr. As usual, his white teeth gleamed behind a wolfish smile. They were both dressed in warm camouflage gear, and Didi's long braid came from beneath her stocking cap to run down the front of her coat. Mattie suppressed a shiver, her broadcloth coverall and tennis shoes doing little to protect her from the frigid temperature.

"I hear you planted a tracker in your clothing and had to change," Didi said. "That wasn't very trustworthy of you. Kind of got us off on the wrong foot."

Mattie splayed her hands in front of her in an open gesture. "I hope you don't blame me for trying. It made my colleagues feel better about me coming to meet you. If it were up to me, I would've left it at home."

Didi gave her a skeptical smile as she gestured toward a chair. "Have a seat."

Mattie sat, hugging her crossed arms close to try to keep from shivering. It was a losing battle, and she gritted her teeth to keep them from chattering. Didi sat in a chair across from her, apparently taking her in while Milo sat in the other chair.

"Go get her a coat from my stuff," Didi said to one of the men behind Mattie before refocusing her attention on her. "Gotta keep you alive for the show."

When the guy came from behind to head for the door, Mattie recognized him as one of the Gaffey brothers—the shorter one named Rope. She should have known. It would have taken at least two people with muscles to carry Juan into the forest and tie him to a tree. It made sense that this party of four could have carried off the crimes committed here in Colorado. There must be others in California who had pulled off kidnapping Julia.

"I appreciate your kindness," she told Didi, actually meaning it. "It is way too cold for this outfit."

Didi tipped her head toward the other room. "Those two are in pretty bad shape, your mother worse than your sister."

"Selenium poisoning will do that to a person. I need some bottled water if I'm going to be able to keep them alive. With unbroken seals, of course."

Didi gave her a sarcastic grin. "I'll have someone run out to the nearest corner store to get it."

Milo snorted.

"And some heat would help too," Mattie said, keeping a conversational tone. "It looks like that fireplace in the corner works. You could move us in here, you know. We're not going anywhere." She thumbed a gesture over her shoulder. "Maybe Kent back there could build us a fire."

"You're getting way ahead of yourself."

Rope came back in and tossed her the coat from a distance of about six feet, apparently giving her a wide berth. They obviously believed they should approach her with caution, so she needed to work to establish some level of trust or at least strengthen their belief that she was on board.

Her cop's mind warned her that there could be something dangerous sprinkled inside the coat or its sleeves, like fentanyl powder or some other type of contact opioid, but her need for heat overrode the warning. This woman had a plan, and it seemed to involve keeping Mattie alive for a while. Mattie glanced at the inside lining, and seeing nothing that raised a red flag, she shrugged on the coat, immediately welcoming its warmth.

"Thank you again," she said to Didi, bowing her head slightly. "If I may ask, what's your purpose in bringing us all together here?"

"So polite, Mattie Wray. Your mother trained you well."

"I remember very little about my mother."

"Huh." Skepticism dripped from the syllable. "I believe you were school age when you parted ways. What . . . about six? That's pretty old to not remember."

Mattie shrugged. "There were extenuating circumstances that created the memory block."

"That's interesting. What would those be?"

It felt like they were having a getting-to-know-you chat. Mattie zipped up the coat, shoved her hands in its pockets, and leaned back in the camp chair, assuming a casual posture. She decided it would be best to lie. "It's complicated, hard to explain. Suffice it to say that Ramona and I have never been close. And I didn't even know Julia existed until a few months ago, so we're not close either."

Didi eyed her as if suspicious. "So . . . do you remember me?"

"From my childhood?" Mattie shook her head. "Not at all."

"Oh . . . that's disappointing." Didi looked anything but disappointed. She looked like a cat toying with a mouse. "You were pretty young when we met."

"And that was when?"

"I can't give you the exact date. But you see . . . I'm the one who killed your dear old dad." Didi paused, an expectant look on her face.

Grateful that she'd already guessed the connection, Mattie still felt a ripple of pain. She could only imagine her anguish if she'd heard those words unexpectedly. She knew Didi wanted to goad her into a reaction, but Mattie wasn't going to let her. She raised her eyebrows as if surprised. "In San Diego?"

"Yes, in San Diego." Didi acted a bit huffy. "You were there, but I guess you were just a little thing. Still . . . I'd think you were old enough to remember. How old were you?"

"Two."

"Doug's youngest child. You were there, watching everything with those big brown eyes. Your mother was too busy screaming to try to shield you." Didi stared at her. "Yeah, I shot him right in the gut. Gave him what he deserved."

Mattie's chest tightened. It was getting hard to remain neutral. For a moment she was speechless. She managed to squeeze out one syllable. "Why?"

"Because no one cheats destiny."

The words rang in Mattie's ears. It was the very same phrase that had awakened her during the night. *No one cheats destiny.* A scary woman shouted the words. Gunshots echoed in her mind. Blood spattered the walls. Her father crumpled to the floor. Her mother screamed.

Didi smiled, evidently reading something she wanted to see on Mattie's face. "I saw you again later in Timber Creek when you were living with my brother. You were older then."

This time Mattie couldn't conceal her shock. "Harold Cobb was your brother?"

"You bet, sweetheart. Before I married Milo, my name was Destiny Cobb." She paused for a moment as if to let that sink in. "I'm Destiny Carino now."

Thoughts chased each other through Mattie's brain. *Destiny? Destiny Cobb? No one cheats Destiny.*

"And I know all about how you and your mother sent Harry to prison." Didi let her anger show as her jaw muscles hardened and her eyes glittered with hatred. "You sent both of my brothers to prison, where they were killed."

Mattie could allow herself only seconds to process what she'd learned. "John almost killed me trying to get information about my mother that I didn't know. Something about money she'd stolen."

Destiny took on a sly look. "I told him your mother stole the money from him and Harold, when in reality I took their share. Milo and I lived off that stash for a long time."

"Both of your brothers landed in prison through acts of their own. I had nothing to do with them being killed, and Ramona had nothing to do with it either."

"You think getting them sent to prison didn't put them in harm's way? That's ridiculous."

"I was a six-year-old kid. All I knew then was that Harold was about to kill my mother."

"Well, isn't that too bad? I should have killed her myself the same night I shot Douglas."

This exchange was getting them nowhere. Mattie had regained her composure enough to know she needed to move away from the topic of the Cobb brothers and back to the night that still piqued her curiosity. "I commend you for knowing as much as you do about my family's history and admit that you know more than I do. Since Ramona and I haven't seen each other in all these years, she's never told me anything about the night that my father died. I'm curious, and you're the only witness that I know who saw what happened. Besides my mother, that is, and she's not talking."

"Ha! Clever girl." Destiny's contempt was obvious. "The only witness, huh? Try the ringleader of the whole operation. How does that make you feel?"

Mattie couldn't afford to let her emotions consume her. "It makes me even more curious. I'd like to understand why killing Douglas was necessary."

Destiny stared at her for a long moment, and Mattie feared she wouldn't talk . . . but then she did. "He made the wrong choice, that's why. Doug seemed very happy to be working with us for months, helping us move products from Mexico into the US and Canada. Guns, drugs, you name it. He acted like he was one of us, and he and I had a thing going."

Milo snorted again. So far he'd had very little to say, but Mattie wondered how much of this story he'd been a part of. Had he been present during the shooting?

"I know, darling," Destiny said, leaning forward to pat his hand. "But that was before you and I fell in love. You've been the only one in my life since then."

"Were you with Destiny that night?" Mattie asked him.

"Sure was. That night and forever after." He smiled at his wife. "But I gotta say, I don't really remember much about it."

Maybe Milo was the alleged Mexican man that the eyewitness had reported. He had a dark complexion and black hair, but Mattie guessed he was probably of Italian or Sicilian descent rather than Mexican. That was the problem with eyewitness reports; they weren't always accurate.

Mattie turned back to Destiny, wanting to keep the conversation on track. "It was you, your two brothers, and Milo who were there that night. Anyone else?"

"No, just the four of us."

"So you said that you and Doug had 'a thing going.' How serious was it?"

"Oh, it was serious, sweetheart. Deadly serious. He told me he loved me and wanted to leave his wife and kids so we could be together. And then . . . for no reason, he changed his mind." Her voice shifted to a high-pitched, mocking tone. "He said he wanted to stay with his family—the namby-pamby wuss."

Mattie raised her brows and thinned her lips, trying to act sympathetic, although she wasn't sure she could pull it off. "And he backed out on his agreement to help you move stuff through his border checkpoint?"

"Yup, you know it. He said he wanted out of the whole operation. I told him he'd made a mistake, and if he didn't change his mind and cooperate, we'd kill his wife and children." Destiny shrugged with a sardonic smile. "But in the end, it seemed best to kill him instead. Gave me a lot of pleasure, anyway."

"Why take Ramona, my brother, and me? I mean, you could have just killed all of us."

Destiny chuckled. "Maybe. But it was so fun getting to tell Doug that we would be keeping his family. And then Harold was such a fool to fall for your mother's *exotic beauty*," she said, using finger quotes. "He wanted her. Oh yeah, he wanted her bad. And she held enough sway with him to keep her two kids alive. Harold was a man who had an interesting appetite. He always wanted us to get into human trafficking with young kids and thought you and your brother would be a good place to start." She shook her head. "But Ramona put a stop to that plan the night she called the police on him."

Well, that was one thing Destiny didn't know. Mattie had called the police instead of Ramona, but she didn't think now was the time to make the correction. "So . . . all of this happened ages ago. Why are we here today? What purpose do you have in bringing us all together now?"

Destiny leaned back in her camp chair and flipped her hand. "It's simple. Ramona has to suffer. You might not feel close to her, but I think she loves her kids, or at least she did at one time. She was pretty broken up when her husband died. You missed the show when we delivered your sister to her, but she turned hysterical over that. I'm sorry she's not well enough to appreciate you being here too."

Mattie flinched inside, hearing about the pain this woman had inflicted on her mother, but she kept her cool. "Like I said, I think I could bring her around if I could get some clean water into her. She's dehydrated and hypothermic. Water and heat could change that."

Destiny narrowed her eyes at her and then gestured toward one of the Gaffeys. "Rope, go get some firewood and get a fire started in here. And get one of those water jugs from the Jeep." She held out a hand toward Mattie as if offering a gift. "One with a sealed cap, of course."

Mattie felt she'd won a battle . . . now to move on to the war. She waited to speak until Rope left the cabin. "So why now, Mrs. Carino? Why go after Ramona now?"

"Oh, sweetheart, please call me Destiny. I'm amazed at how polite you are. Who taught you such manners?"

Mattie would never give up Mama T's name to this woman. "We learn respect for others at police academy. I'm sure you've heard about it—to protect and serve and all that."

"Oh, all right. I think it goes deeper than that, but never mind. Let's get back to your question. Why go after Ramona now?" Destiny tapped her chin with her index finger. "At first I didn't know where she was, and that went on for decades. Then Milo got hurt."

She reached out her hand, and Milo grasped it for a brief moment, smiling at her as he did. When Destiny tried to return his smile, her lips trembled and a shadow of pain crossed her face.

"I told your partner that Milo got kicked in the head by a horse, but the truth is that he butted heads with a bullet. Right, honey?"

Mattie wondered if this despicable woman truly loved her husband. Mattie thought the bullet that damaged Milo's brain must have wounded Destiny on some level too. Destiny's gaze turned melancholy as it lingered on Milo.

But with a mercurial change of mood, Destiny spread her hands and grinned. "So . . . we've been busy. You know . . . life. What are ya gonna do?"

The way Destiny shifted back and forth between venom, sadness, and humor struck Mattie as clearly unstable. Her motives seemed to be a mixture of love, disappointment, and revenge combined with a mean spirit.

She'd lied to and stolen from her own brothers, so Mattie didn't believe Destiny was all that concerned about their demise. This was a woman whose moral compass was way off-kilter, and she would use any excuse to justify her own evil behavior.

Destiny continued. "But then that one detective reopened the cold case. He was pretty good, actually. He found out the village in Mexico where Ramona was hiding and sent word out on the grapevine. Before I knew it, John was killed in prison, and then Ramona's name came up among our little band of brothers. I knew it was time to, well, let's say . . . reach out."

Milo chuckled again. It was obvious that Destiny's husband was her biggest fan.

Time to play dumb. "I'm confused. You say you found her in Mexico?"

"In a little village called Pueblo del Sol. First I sent a scout, and I think she got word someone was looking for her and got spooked. She and her hubby were driving south, headed for parts unknown, when we stopped them. Such rabbits . . . they didn't stand a chance."

It gave Mattie a small sense of relief that she wasn't the one who had inadvertently tipped them off to Ramona's whereabouts. "What about our game warden, the one who got shot at Cedar Canyon Campground?"

Destiny gazed sadly at Milo again. "We got a little trigger happy, didn't we?"

He shrugged and tilted his head as if in reluctant agreement.

"We had pulled in there so we could stay close," Destiny explained, "but then she came snooping around. Milo got an itchy finger before I had a chance to talk with her. I pulled us out of there fast but then decided it was a good idea to go back after we saw you return. Just in case you found our tire prints. Better to look like we'd just arrived rather than let you track us down."

"But where was the rifle Milo used?"

"Oh, sweetheart, there's a false back to the gun cabinet." Destiny tried to look sympathetic. "Don't feel bad that you missed it—it's impossible to see, and there's no way to tell how deep the cabinet should be in an RV like that."

Mattie was disappointed in herself that she hadn't discovered such a thing. Robo had indicated the gun cabinet. It was her mistake that she'd missed it.

Rope came back into the cabin, carrying a jug of water and an armful of firewood. The conversation lapsed while he crossed the room to the fireplace, dropping the jug off by Destiny's feet as he went. He began the process of starting a fire on the hearth.

"So, one thing led to another, and I got Ramona, then Julia, and now you." Destiny refocused on Mattie, her expression more of a leer than a smile as she withdrew a small LadySmith .38-caliber revolver with a turquoise grip from her pocket. "And I get to use all three of you for target practice. Ramona last, of course, so she can watch her children die. And you're going to help get her ready for the show."

THIRTY

It took a while to move Julia, Ramona, and the mattress from one room to the other. In the light provided by the electric lantern, Mattie learned that Julia was capable of walking, although it was more of a stagger, while Ramona had to be carried. Her mother didn't regain consciousness during the transition, and Julia remained silent, letting Mattie do the talking.

Kent and Rope did the heavy lifting while Mattie knelt on the filthy mattress to settle Ramona into the most comfortable position possible. Destiny and Milo watched from the comfort of their camp chairs, both apparently enjoying this part of what Destiny called "the show."

Kneeling beside her mother, Mattie looked up at the ringleader. "I'm going to need a first-aid kit."

"Oh no, sweetheart," Destiny said. "Now you're overstepping your boundaries."

"What I actually need is a small syringe, no needle. I know you can't give me anything sharp. I'll give her little sips with the syringe to make her swallow. I don't know how else to bring her around, since we can't run an IV."

"What are you? Some kind of paramedic?"

"No, I've only taken first aid. But I know about hypothermia and dehydration. They often go hand in hand."

"All right, all right, I guess we have to keep her alive," Destiny said, her face filled with disgust as she gestured with her head toward the door. "Kent, go get a syringe out of the kit in the Jeep. That's all. Make sure there's no needle on it."

When Kent opened the door, Mattie could tell that dawn wasn't too far off. The sky had lightened slightly. Looked like sunrise might be an hour away. Though it pained her to think this way, she realized she was lucky her mother was unresponsive. It would buy them some time. She just prayed Ramona wasn't too far gone to bring back. Her mother needed a hospital and a doctor who knew how to move the poison out of her system as quickly as possible.

"Bring a cup too, Kent," she called to him before he stepped over the threshold and shut the door.

He turned and gave Destiny a look as she muttered, "Sheesh." Then she said, "Bring it," and sent him on his way.

Julia and Mattie exchanged a quick glance. Though Julia looked pale and wan, she still seemed alert, so Mattie hoped for the best. She wasn't sure why Destiny would want to poison Julia too, but she suspected it was from sheer evilness.

Needing to ask, Mattie looked at Destiny. "Why use the selenium poison?"

Destiny shrugged. "To make them suffer, but also to keep them under control. When the husband died, this one fell apart," she said, gesturing toward Ramona. "I had to dose her to settle her down. Then I had to do it again when she flew off the handle when we brought that one in." She gestured toward Julia. "Maybe I gave her too much. We'll see. I'll wait a couple hours until she comes around, and then I'll proceed with the show. You both deserve to suffer too—especially you, Mattie. Maybe you'll be last."

Mattie decided not to respond, because she needed a little more time. When the sun rose, it would be time to act. She remembered the poisoned stock tank. "Why did you put poison in the tank at Shadow Ridge?"

Destiny slid a glance at Rope, making him squirm. "One of my helpers washed out a container while I was involved elsewhere. More collateral damage."

Ever the K-9 handler, Mattie wanted to determine whose track Robo had followed to the parking lot and then to the stock tank. "So did Rope and Kent take Juan Martinez into the woods?"

Destiny frowned. "You're full of questions, aren't you?"

Might as well tell the truth. "My dog followed a track from Martinez to the parking lot and then to the tank, but he didn't seem to recognize you two the next morning. I just want to confirm that it was Kent and Rope who handled the body."

Destiny looked from Mattie to Rope, who was giving Mattie a mean look. "I guess it won't hurt to answer. Your K-9 cop days are over anyway. It was the Gaffeys."

Kent interrupted by bringing the cup and syringe from outside and handing them to Mattie. She eyed the jug of water near Destiny's feet but didn't want to approach the woman and inadvertently signal a threat. She remained kneeling at Ramona's side and said, "Kent, could I trouble you to give me that jug of water?"

Destiny toed the jug. "Go ahead."

Mattie tore open the seal, surreptitiously inspecting the top of the bottle for any puncture marks that might indicate contamination. There were none that she could see, so she poured a small amount into the paper cup. She handed it to Julia. "Just take small sips at first."

After Julia finished half a cup, Mattie refilled it and placed the syringe, tip downward, into the cup. She turned to Ramona to try to lift her enough to get her into a more upright sitting position. Julia struggled to help.

"Can you sit behind her and lean against the wall?" Mattie murmured to her sister, helping to situate her so that Julia straddled their unconscious mother to support her from the back.

Mattie drew up a few cc's in the short syringe and placed the tip at the edge of Ramona's mouth. She depressed the plunger to deliver a sip of water. It dribbled from Ramona's mouth and down her chin.

Destiny exploded with curse words and stood up from her chair. "This is driving me batshit crazy. This isn't going to work."

"It will work," Mattie said. Destiny's emotional volatility pointed further toward her instability. Mattie tensed, preparing to defend her mother physically if needed. "Just give me a few minutes."

"I can't stand to sit here and watch," Destiny said. "Let's go, Milo. Kent, you come with us. Rope, you stay here and keep an eye on these two girls and their mother."

It didn't surprise her that a guard would be left with them, but Mattie would have preferred Kent, since he seemed more sympathetic.

Mattie set her concerns about implementing the plan she'd formed with her teammates onto the back burner while she focused on trying to give her mother liquid. She refilled the syringe and, remembering how Cole had fed the weak puppy named Velvet after delivery, patiently used one hand to hold her mother's chin and jaw. With the other hand, she slowly plunged a sip of water between her lips. This time, she felt her mother swallow against the finger she held beneath her chin.

Encouraged, she continued the process, finding that her mother swallowed more readily as they progressed. Mattie didn't stop until Ramona had consumed at least a quarter of a cup. She looked up at Julia and saw that her sister's strength was flagging. "We can take a break and give her more in about fifteen minutes, okay?" Mattie murmured.

Ramona's eyes didn't open as Mattie repositioned her on the mattress. "Go ahead and lie down," she told Julia. "I'll stoke the fire."

She covered the two of them with the space blanket. Destiny and Milo had taken their camp chairs with them when they left, but Rope had dragged the third over to the door and was sitting in it. When Mattie arose from the mattress, he stood as if on guard.

Mattie raised her hands to keep them in plain sight. "Don't worry. All I want to do is stoke up the fire to give them more warmth."

Without a word, Rope gestured for her to go ahead.

This felt like another small victory. She needed to have some freedom to move about the cabin if she was to pull off her part of the plan. She crossed over to the fire, fed it a couple of short logs, and used a longer stick to probe the coals beneath the flame. "This is a good fire you made," she said to Rope.

Silence.

She poked around the fire for a few seconds. "How long have you worked for the Carinos?"

"Shut up."

Mattie raised her hands with fingers spread as an apology. She crossed back over to the mattress, keeping her hands well away from her body to show they were empty. She sank down on the edge of the mattress with her back against the rough plank wall, bent her knees, and placed her elbows on them, her fingers against her head as if resting. She stayed in the position for about five minutes, wanting Rope to get used to seeing her with her hands at her head.

She almost dozed off. She'd been up all night and had gotten limited sleep the night before. She roused herself and nudged Julia, and they resumed the job of trying to help Ramona drink. This time brought more success, and she was glad to see that her mother took about half a cupful through the syringe. Mattie made sure Julia drank too, and then went back to resting with her hands on the French braids at the top of her head.

In this way, she alternated caring for her mother and sister, resting, and feeding the fire. She didn't try to initiate conversation with Rope again but noticed that he no longer stood when she rose to tend the fire, and he was beginning to look sleepy as the cabin air warmed. She hoped to lull him into this routine and decrease his diligence with his guard duties.

Everything seemed to be going smoothly as Mattie waited for sunrise. But then Destiny and Milo returned to the cabin.

"What's going on here?" Destiny asked as she entered. "Did she wake up yet?"

Rope stood, but Mattie decided not to rise and remained seated on the mattress. She lifted her head and let her arms dangle between her raised knees, propped at the elbows, assuming an air of exhaustion. "Not yet, but I'm sure she will soon. She's drinking fluid better and she feels warmer. I think we've turned a corner and she'll be awake in maybe an hour."

"You think, but you don't know."

"That's true, but she seems to be getting better fast. I think she'll rally soon." Mattie was blowing smoke at this point. The amount of sunlight she saw when Destiny opened the door indicated the sun had risen. Mattie wanted to get rid of Destiny and Milo so she could execute her plan.

The two hadn't brought their chairs, so it looked like they weren't planning to stay. Destiny groused around for a minute or so, even toed Ramona's foot to see if she could get a response. Ramona lay still and quiet, her eyes closed.

"Shout out the door when she wakes up," Destiny told Rope. "Kent will come get us. Don't leave these gals unsupervised."

And with that the two of them left again, much to Mattie's relief. She felt she could handle Rope, but not all four of them.

She and Julia looked at each other. Mattie hadn't shared the plan with her sister during the night in case their room was bugged, so now she could read the hopelessness in Julia's eyes. Things would seem impossible to her, and in fact all of them were still in grave danger. But Mattie had hope, and she refilled the cup to give to her sister, urging her to drink again.

They tended to Ramona, succeeding in giving her another half cup, and afterward Mattie sank against the wall with her hands on her braids.

It was time. She closed her eyes and drew a breath, trying to slow the increased rate of her heartbeat.

Moving ever so slightly, Mattie wiggled her fingers under the edge of her right braid. The tracker was under the left, and what she searched for was well within her reach under the right. She felt the thin long packet encased in plastic, and slowly, ever so slowly, she drew it out and hid it under her fingers.

Rope didn't make a move. He had tipped his head back against the wall and was staring at a spot someplace above Mattie, his eyes glazed with sleepiness.

She tucked the plastic tube into her pocket and rose. Heading toward the fire, she kept her hands raised and visible in the position that she had trained Rope to expect. *It's like dog training*, she thought. *Repeat something over and over until you condition the response.*

And in this case, Rope's response was nothing. She squatted in front of the hearth with her back turned slightly sideways to hide the fact that she inserted her hand into her pocket. Picking up the stick she'd been using as a poker, she stirred the coals, making the flames leap. She placed a small log on the fire and left a heavier one on the floor beside her.

She tossed the tubular packet into the fire, keeping her back to Rope and shielding the fire from his view as much as possible. The plastic melted on contact, and black smoke billowed up and out the chimney—her signal to the team that would indicate where she was and that the operation could begin. This step wasn't critical—Rick would give the go-ahead even without it—but the team had figured that a campfire would be highly likely in this terrain and it would be beneficial to know where she and her family were located.

Rick had fashioned the chemicals in the tube from his recipe of potassium chlorate, lactose, magnesium carbonate, sodium bicarbonate, and an industrial black colorant. They could have chosen from a variety of colors but had selected black, since it wouldn't be as readily apparent that Mattie had signaled should one of her captors notice the change in the smoke pattern. Black smoke from a campfire wasn't that unusual.

But her teammates would notice it. If the tracker she had under her left braid was working as it should, her colleagues and their reinforcements would have formed a perimeter around the cabin by now and would have eyes trained on her location. At least that's what would happen in theory. But she truly had no idea if they had surrounded the cabin or not.

She was acting on trust.

It was time for her team of law enforcement officers to close in. Mattie remained in front of the fire, stirring it listlessly while the black smoke continued to rise. The team wouldn't miss the thick, dark smoke. She remained hunkered down at the hearth and waited.

The sharp report of gunfire sounded. This was it!

Rope leapt to his feet with his rifle in hand. He turned his back on Mattie and opened the door a crack to peek outside.

Mattie didn't hesitate. She snatched the short log beside her foot and ran lightly across the room, grateful for the silence provided by her sneakers. Rope must have sensed her coming though, because he turned toward her. She smashed him broadside over the head with the piece of firewood.

He staggered to one knee but didn't drop the rifle.

This fight would end in life or death for Mattie. This man was strong and stout, and she'd never be able to fight him if he closed in on her. She swung the log again and hit him square on the nose. Blood gushed. He raised his rifle in both hands.

Like Robo, Mattie knew she had to go for the gun. She risked delivering a kick to Rope's face. His head snapped back and hit the wall behind him. Stunned, he started to topple. Mattie rushed in close and kicked him hard in the crotch. He dropped the rifle and fell into a fetal position, his hands between his legs.

Mattie grabbed the gun. "Do not move or I'll put a bullet in your head."

He was sucking air, his eyes partly closed. He reached out to grab at her legs. She jumped away but not fast enough. He snagged her foot, and she fell backward onto her tailbone.

She shifted her grip on the gun and crunched her abs to sit up. Using the momentum from her movement, she clubbed him with the rifle butt. Breathing hard, she scrambled backward so he couldn't reach her.

But Rope had no more fight in him. He lay still and unconscious.

Mattie realized that Julia was at her side. Mattie stood and did a quick check of the status of the rifle and its ammo before training the barrel on Rope's face. Since he was so hardheaded, she worried he would regain consciousness before she could immobilize him. "Look in his coat pockets," she said to her sister. "He had zip ties in them earlier."

Julia found the ties. Mattie rolled him onto his stomach, grabbed one hand, and bent his wrist forward so she could control him should he wake up. But he was definitely down for the count, and she managed to zip his hands together behind his back.

Quickly she zipped a tie around each ankle and then bound them together with a third tie. If he came to now, he wouldn't be able to go anywhere.

More shots rang from outside, close to the cabin.

"Go stay by Mom and huddle against the wall. Don't leave that mattress," Mattie told Julia.

Mattie's role was to keep her mother and sister safe. Her teammates would *not* be shooting toward the cabin, she knew that much. Her signal had told them where she was, so friendly fire wasn't an issue. But where were the other three in this gang?

Taking the rifle with her, Mattie cracked open the door to peek out. It was her first time to see the terrain around the cabin. There was a fire ring outside and a flat stretch littered with boulders and dotted with pine trees. Snow covered the ground.

Kent darted from tree to tree, coming toward the cabin, firing his rifle each time he took cover.

Her teammates were hampered by not being able to shoot toward the cabin. Kent was gaining ground. Mattie knew it was up to her to pick him off from inside the cabin, but fear for the safety of her teammates held her back. If she didn't hit her target, a stray bullet could just as well injure one of them.

As loud as she could, she shouted out the door the code words they'd all agreed on, "All secure! All secure!" It was her signal that Julia and Ramona were safe. Now law enforcement would know that she and her family were secure in the cabin.

Kent looked at her and took another run toward the cabin, bearing down on her at full speed. She prepared to slam the door and hold it, hoping she could keep him from pushing it open. She had nothing inside to barricade it with.

But a black streak caught her eye, coming from a clump of mountain juniper off to the right. Robo! Her dog hit Kent before he saw him coming, slamming into him from the side and slightly behind. Kent went down to his knees. Robo's mighty jaws clamped down on Kent's gun arm, and he held it the way he'd been taught.

Kent shrieked and dropped his gun. Mattie was about to leap from the cabin porch to help her partner when Cole came barreling from the bushes. He crashed onto Kent's back, knocking him to the ground. Brody came from the other side of the cabin and leaped up onto the porch.

Mattie and Brody's eyes met. "All secure here," Mattie told him, and he turned to help Cole.

Robo was still tugging at Kent's arm, trying to stretch him out while Cole rode Kent's back. Cole grabbed Kent's free arm and twisted it hard up toward his shoulder blades. It became clear that Cole seemed at a loss for what to do next.

Brody took over while Mattie continued to stand guard at the cabin door. There were still two people who were unaccounted for, and she couldn't back off from guarding her family yet.

"Robo, out!" Brody shouted.

But Kent was still fighting, and Mattie knew her dog wouldn't let go until Kent gave up.

"Tell Kent to quit fighting," she shouted, holding her rifle ready and scanning the perimeter around them for a sign of Destiny and Milo.

Brody had assisted in enough takedowns that he revised his process quickly, evidently remembering the steps Robo had been taught. Once Kent stopped fighting, Brody repeated the "Out" command, and Robo dropped Kent's arm and backed up.

Robo's eyes darted between Mattie and the man he'd taken down. Mattie could tell he wanted her to give him his next command, so she did.

"Good boy," she called to him. "Guard."

He dug his toenails into the snow and stared at Kent, saliva dripping from his open mouth, his sharp teeth gleaming against his black lips and pink tongue. Brody and Cole cuffed Kent's hands behind his back. Brody raised his rifle, keeping Kent under guard while Cole hauled him to his feet. The two of them hustled Kent up the porch steps and into the cabin. Robo followed them inside, tail wagging, and Mattie shut the door behind them. She sank to her knees and hugged her dog, murmuring what a good boy he was into his ear.

When Rope groaned, his eyes fluttering open, Brody took in the man on the floor. He told Kent, "Sit down there by your brother." He trussed up Kent's ankles with zip ties and left the two of them against the cabin wall, completely out of commission.

Mattie stood and hugged Cole fiercely—a hug that he returned just as fiercely—before taking a step back and looking him in the eye. "You did great!"

She held Cole's hand while she turned to Brody. "It's Didi and Milo Carr, also known as Destiny and Milo Carino."

Brody gave a curt nod. "We've had them under surveillance since sunrise. They're in a cabin across the road, pinned down by Rick and his men. They're not going anywhere."

"Do they know they're surrounded?"

"They do. It's a standoff at this point. We might have to wait until they run out of food and water. Or in this temperature, firewood."

Mattie glanced at Julia, who had been watching, her eyes dark and wide. "Can you take a look at my mom and sister?" she asked Cole.

"Yes. Dr. McGinnis sent fluids and an IV kit. They're out in my backpack that I left behind the trees where Robo and I waited."

"I'll get it," Brody said, and he left, barely opening the door wide enough to slip through.

Mattie hurried to the mattress and reached to grasp Julia's hand. "I'm sorry I couldn't tell you. I thought the room could be bugged."

"No problem." Julia raised Mattie's hand to her lips and kissed the back of it. "You are amazing."

Cole knelt beside Ramona, placing his fingers at her wrist and then at her neck as if searching for a pulse. Mattie's breath caught as he frowned in concentration. Fear that her mother had passed rose inside her.

"Her pulse is faint and irregular. We need to move her as soon as we can," he said, meeting Mattie's eyes, his filled with compassion.

Brody reentered the cabin with McCoy following. Brody carried the backpack to Cole.

"Rick and his team have the others pinned down," McCoy said. "We observed only four captors earlier, Mattie. Do you know if there were others?"

"I only interacted with four. If there were others, I don't know about them."

"What's the status of your mother and sister?"

"Ramona's unconscious. Julia is weak and can barely walk."

McCoy turned to Brody. "Can you circle back to the Jeep? Drive it as close as you can without being in danger of a shot from the other cabin. Get the stretcher and bring it here. You and Cole evacuate Mattie and her family as soon as you can. I'll radio Stella to call in medevac to meet you at the trailhead. I'll stay up here to watch over these two and back up Rick until we end this thing."

But Mattie felt she couldn't leave until Destiny and Milo were taken into custody. Destiny would have an escape plan, and if a K-9 team could block it, she and Robo needed to remain on duty. "Robo and I might be needed," she said. "I have to stay." She knelt on the mattress beside her mother on the opposite side from Cole. "Can I help before I go?"

Cole had already broken the seal on the IV kit and was well on his way to establishing an IV in Ramona's arm. "I can manage. Do what you need to do."

Gunshots had ceased outside. Voices shouted a short distance away, but Mattie couldn't make out words. With Robo at her side, she arose from the mattress and joined McCoy at the door. Brody had already left to get the Jeep.

McCoy remained focused on watching outside the door. "I made radio contact with Rick to tell him that you and Robo are coming." He pointed outside. "See the cabin over there about a hundred yards?"

Through the pines, Mattie could see an old, boxy log cabin. "Yes."

"Rick is on this side about fifty yards away. See him?"

She couldn't at first but then made out movement from a man in camouflage gear that blended into the evergreens; he was waving at her. "Got him."

"I'll stay with Cole until he and Brody can evacuate your family."

"Thank you," Mattie said, as she slipped out the door into the cold air. "Robo, heel."

Bending low, Mattie kept trees between her and the cabin while she ran to Rick's position. The six-inch snow cover chilled her feet inside her thin sneakers.

"The female said they'll never surrender," Rick said as she came to a stop beside him. "It's just her and a male inside there."

"Destiny and Milo Carino. They're the only two left, to my knowledge," Mattie said. "The other two males are in custody."

Rick gestured toward the cabin. "They're both armed with rifles."

"And she also has a revolver. I don't know if he has a handgun." Mattie spotted two snowmobiles sitting beside a narrow trailer parked next to the Jeep in front of the cabin. "So I guess their escape strategy was to continue over the pass?"

"Maybe. But we have a SWAT sniper guarding that door, and it's the only one out of the cabin. We have all the windows covered too."

"I think she's unstable and a danger to her husband or to herself, Rick," Mattie said. "I want to talk to her. See if I can get her to surrender."

"Go ahead and try."

"Destiny," Mattie shouted. "Can you hear me?"

The cabin door opened a few inches, but no one appeared. "I hear you, you little snake," Destiny screamed, her voice filled with rage. "I hate you!"

"Destiny, listen to me. Let's talk."

"There's nothing I want to say to you. You're a cheater, just like your father."

Mattie had a bad feeling about this situation, but she didn't know how she could deescalate it. "I don't think my father meant to harm you, and I don't want to harm you either. I just want all of us to get out of this alive. Are you and Milo both okay?"

"Don't even think you can get us to give up." The door closed with bang.

Mattie glanced at Rick, and he shrugged. She decided to try again. "Destiny! Destiny, let's talk!"

Mattie waited for an answer. After a minute, a gunshot sounded from inside. Within seconds, another shot fired.

Robo stiffened beside her. To him, gunshots meant, "Go! Find the shooter!" Mattie held him by the handle on his Kevlar vest while her heart pounded in her ears. Those shots weren't directed at anyone *outside* the cabin.

She stared at the door while Rick radioed some of his key teammates, but no one could see what had gone down behind the cabin walls. After a long moment, Rick decided to send in the SWAT team.

Three men in full tactical gear came from behind trees and boulders and rushed the cabin, making it to the front wall without drawing gunfire. Two of them took positions on each side of the door while the third kicked it in before dodging back behind the cover of his teammates. Rifles forward, they swept through the open doorway in tandem. Within seconds, one of the men stepped outside and signaled an all clear. "Two down inside," he shouted to Rick. "Both dead."

Mattie hung her head, dealing with the slew of emotions that assaulted her. She sorted out relief, disappointment, anger, and even a degree of sympathy for Milo. Destiny had probably shot him before killing herself.

Mattie had never planned for it to end this way.

THIRTY-ONE

After the medevac helicopter airlifted Julia and Ramona away from the trailhead, Cole and Mattie drove Frank Sullivan's Jeep back to the station to pick up her Explorer.

Ramona had still been alive when they turned her over to the medevac crew, but Cole suspected her life was hanging in the balance. Julia, on the other hand, appeared to stand a decent chance of survival as long as there were no complications. Both women had been loaded into the chopper and were on their way to the hospital in Willow Springs.

And that's where Cole and Mattie were now headed with Cole behind the wheel. Mattie had been checked out by the EMTs, who had treated her injured wrists and approved her decision to not be admitted to the hospital. She sat in the passenger seat, looking pale and exhausted, her head leaning against the headrest. Robo was in the back, curled up in a furry ball on his cushion.

Mattie's eyes were open, and she was staring out the windshield. Cole reached for her hand, and she took his in a firm grip. "Are you thinking?" he asked. "Or just resting."

"I was thinking," she responded in a quiet voice. "I was wondering why Destiny felt she needed to kill Milo and then herself. But I think I know the answer."

"What did you come up with?"

"They've led a long life of crime together and gotten away with it. She must have suspected that someday that would come to an end. I think she truly loved Milo and didn't want them to be separated. He would have been vulnerable without her in prison."

"Do you feel sorry for them?"

Mattie sighed. "It's complicated. After everything they've done, I'm relieved not to have to worry about them anymore. But Destiny had become obsessed with old events and past traumas. Milo's gunshot injury seemed to have been painful for her, and perhaps it stirred up dark memories. I think she became unhinged."

"I suppose it's hard to have any mission end in death, but I'm thankful it didn't happen to any of the good guys." Cole squeezed her hand.

"Yes, there's that to be thankful for." She paused for a long moment before continuing. "She died hating me because she thought I double-crossed her. I guess she felt entitled to kill all three of us with her fancy LadySmith revolver and wanted me to let her do it. That's another indicator of her skewed reasoning."

"You're right."

"I can't help but wonder what kind of childhood the Cobb siblings had. What shaped them into the vicious and corrupt people they became?"

"They were quite a family. They'd make a good case study for a forensic psychologist."

"They would, wouldn't they? I hope there aren't any other siblings left."

"I agree with you there." Cole let the silence linger until they hit the pass leading to Willow Springs. "The girls and Mrs. Gibbs want to go back home, but I asked them to wait until I can meet them there this evening. Destiny's reach extended beyond the two Gaffey brothers. I don't know if we should expect some type of retaliation."

Mattie looked at him with pain in her eyes. "I know. Rick and Stella are following up on that today."

After a few miles, Mattie broke the silence again. "I've been thinking about my father's infidelity and how it set this whole thing in motion for our family thirty years ago."

Cole nodded, knowing this was a hard subject for Mattie to broach.

"I think finding out about his affair the night he was killed left my mother feeling betrayed and vulnerable. Then after suffering years of abuse at the hands of Harold Cobb, I guess I can understand why she thought Child Protection Services could care for her children better than she could. It must have felt like her only choice."

He knew Mattie had struggled with Ramona's abandonment most of her life. It felt good that she was coming to terms with it. "I think you're right."

Mattie shuddered, as if shaking off her demons. "I told Rainbow to either go home with Stella or wait until I come home so she can stay with me."

"She's welcome at my house. You too."

Mattie nodded. "Thank you. Let's see how my mom and sister are doing by the end of the day. I might want to stay at the hospital tonight."

He squeezed her hand. "Whatever you want, we'll work it out." And as he released her hand so he could use both of his to steer around the curves on their way up the pass, he decided that his words should be his guidepost for dealing with things the next few days. *Hey, maybe even my lifetime.*

★ ★ ★

Several days later Mattie stopped by the station on her way home from the hospital. Blood testing had confirmed that both her mother and sister had been poisoned with selenium, and treatment with dimercaprol had begun immediately. Dimercaprol acted as a chelating agent to bind selenium so it could be excreted through the kidneys. Julia had responded well, but Ramona had taken a couple of days to fully regain consciousness, and it was still uncertain if she would have permanent damage to her organs.

Julia's husband, sons, and their grandmother had arrived from California and had relieved Mattie of her constant bedside vigil. Glenna had recovered enough to be released from the hospital under her sister's care, and Mattie had heard that Moose had been overjoyed to be reunited with her at home.

Mattie greeted Rainbow with a hug as she entered the lobby, and after catching up, she went to find Stella, who was working in her office with her reading glasses perched on the end of her nose. She looked at Mattie over the top of them before pushing them to the crown of her head and getting up to exchange a hug. "It's wonderful to see you. How are your mother and sister doing?"

Mattie told her about their improved condition while they both settled into chairs. "I'm on my way to Cole's, but I thought I'd stop in to get an update on everything."

Stella nodded, put her glasses back on her nose, and looked at her computer screen. "Sonia Alvarez, Rick's contact at the Attorney General's Office, and the FBI have teamed up to do some remarkable work tracking down Julia's kidnappers. They finally found a surveillance camera that gave them a make, model, and license plate number of the car that Julia was transferred into from the van. This gave them a lead on the two thugs who took Julia from the parking lot, and they've made an arrest. These two guys used to have connections to the cartel but haven't been active for a while. And it looks like Destiny and Milo were in the same boat."

"How so?"

"They've been living in Mexico for the last ten years, probably on that money she said she stole from her brothers. She pulled these two guys back into the fold to make a run at your family, but even though they were good, they weren't *that* good. I hope they'll be put away for a long time."

A weight lifted from Mattie's shoulders as she leaned back in her chair. It sounded as if it would be safe for Julia's family to return to California once she and Ramona were well enough. That's what the family all wanted, at least for now—to live together at Julia's house, including their mother and grandmother.

"Sounds like we'll be safe in our own homes again," Mattie said. "Rainbow is eager to get back out to her place, although I convinced her to stay with me at Cole's tonight. I promised the kids we'd have a big slumber party in the great room. Tomorrow will be soon enough to get back to normal."

"Good plan."

"Do you want to join us?"

Stella raised an eyebrow. "I'm not exactly the slumber party type. Besides, I'm getting together with Rick tonight before he has to go back to Denver."

Mattie nodded and leaned forward to stand up.

"Wait a minute," Stella said, a grin crossing her face. "I have more good news."

Mattie settled back in her chair. "I could use all the good news I can get."

"The DNA Robo found at Juan's crime scene came back as a match to Rope Gaffey." Stella's smile indicated how pleased that made her.

Mattie returned her grin. "That *is* good news. Now we can place him directly at the crime scene."

"With you as a witness, both Kent and Rope will be going away for a good long time."

After they celebrated for a few minutes, Mattie and Stella said their good-byes. Mattie was eager to go to Cole's house to see Robo . . . and Cole and the kids too, of course. As she passed back through the lobby, she confirmed the arrangements with Rainbow to meet at Cole's when her shift ended.

Cole had texted her to meet him at the clinic, so she drove past his house and on up the lane. As she approached the clinic, she pulled over to the edge of the lane to allow a horse trailer and the Rattler SUV to drive past. Althea Rattler stopped and rolled down her window, deep frown lines on her face.

Mattie groaned softly before rolling down her own window. Remembering Althea as rather arrogant and pushy, she really didn't want to talk to the woman right now.

"I hear you apprehended the guy who poisoned the stock tank," Althea said.

Mattie nodded, wondering if Althea had heard the news through official channels. "Where did you hear that?"

"From the sheriff himself."

That's about as official as you can get, Mattie thought, waiting to see what else the woman had to say.

"So . . . well done," Althea said, still frowning. "I'm glad you caught the guy."

Mattie nodded again. "Me too. Are you headed home now?"

"Yes. With both horses."

"I'm glad things worked out and they both survived."

"They've had good care."

And though it was said almost begrudgingly, Mattie was pleased Althea recognized Cole's efforts and expertise. "Safe journey," she said, wanting to end the conversation and get to the clinic.

Althea raised a hand in farewell and drove on.

Mattie parked in front of the clinic, noting that Cole's truck was the only vehicle there. She hoped he was about to wrap up his day. As she entered the front door, Robo dashed from the exam room and launched himself into her open arms. She laughed as she absorbed the impact of his weight and then knelt to wrap his wiggly body in a hug. His tail was wagging so hard it beat a staccato rhythm against the side of the desk.

Cole came into the lobby after him. "I guessed it was you by the way your dog reacted."

Mattie looked up at him with a grin and then tousled Robo's ruff. "We're happy to see each other. Aren't we, big guy?"

Robo swiped her cheek with his tongue as she continued to kneel on the floor with him. After a playful minute, she rose to give Cole a hug too, and he pulled her close for a kiss.

"I have one more call to make. Will you go with me?" Cole asked.

"Should I stay and help Mrs. Gibbs get dinner ready?"

"I just talked to her, and she said she had things well in hand. Besides, this will take only about a half hour. I'm going to go do a last check on Sassy and her pups, and I plan to offer Hannah a job too. That should make her happy."

Mattie's heart soared. "Yes! I'll go. Can Robo come too?"

"Sure. I doubt if Sassy and the pups are still contagious, but he'd better stay in the truck, just to be on the safe side."

They loaded into Cole's truck with Robo in the back seat. As Cole drove past the house, he said, "I'd ask the kids to go with us, but I wanted a few minutes alone with you so we could talk."

"Our time together has been short lately, hasn't it?"

"That's okay—you were needed at the hospital." At the end of the lane, Cole turned onto the highway. "But I've been thinking about it. You know . . . our limited time together. I was wondering if we could fix that sooner rather than later."

Mattie figured he was talking about a date for their wedding. She'd had a lot of time to think about marrying Cole while she waited in the room that her mother and sister shared at the hospital. It was awkward having two places to live, and besides, she'd been thinking of asking Rainbow to move into her house in town. Her heart picked up its pace as she waited for Cole to continue.

"Do you want a big wedding, Mattie?" Cole said, taking her hand as he kept his eyes on the road.

She held his warm hand between both of hers. "No, I don't. I want just our close friends and family. How about you?"

"That sounds good to me, but I want you to have a big wedding if you want one."

"No, Cole. You know me. Something simple is better. What were you thinking?"

He glanced at her. "I'd love to get married around Christmastime. Have a close circle of friends and family in our great room along with a big tree and all the decorations."

"That sounds lovely." She squeezed his hand. "That's about a month away, but probably enough time for my mother to regain enough strength to come."

"I think so too. We could ask your family and mine, the Hartmans, Mama T, and all the gang at the station. And, of course, anyone else you want to add to the list. I was even wondering if Abraham might officiate."

Nothing would please Mattie more than having the sheriff marry them. "I'd like that."

Cole was grinning from ear to ear. "Maybe Mrs. Gibbs would make a couple of her chocolate cakes."

"And the girls could help us with decorations. Maybe they'd like to stand up with us."

"And Robo could be the ring bearer," Cole said, as Robo leaned over the console and stuck his wet nose between them to sniff their hands.

Mattie laughed, feeling more joy than she'd felt in her entire lifetime.

They pulled up in front of the Vaughn home and parked. "You stay here," Mattie told Robo as she exited her side of the truck.

Cole grabbed his stethoscope and a small bag, and they walked hand in hand around the side of the house. At the gate to the backyard, Mattie spied Hannah and the pups playing in the grass.

The latch clanked as Cole unhooked it, and eight little heads popped up, ears pricked as the pups alerted. When they spotted Cole and Mattie, they came running, eight furry bodies bobbing up and down as they scrambled across the lawn. Little Velvet tripped and sprawled headlong but picked herself up quickly and scurried after the pack.

Mattie giggled as she and Cole entered the yard, watching the little ears flop as the puppies raced toward them. She sank to her knees to greet the eight fur balls, who leaped into her arms and shared with her their unrestrained happiness.

Wedding plans and puppies . . . what more could she ask for in one afternoon?

Acknowledgments

Heartfelt thanks to all who've supported this series: readers, librarians, other writers, book reviewers and bloggers, podcast and radio hosts, as well as others who've enjoyed the books and helped spread the word about them.

I'm forever grateful to those who helped me with professional content in this book: Lieutenant Glenn J. Wilson (Ret.); Charles Mizushima, DVM; Kathleen Donnelly, K-9 handler and co-owner of Sherlock Hounds as well as author of the National Forest K-9 series; and Sheila Lowe, handwriting examiner and author of the Forensic Handwriting suspense series as well as non-fiction books about handwriting and behavior. Any inaccuracies or fictional enhancements of professional content are mine alone.

Huge thanks to my publishing team: my agent, Terrie Wolf of AKA Literary Management; publisher Matthew Martz and the team at Crooked Lane Books, Melissa Rechter, Madeline Rathle, and Rebecca Nelson; my editor, Martin Biro; my copy-editor, Rachel Keith; and my publicist, Maryglenn McCombs. It is such a pleasure to work with all of these fine people.

I owe a hearty thank-you to Scott Graham, author of the National Parks Mysteries; the aforementioned author, Kathleen Donnelly; and to Bill Hazard for assistance with early drafts.

Hugs, love, and gratitude go to friends and family who've supported me throughout the years. Your support means the world to me.

And to my husband, Charlie; daughters, Sarah and Beth; and son-in-law, Adam: sending my love and a huge thank-you for always being there.